SPILL

ZONE

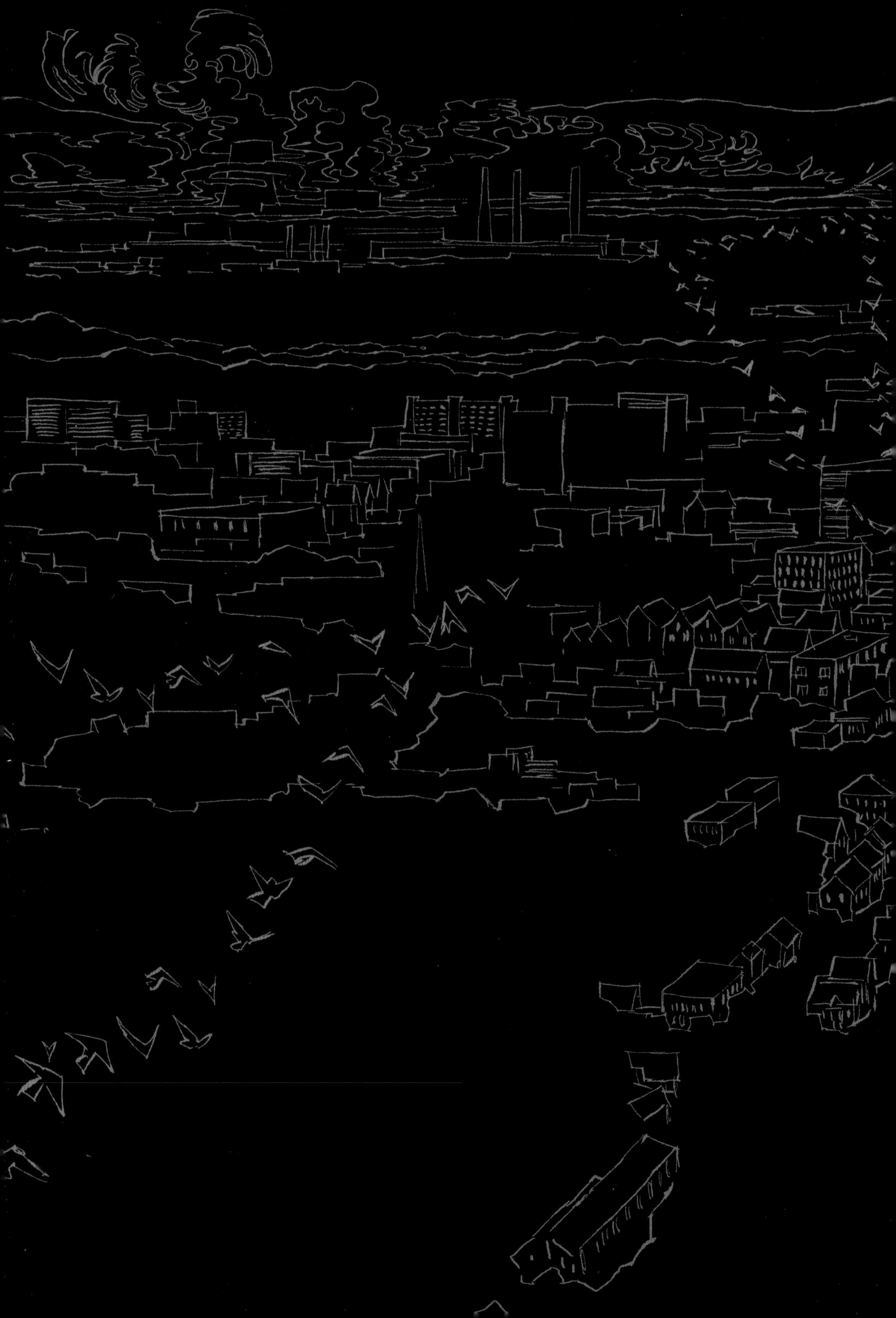

SCOTT WESTERFELD

SPILL ZONE

ALEX PUVILLAND

Colors by
HILARY SYCAMORE

:01
First Second
NEW YORK

To everyone who creates fan art,
thanks for putting drawing, painting, costuming,
and building at the center of your reading
—S.W.

To my petit nenuphar
—A.P.

SPILL

ZONE

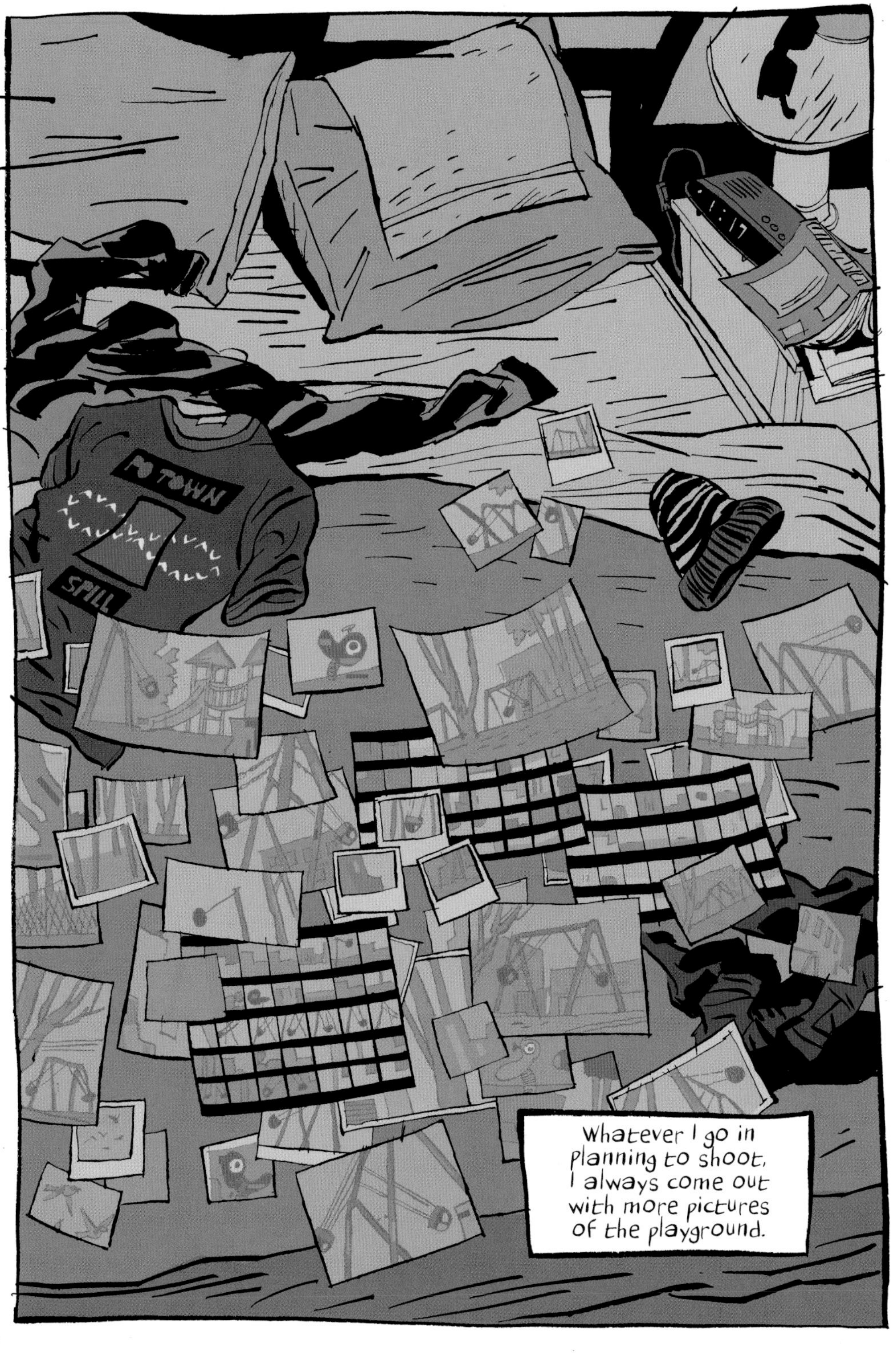
SPILL
Whatever I go in planning to shoot, I always come out with more pictures of the playground.

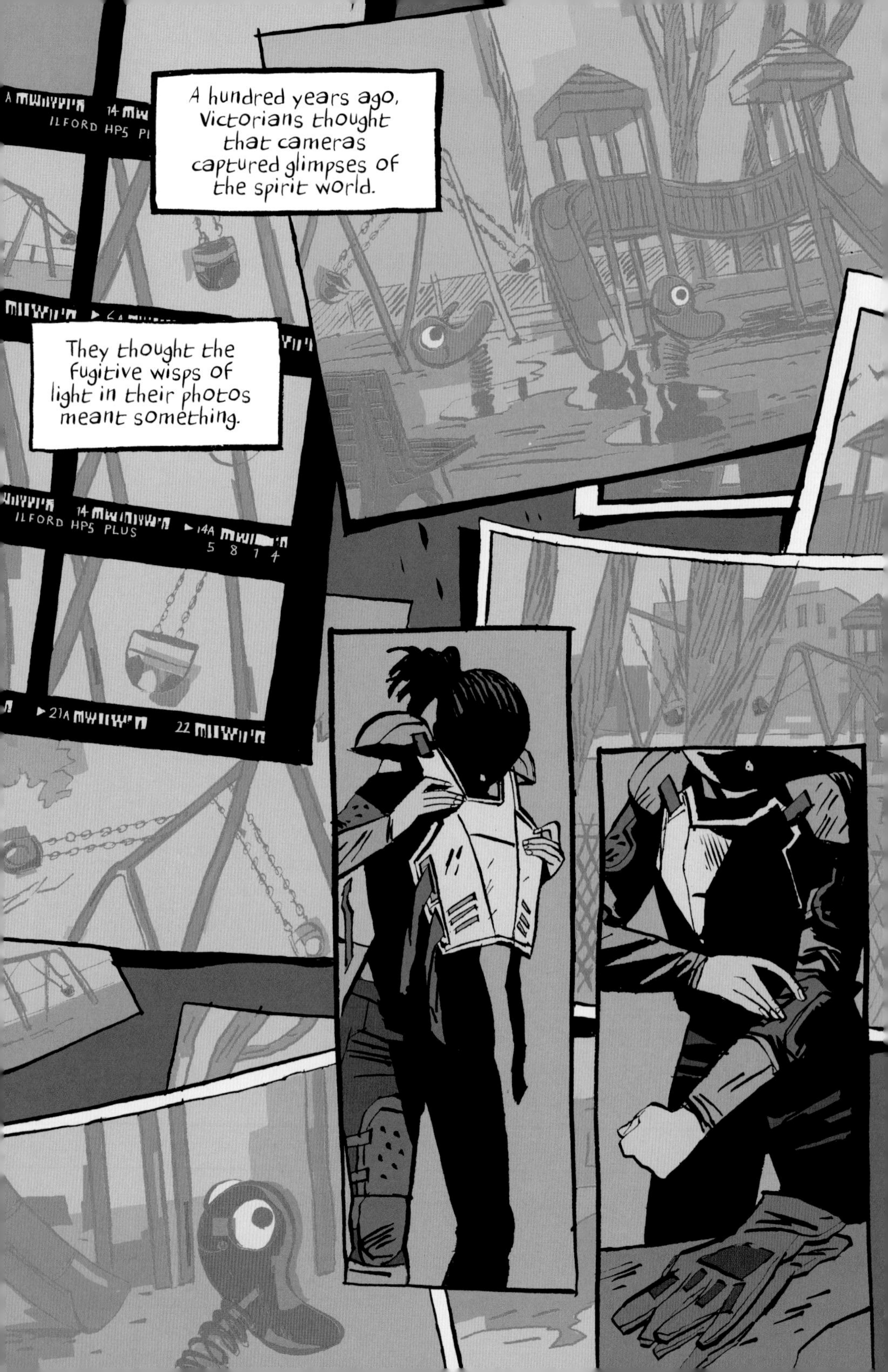
A hundred years ago, Victorians thought that cameras captured glimpses of the spirit world.
They thought the fugitive wisps of light in their photos meant something.
ILFORD HP5 PLUS
14A
5 8 1 4
21A
22

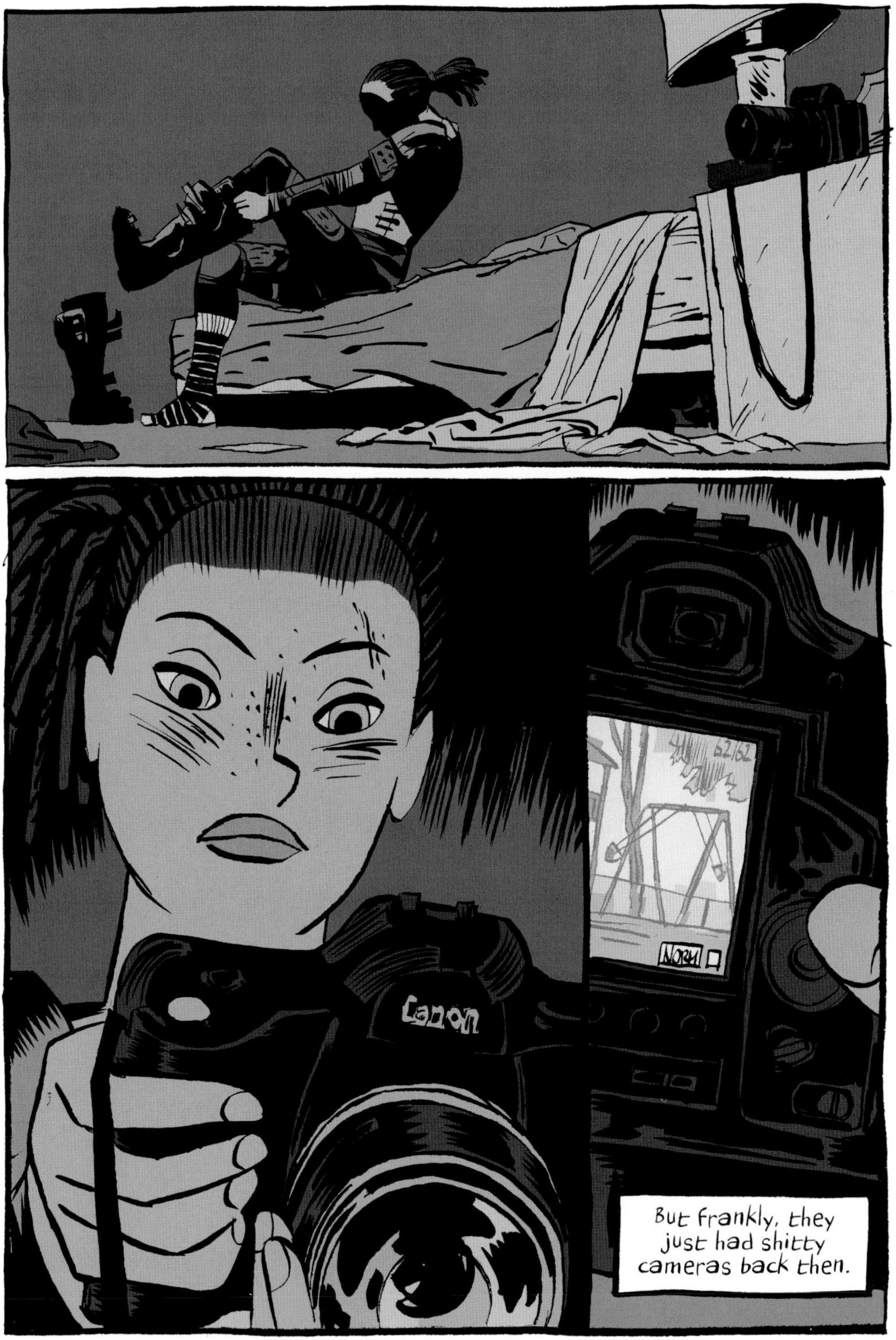
62/62
NORM
Canon
But frankly, they just had shitty cameras back then.

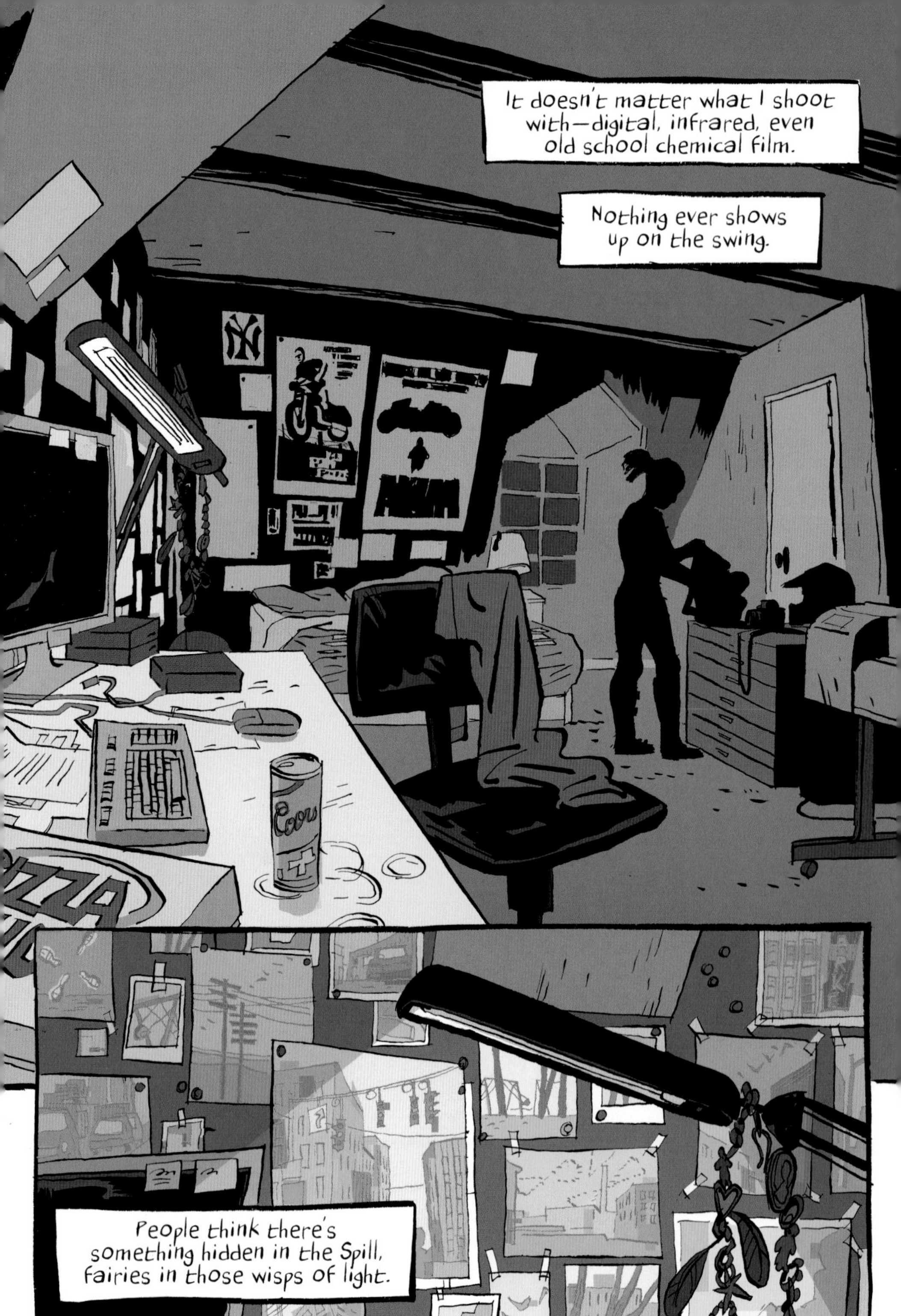
It doesn't matter what I shoot with—digital, infrared, even old school chemical film.
Nothing ever shows up on the swing.
People think there's something hidden in the Spill, fairies in those wisps of light.

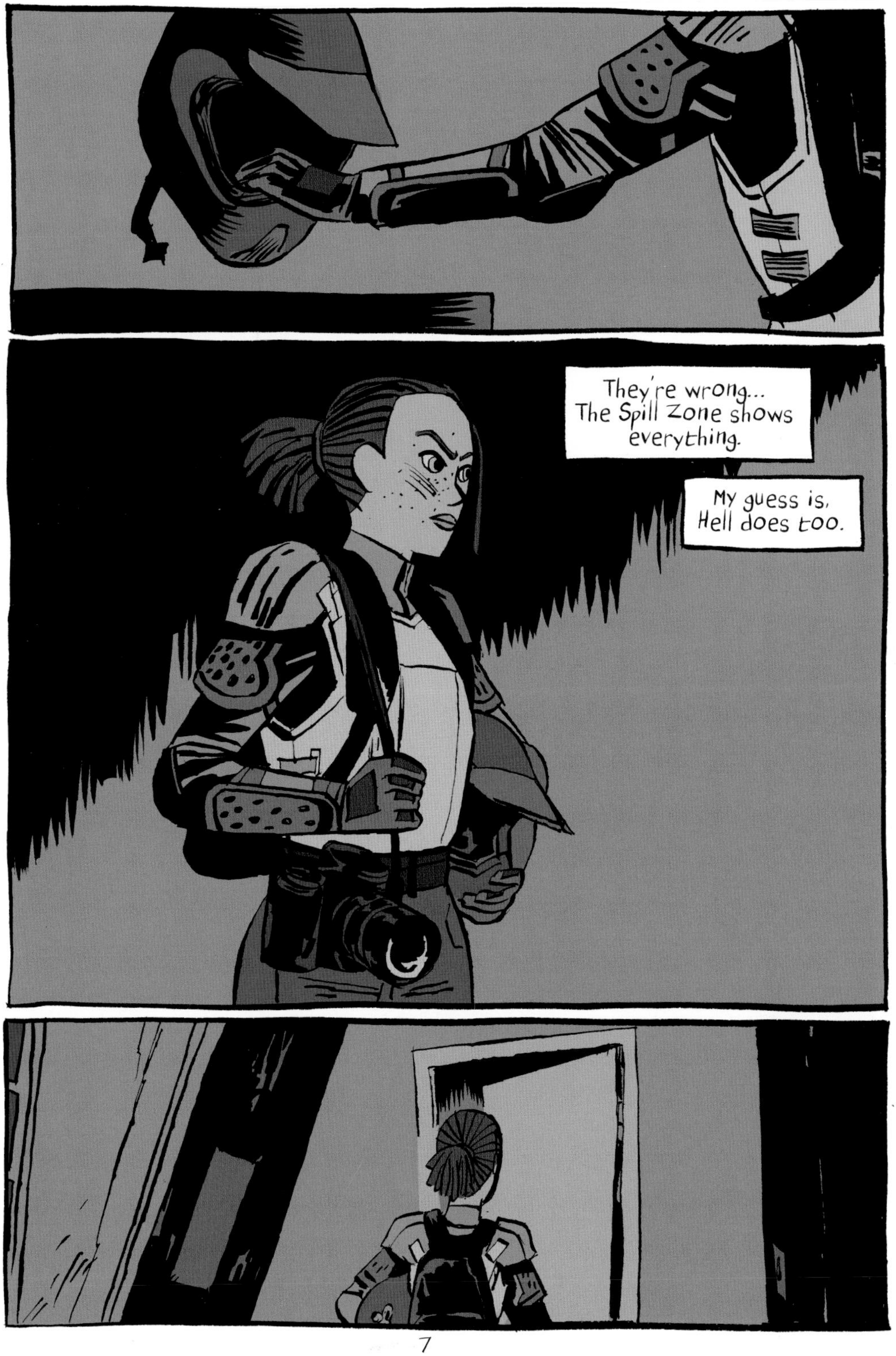
They're wrong...
The Spill Zone shows everything.
My guess is, Hell does too.

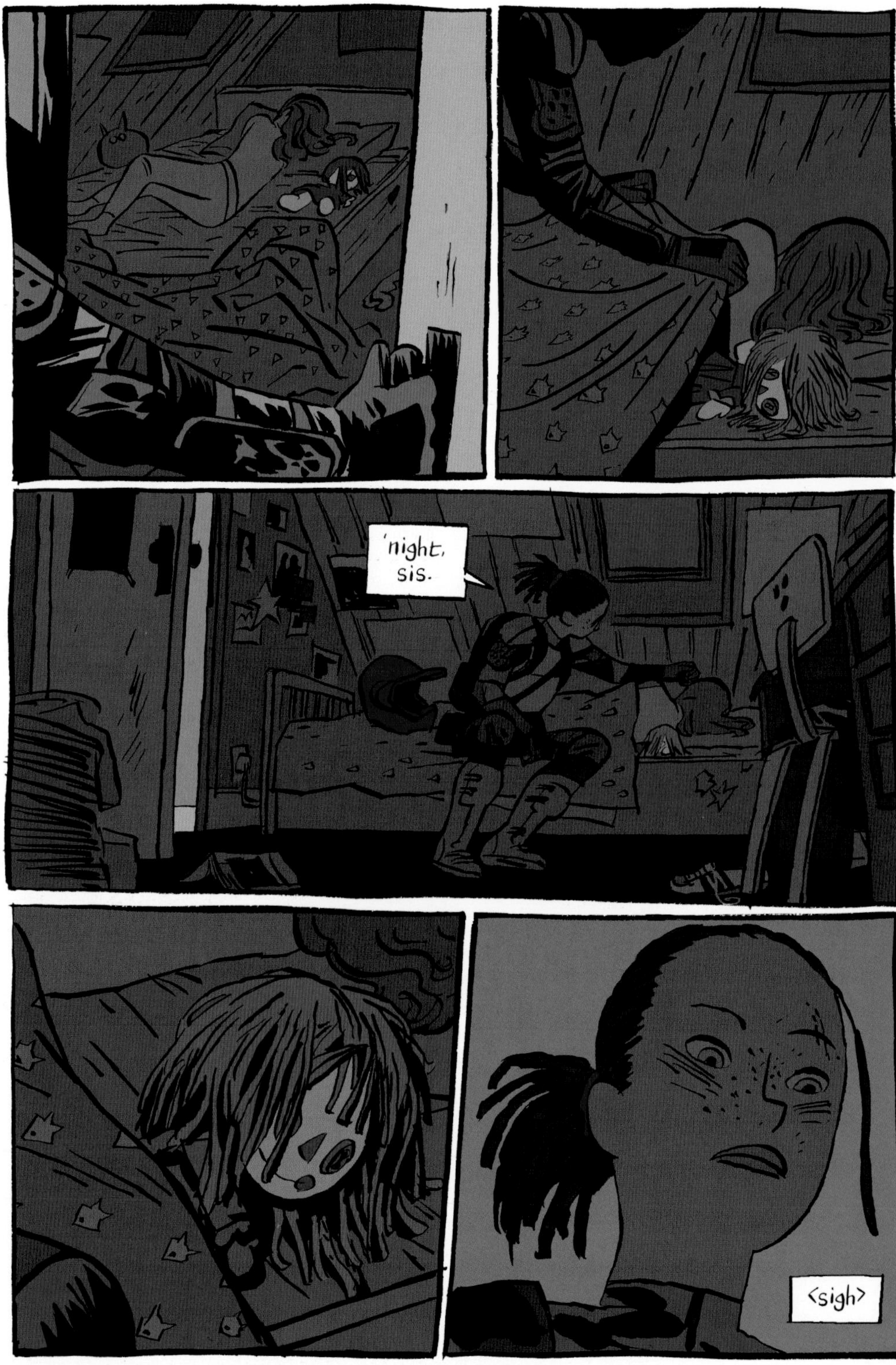
'night,
sis.
<sigh>

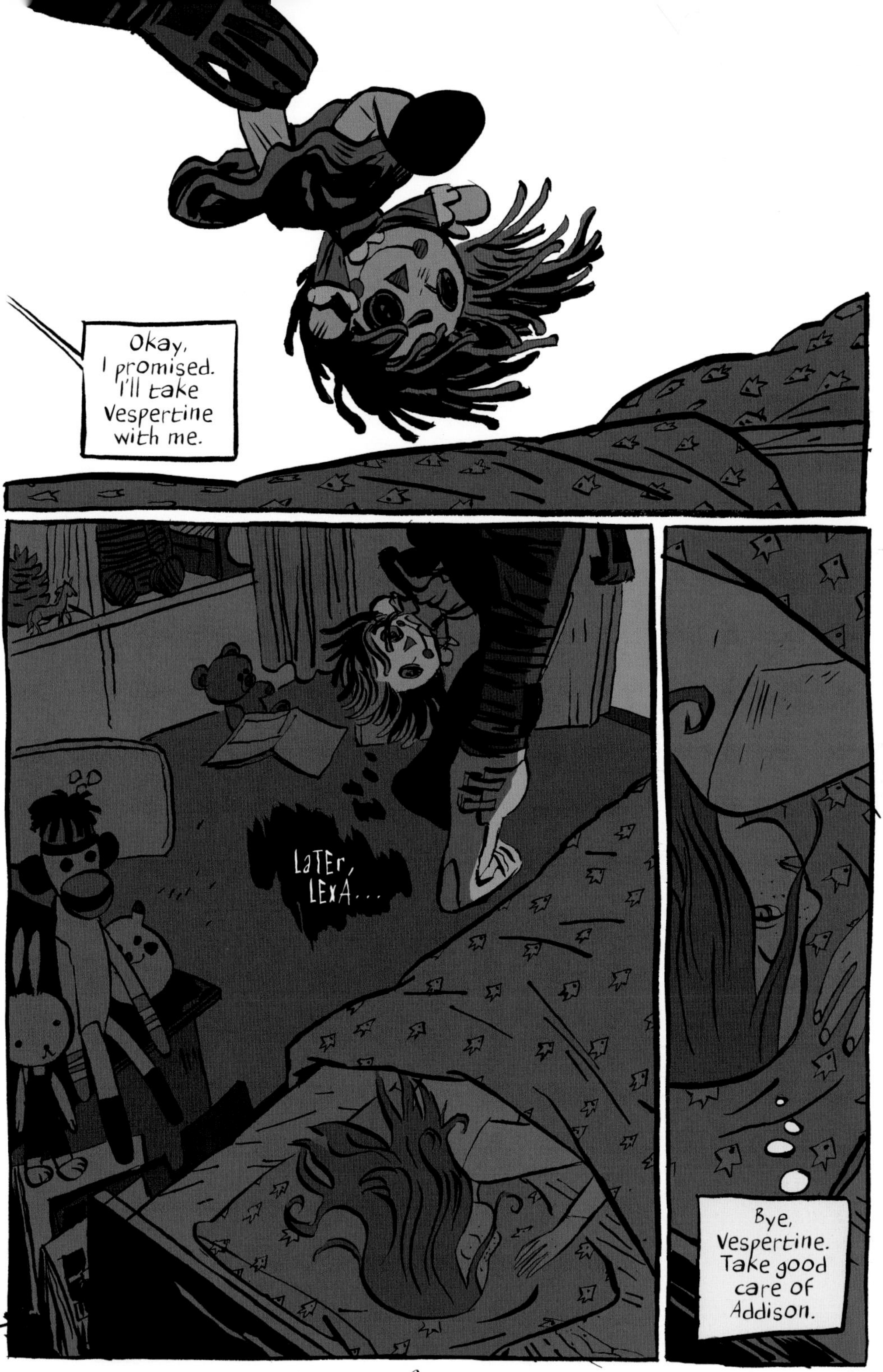

Okay, I promised. I'll take Vespertine with me.
LaTer, LExA...
Bye, Vespertine. Take good care of Addison.

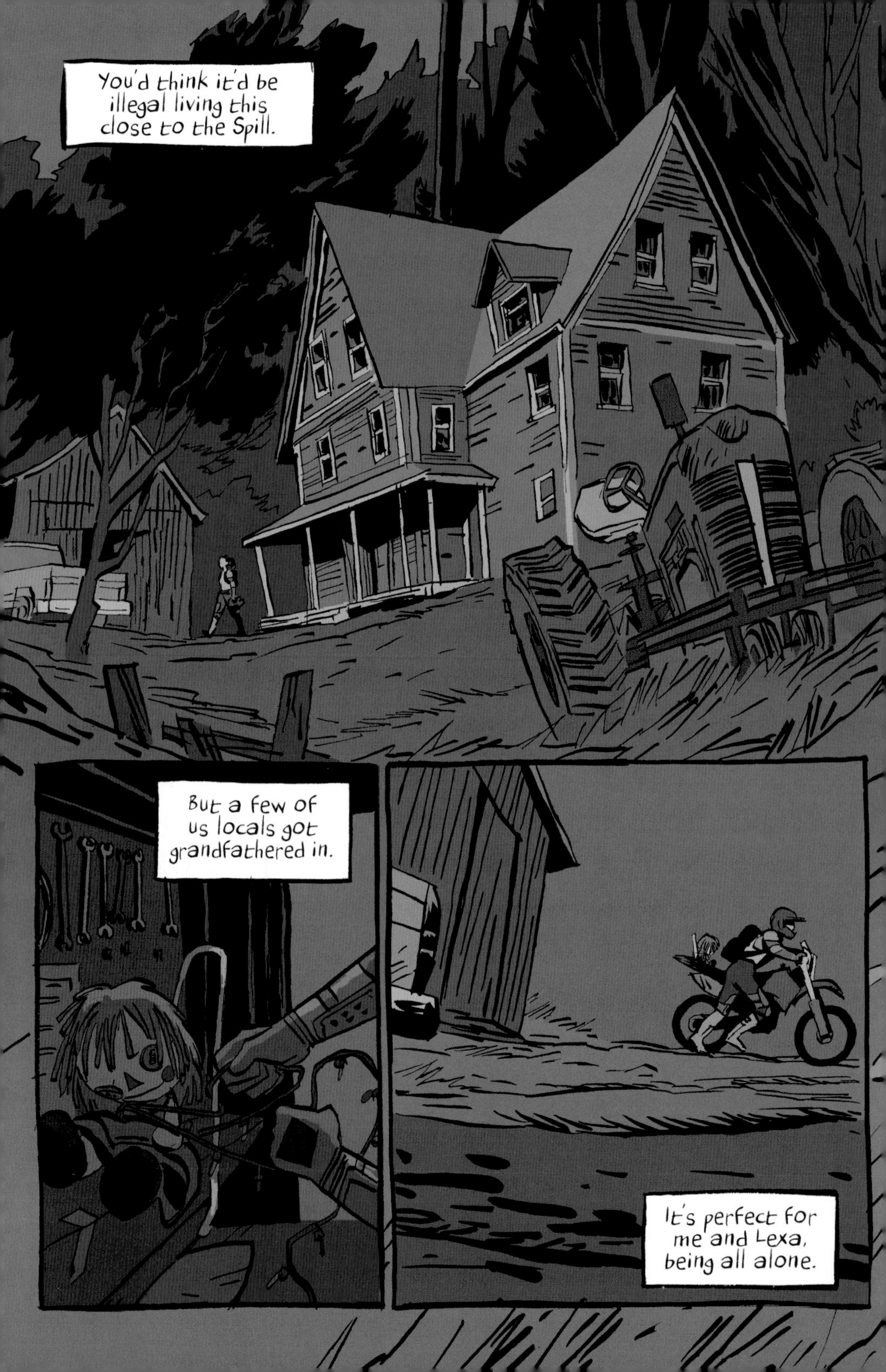
You'd think it'd be illegal living this close to the Spill.
But a few of us locals got grandfathered in.
It's perfect for me and Lexa, being all alone.

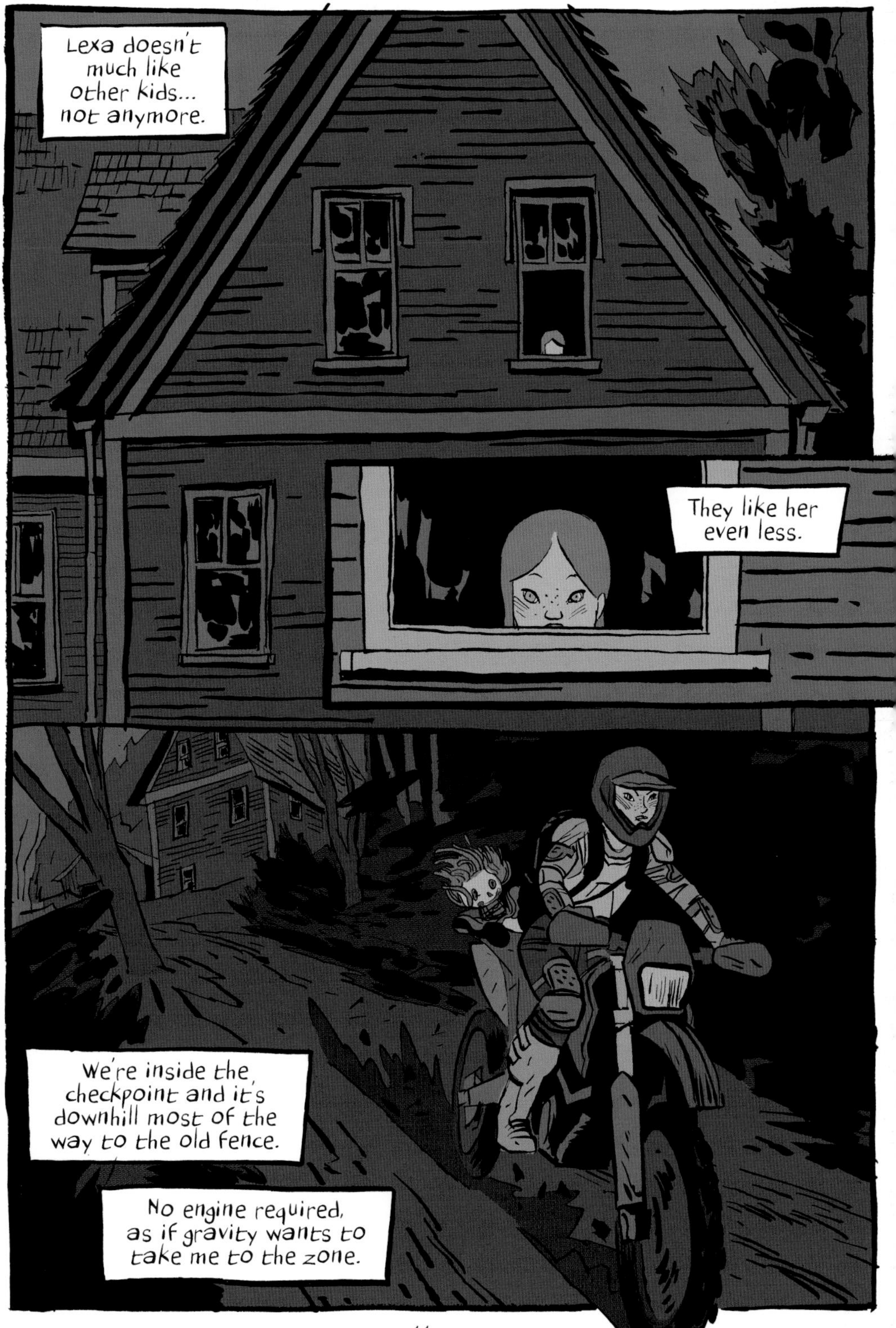
Lexa doesn't much like other kids... not anymore.
They like her even less.
We're inside the checkpoint and it's downhill most of the way to the old fence.
No engine required, as if gravity wants to take me to the zone.

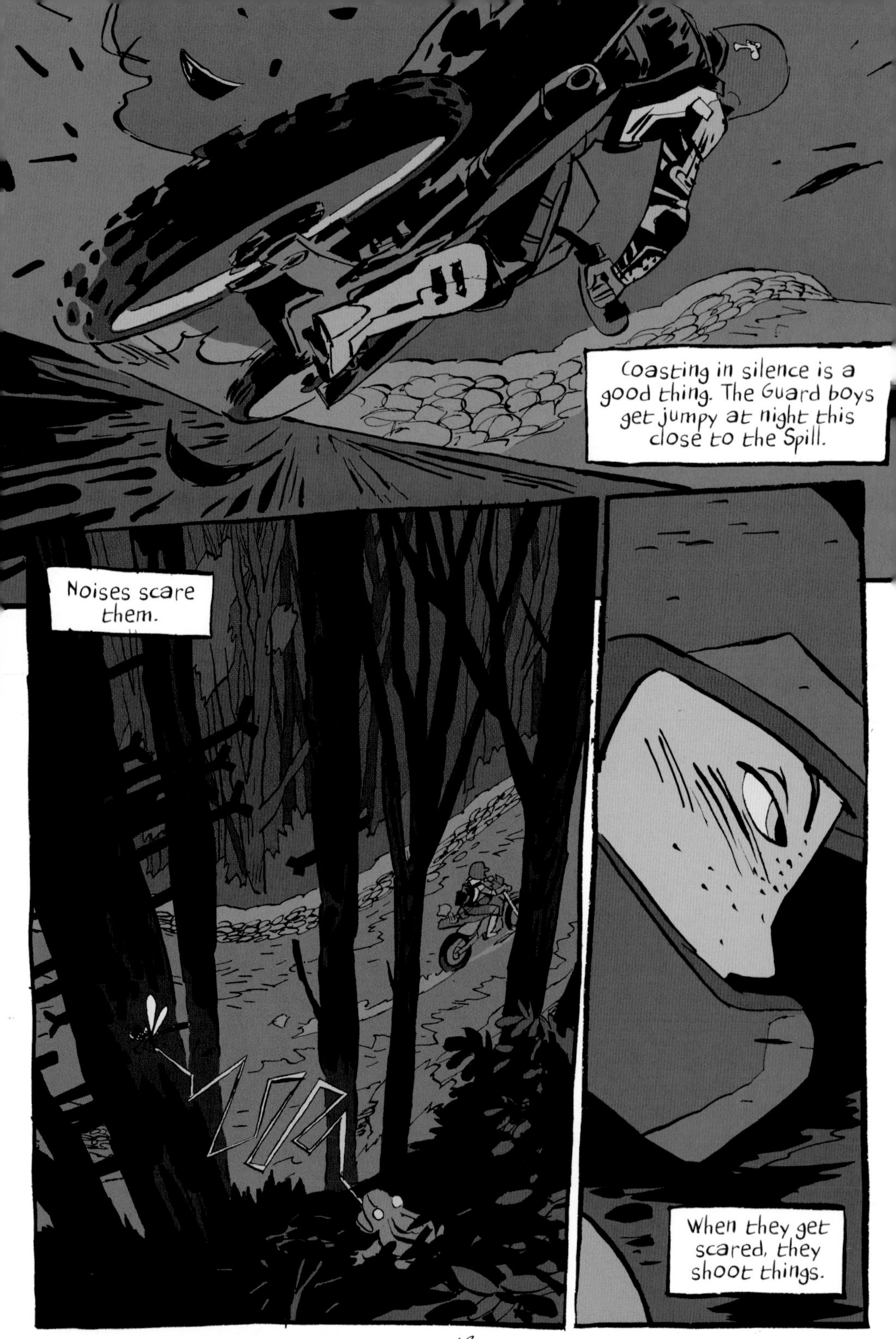

Coasting in silence is a good thing. The Guard boys get jumpy at night this close to the Spill.
Noises scare them.
When they get scared, they shoot things.

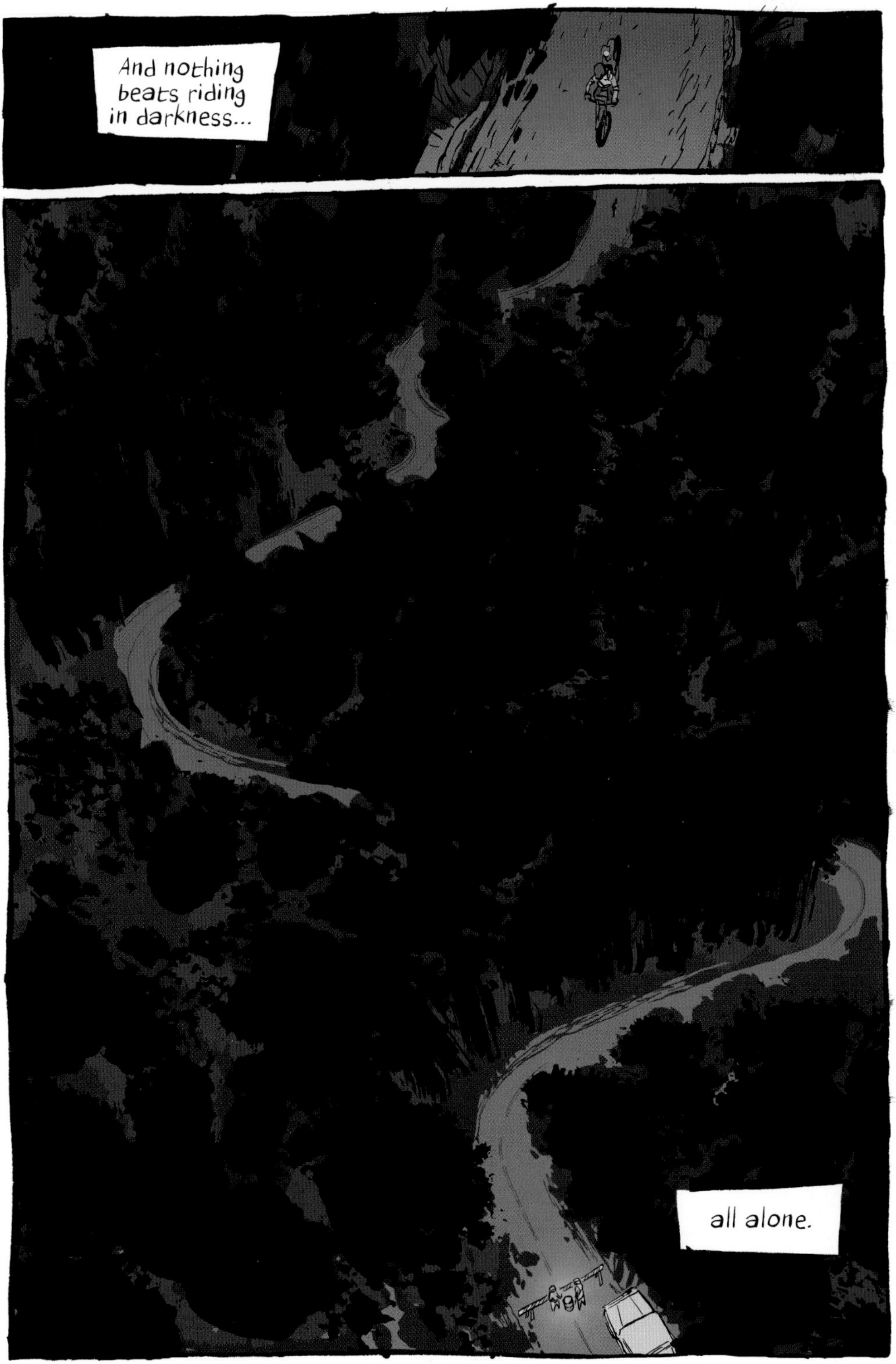
And nothing beats riding in darkness...
all alone.

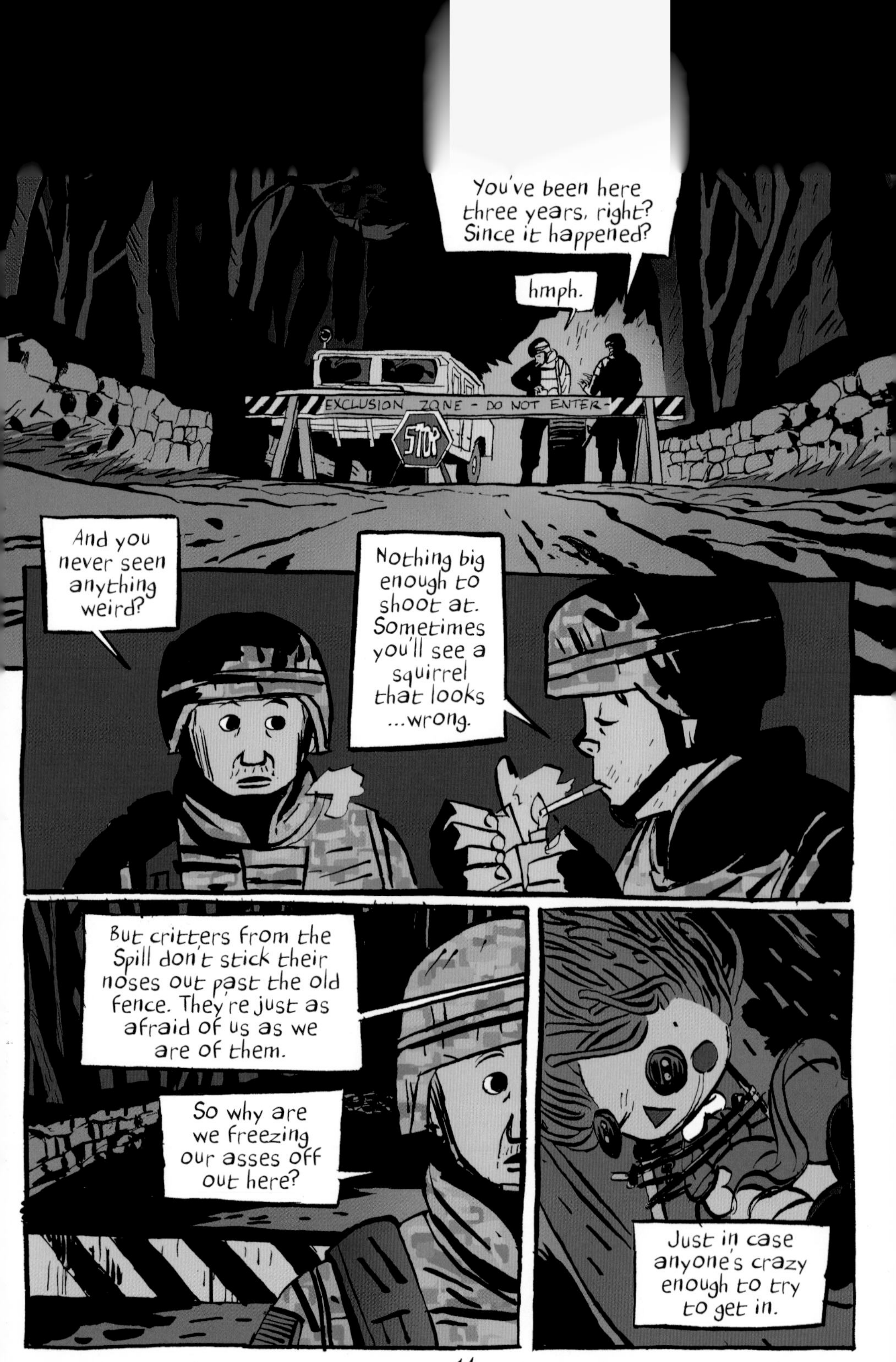
You've been here three years, right? Since it happened?
hmph.
EXCLUSION ZONE - DO NOT ENTER
STOP
And you never seen anything weird?
Nothing big enough to shoot at. Sometimes you'll see a squirrel that looks ...wrong.
But critters from the Spill don't stick their noses out past the old fence. They're just as afraid of us as we are of them.
So why are we freezing our asses off out here?
Just in case anyone's crazy enough to try to get in.

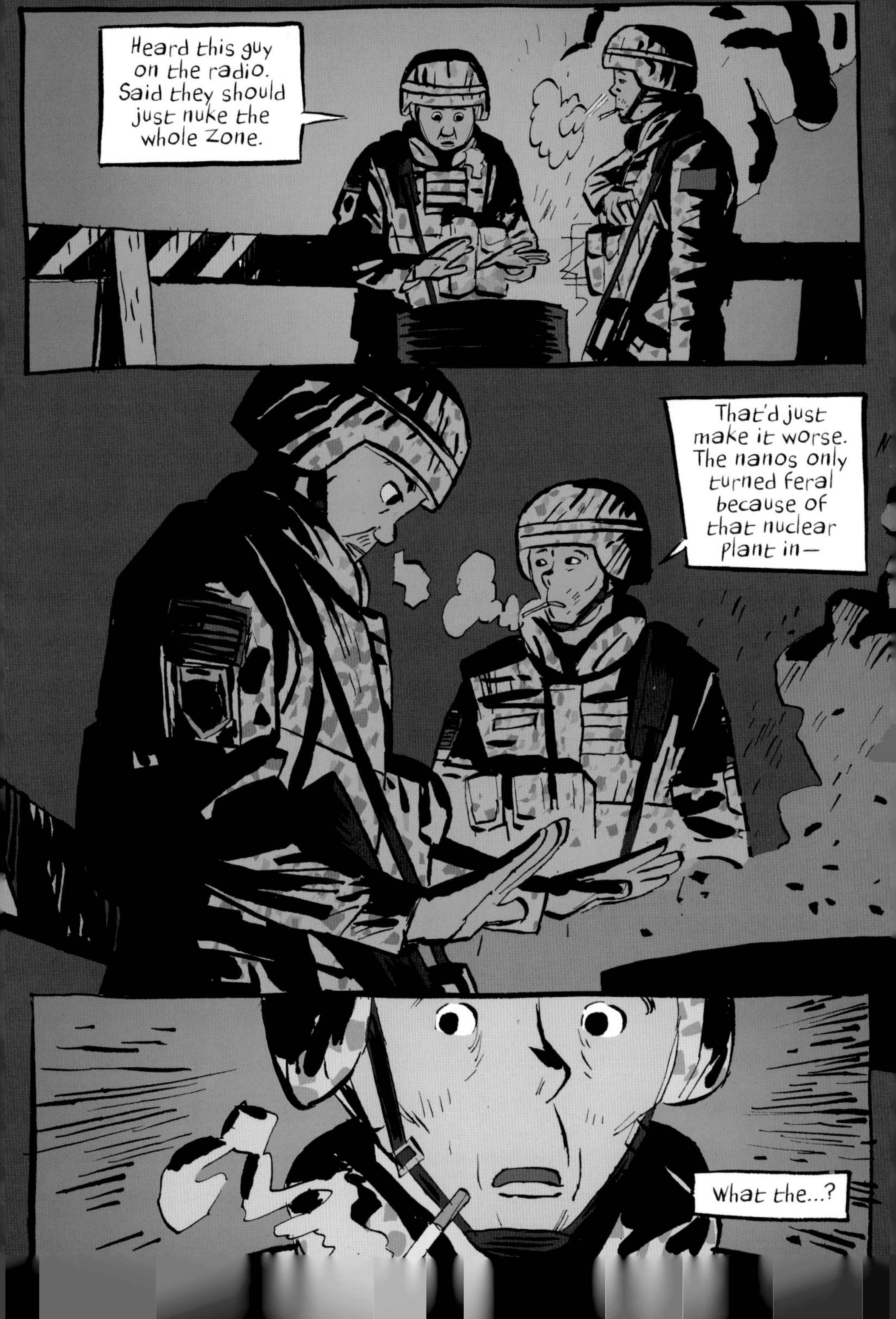
Heard this guy on the radio. Said they should just nuke the whole Zone.
That'd just make it worse. The nanos only turned feral because of that nuclear plant in—
What the...?

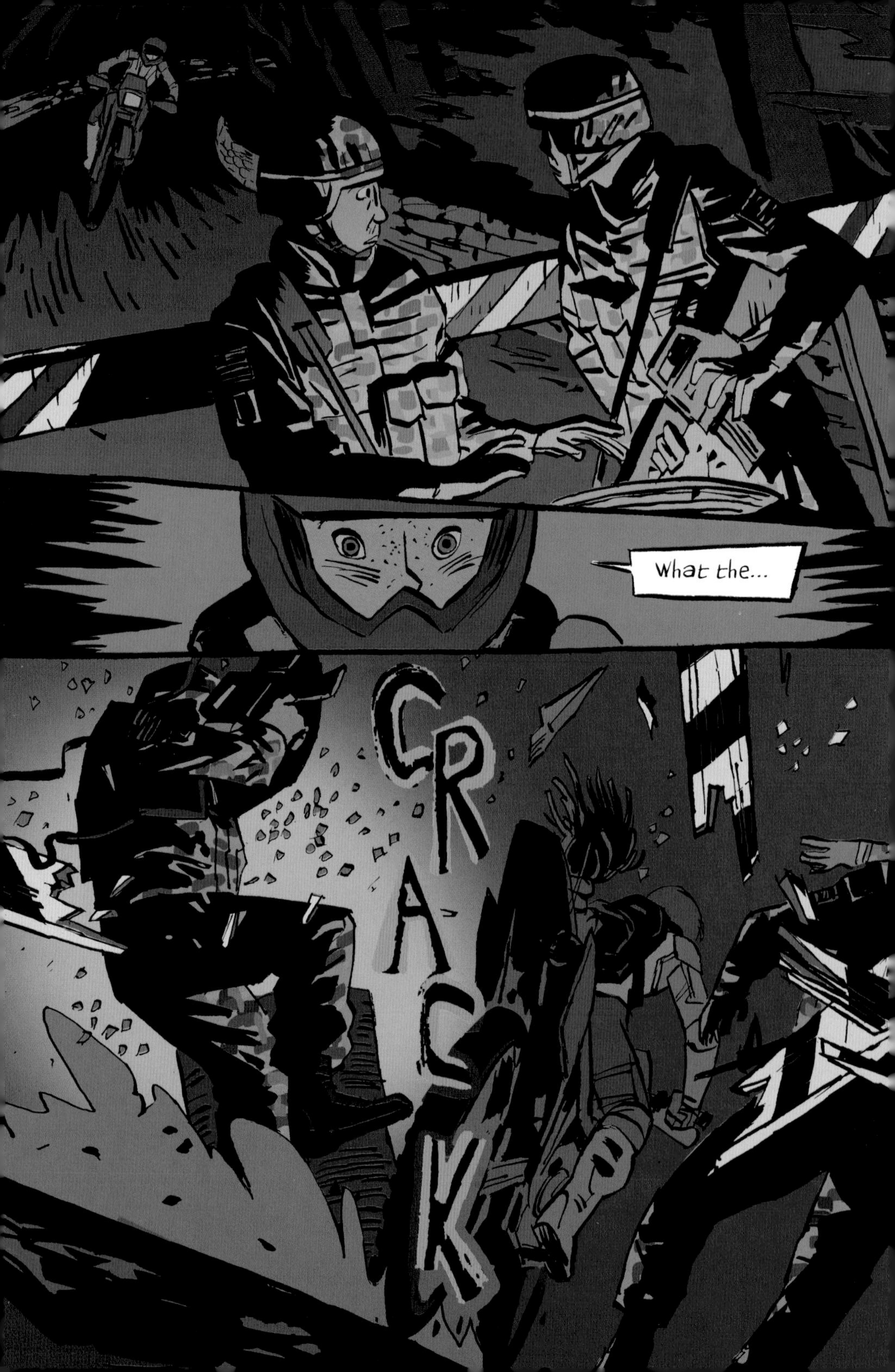
What the...
CRACK

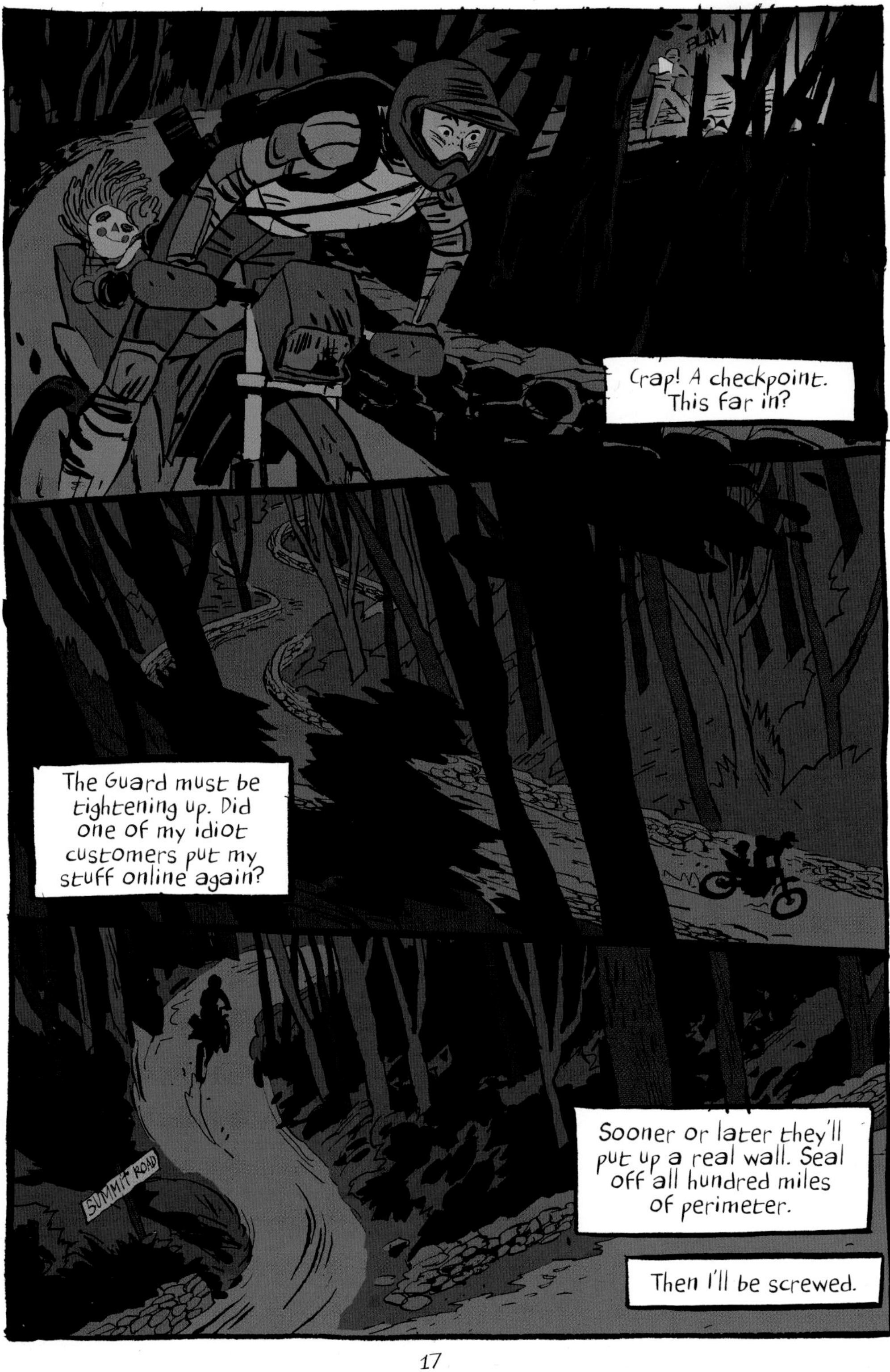
BLAM
Crap! A checkpoint. This far in?
The Guard must be tightening up. Did one of my idiot customers put my stuff online again?
SUMMIT ROAD
Sooner or later they'll put up a real wall. Seal off all hundred miles of perimeter.
Then I'll be screwed.

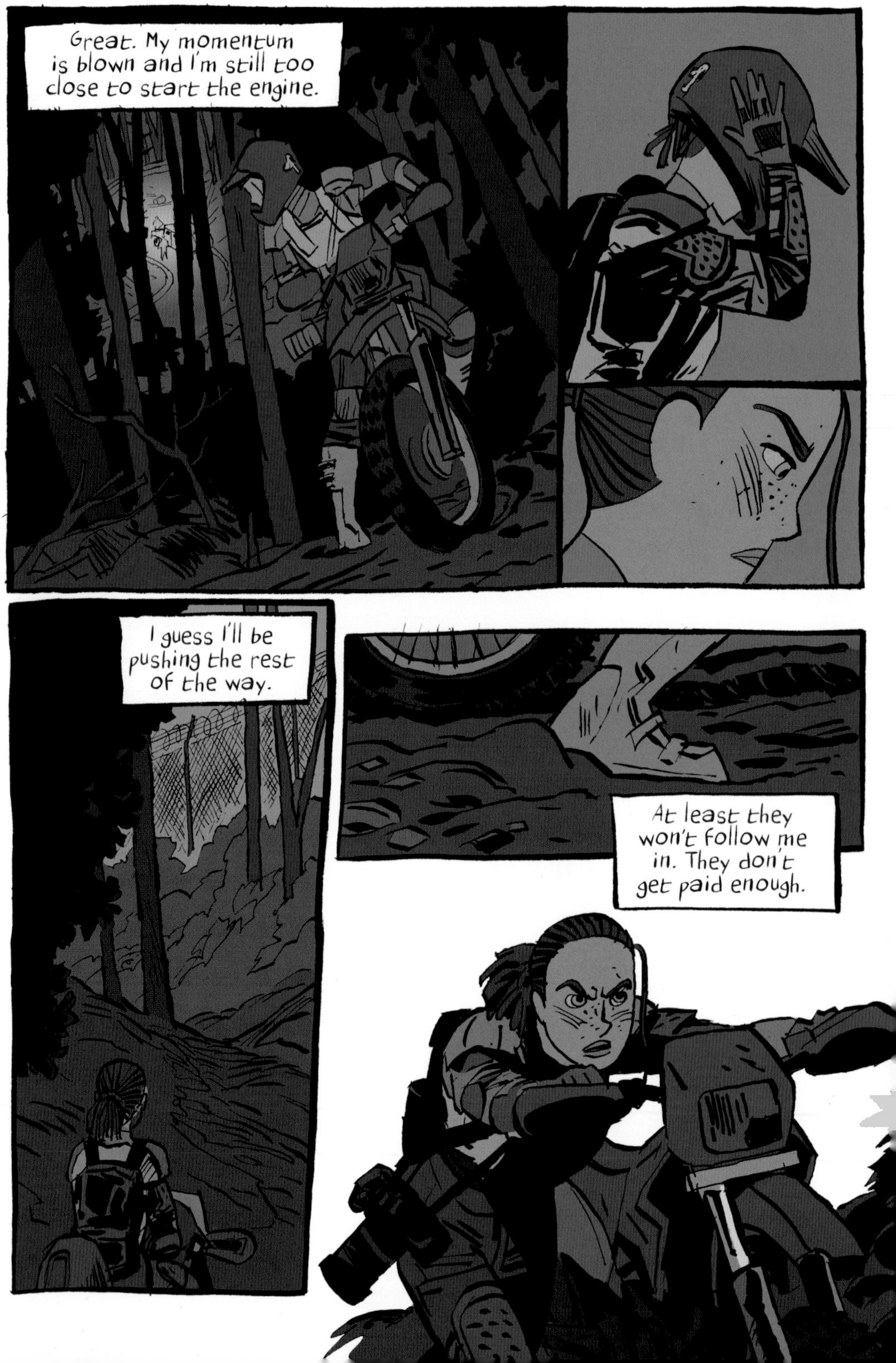
Great. My momentum is blown and I'm still too close to start the engine.
I guess I'll be pushing the rest of the way.
At least they won't follow me in. They don't get paid enough.

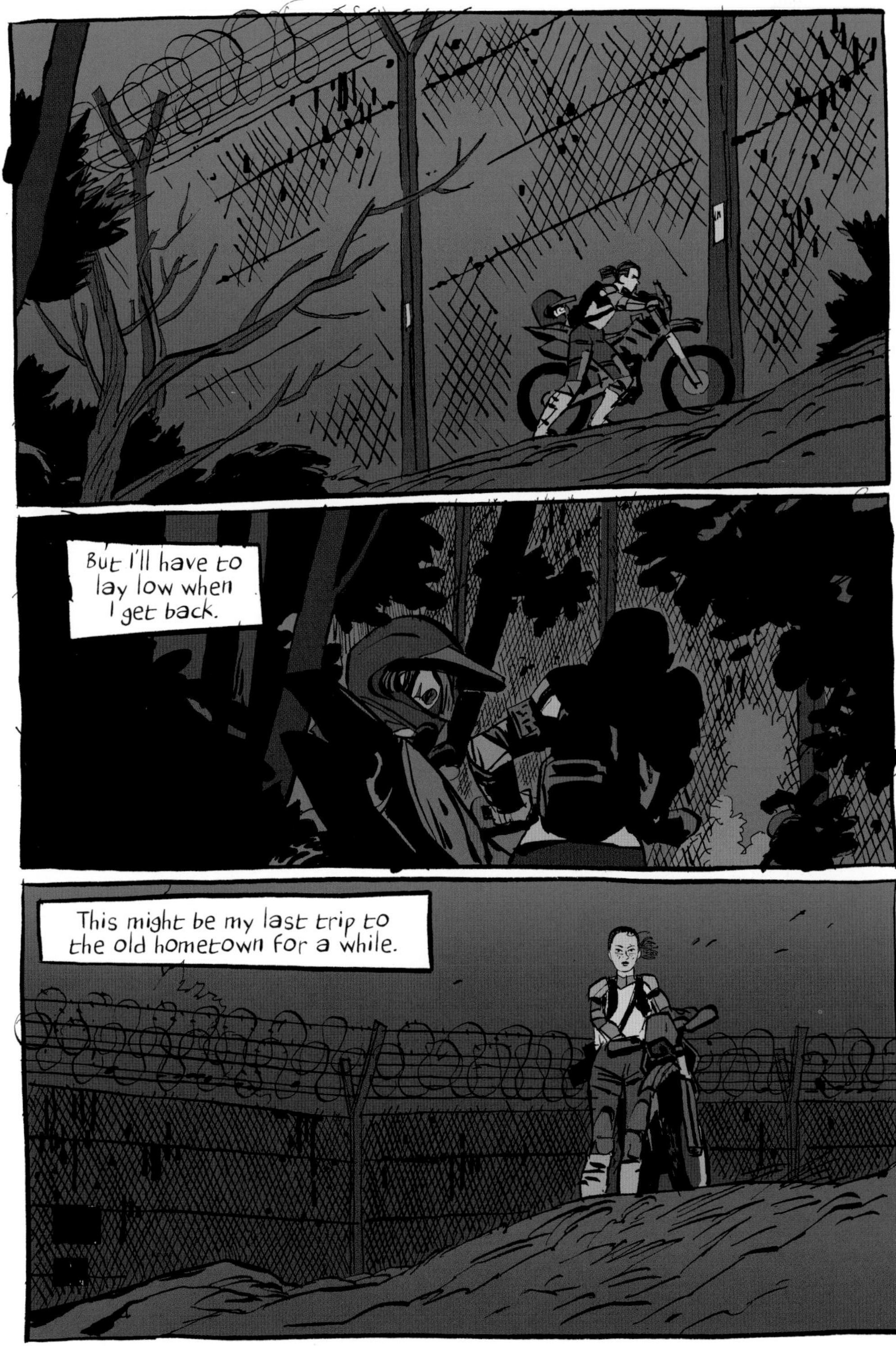
But I'll have to lay low when I get back.
This might be my last trip to the old hometown for a while.

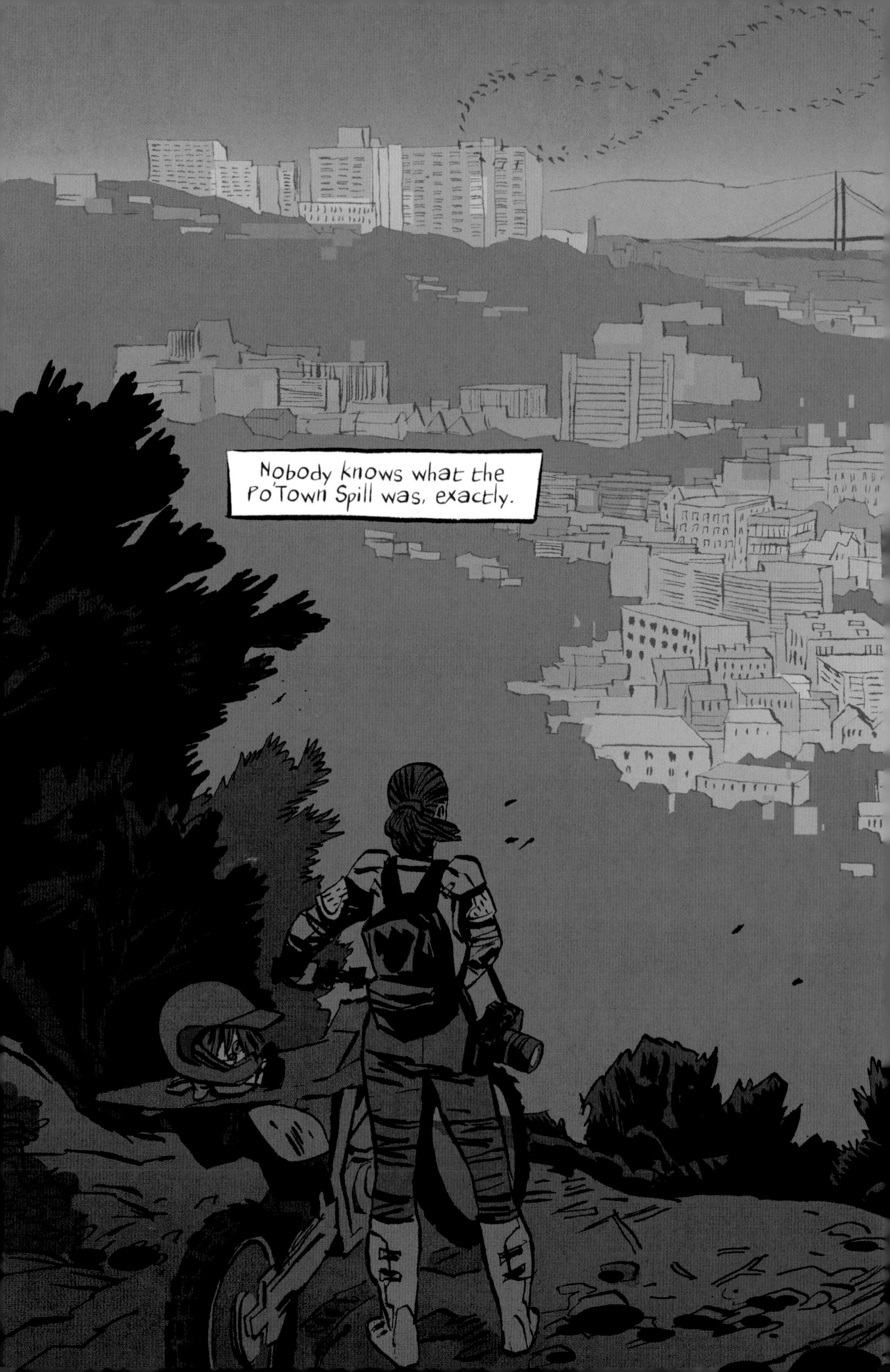
Nobody knows what the Po'Town Spill was, exactly.

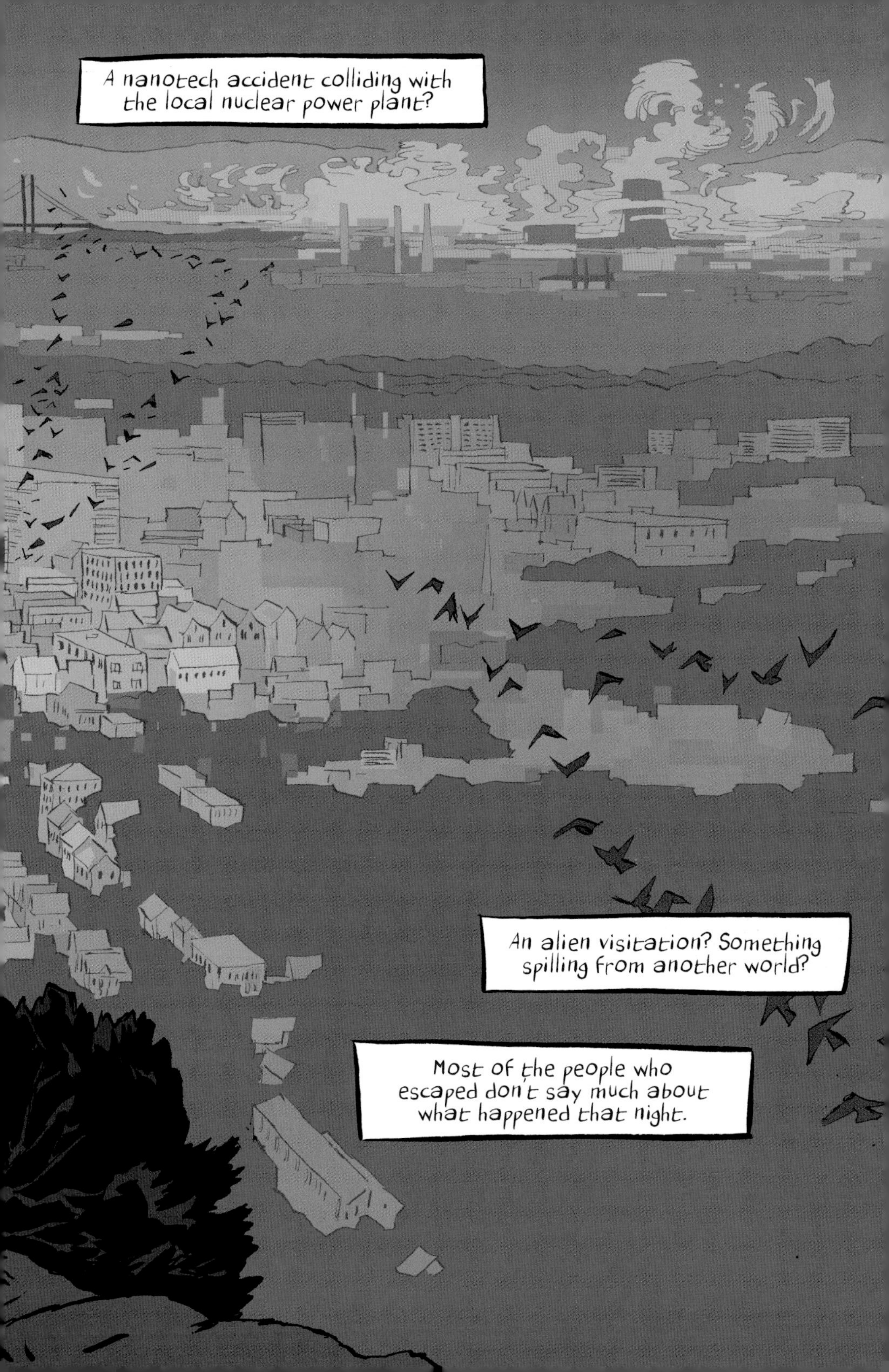
A nanotech accident colliding with the local nuclear power plant?
An alien visitation? Something spilling from another world?
Most of the people who escaped don't say much about what happened that night.

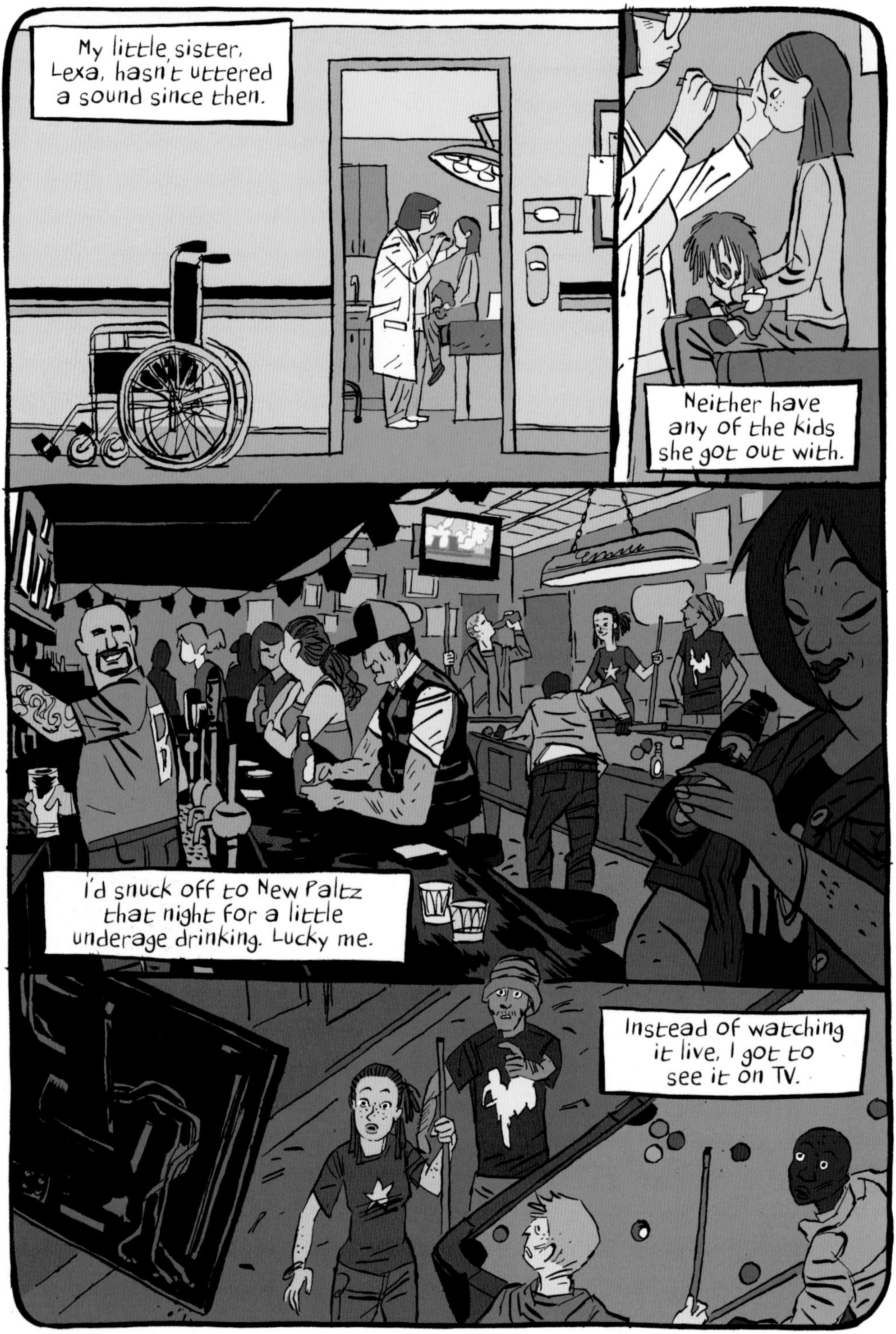
My little sister, Lexa, hasn't uttered a sound since then.
Neither have any of the kids she got out with.
I'd snuck off to New Paltz that night for a little underage drinking. Lucky me.
Instead of watching it live, I got to see it on TV.

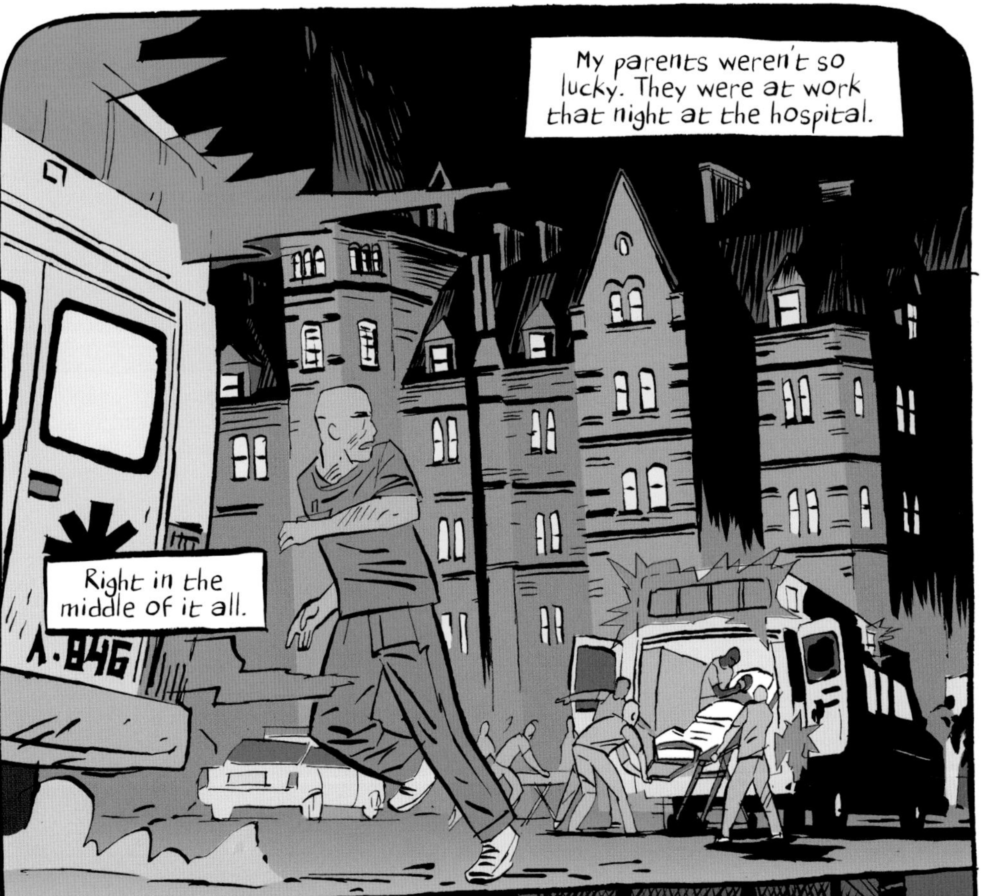
My parents weren't so lucky. They were at work that night at the hospital.
Right in the middle of it all.
A-846

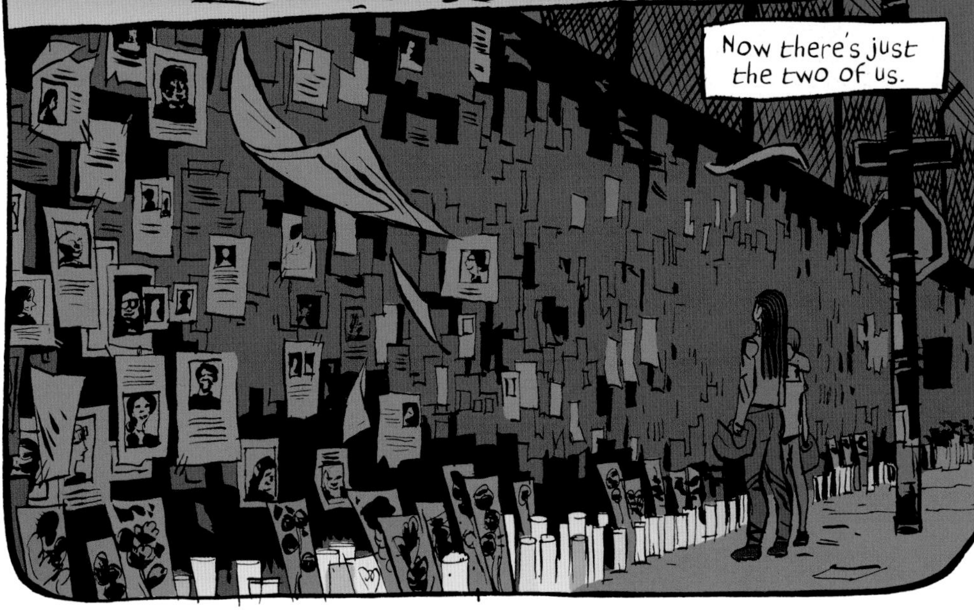
Now there's just the two of us.

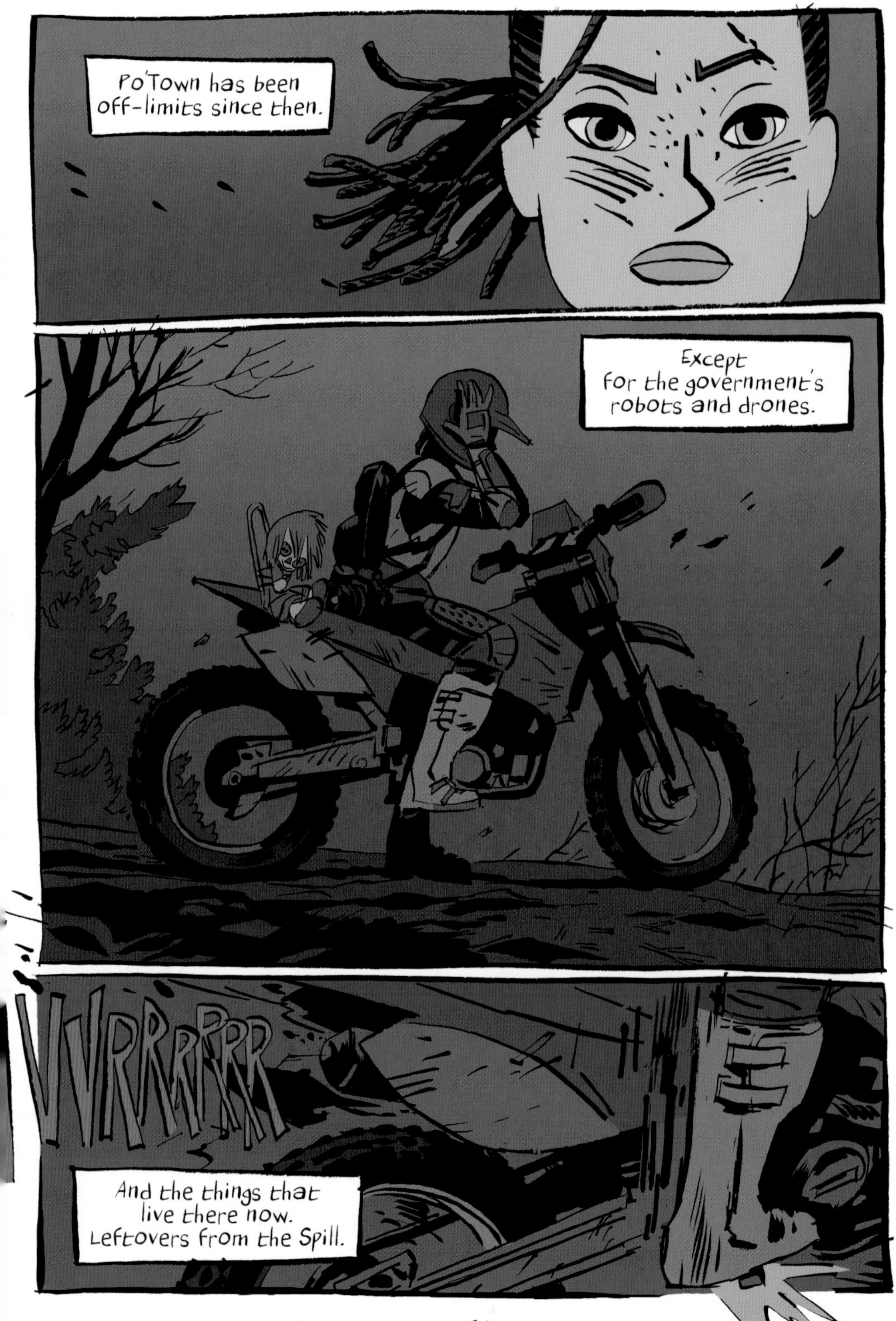
Po'Town has been off-limits since then.
Except for the government's robots and drones.
VVRRRRRR
And the things that live there now. Leftovers from the Spill.

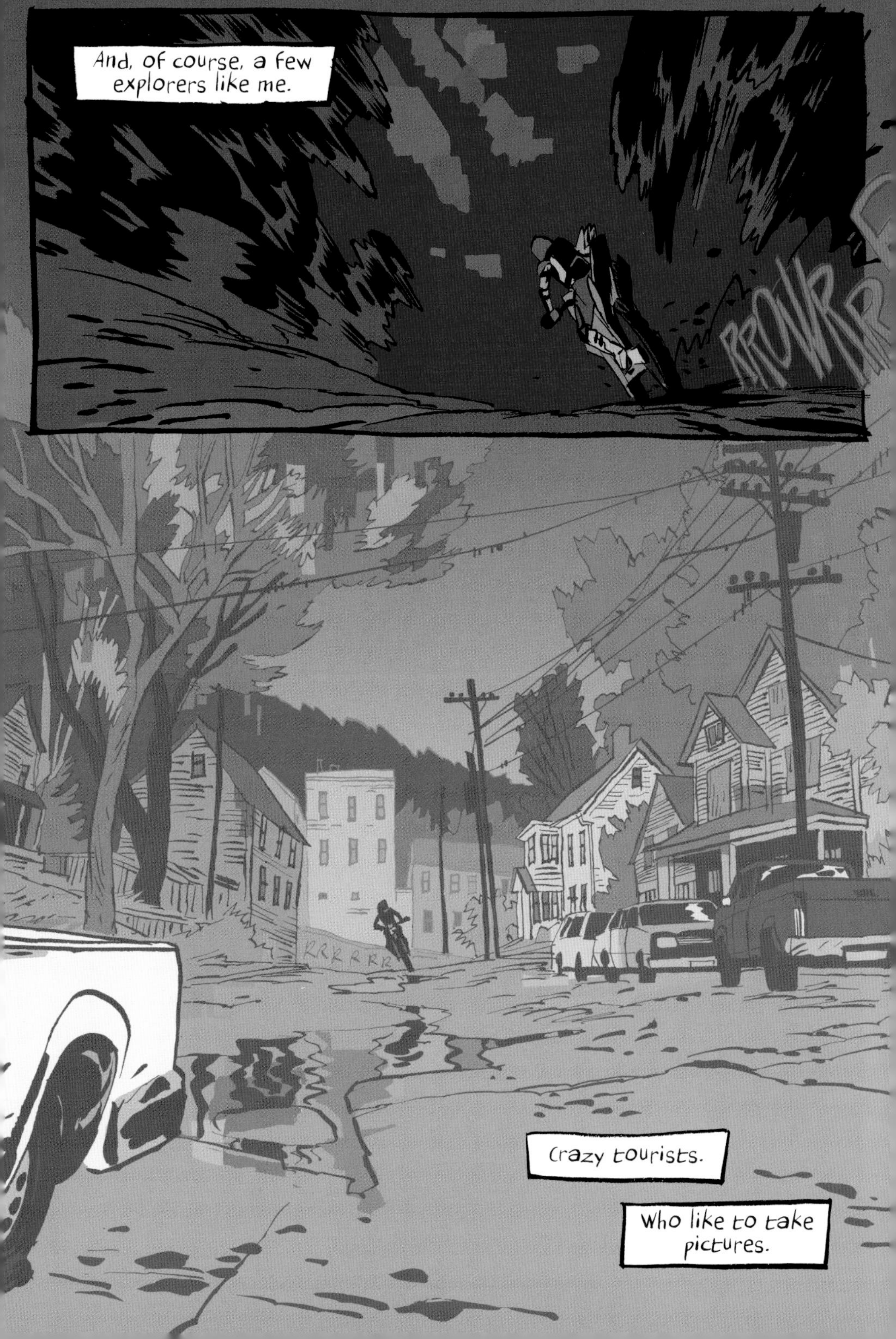
And, of course, a few explorers like me.
Crazy tourists.
Who like to take pictures.

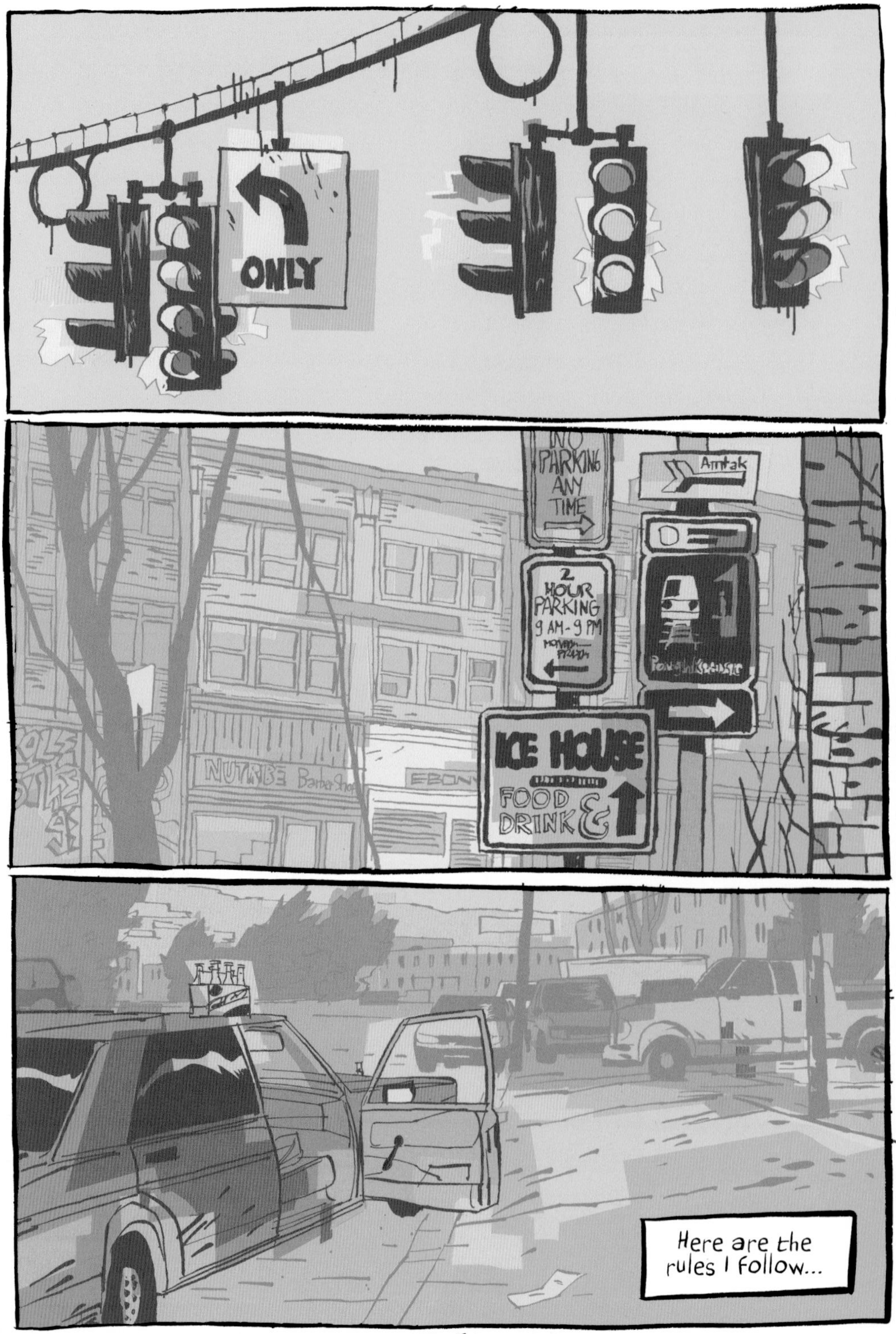
ONLY
NO PARKING ANY TIME
Amtrak
2 HOUR PARKING 9 AM - 9 PM
ICE HOUSE
FOOD & DRINK
Barber Shop
Here are the rules I follow...

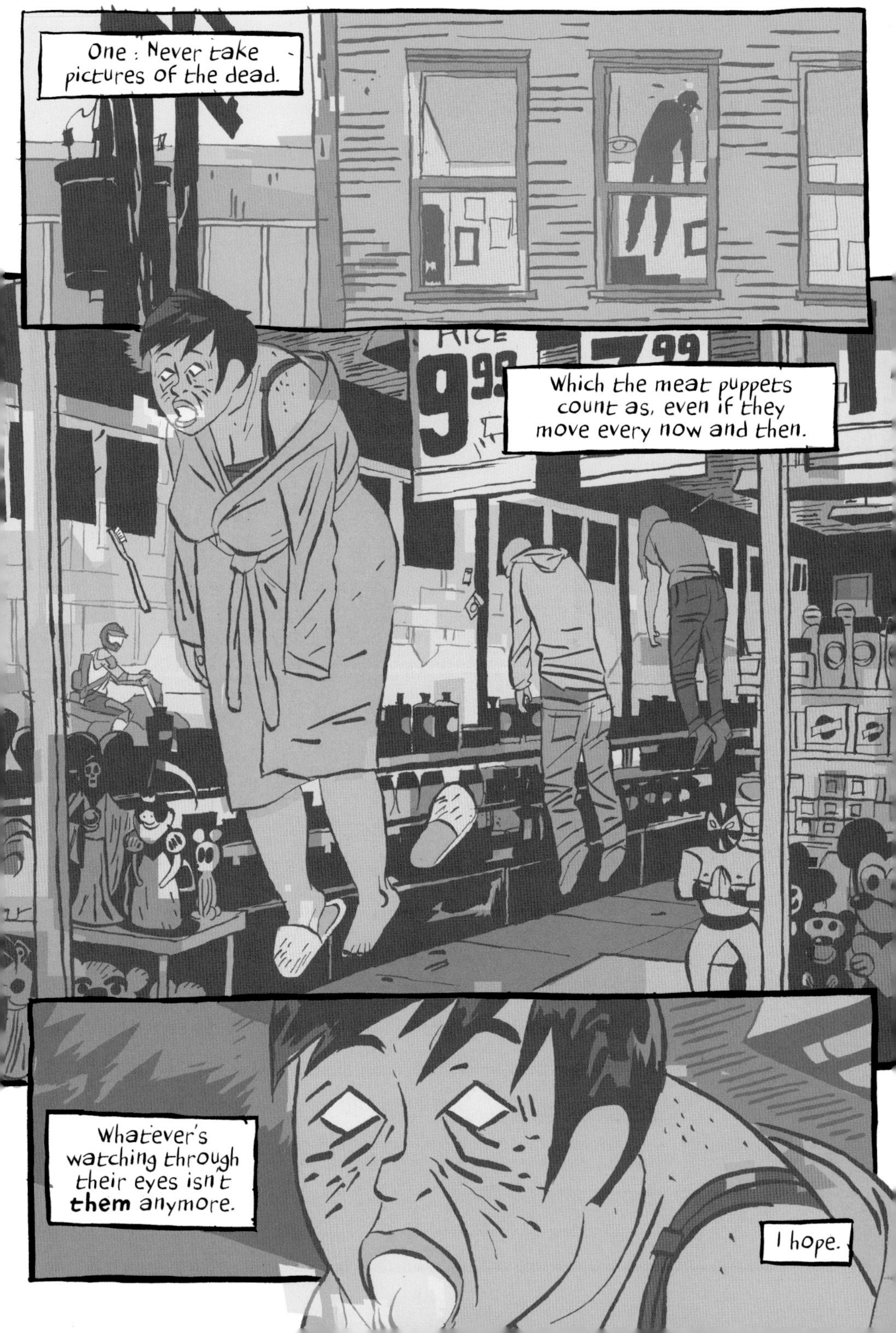

One : Never take pictures of the dead.
RICE
9.9
7.99
Which the meat puppets count as, even if they move every now and then.
Whatever's watching through their eyes isn't **them** anymore.
I hope.

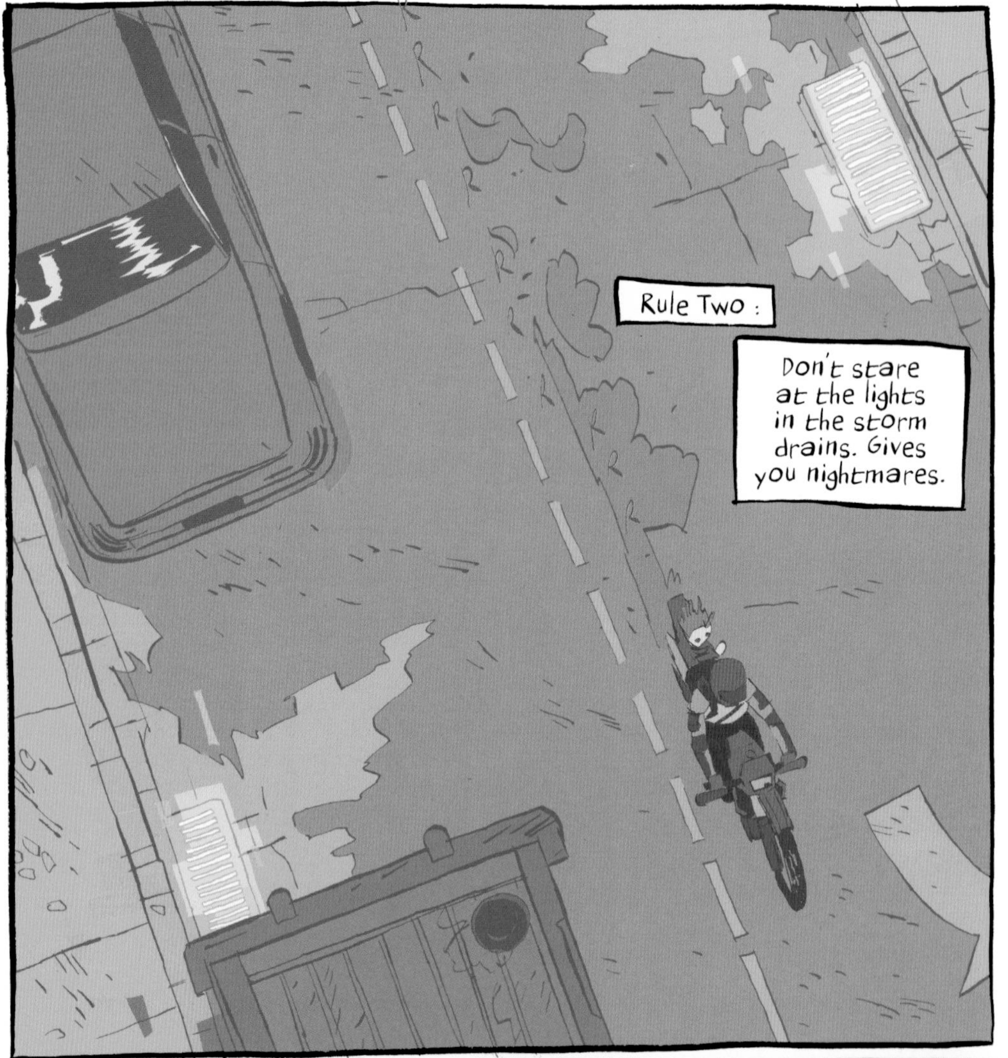
Rule Two:
Don't stare at the lights in the storm drains. Gives you nightmares.

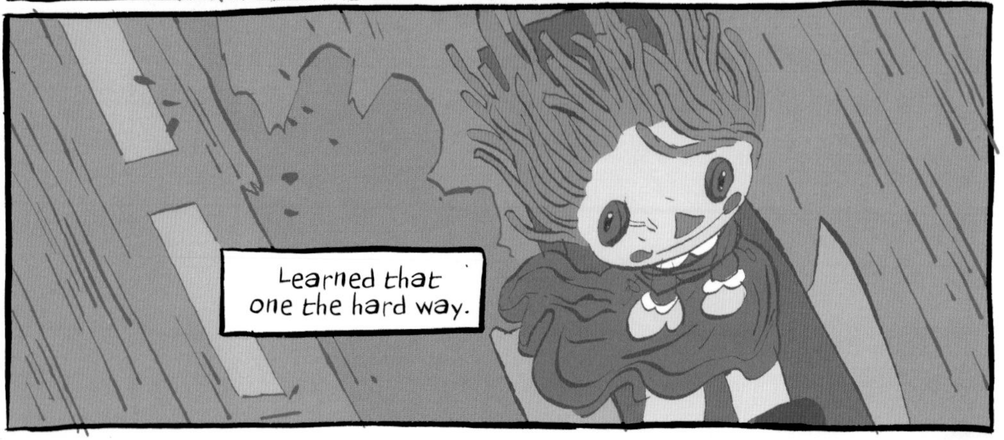
Learned that one the hard way.

Rule Three : Stay away from the factories. The rats there are like little meat puppets.

Except they'll chase you some days.

Four : Don't listen to cats' cries too closely, or they start to sound like words.

WRRRRRONG

PO G NESIA ELEMEN RY SC OOL

29

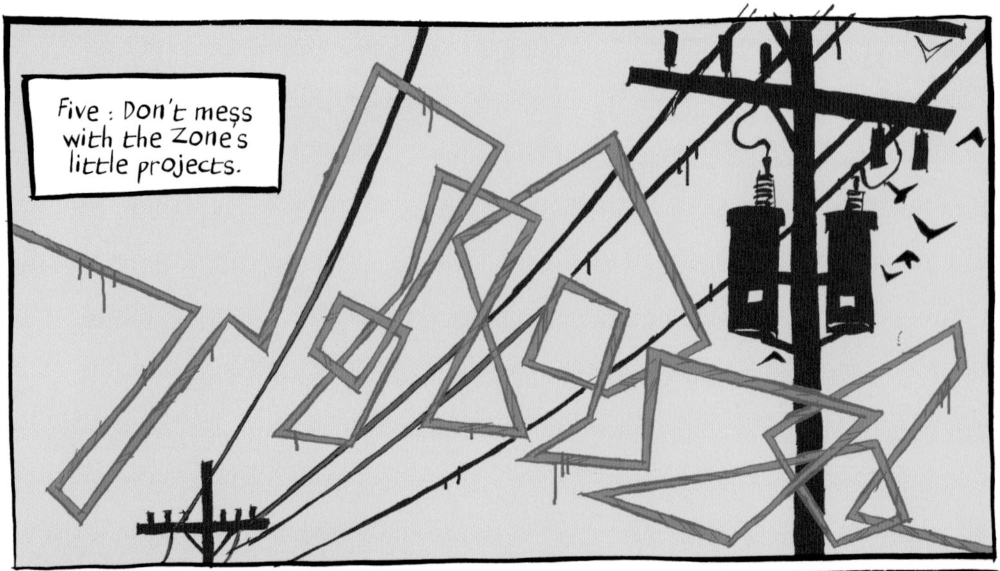
Five : Don't mess with the Zone's little projects.

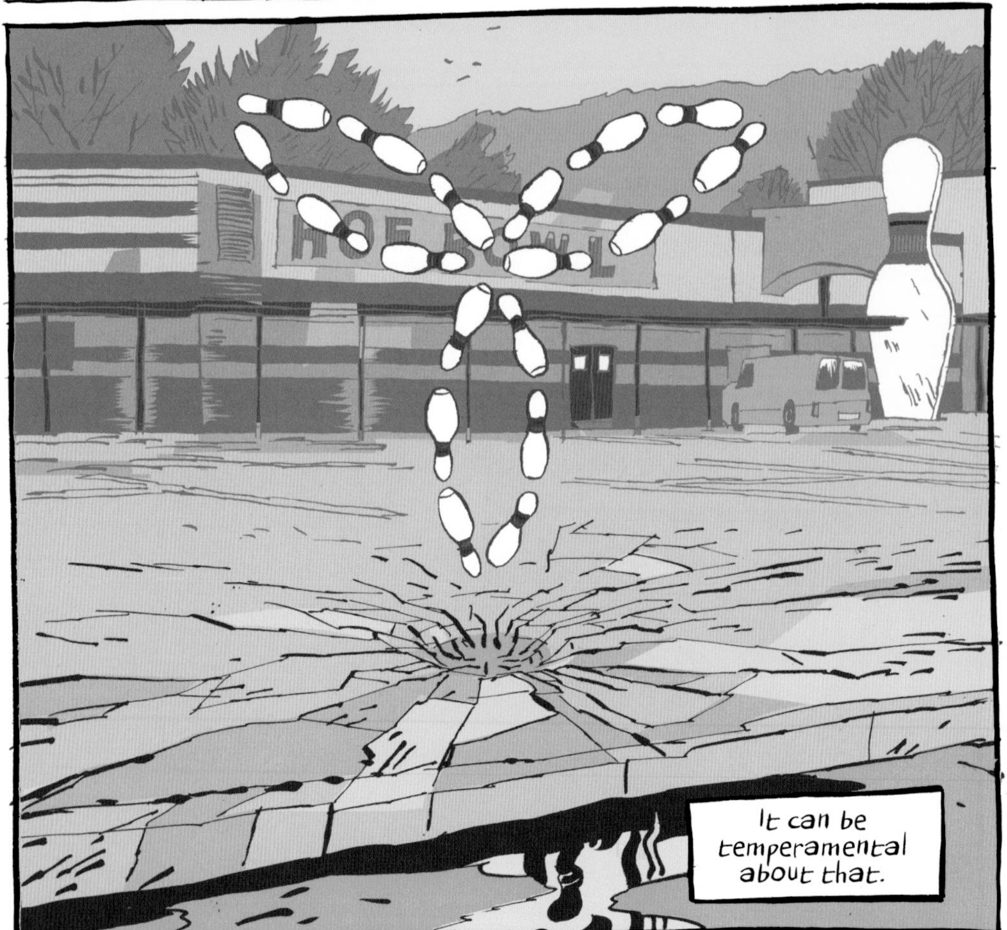
It can be temperamental about that.

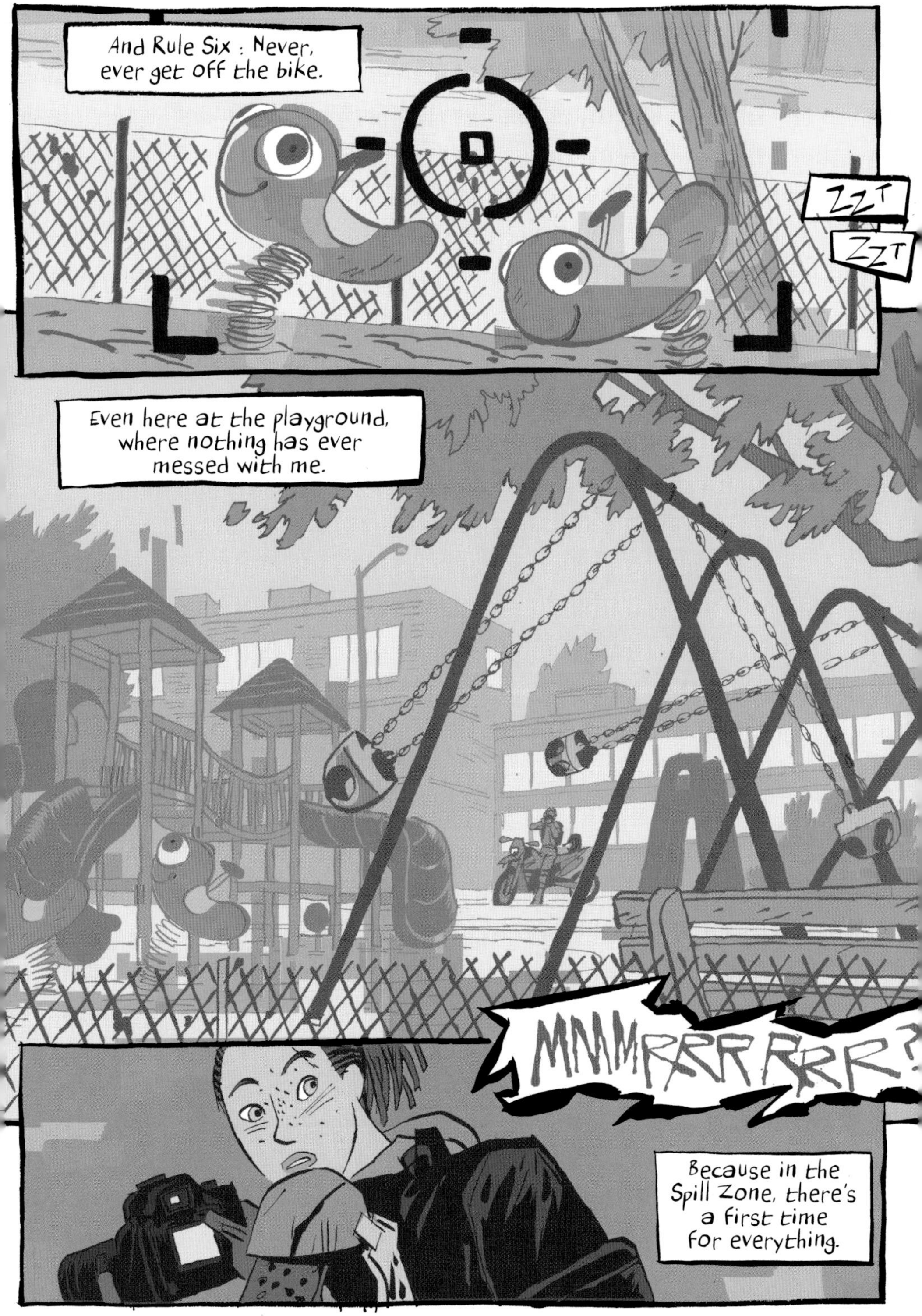
And Rule Six : Never, ever get off the bike.
ZZT
ZZT
Even here at the playground, where nothing has ever messed with me.
MMMRRRRRRR?
Because in the Spill Zone, there's a first time for everything.

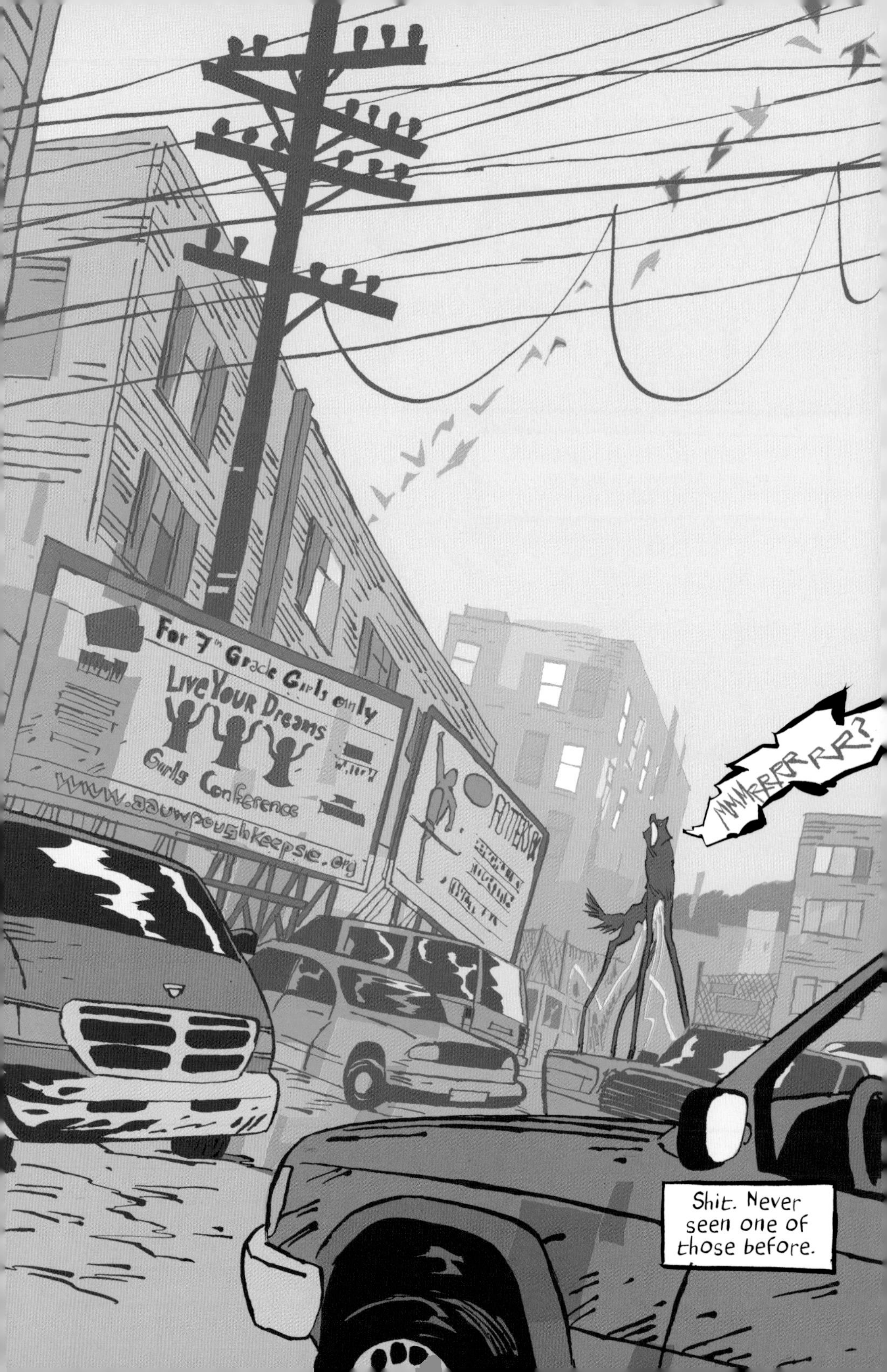
For 7th Grade Girls only
Live Your Dreams
Girls Conference
www.aauwpoughkeepsie.org
MMMRRRRRRR?
Shit. Never seen one of those before.

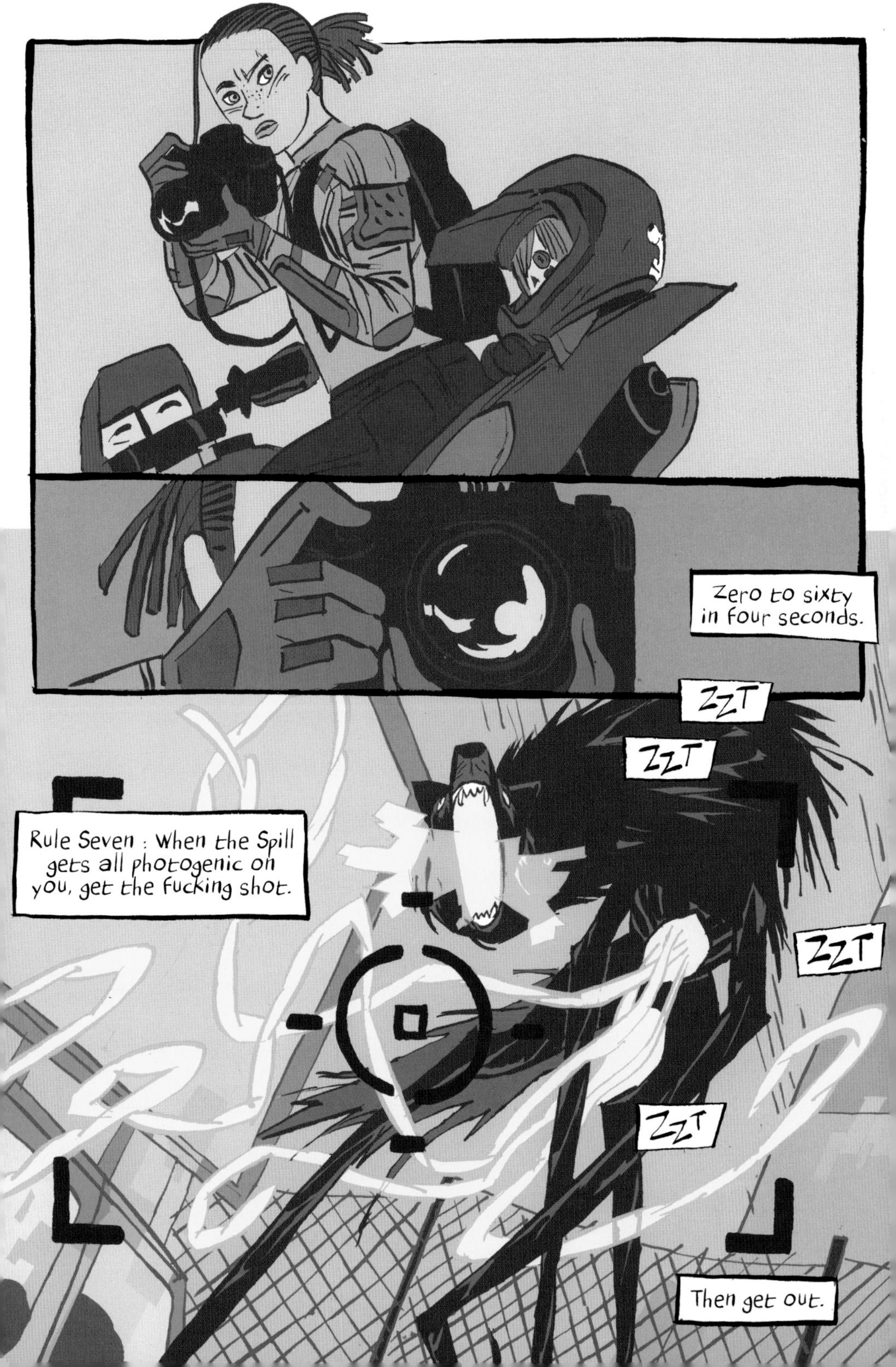
Zero to sixty in four seconds.
ZZT
ZZT
Rule Seven : When the Spill gets all photogenic on you, get the fucking shot.
ZZT
ZZT
Then get out.

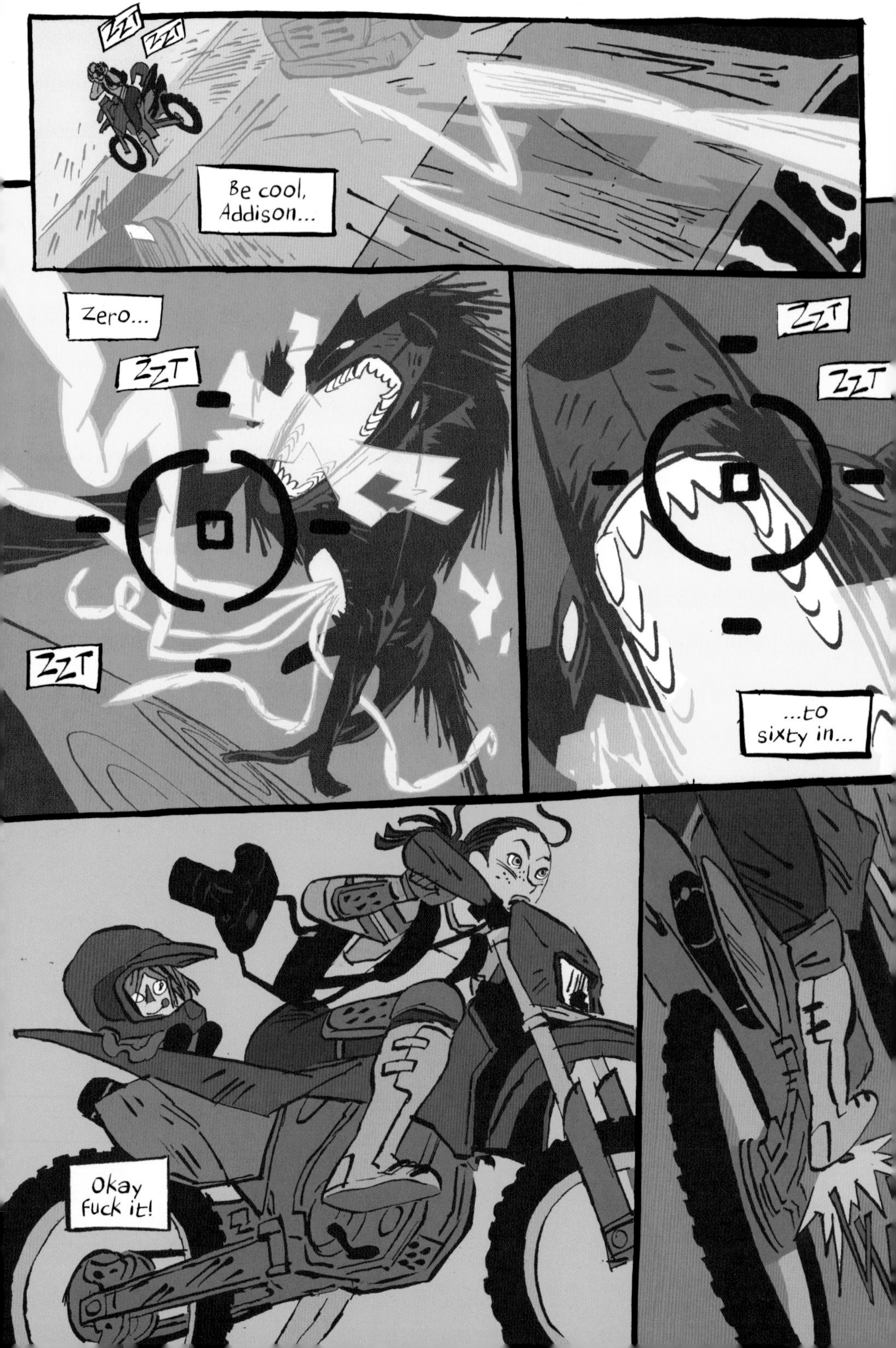
ZZT
ZZT
Be cool, Addison...
Zero...
ZZT
ZZT
ZZT
ZZT
...to sixty in...
Okay fuck it!

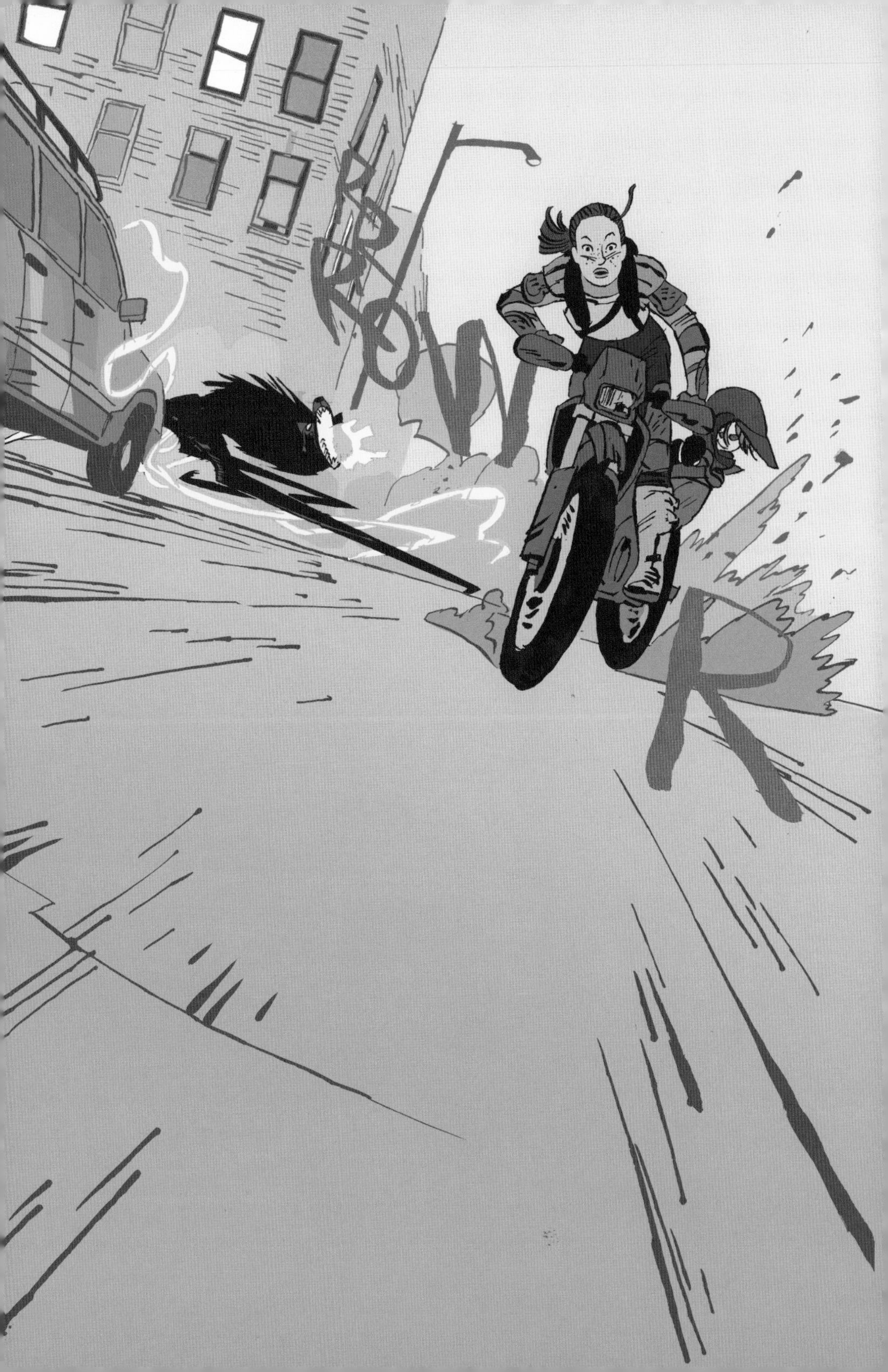

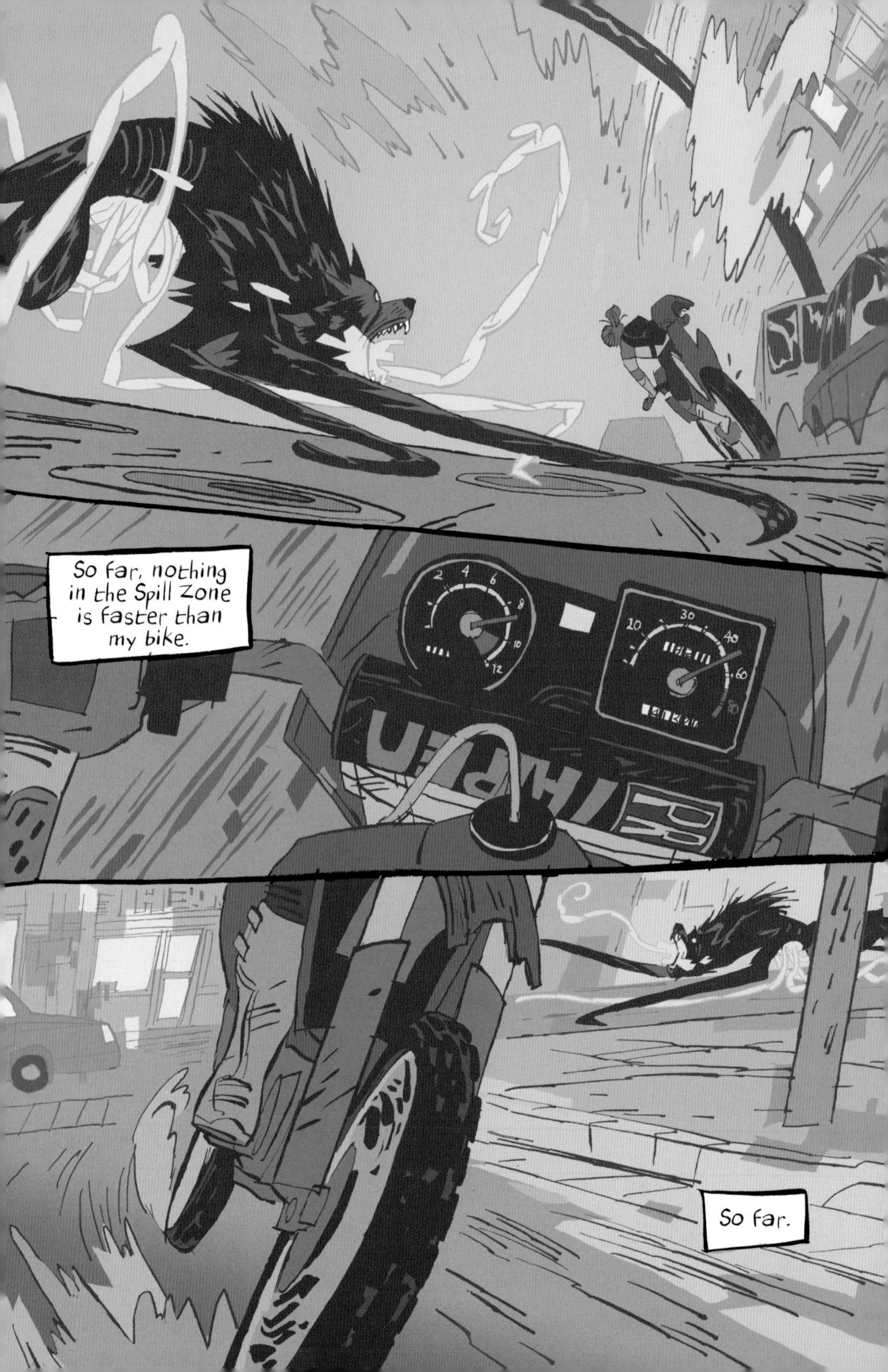
So far, nothing in the Spill Zone is faster than my bike.
So far.

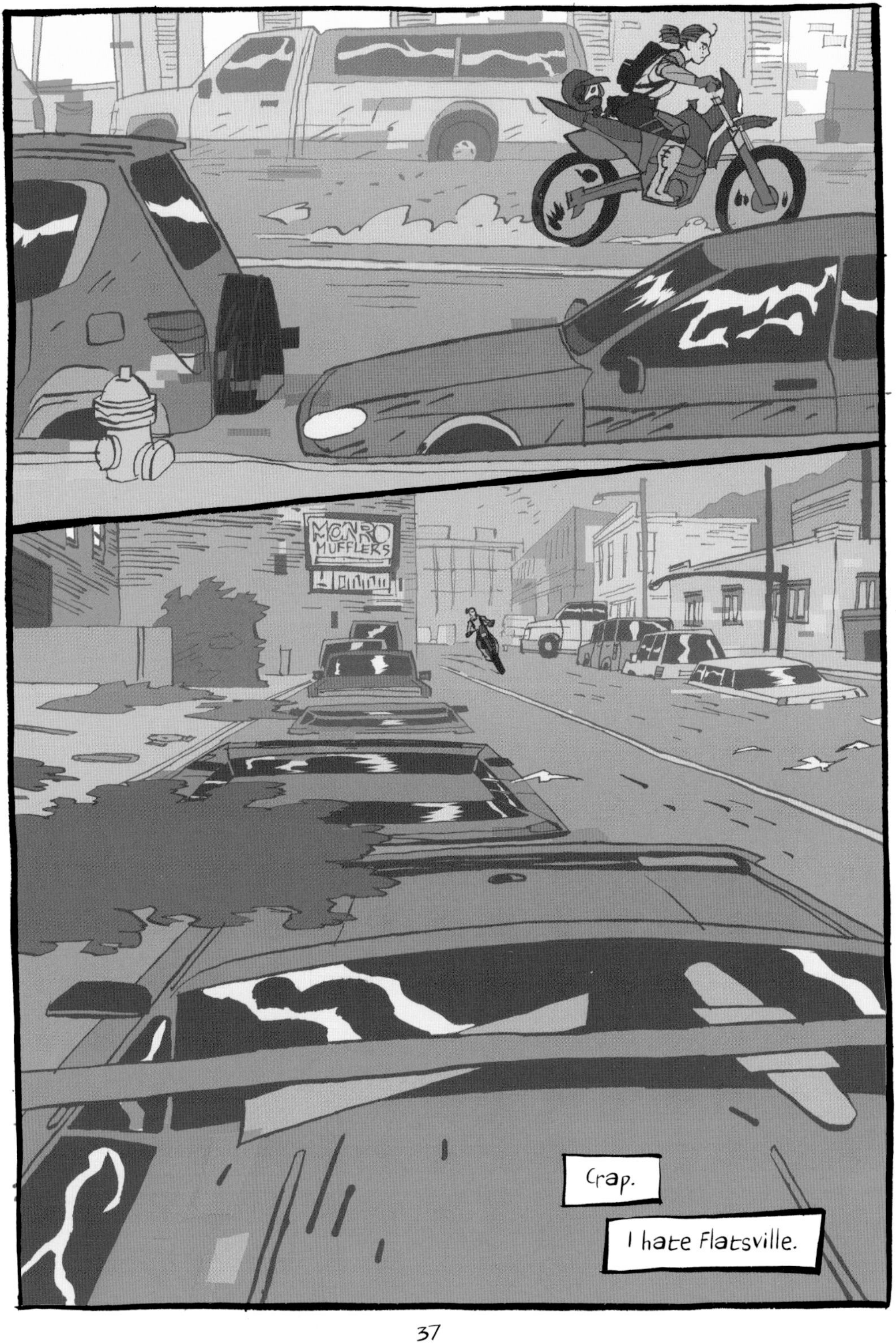
MONRO MUFFLERS
Crap.
I hate Flatsville.

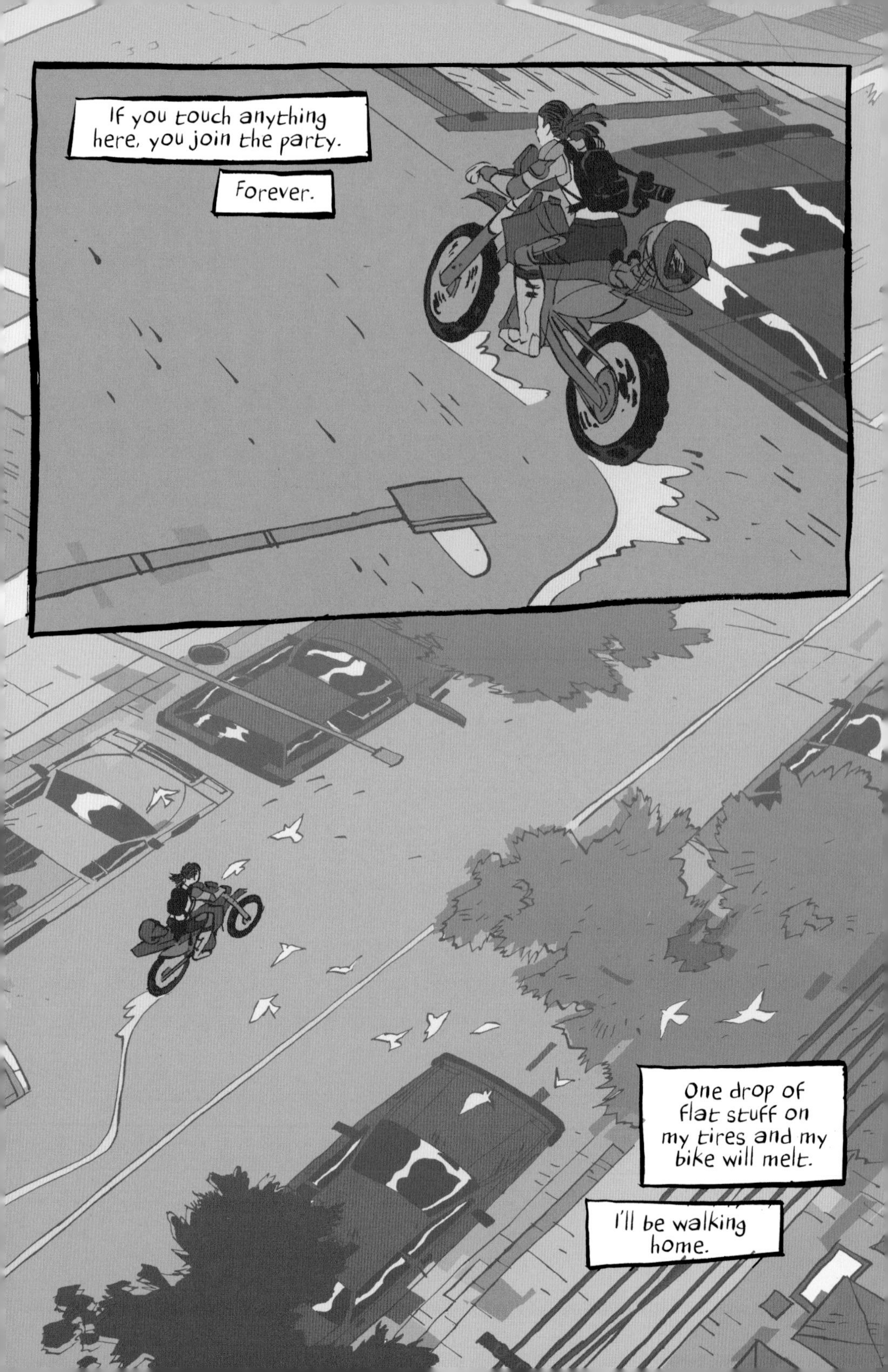
If you touch anything here, you join the party.
Forever.
One drop of flat stuff on my tires and my bike will melt.
I'll be walking home.

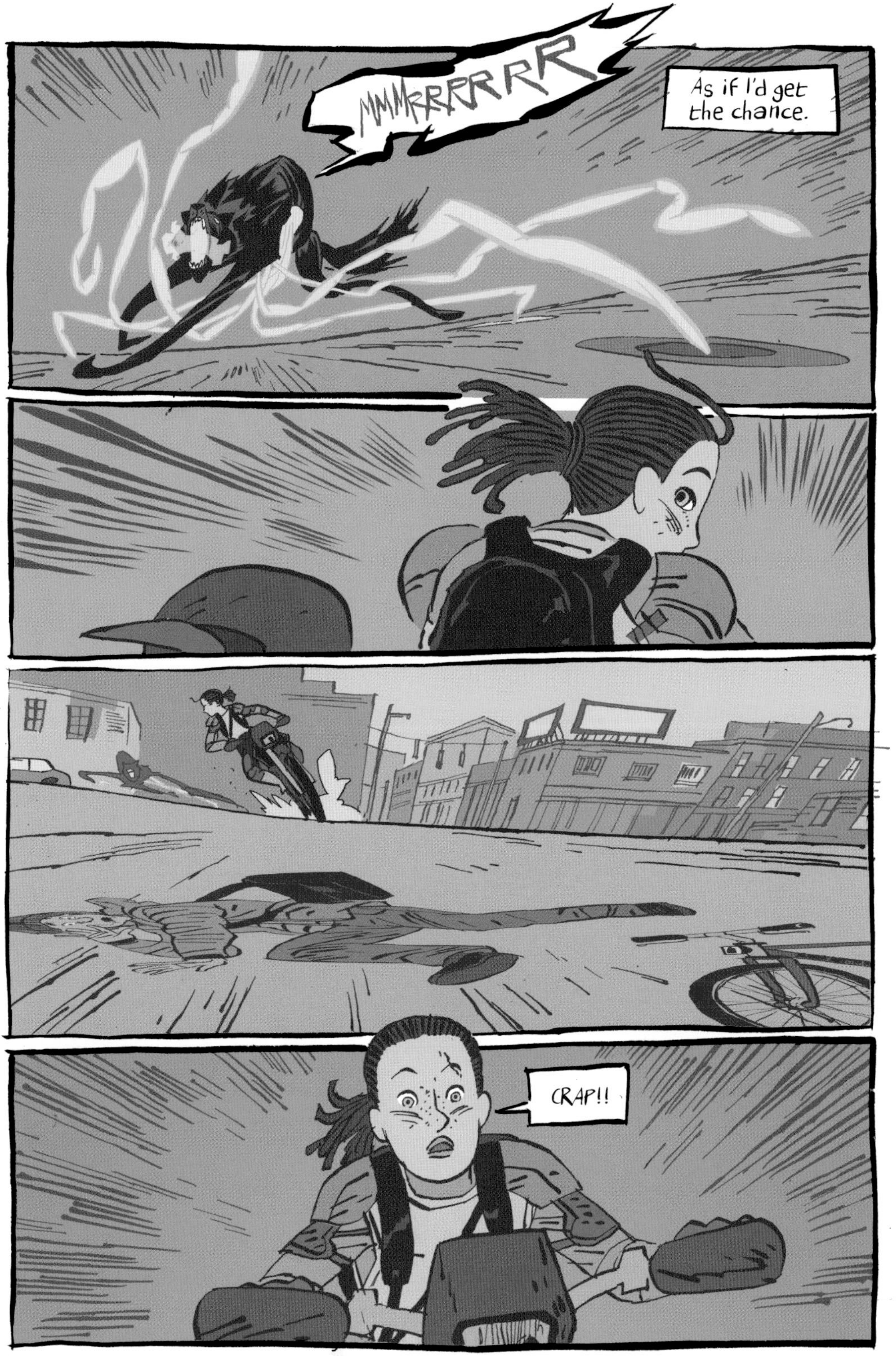
MMMRRRRRRR
As if I'd get the chance.
CRAP!!

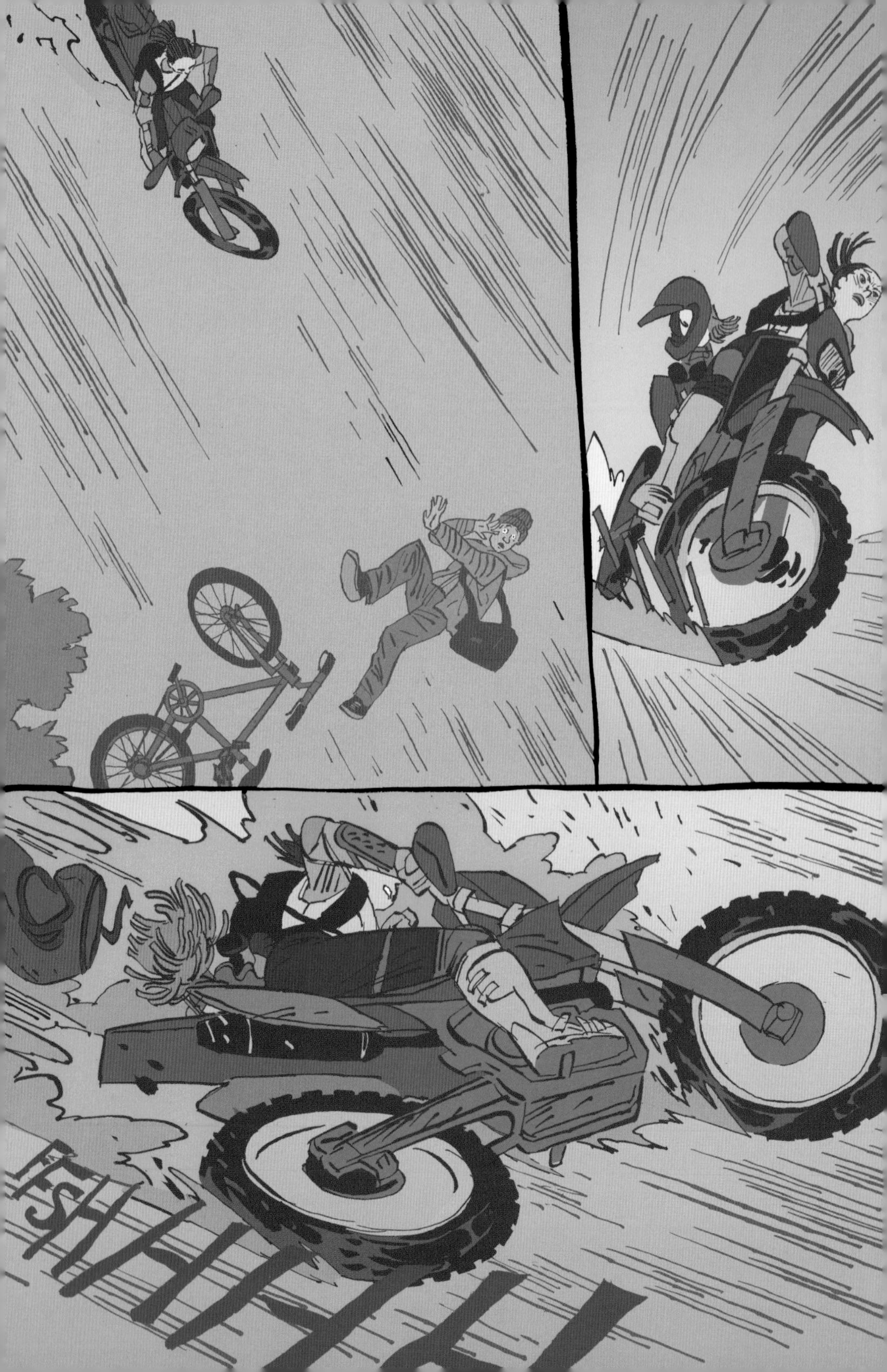
FSHHHH

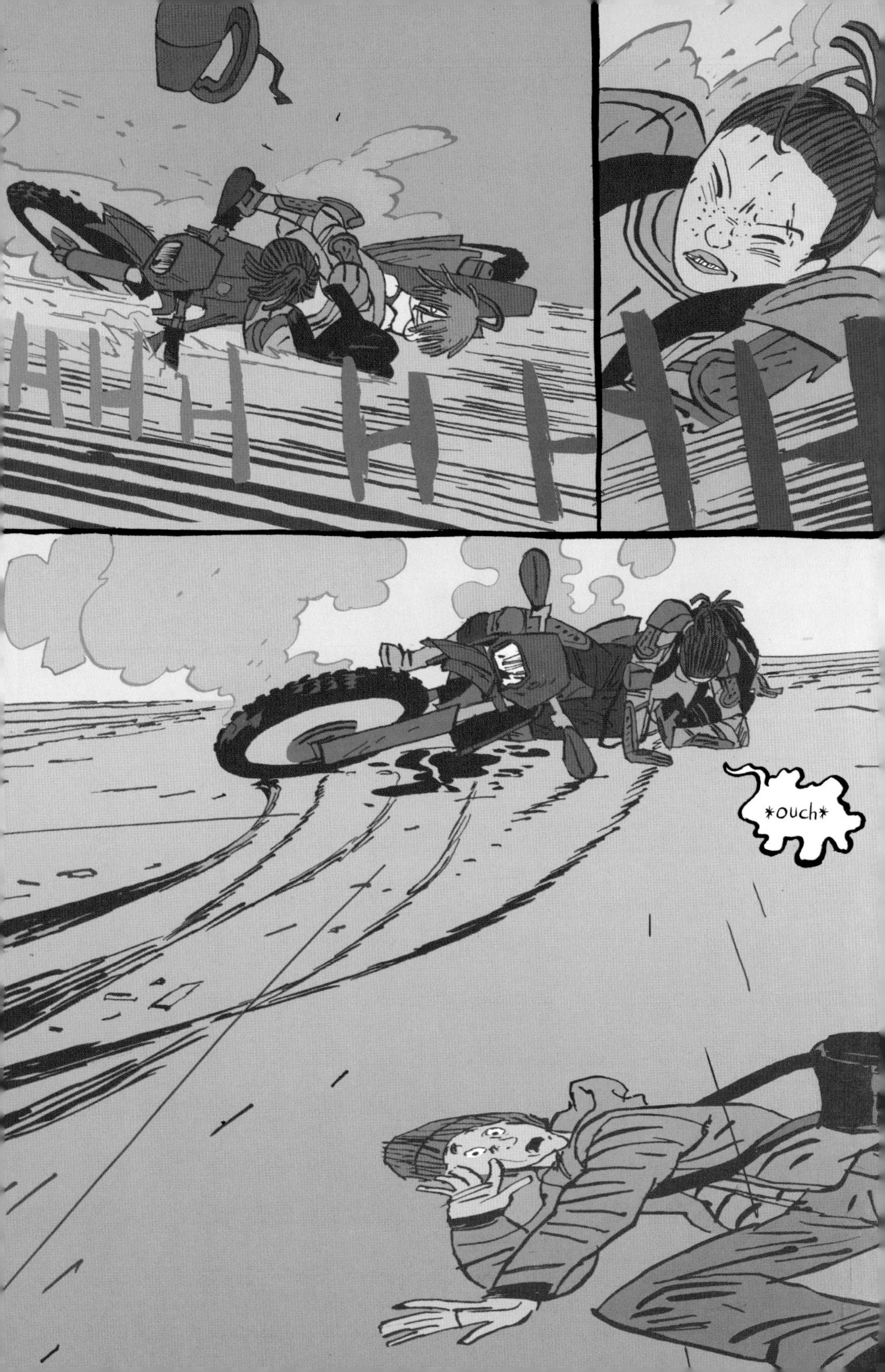
ouch

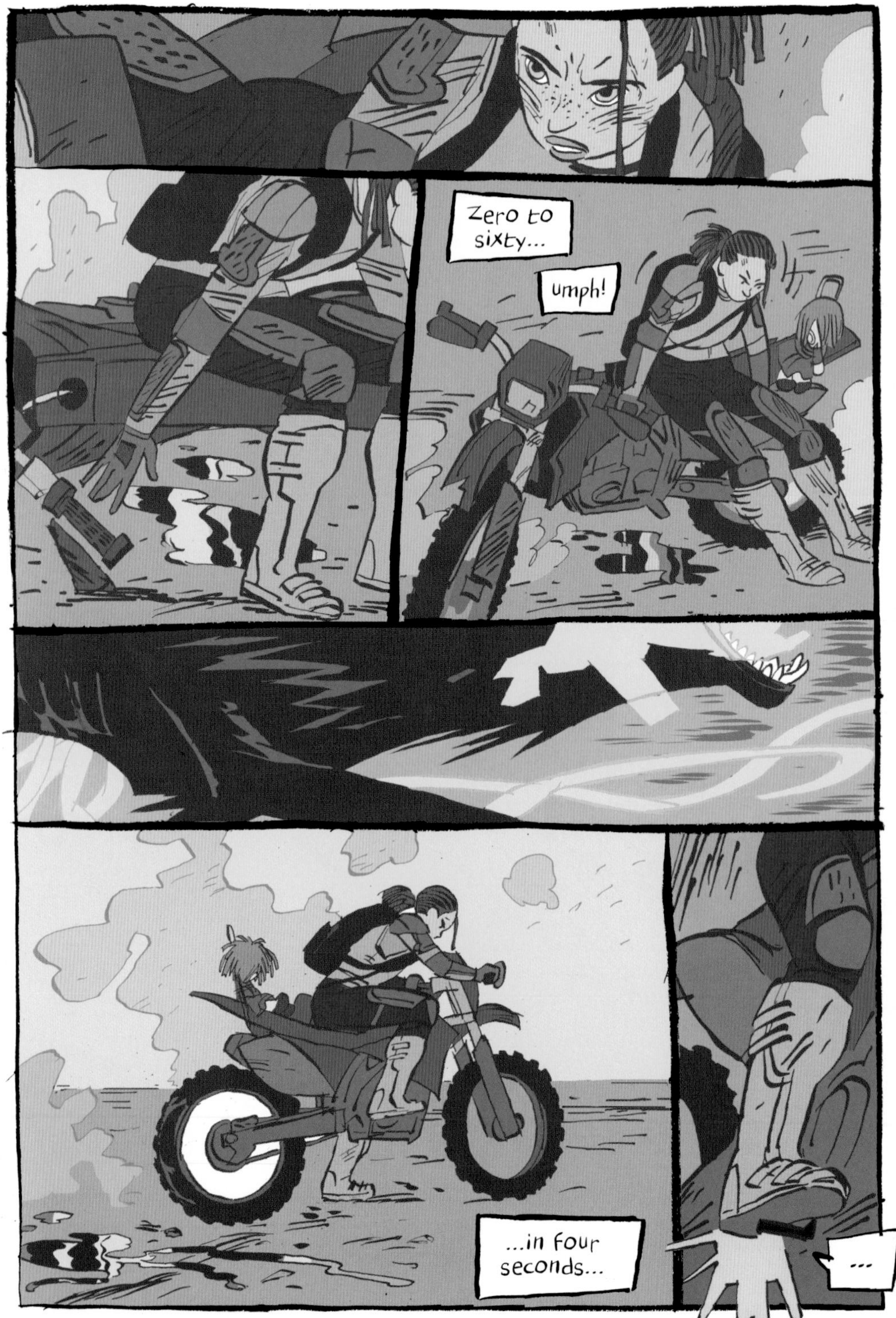
Zero to sixty...
umph!
...in four seconds...
...

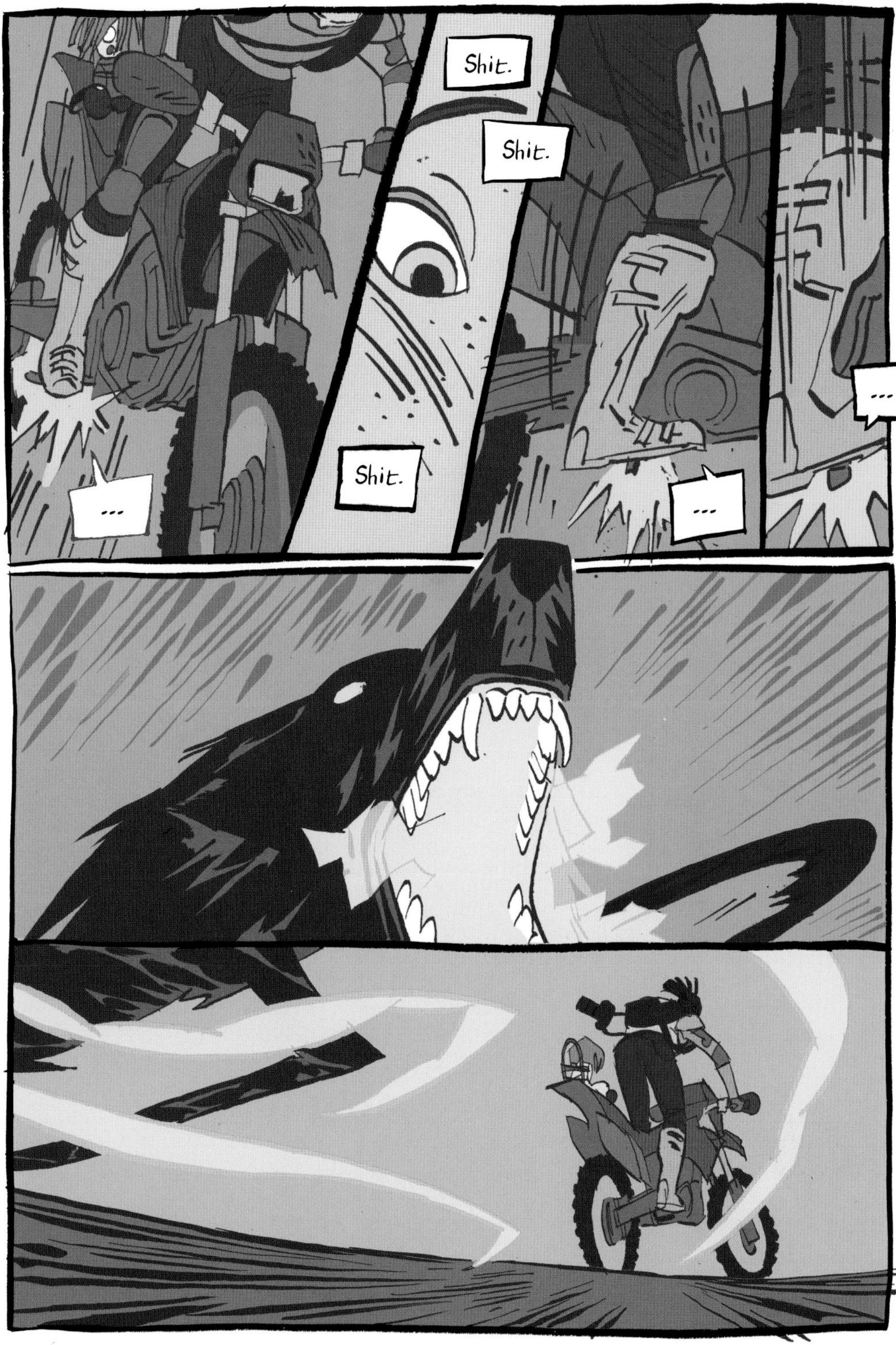
Shit.
Shit.
Shit.
...
...
...

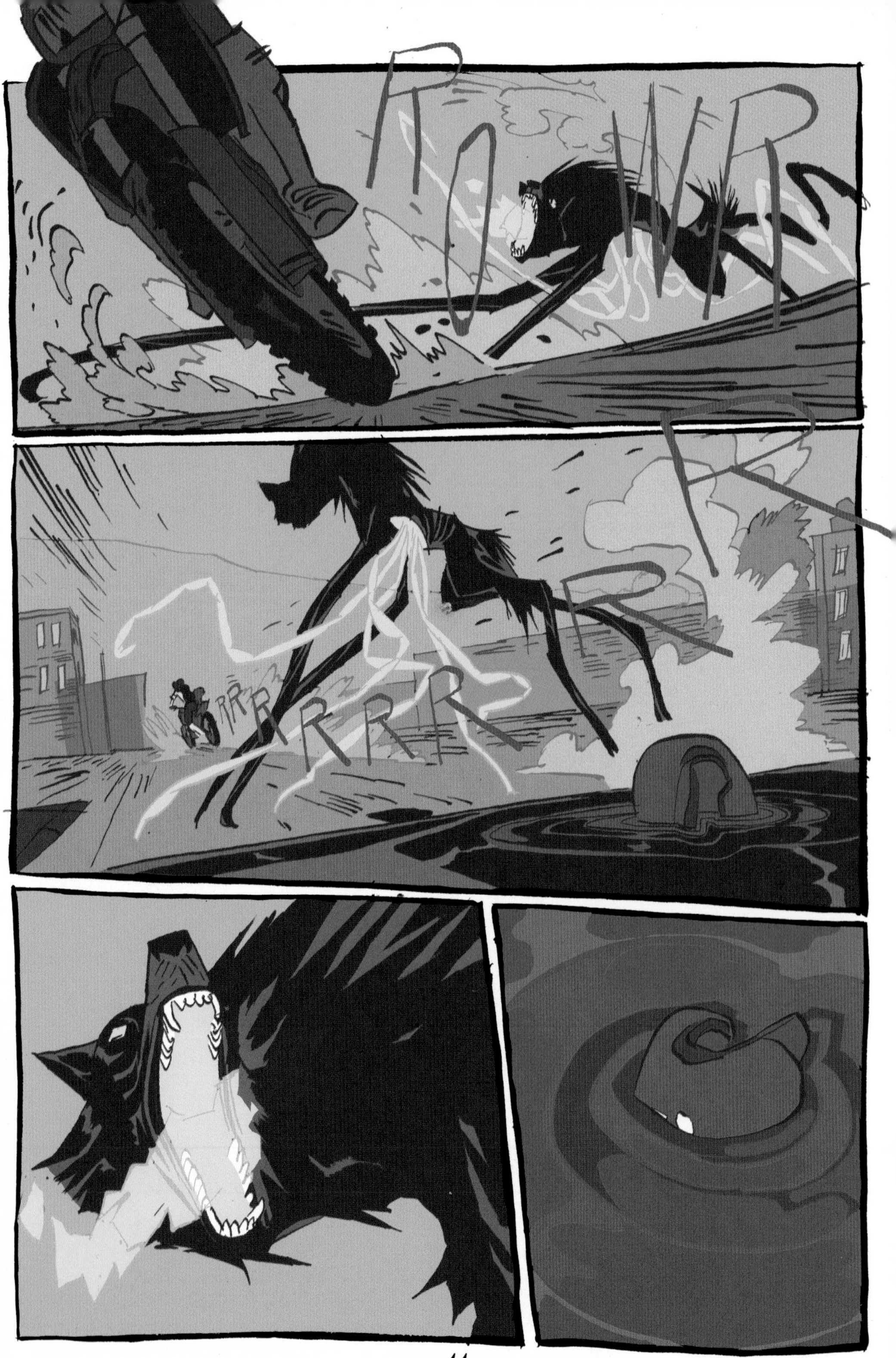

ROWR
RRRRRR

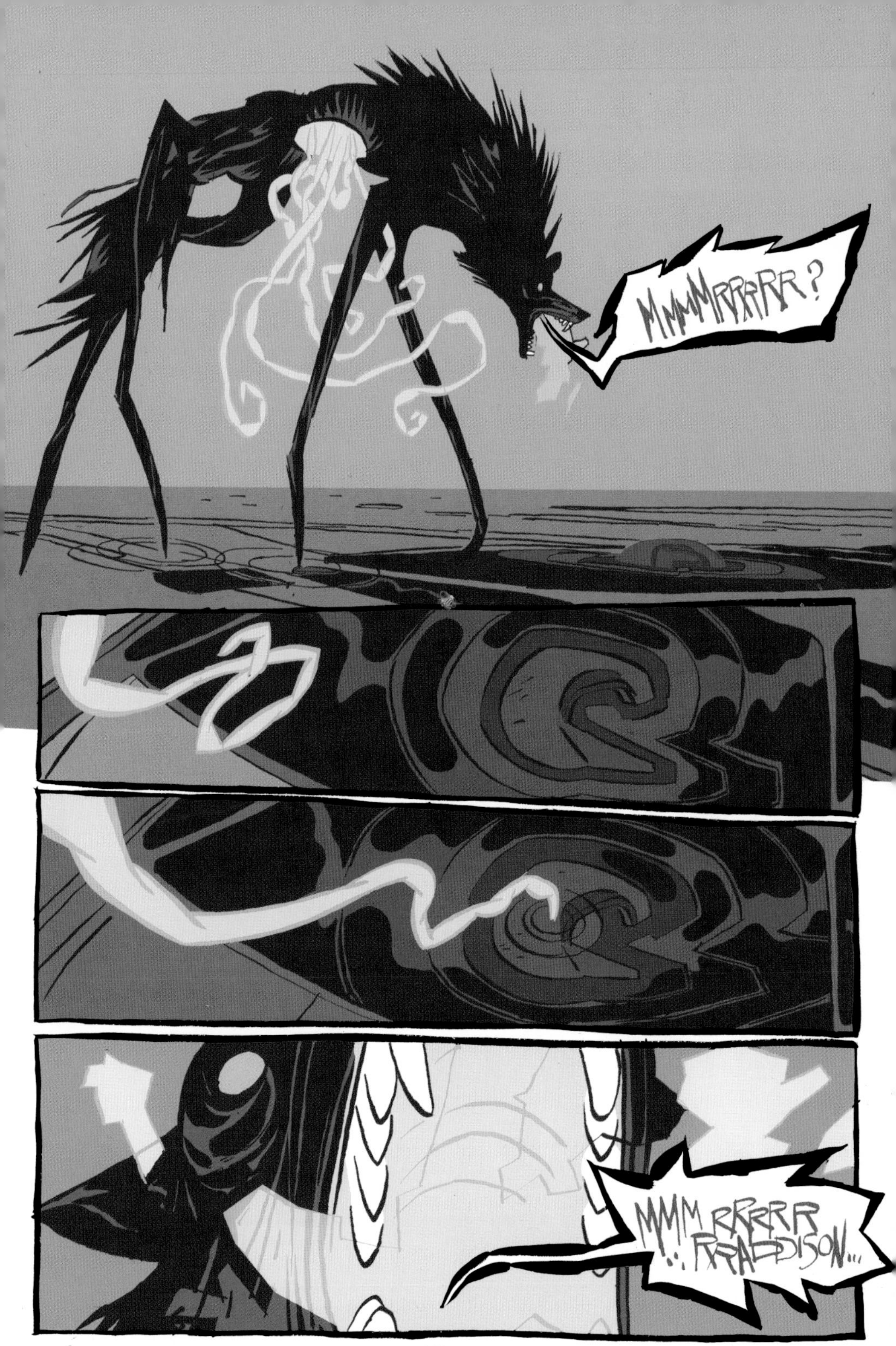
MMMMRRRRRR?
MMM RRRRR !.. RRRADDISON...

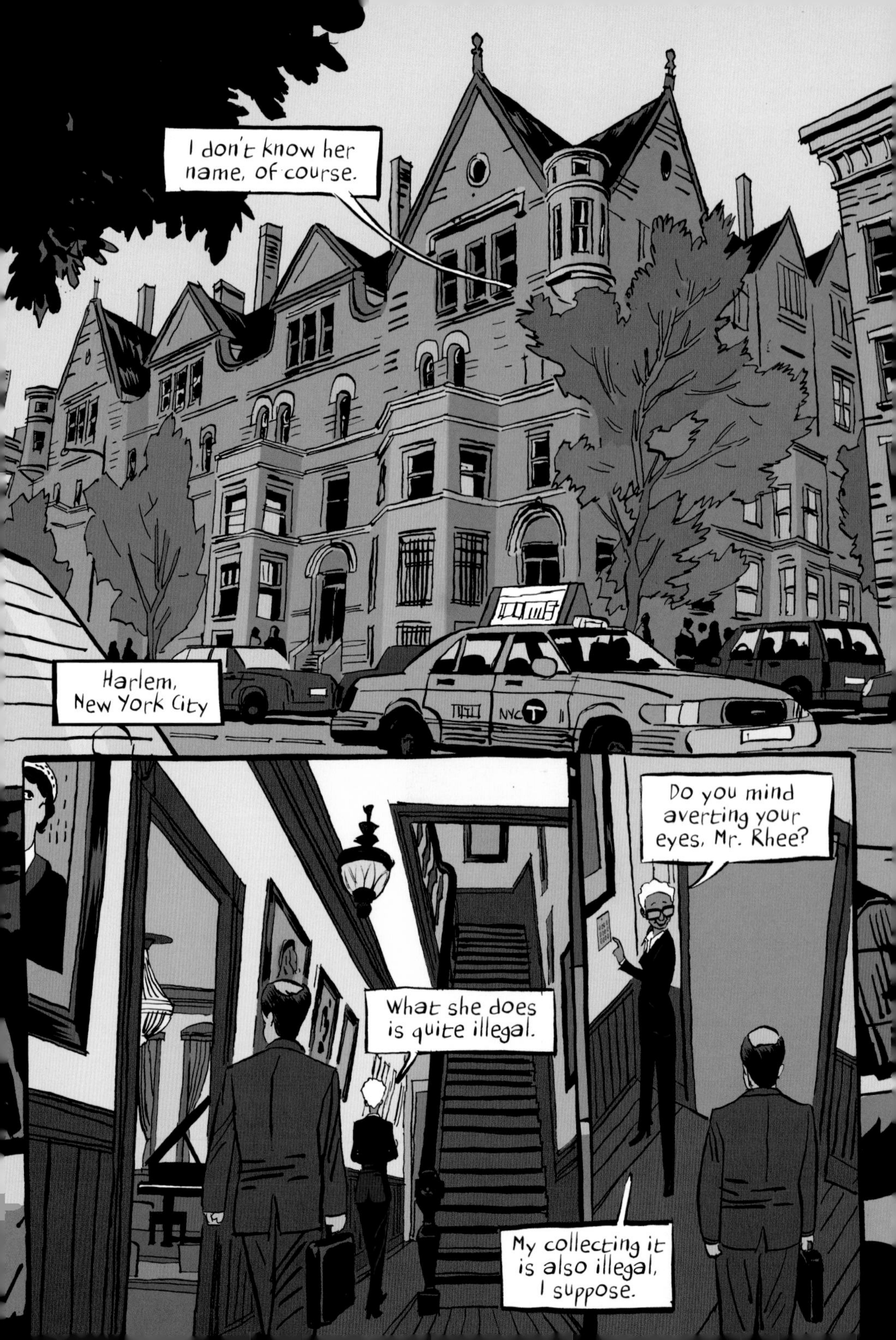
I don't know her name, of course.
Harlem, New York City
Do you mind averting your eyes, Mr. Rhee?
What she does is quite illegal.
My collecting it is also illegal, I suppose.

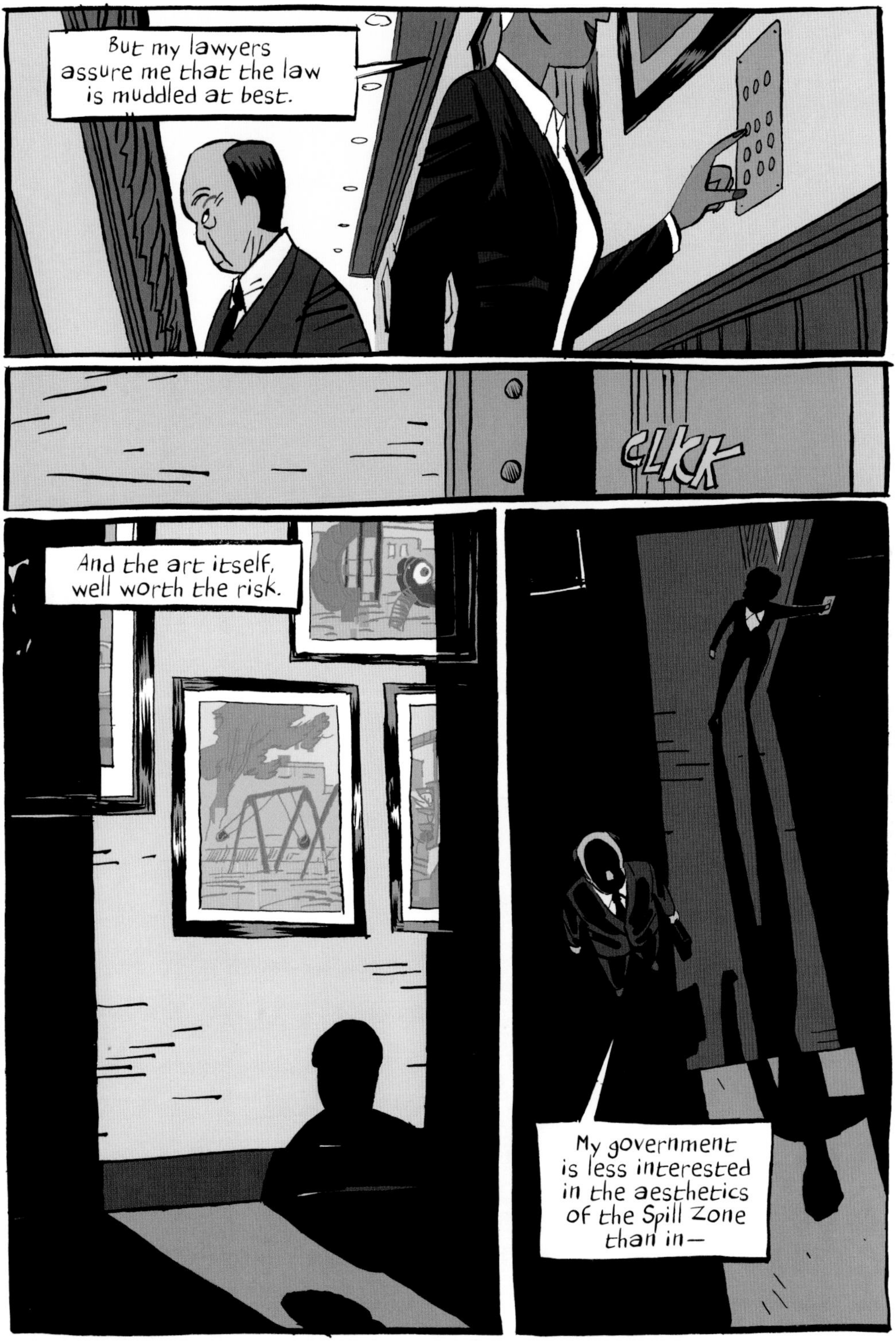

But my lawyers assure me that the law is muddled at best.
CLICK
And the art itself, well worth the risk.
My government is less interested in the aesthetics of the Spill Zone than in—

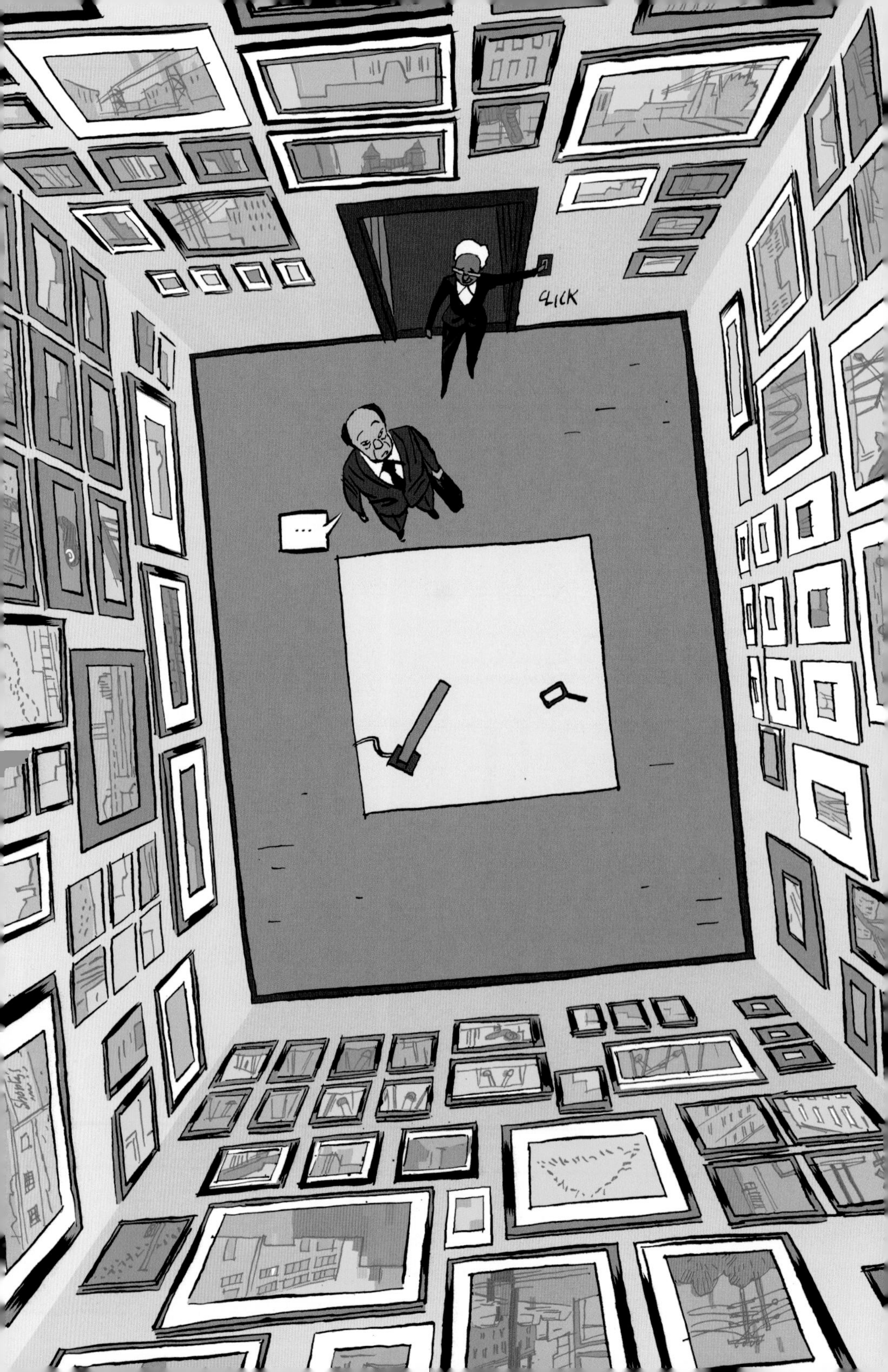
CLICK
...

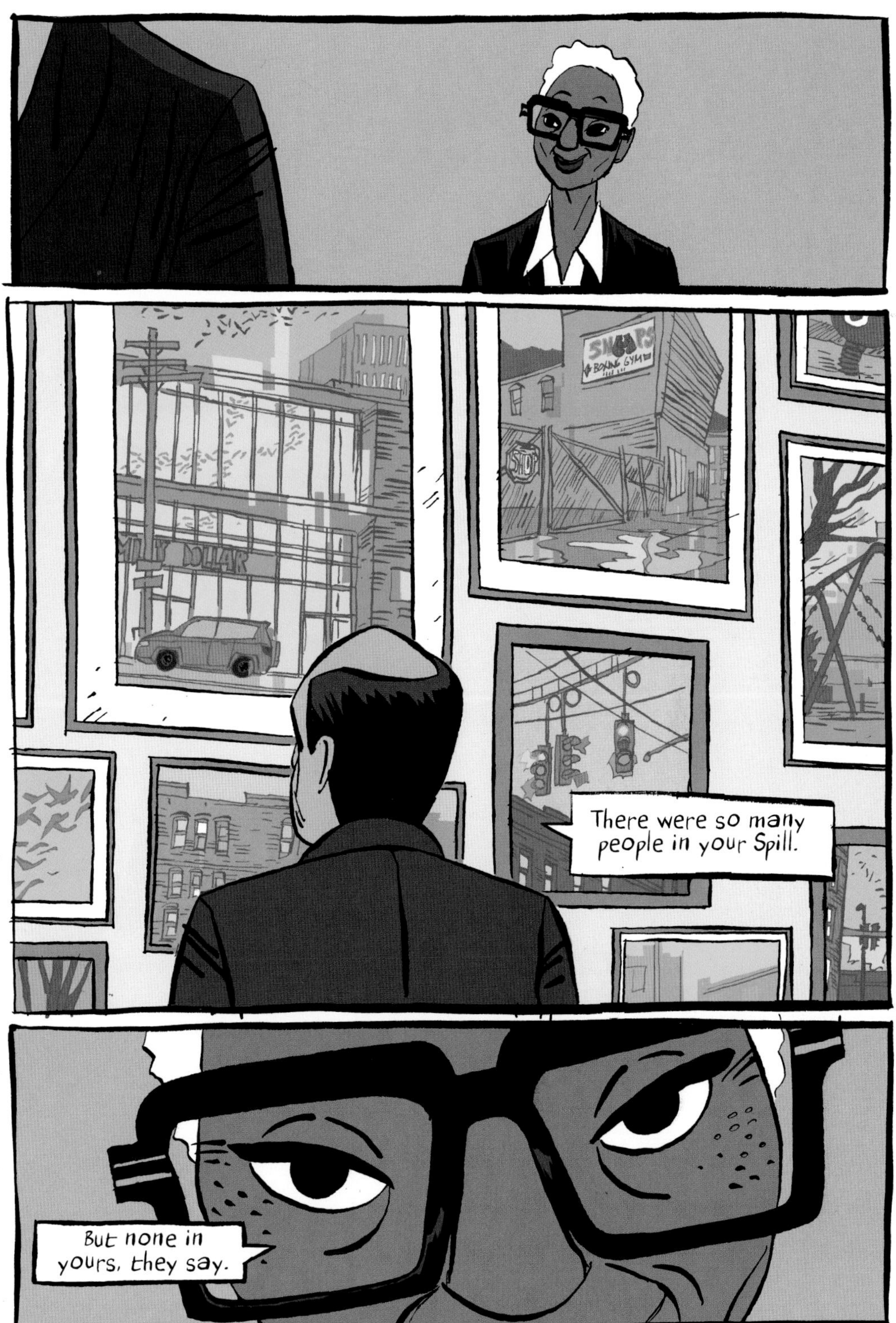
SNAPS
BOXING GYM
STOP
DOLLAR
There were so many people in your Spill.
But none in yours, they say.

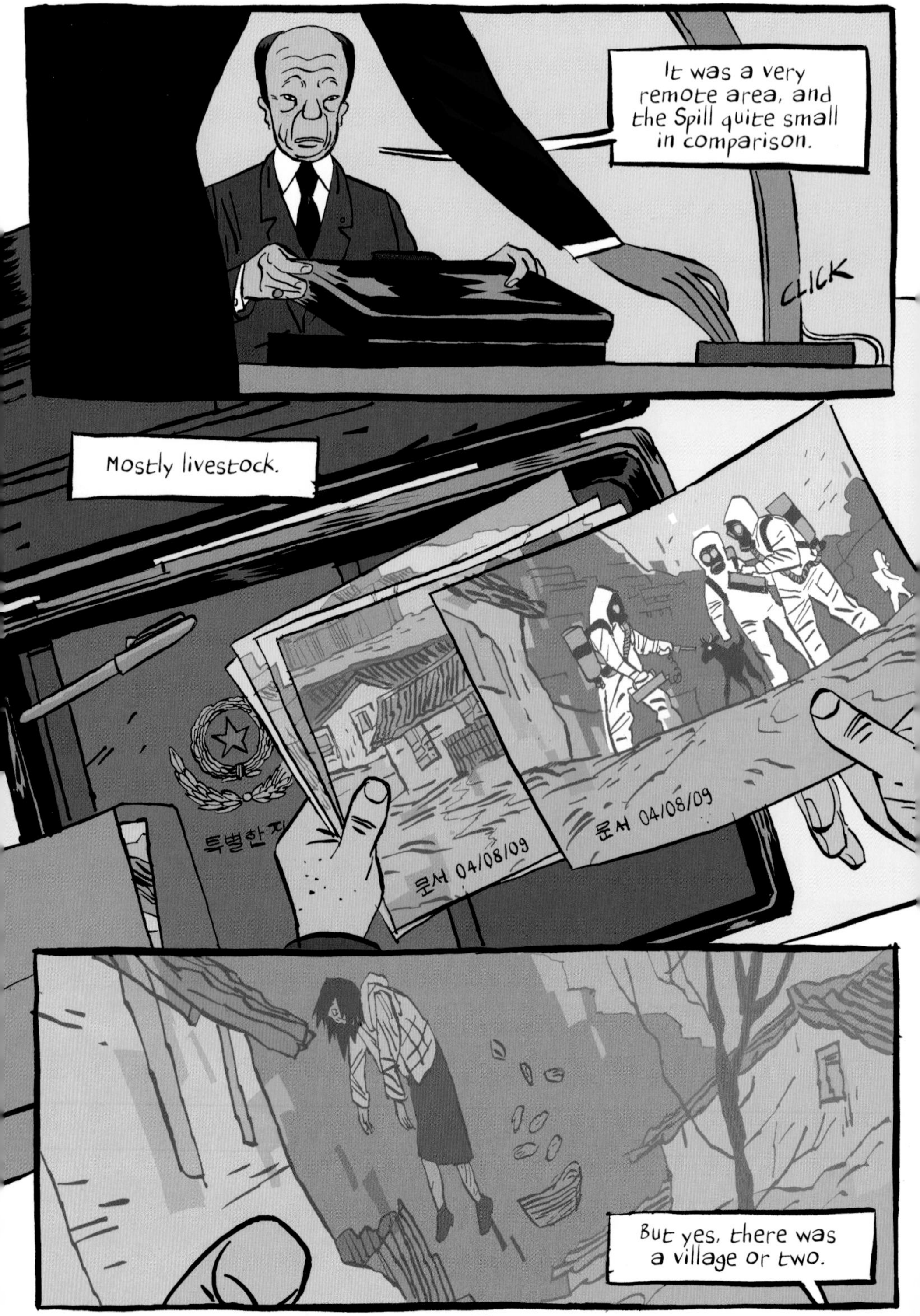

It was a very remote area, and the Spill quite small in comparison.
CLICK
Mostly livestock.
투별한 지
문서 04/08/09
문서 04/08/09
But yes, there was a village or two.

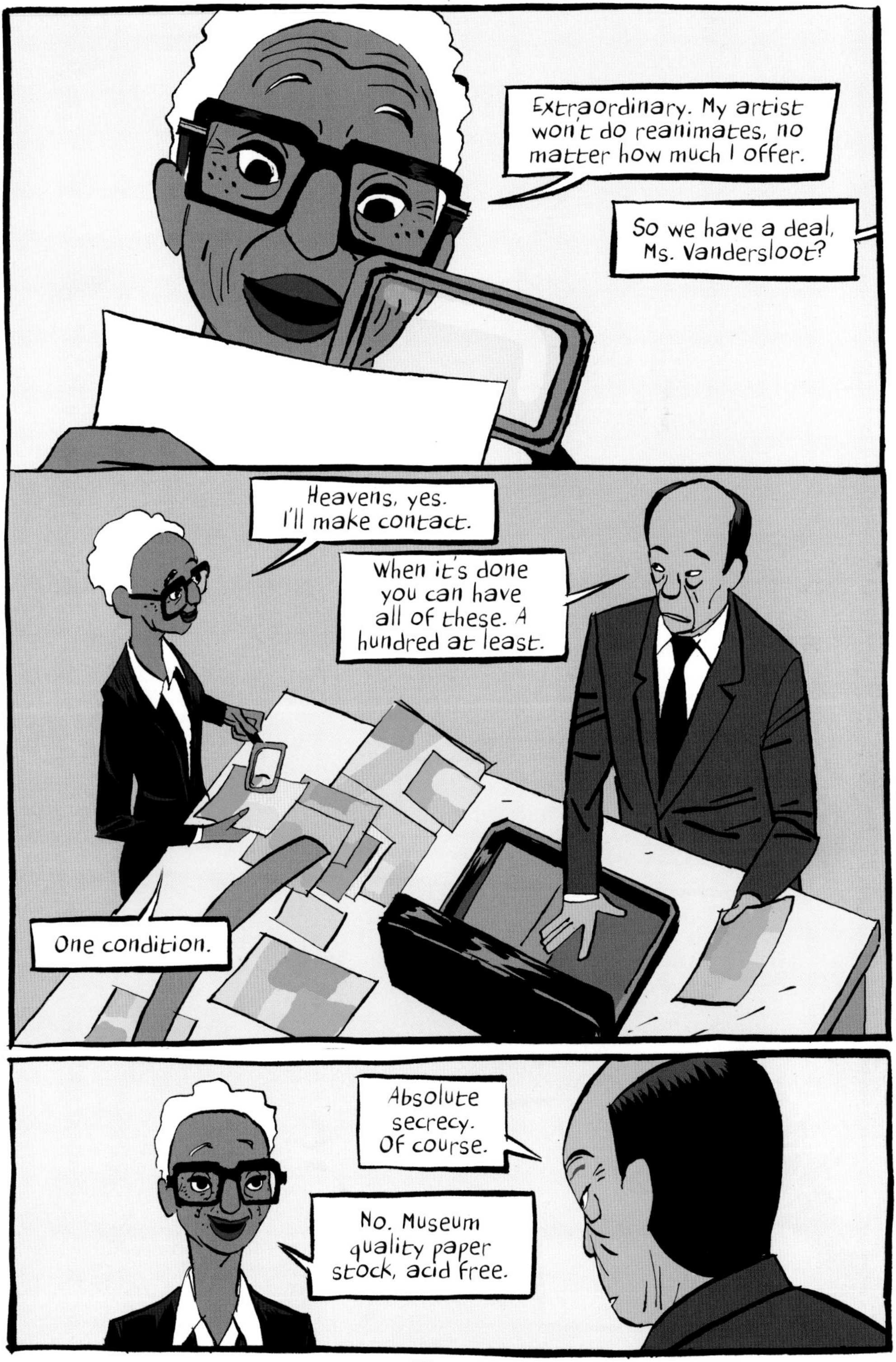
Extraordinary. My artist won't do reanimates, no matter how much I offer.
So we have a deal, Ms. Vandersloot?
Heavens, yes. I'll make contact.
When it's done you can have all of these. A hundred at least.
One condition.
Absolute secrecy. Of course.
No. Museum quality paper stock, acid free.

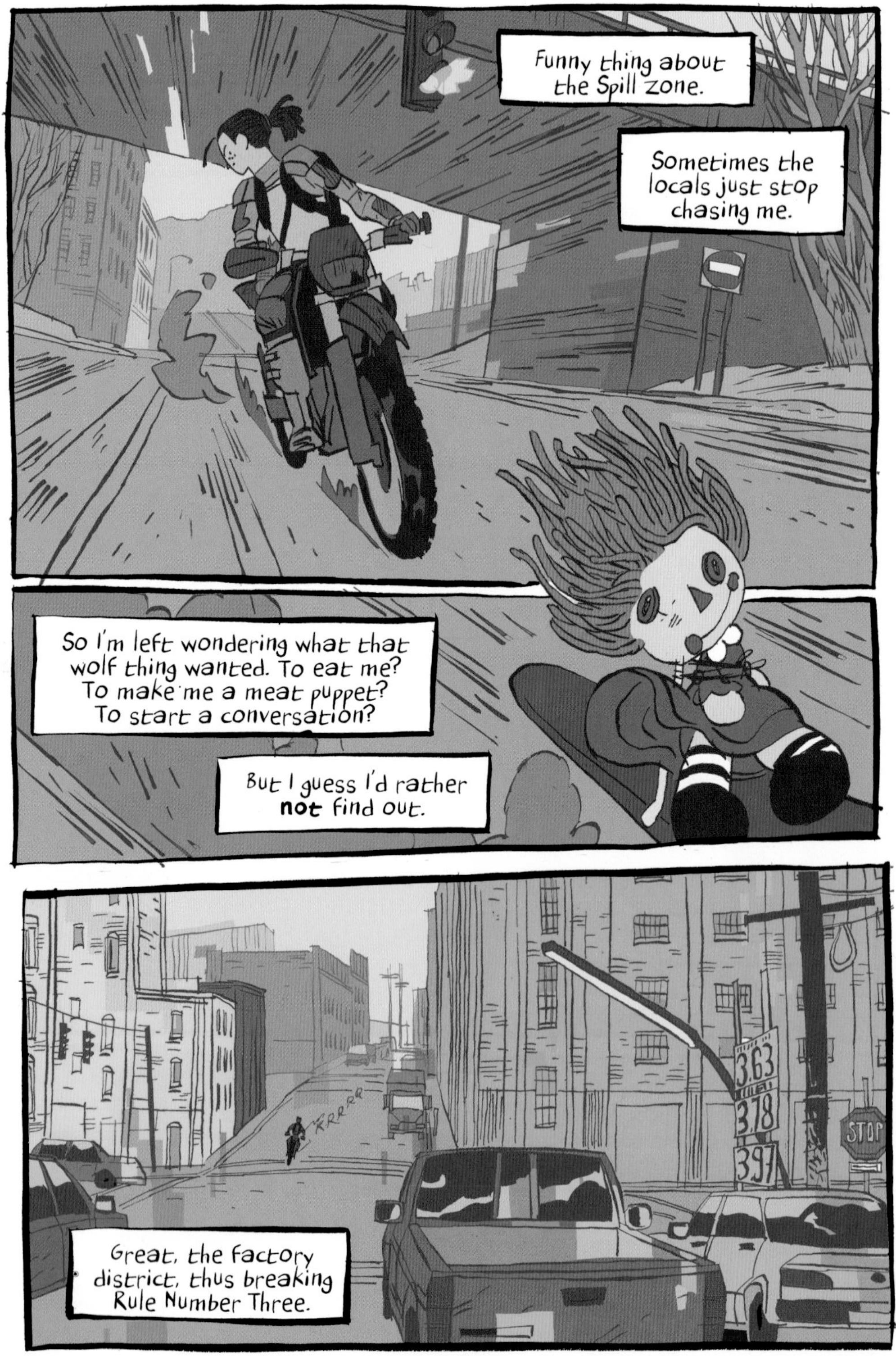
Funny thing about the Spill zone.
Sometimes the locals just stop chasing me.
So I'm left wondering what that wolf thing wanted. To eat me? To make me a meat puppet? To start a conversation?
But I guess I'd rather **not** find out.
3.63
3.78
3.97
STOP
Great, the factory district, thus breaking Rule Number Three.

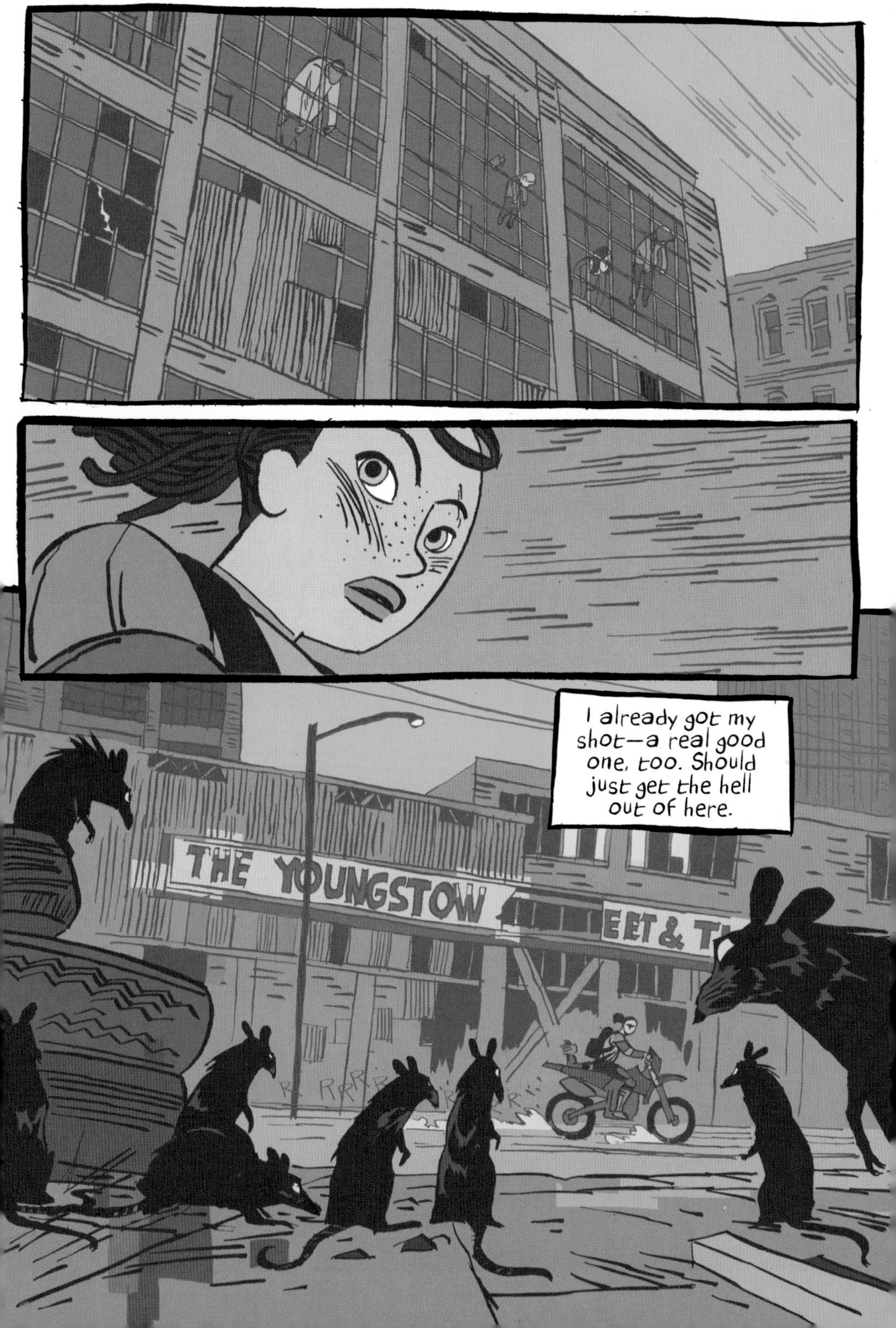
I already got my shot—a real good one, too. Should just get the hell out of here.
THE YOUNGSTOW
EET & T
RRRRRR

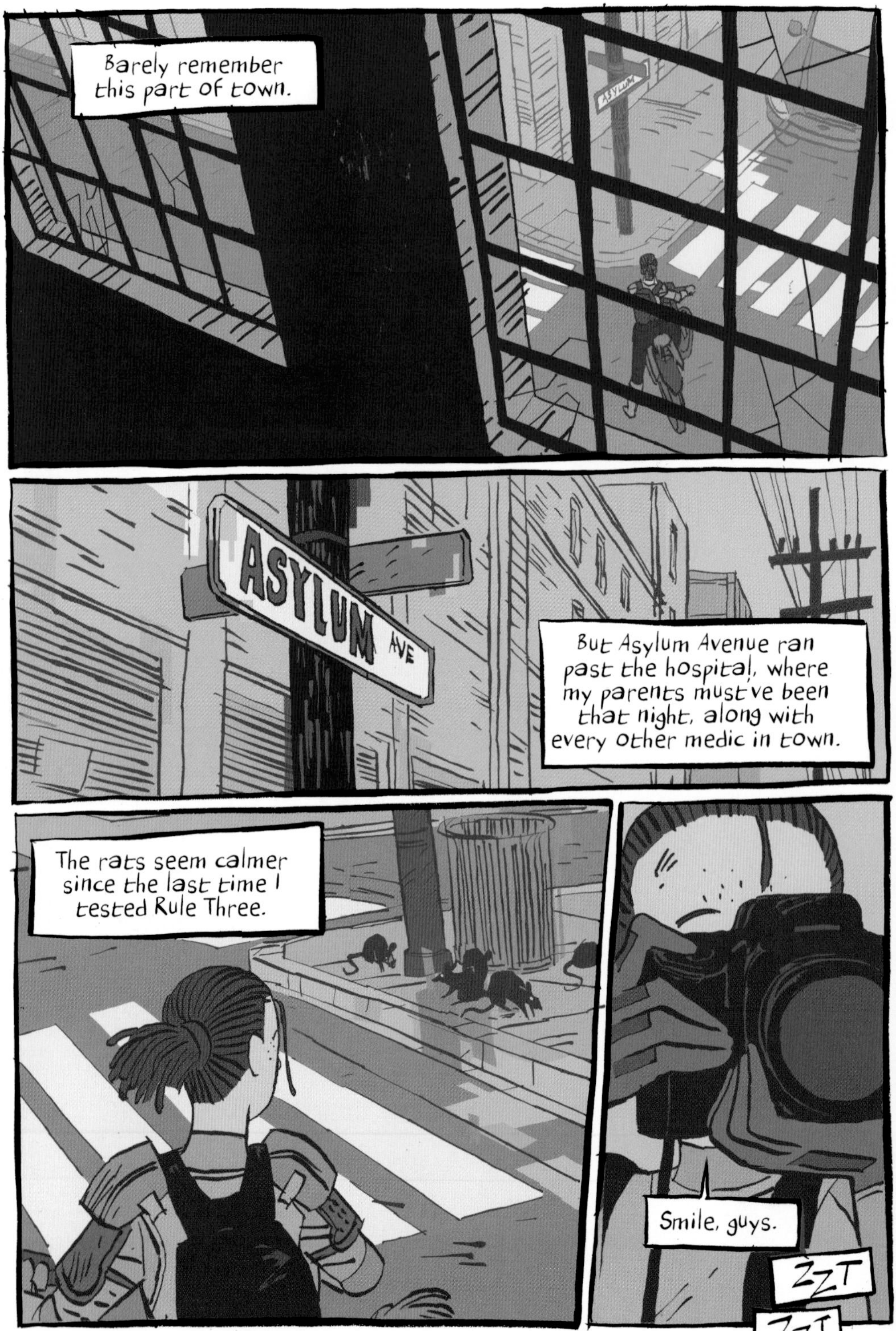
Barely remember this part of town.
ASYLUM
ASYLUM AVE
But Asylum Avenue ran past the hospital, where my parents must've been that night, along with every other medic in town.
The rats seem calmer since the last time I tested Rule Three.
Smile, guys.
ZZT
ZZT

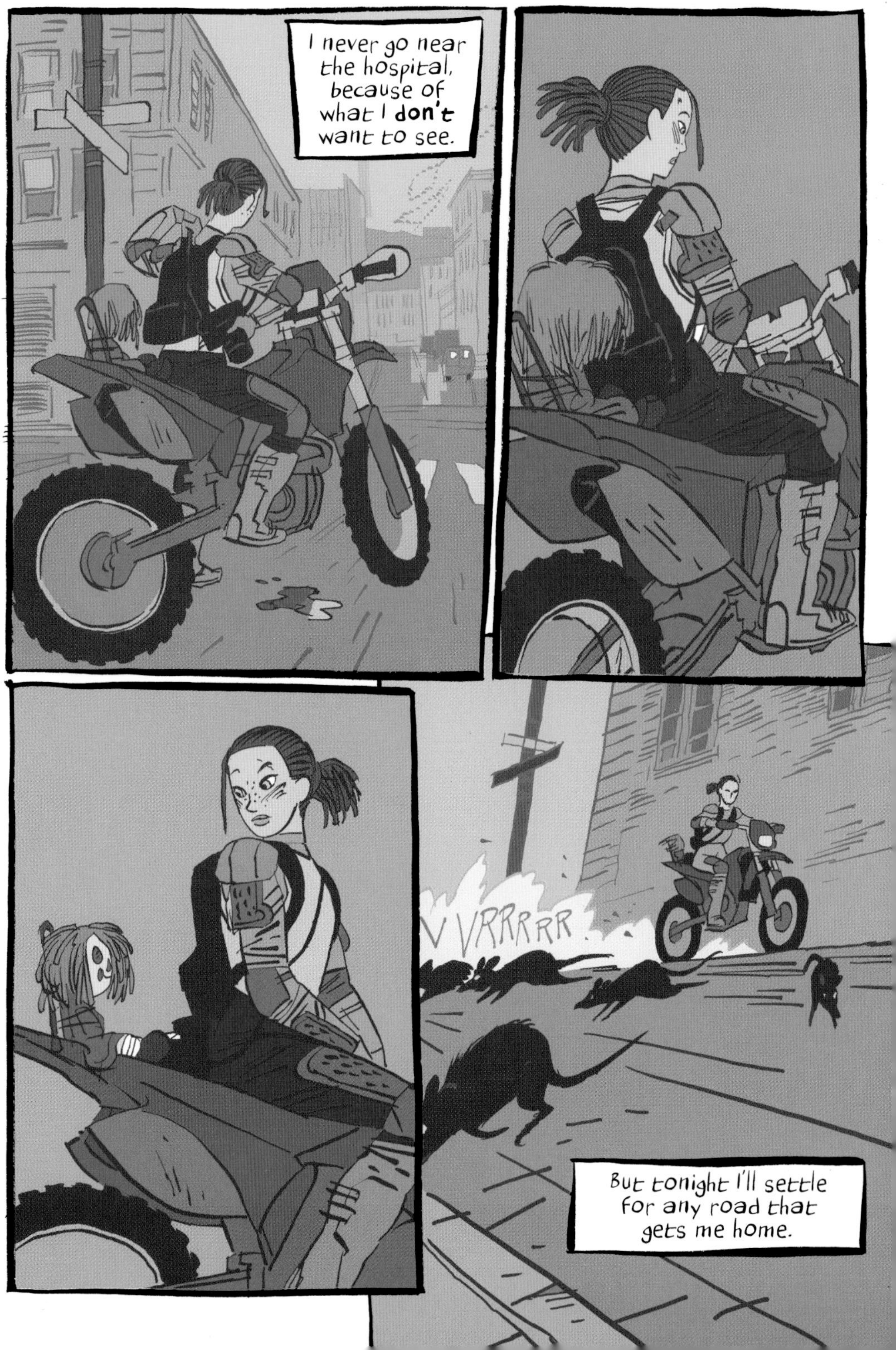
I never go near the hospital, because of what I **don't** want to see.
VRRRRR
But tonight I'll settle for any road that gets me home.

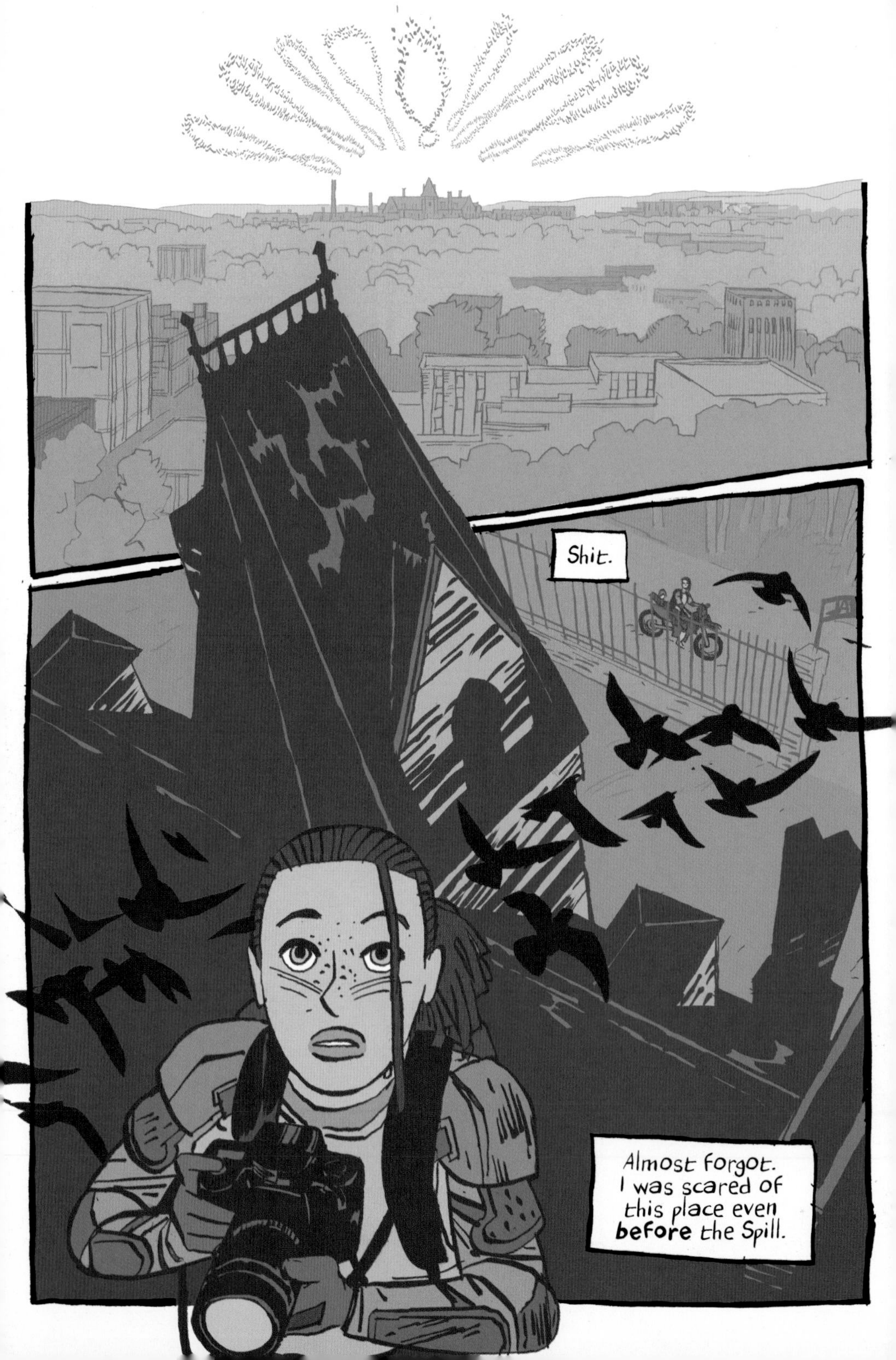
Shit.
Almost forgot. I was scared of this place even **before** the Spill.

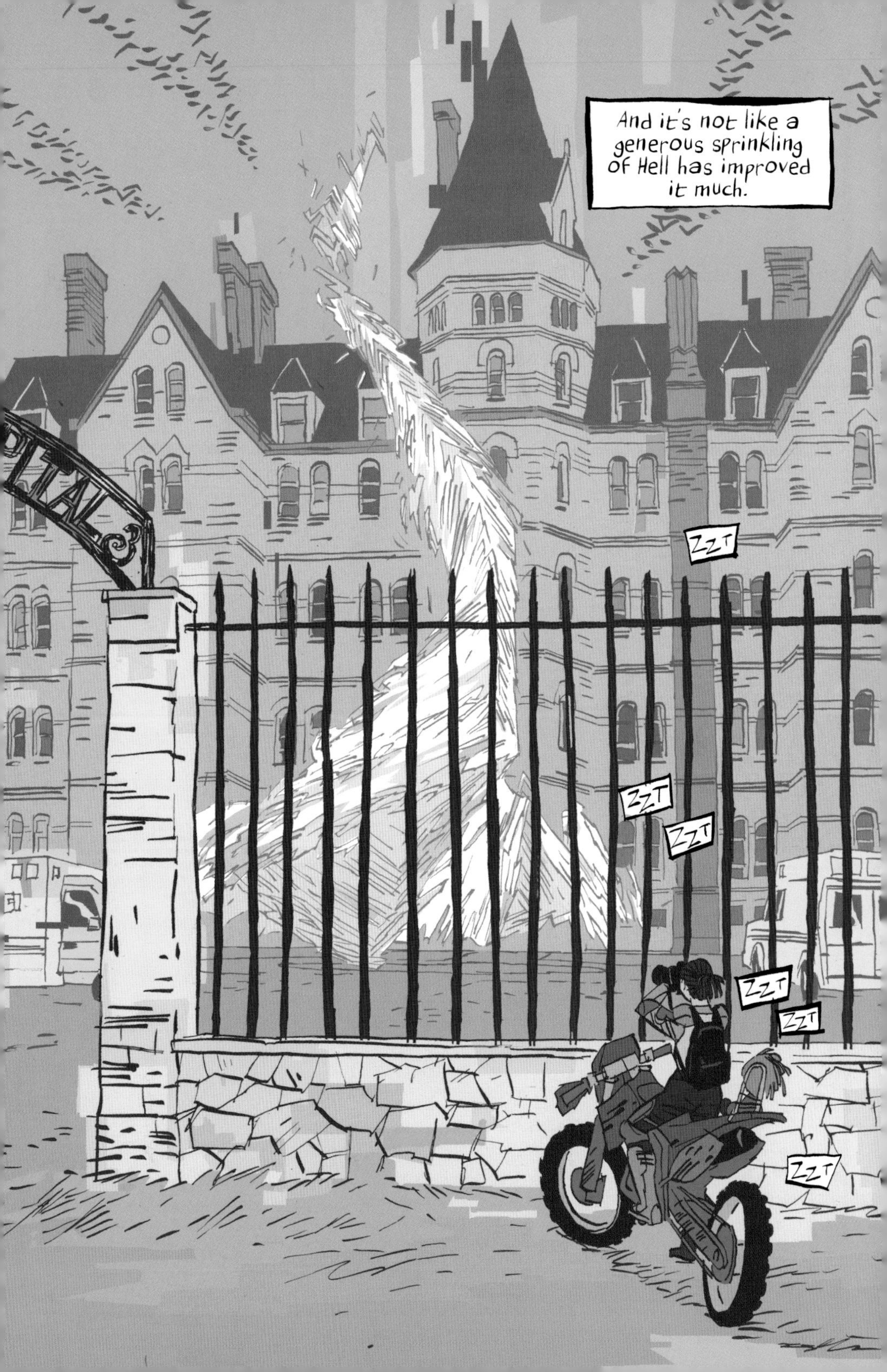
And it's not like a generous sprinkling of Hell has improved it much.
ZZT
ZZT
ZZT
ZZT
ZZT
ZZT

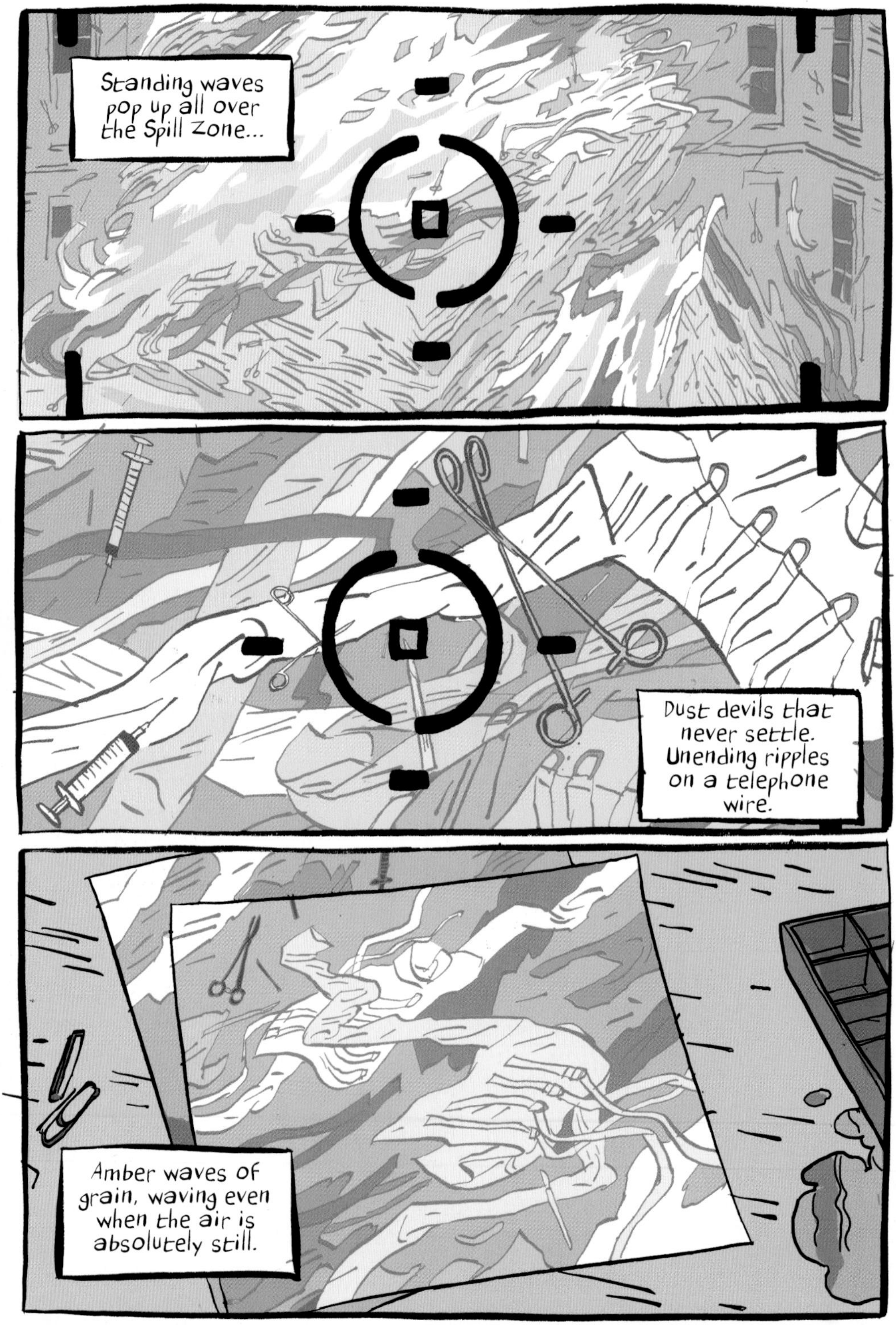
Standing waves pop up all over the Spill Zone...
Dust devils that never settle. Unending ripples on a telephone wire.
Amber waves of grain, waving even when the air is absolutely still.

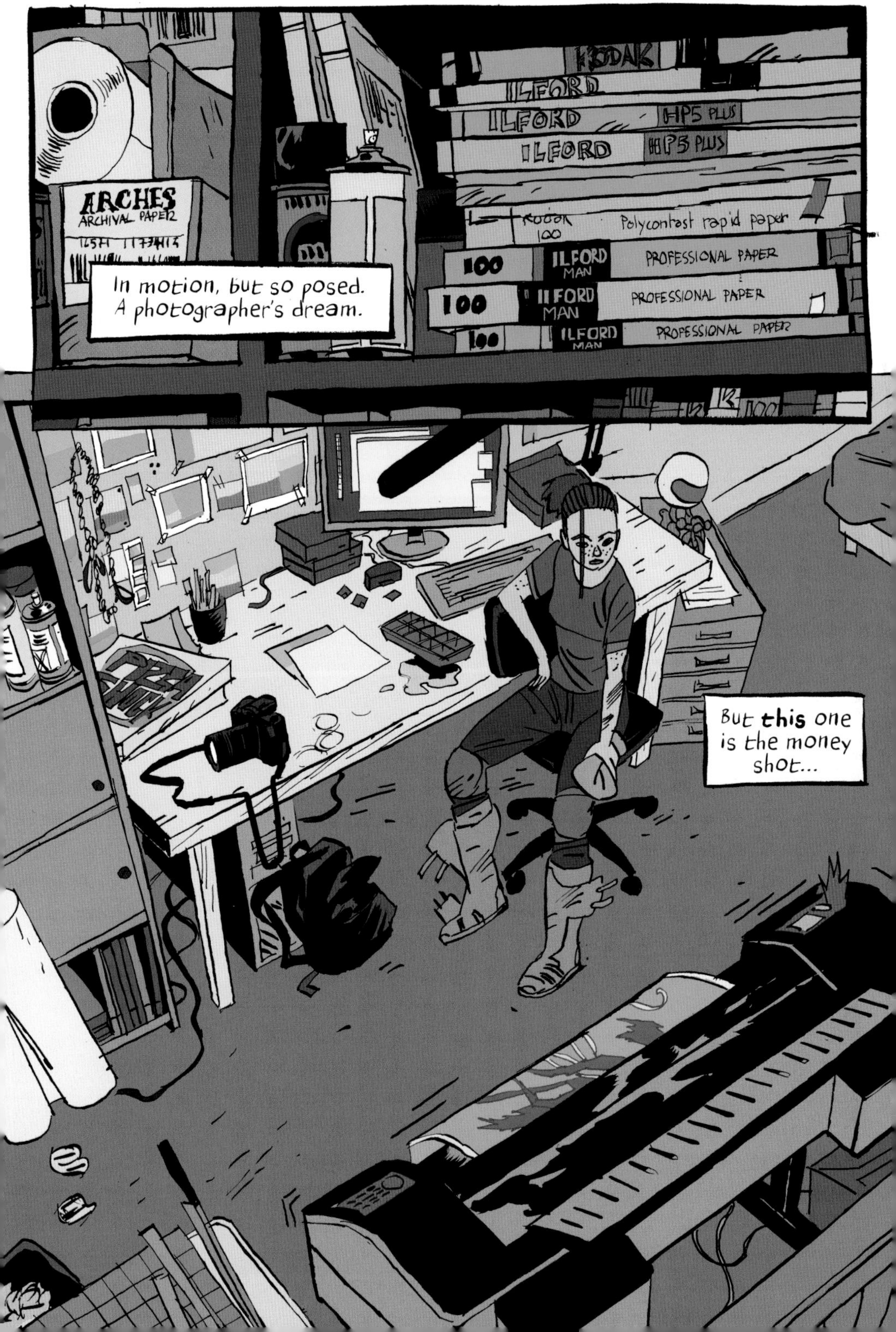
KODAK
ILFORD
ILFORD
HP5 PLUS
ILFORD
HP5 PLUS
ARCHES
ARCHIVAL PAPER
Polycontrast rapid paper
100
ILFORD MAN
PROFESSIONAL PAPER
100
ILFORD MAN
PROFESSIONAL PAPER
100
ILFORD MAN
PROFESSIONAL PAPER
In motion, but so posed. A photographer's dream.
But **this** one is the money shot...

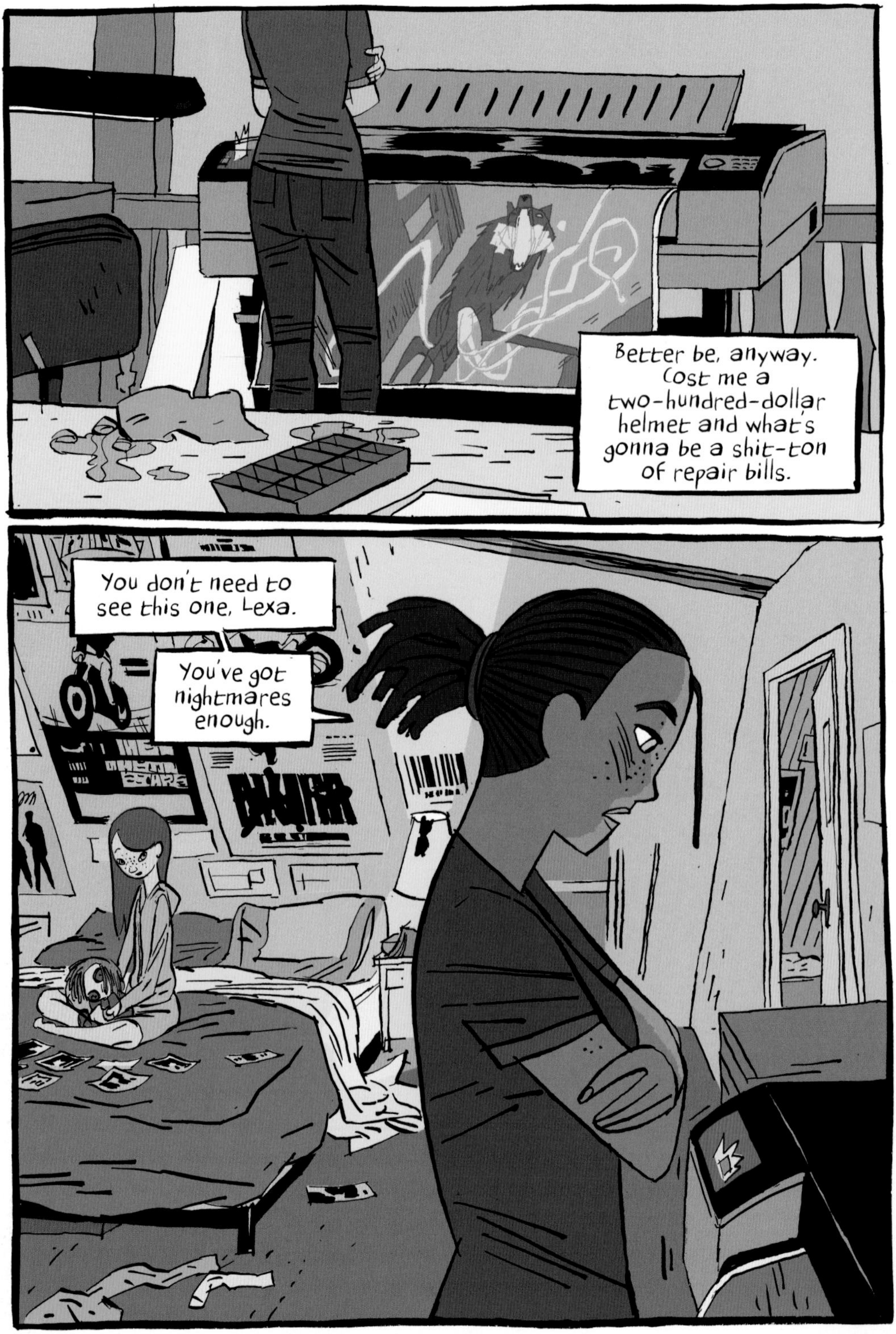
Better be, anyway. Cost me a two-hundred-dollar helmet and what's gonna be a shit-ton of repair bills.
You don't need to see this one, Lexa.
You've got nightmares enough.

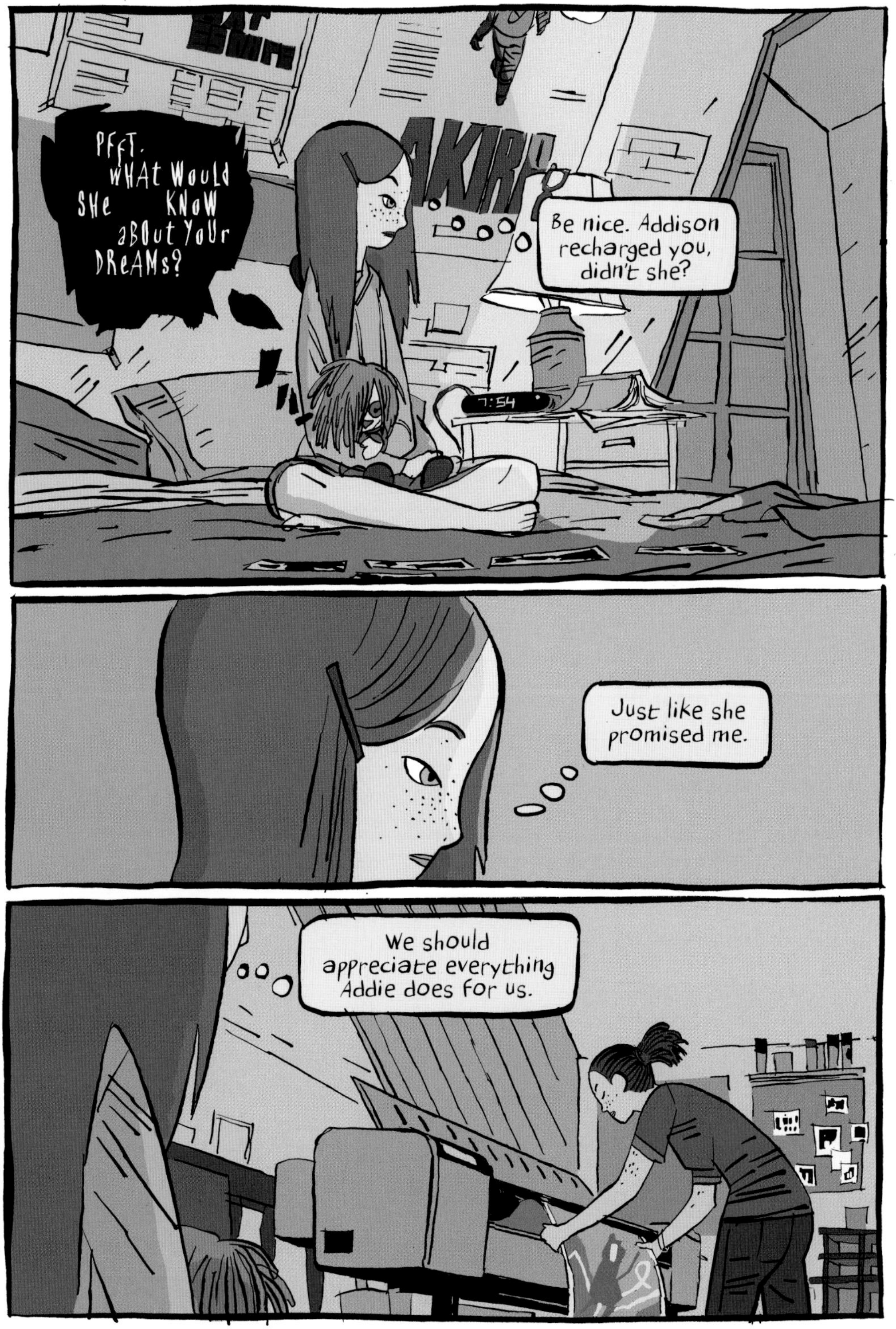
PFFT. WHAT WOULD SHE KNOW ABOUT YOUR DREAMS?
Be nice. Addison recharged you, didn't she?
7:54
Just like she promised me.
We should appreciate everything Addie does for us.

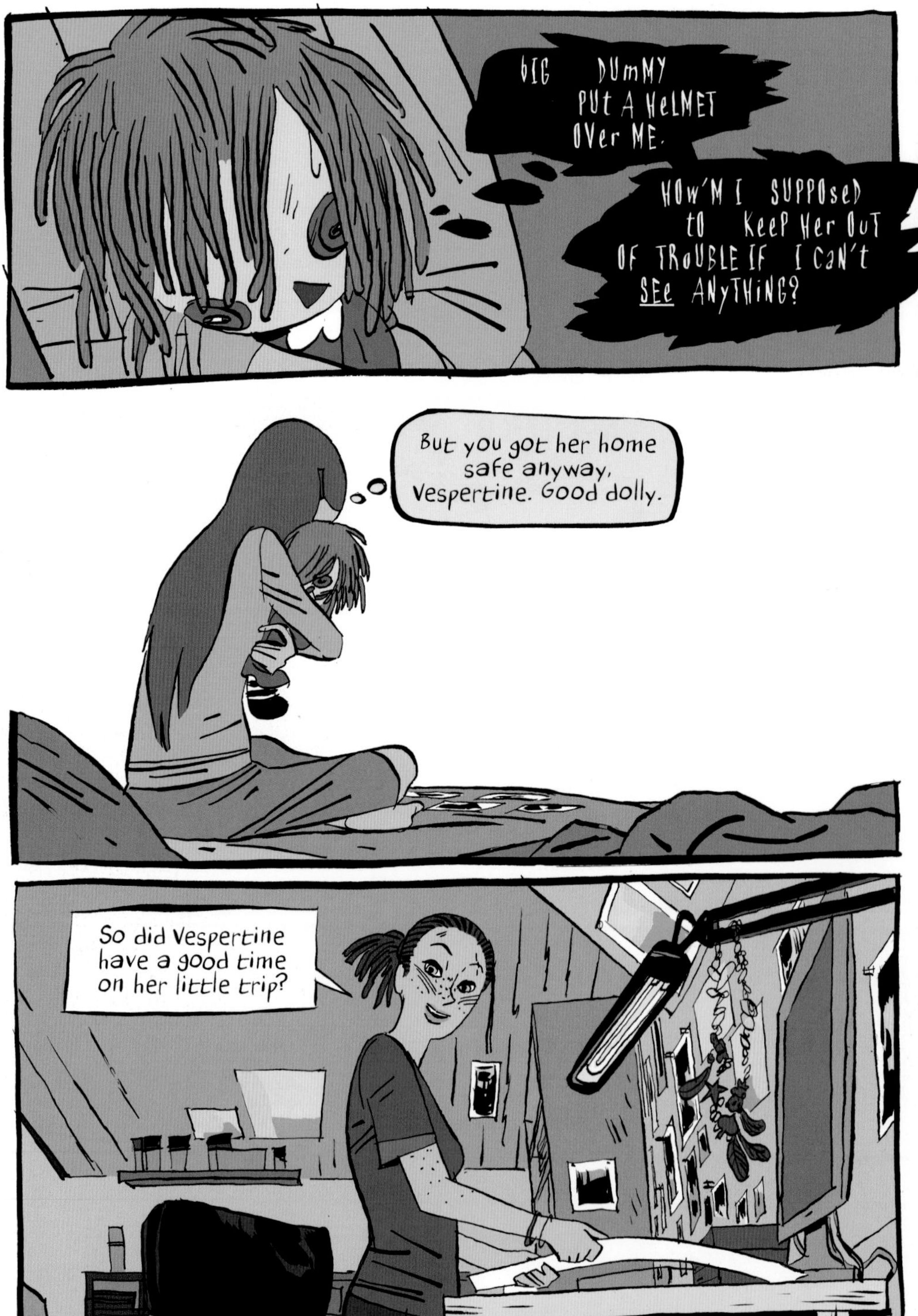
BIG DUMMY PUT A HELMET OVER ME.
HOW'M I SUPPOSED TO KEEP HER OUT OF TROUBLE IF I CAN'T SEE ANYTHING?
But you got her home safe anyway, Vespertine. Good dolly.
So did Vespertine have a good time on her little trip?

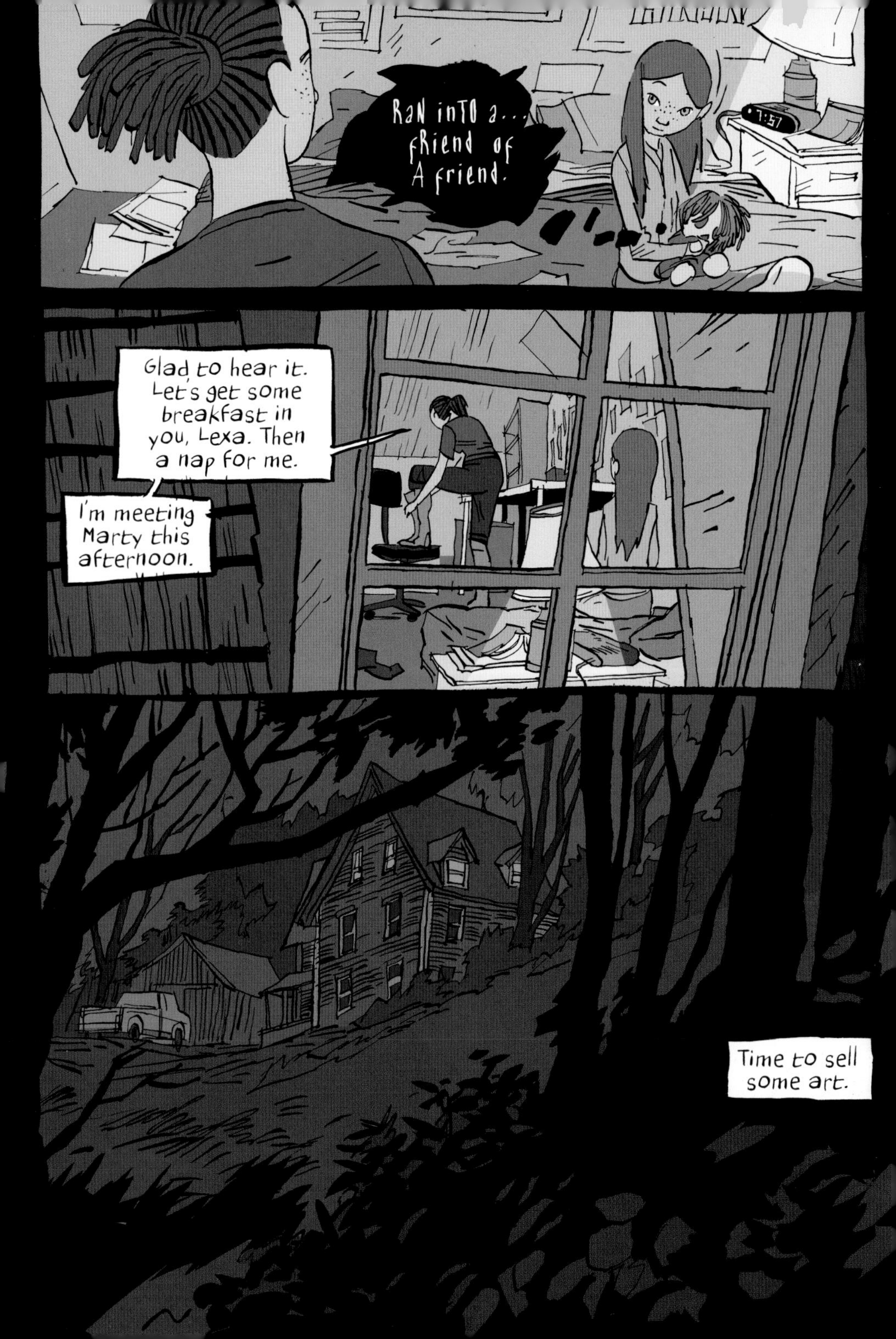
Ran into a... friend of a friend.
7:57
Glad to hear it. Let's get some breakfast in you, Lexa. Then a nap for me.
I'm meeting Marty this afternoon.
Time to sell some art.

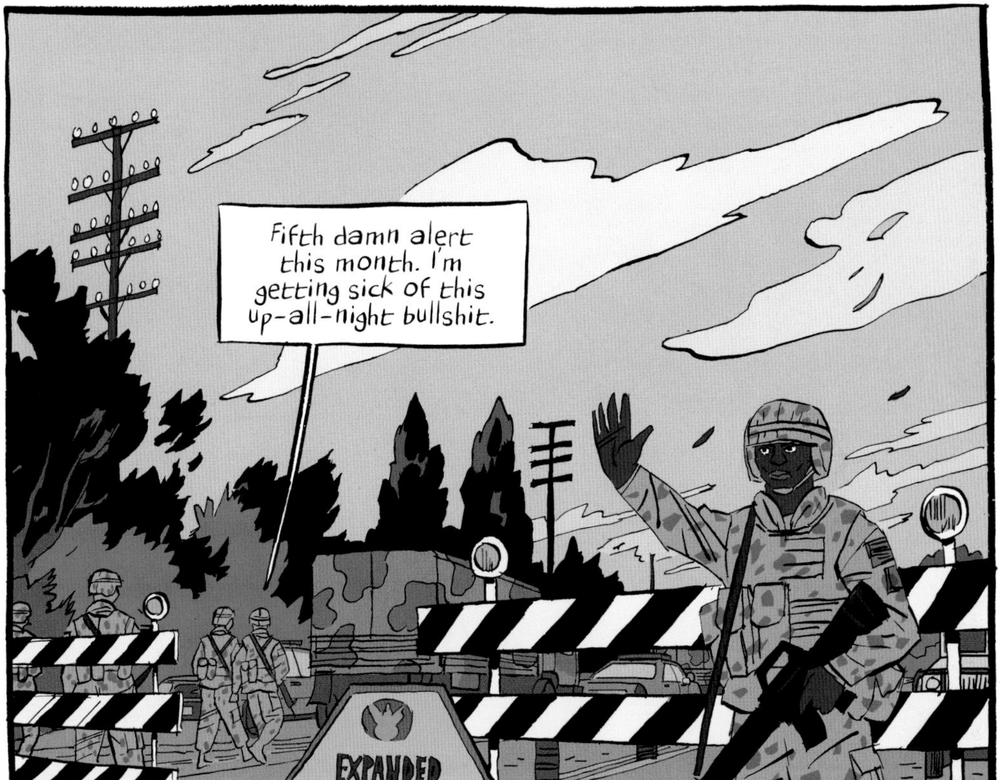
Fifth damn alert this month. I'm getting sick of this up-all-night bullshit.
EXPANDED EXCLUSION ZONE
FOR RESIDENTS ONLY

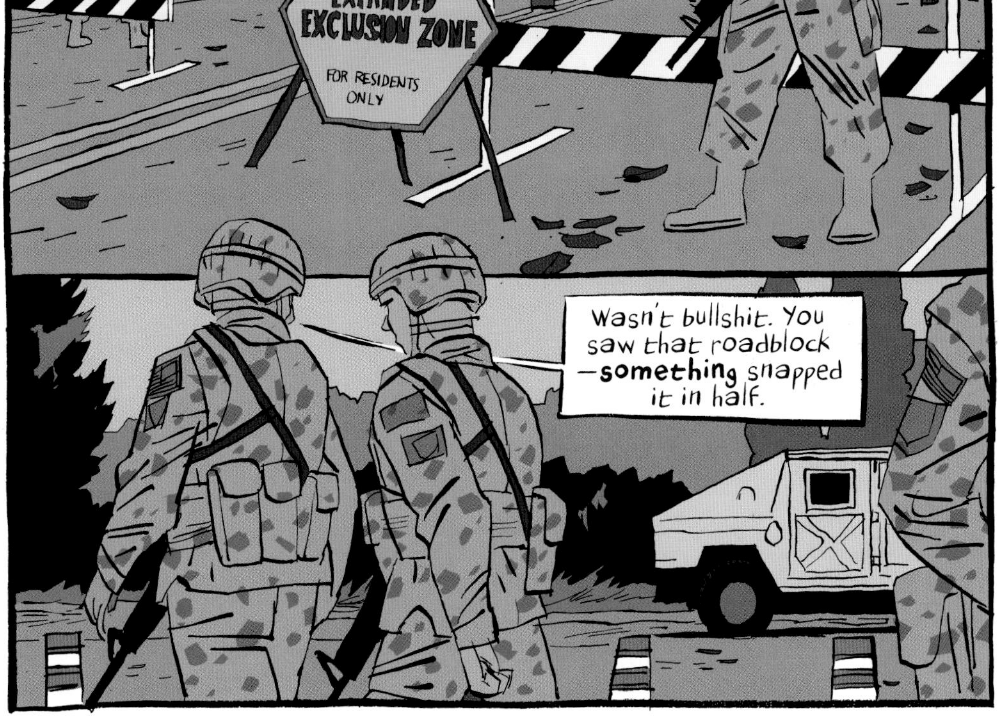
Wasn't bullshit. You saw that roadblock—**something** snapped it in half.

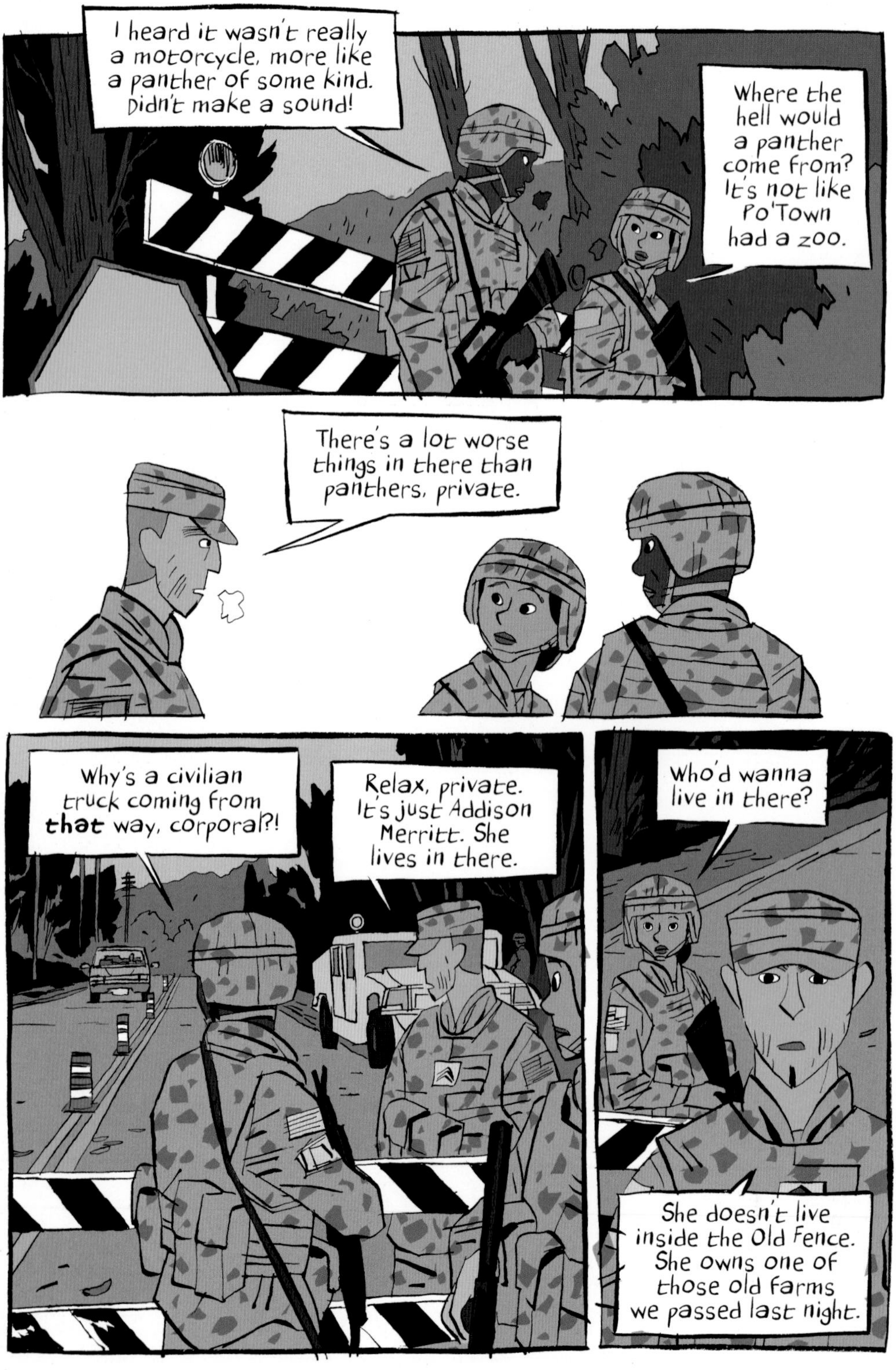
I heard it wasn't really a motorcycle, more like a panther of some kind. Didn't make a sound!
Where the hell would a panther come from? It's not like Po'Town had a zoo.
There's a lot worse things in there than panthers, private.
Why's a civilian truck coming from **that** way, corporal?!
Relax, private. It's just Addison Merritt. She lives in there.
Who'd wanna live in there?
She doesn't live inside the Old Fence. She owns one of those old farms we passed last night.

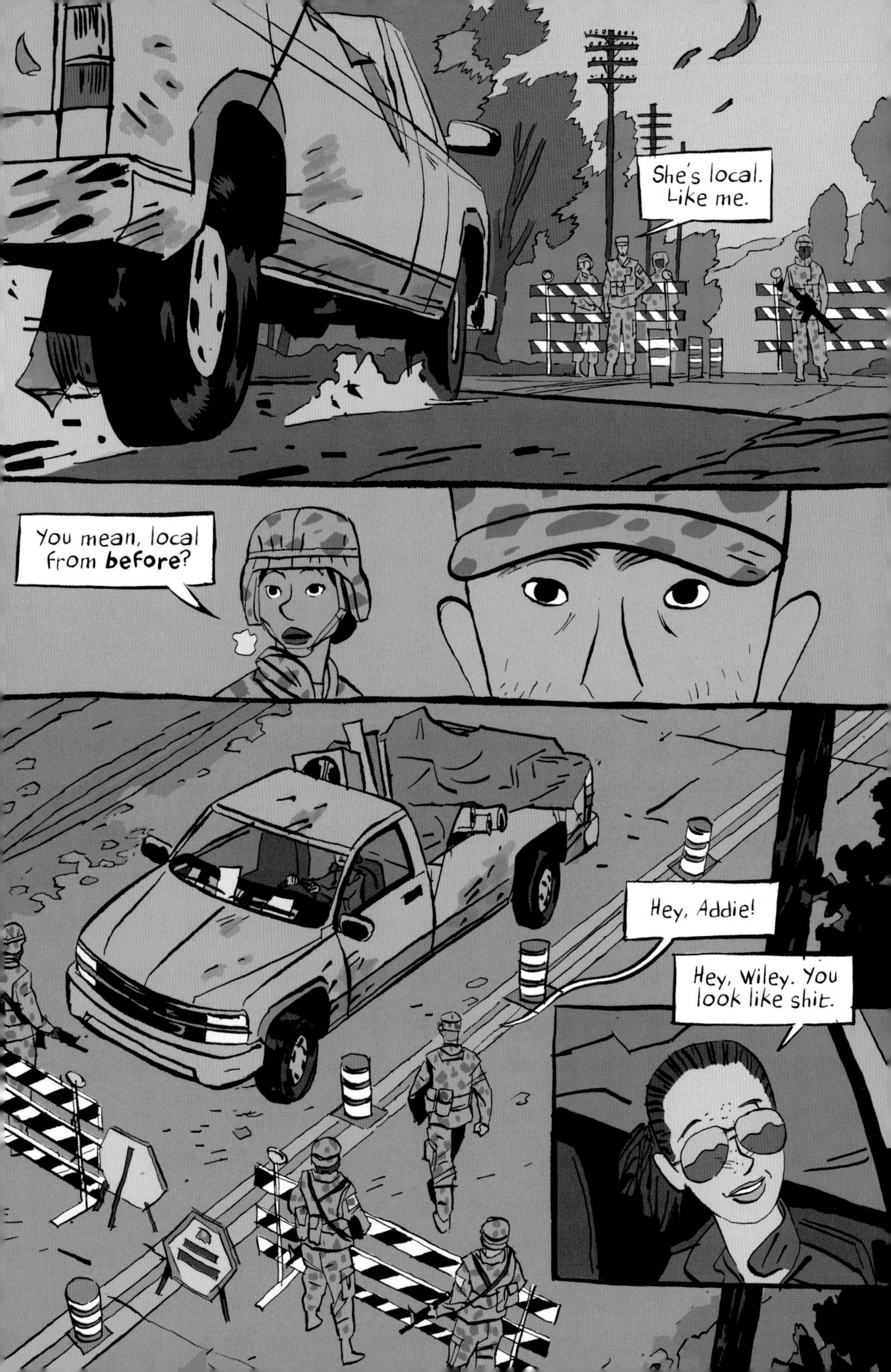
She's local. Like me.
You mean, local from **before**?
Hey, Addie!
Hey, Wiley. You look like shit.

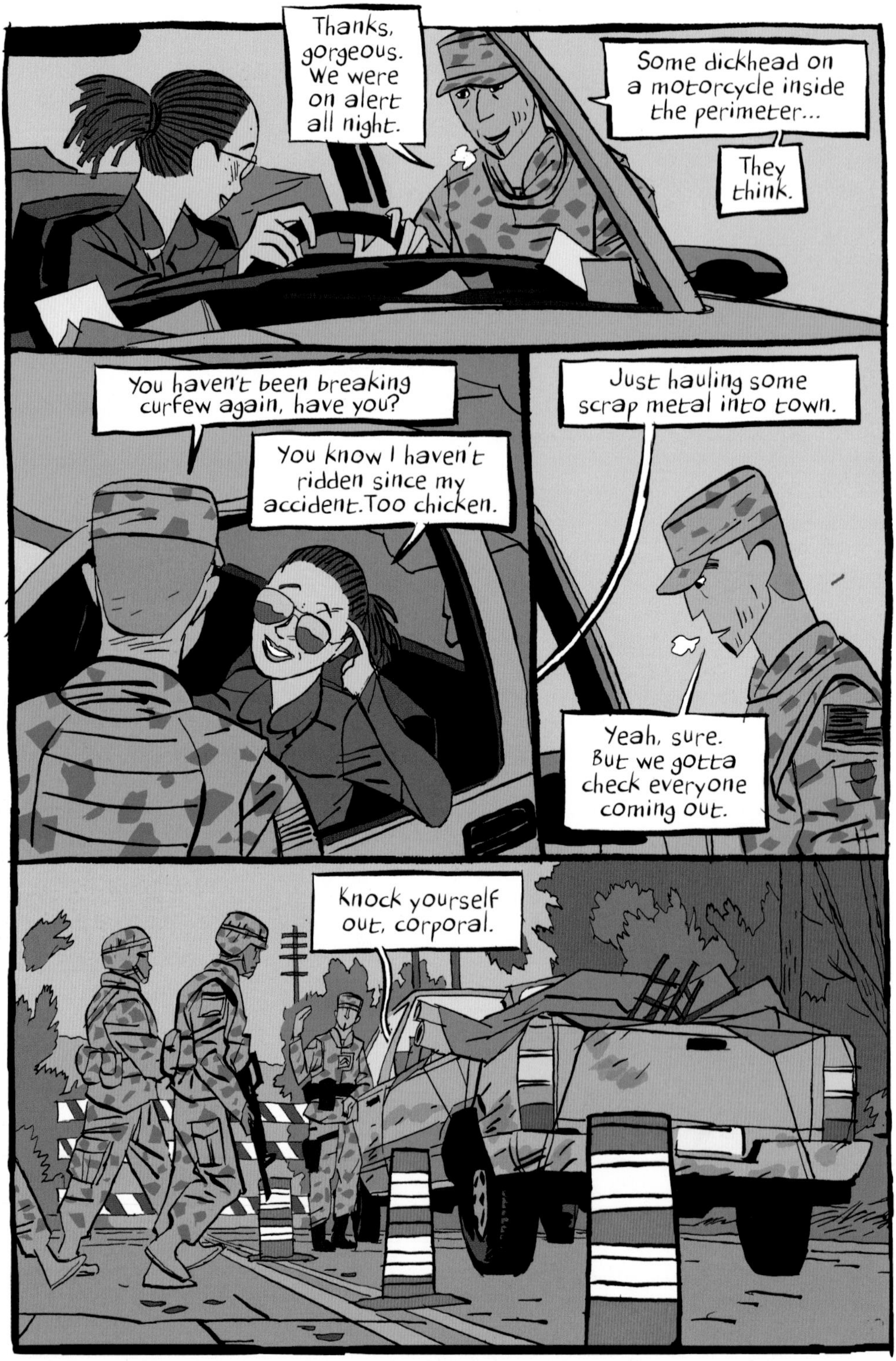
Thanks, gorgeous. We were on alert all night.
Some dickhead on a motorcycle inside the perimeter...
They think.
You haven't been breaking curfew again, have you?
You know I haven't ridden since my accident. Too chicken.
Just hauling some scrap metal into town.
Yeah, sure. But we gotta check everyone coming out.
Knock yourself out, corporal.

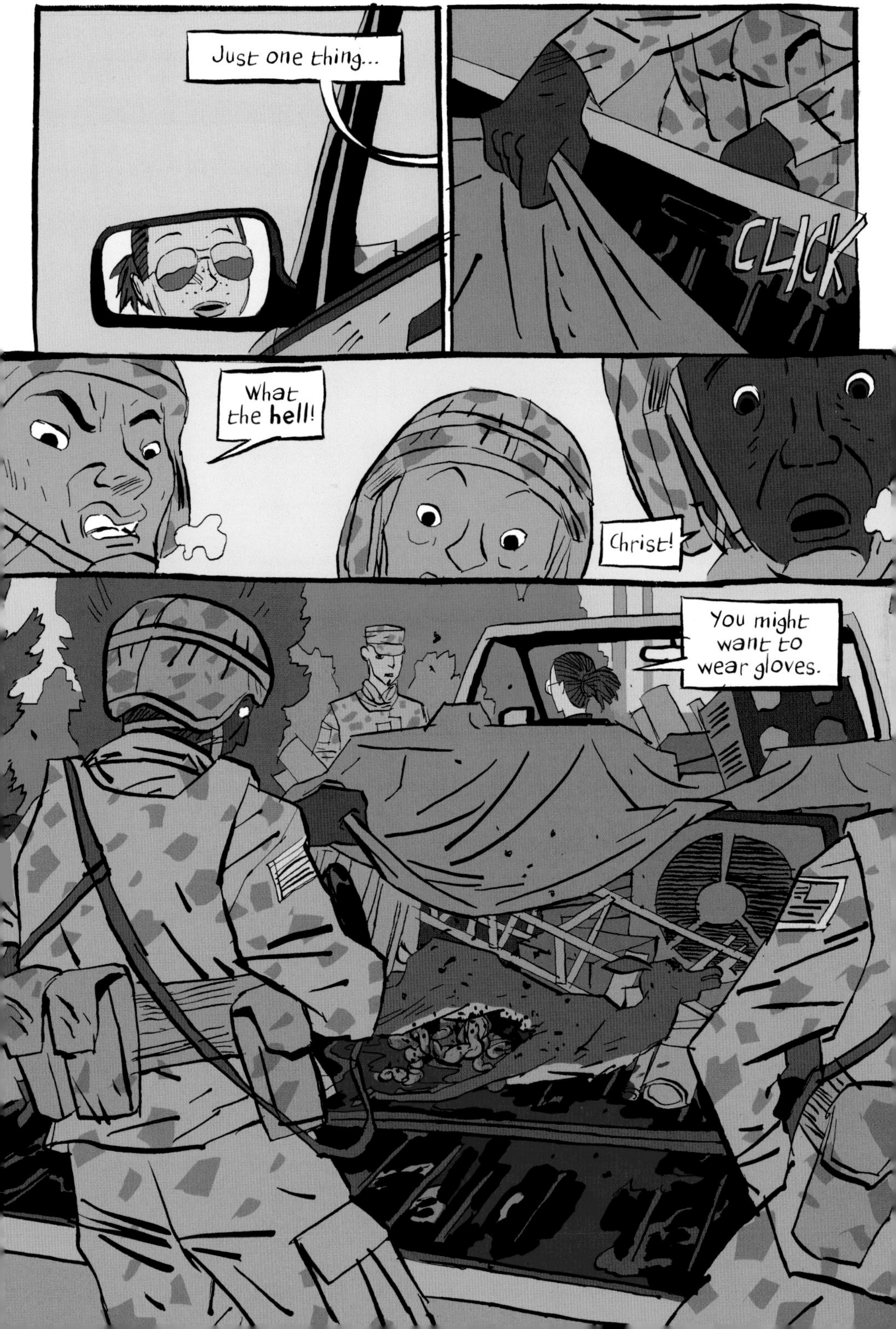
Just one thing...
CLICK
What the **hell**!
Christ!
You might want to wear gloves.

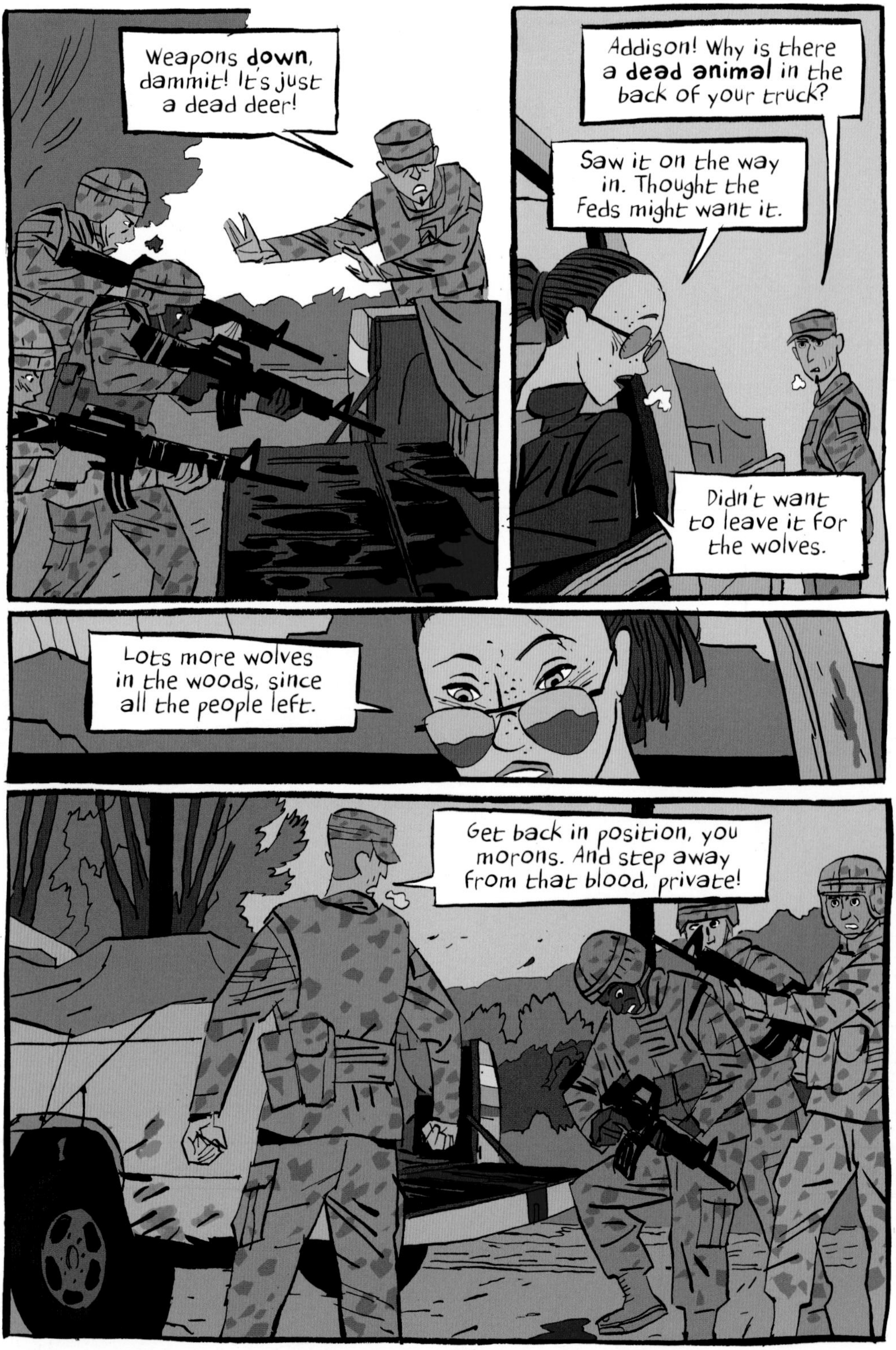
Weapons **down**, dammit! It's just a dead deer!
Addison! Why is there a **dead animal** in the back of your truck?
Saw it on the way in. Thought the Feds might want it.
Didn't want to leave it for the wolves.
Lots more wolves in the woods, since all the people left.
Get back in position, you morons. And step away from that blood, private!

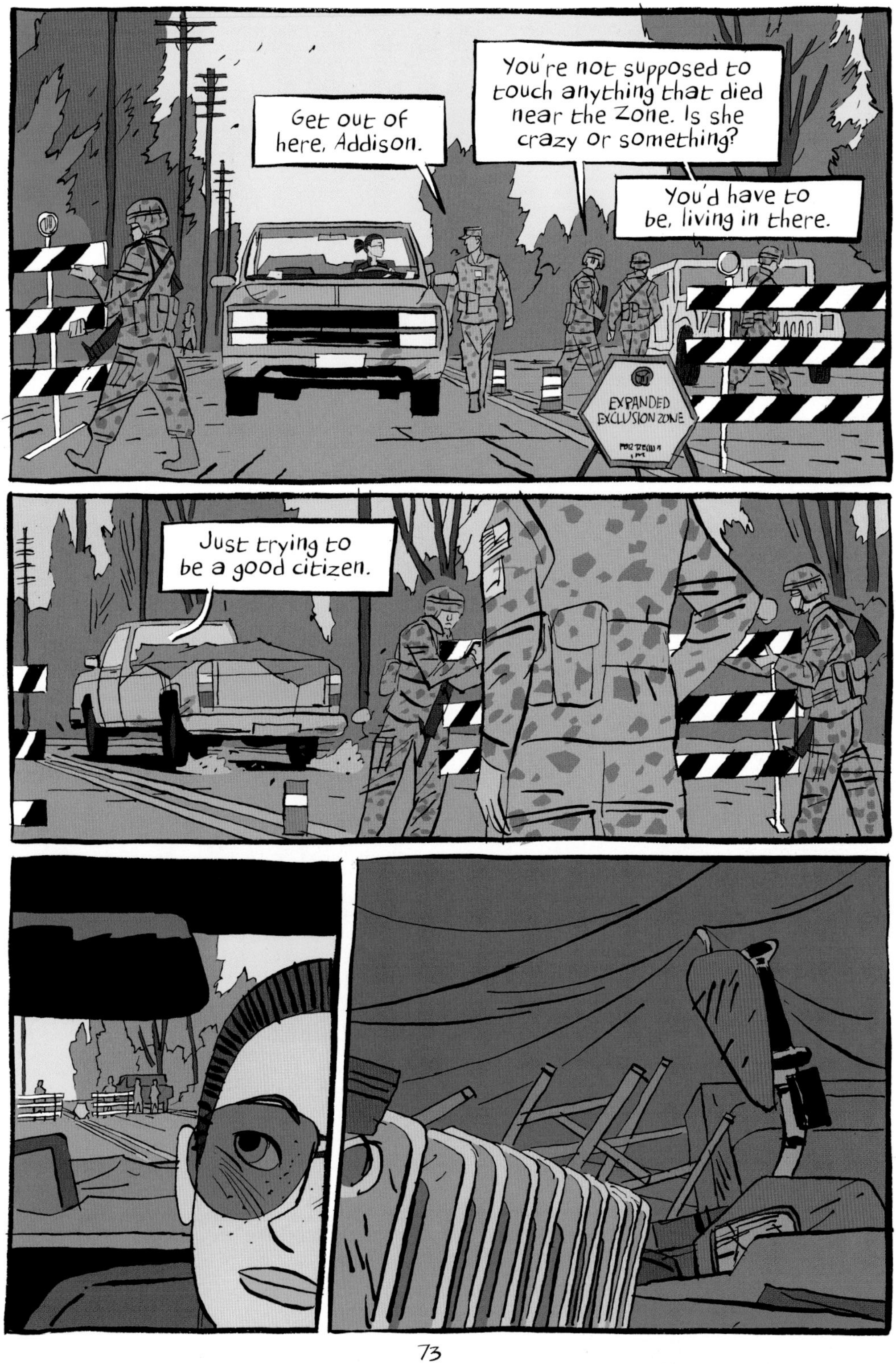
Get out of here, Addison.
You're not supposed to touch anything that died near the Zone. Is she crazy or something?
You'd have to be, living in there.
EXPANDED EXCLUSION ZONE
Just trying to be a good citizen.

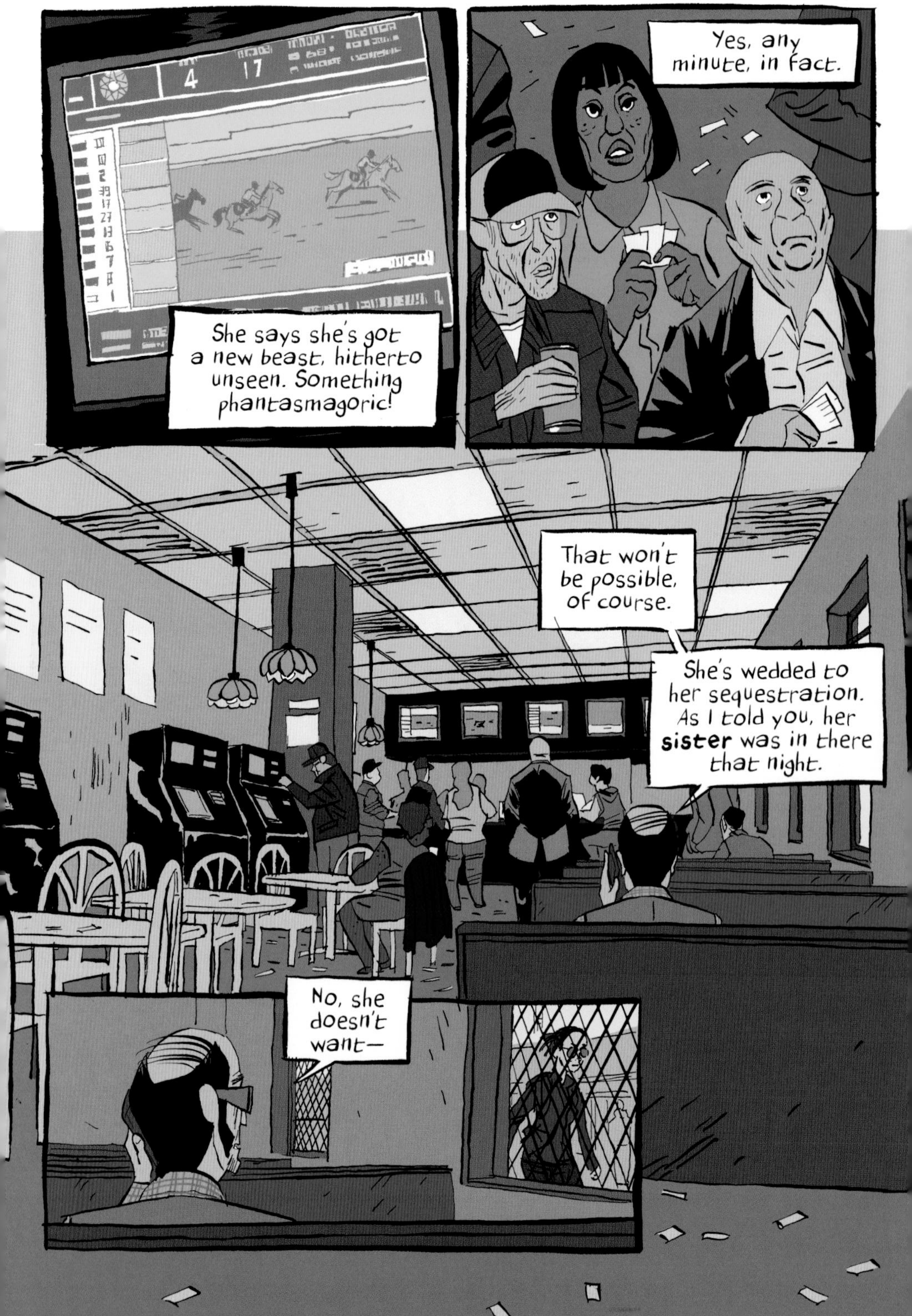

She says she's got a new beast, hitherto unseen. Something phantasmagoric!
Yes, any minute, in fact.
That won't be possible, of course.
She's wedded to her sequestration. As I told you, her **sister** was in there that night.
No, she doesn't want—

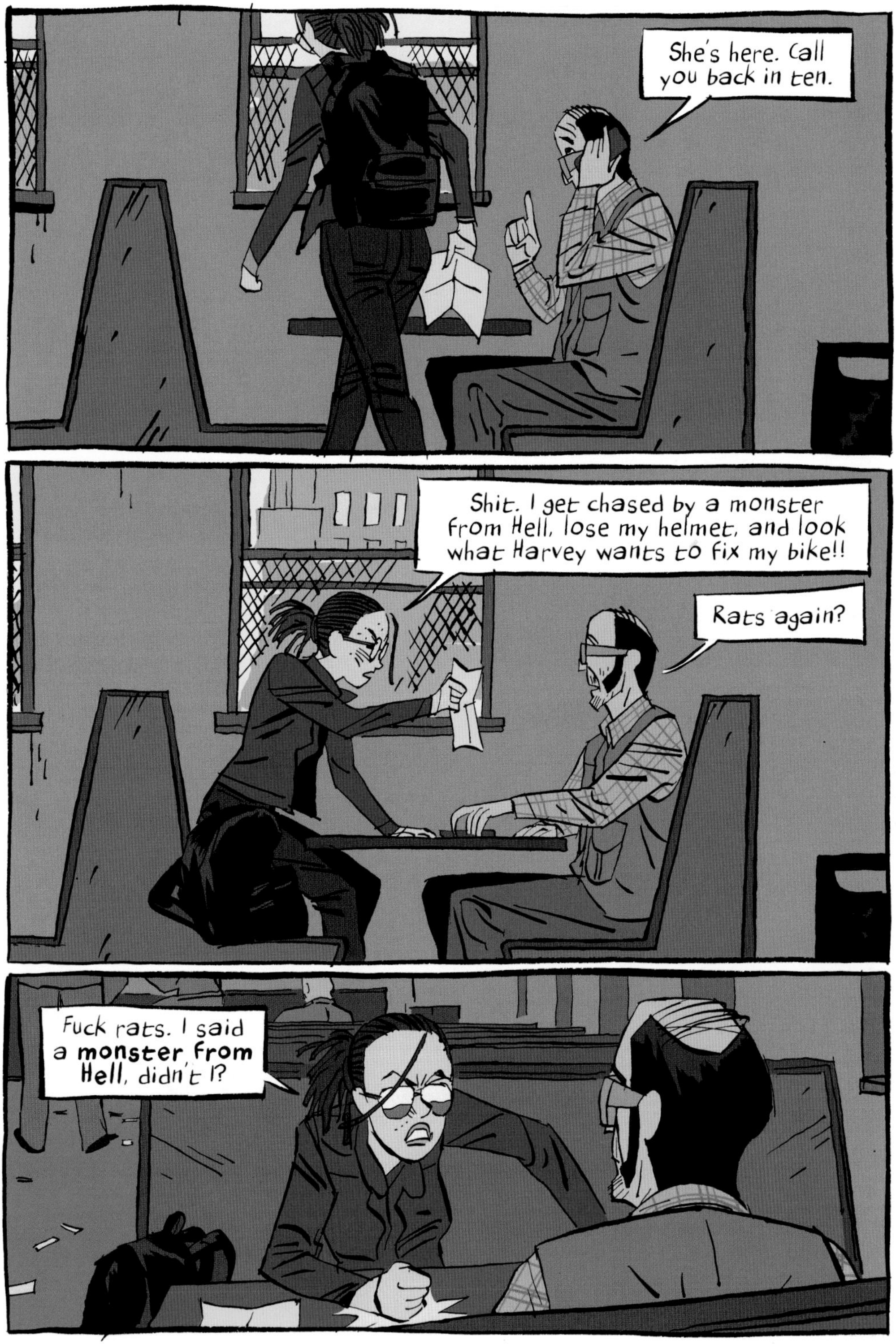
She's here. Call you back in ten.
Shit. I get chased by a monster from Hell, lose my helmet, and look what Harvey wants to fix my bike!!
Rats again?
Fuck rats. I said a **monster from Hell**, didn't I?

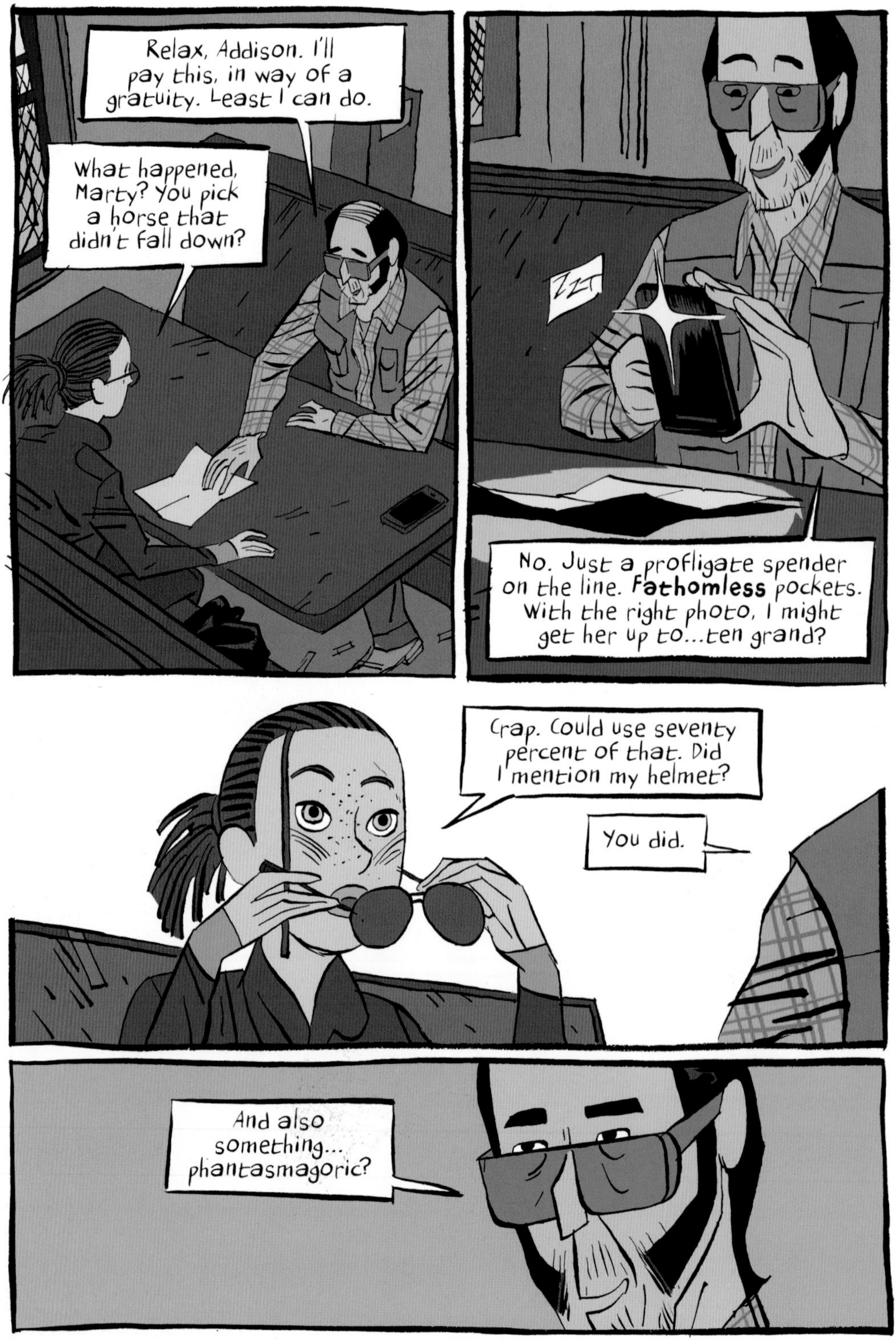
Relax, Addison. I'll pay this, in way of a gratuity. Least I can do.
What happened, Marty? You pick a horse that didn't fall down?
ZZT
No. Just a profligate spender on the line. **Fathomless** pockets. With the right photo, I might get her up to...ten grand?
Crap. Could use seventy percent of that. Did I mention my helmet?
You did.
And also something... phantasmagoric?

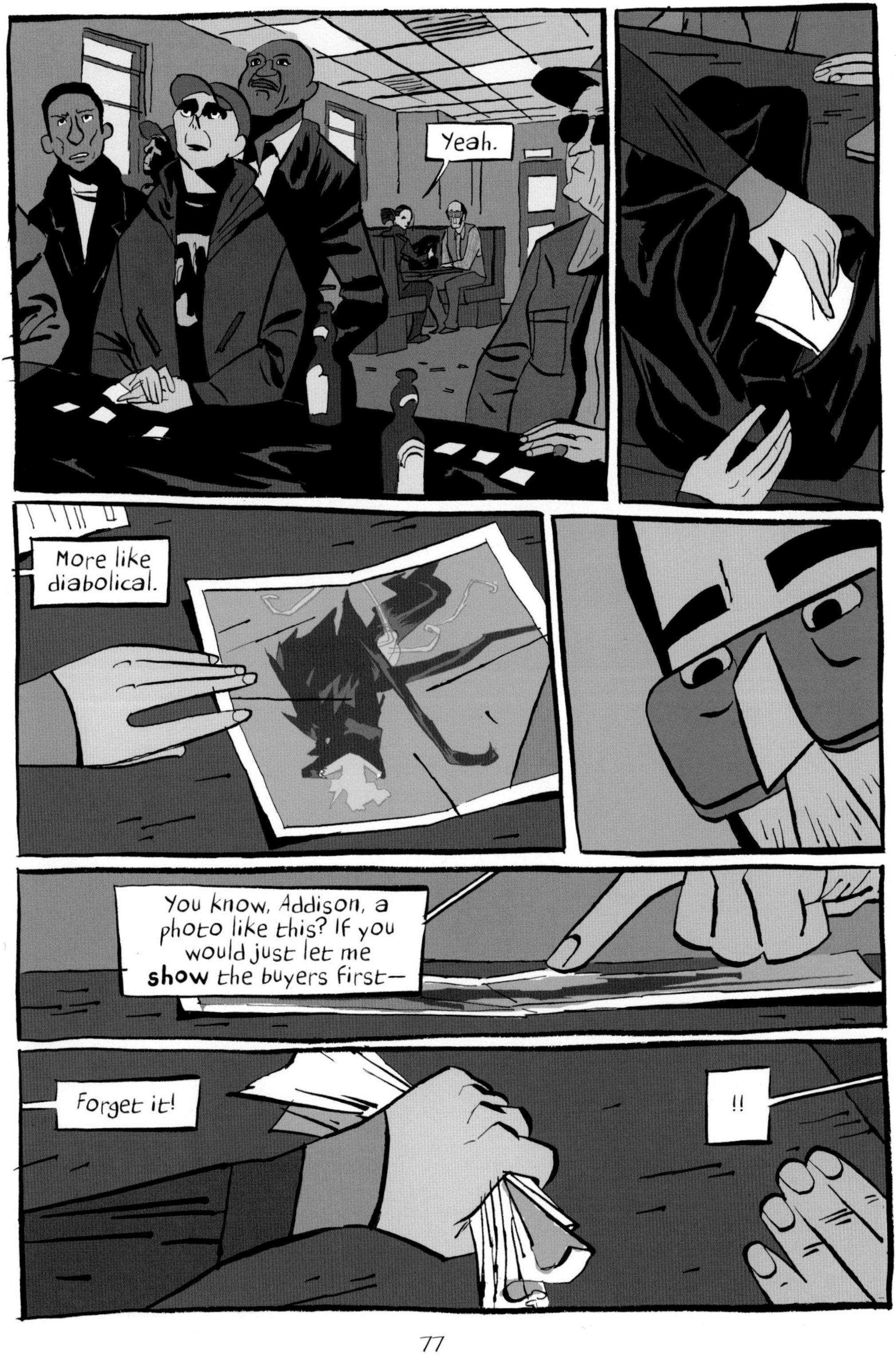
Yeah.
More like diabolical.
You know, Addison, a photo like this? If you would just let me **show** the buyers first—
Forget it!
!!

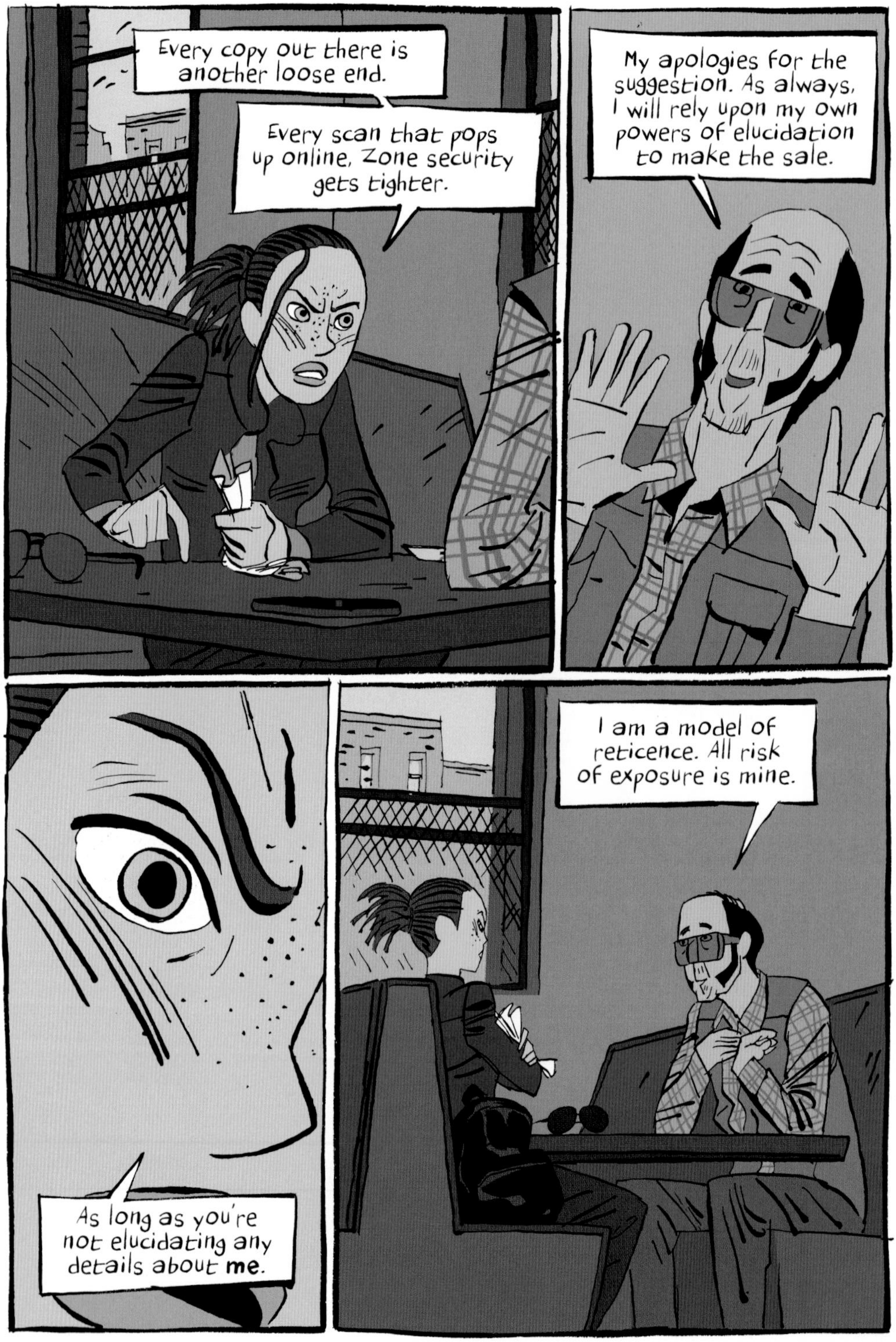
Every copy out there is another loose end.
Every scan that pops up online, Zone security gets tighter.
My apologies for the suggestion. As always, I will rely upon my own powers of elucidation to make the sale.
As long as you're not elucidating any details about **me**.
I am a model of reticence. All risk of exposure is mine.

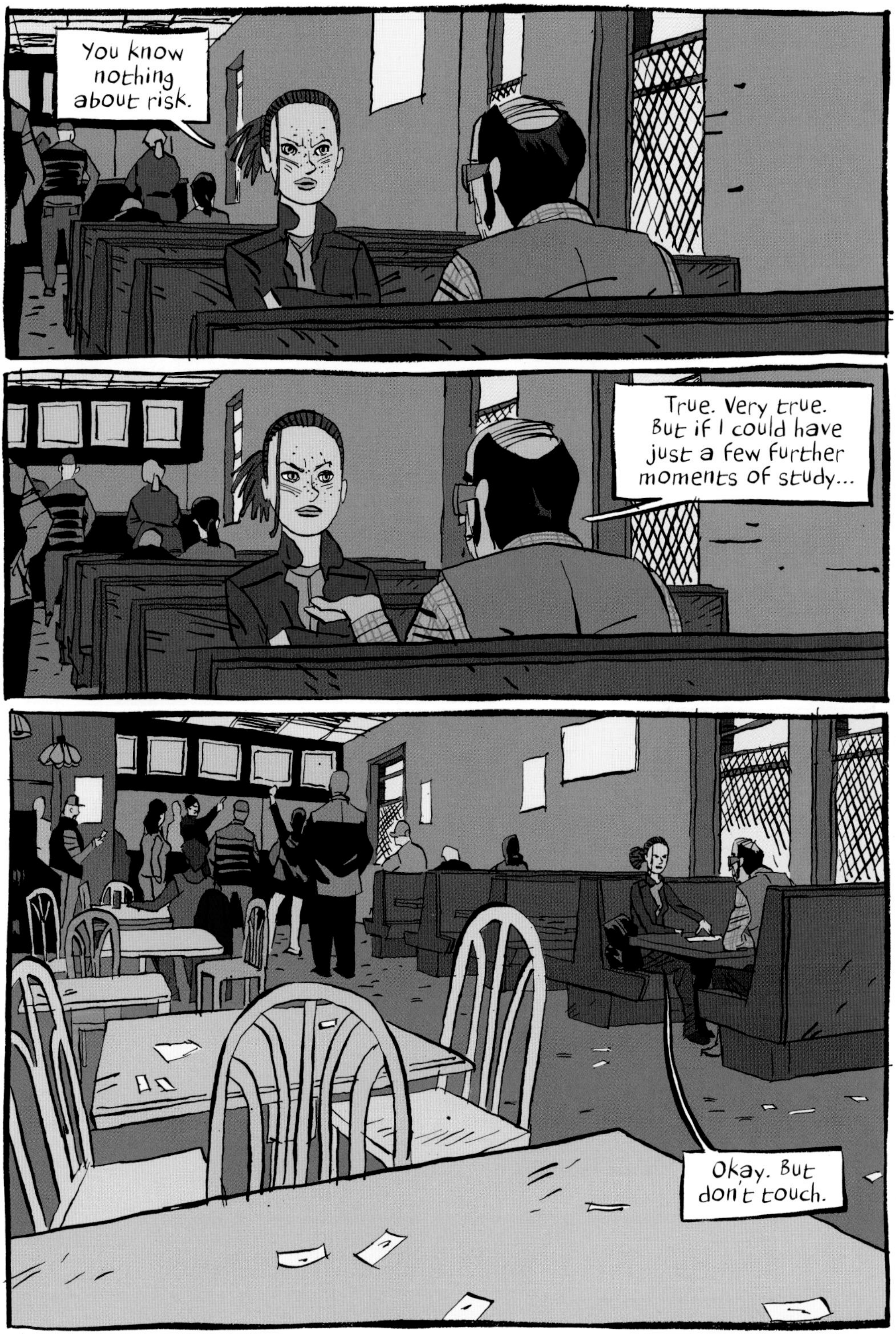
You know nothing about risk.
True. Very true. But if I could have just a few further moments of study...
Okay. But don't touch.

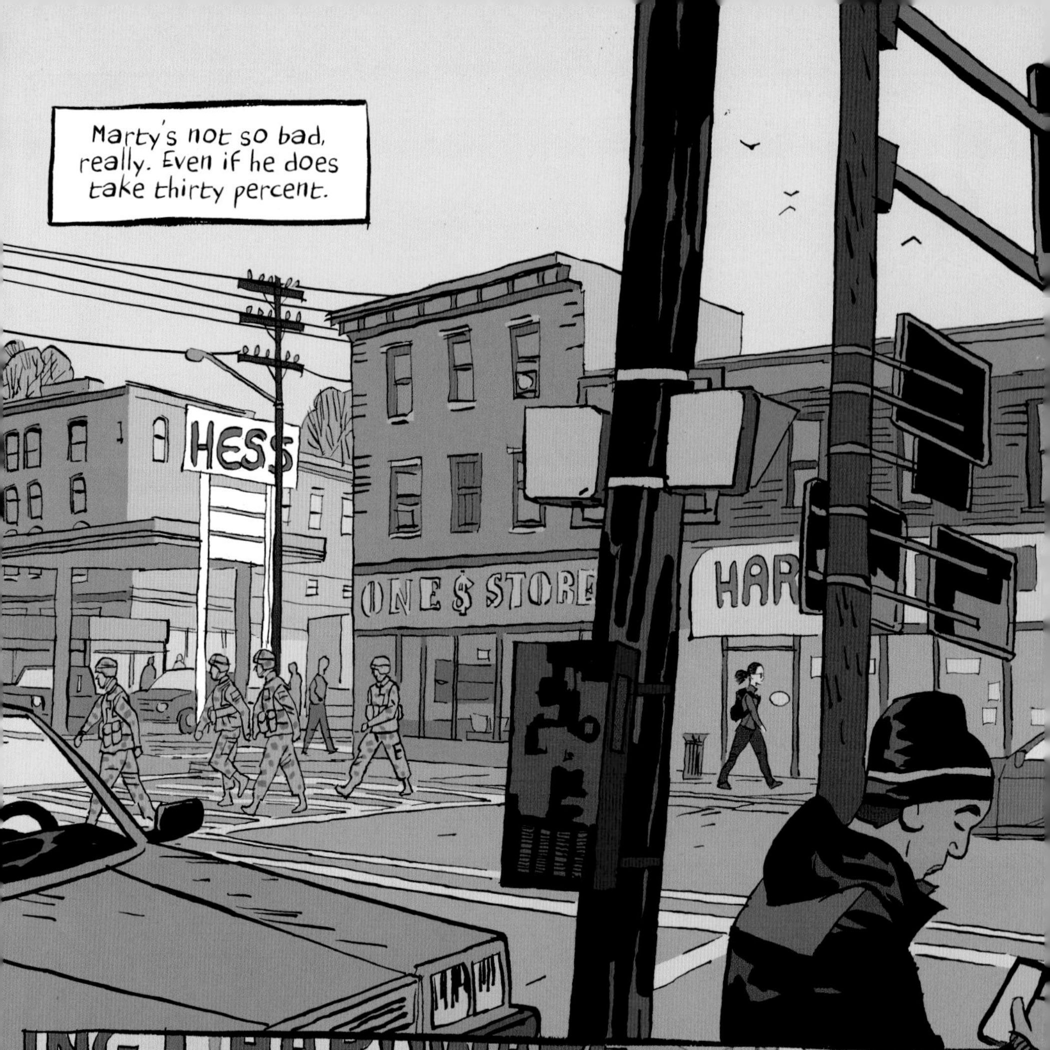
Marty's not so bad, really. Even if he does take thirty percent.
HESS
ONE $ STORE
HAR

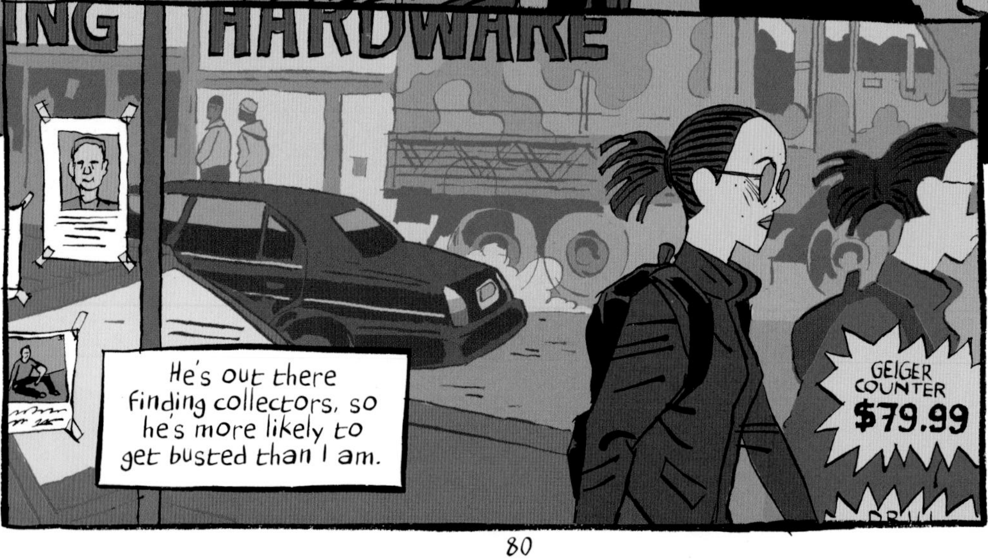
ING
HARDWARE
He's out there finding collectors, so he's more likely to get busted than I am.
GEIGER COUNTER $79.99

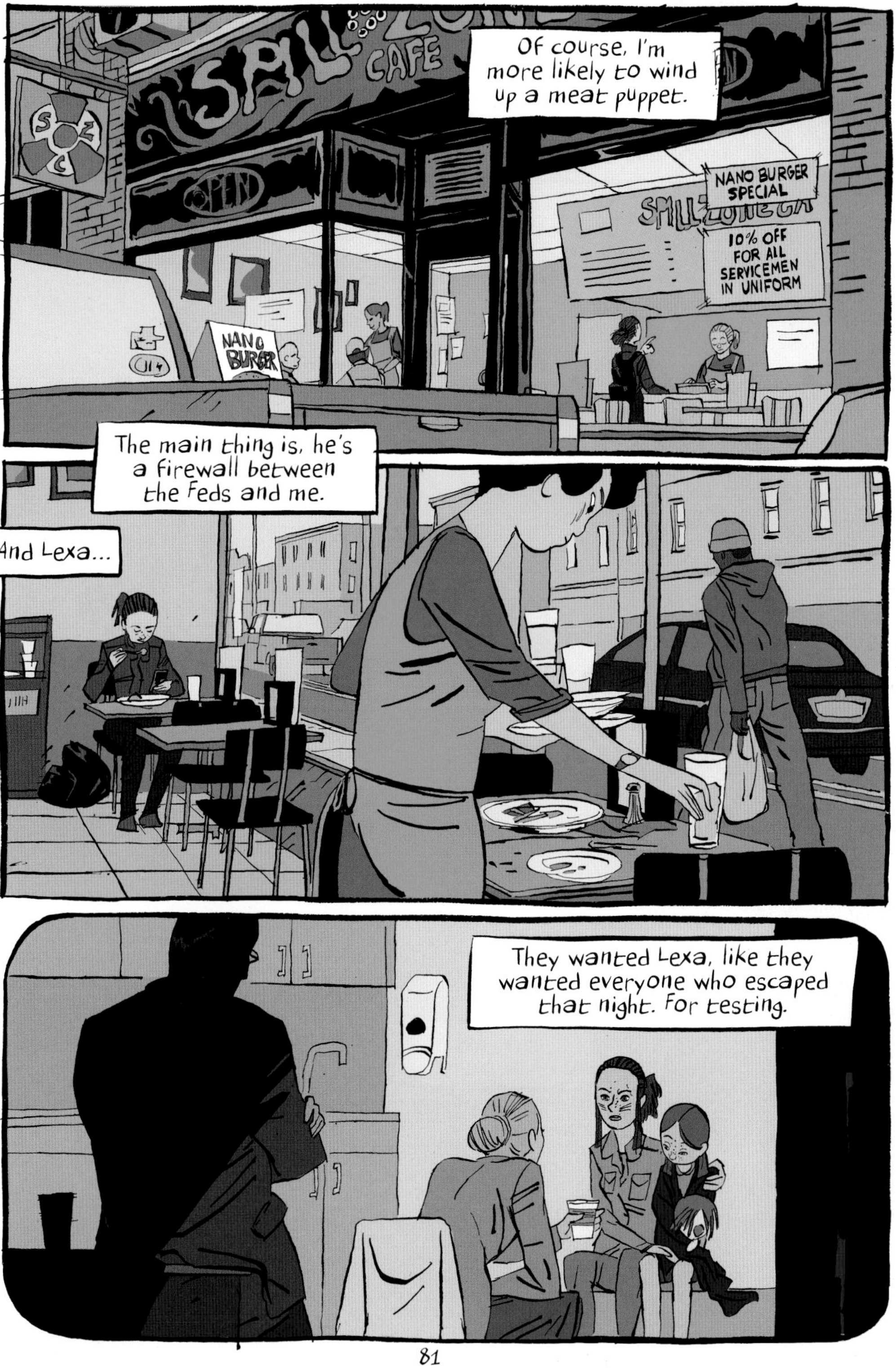
SPILL ZONE
CAFE
Of course, I'm more likely to wind up a meat puppet.
OPEN
NANO BURGER SPECIAL
10% OFF FOR ALL SERVICEMEN IN UNIFORM
NANO BURGER
The main thing is, he's a firewall between the Feds and me.
And Lexa...
They wanted Lexa, like they wanted everyone who escaped that night. For testing.

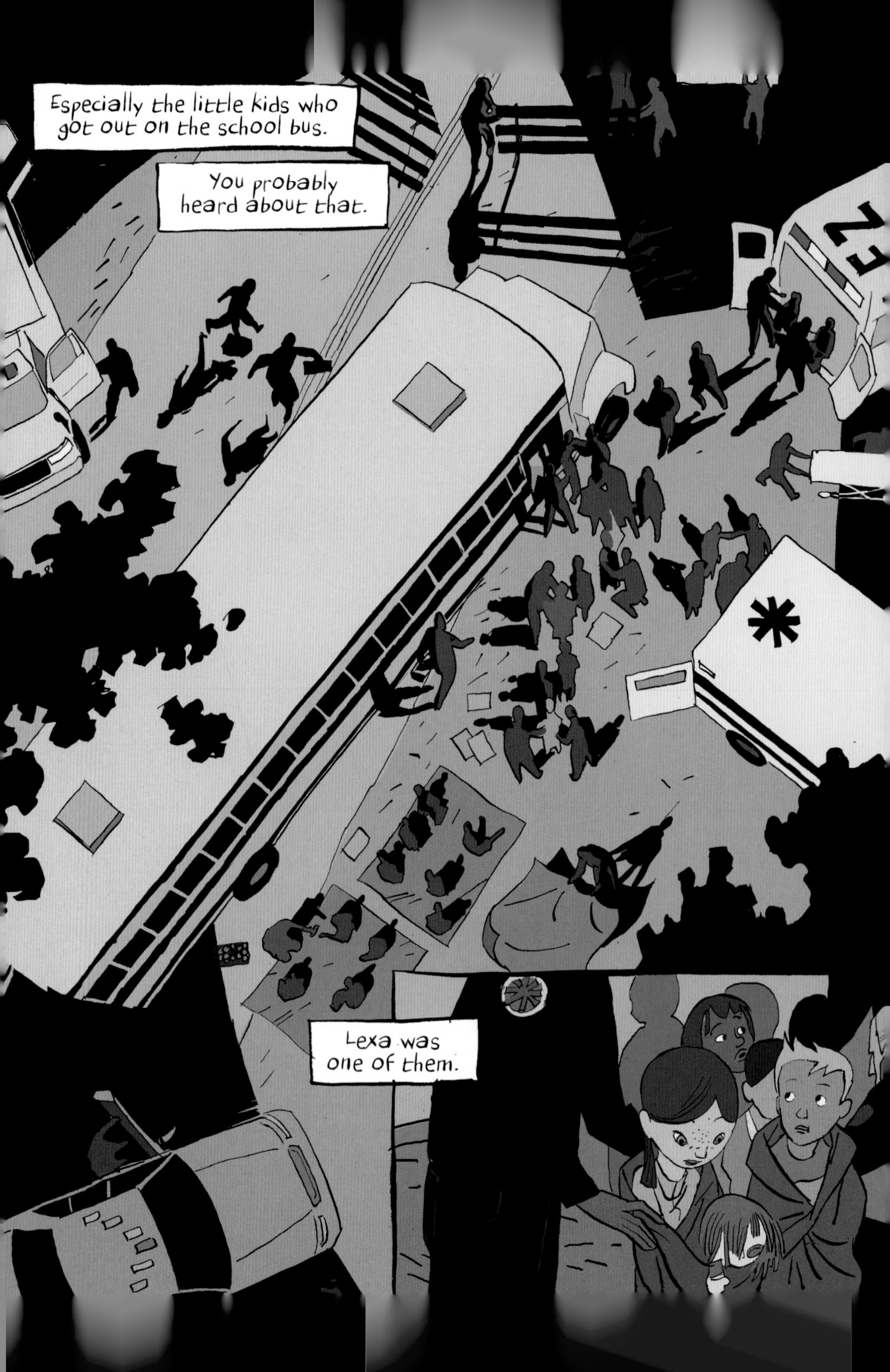
Especially the little kids who got out on the school bus.
You probably heard about that.
Lexa was one of them.

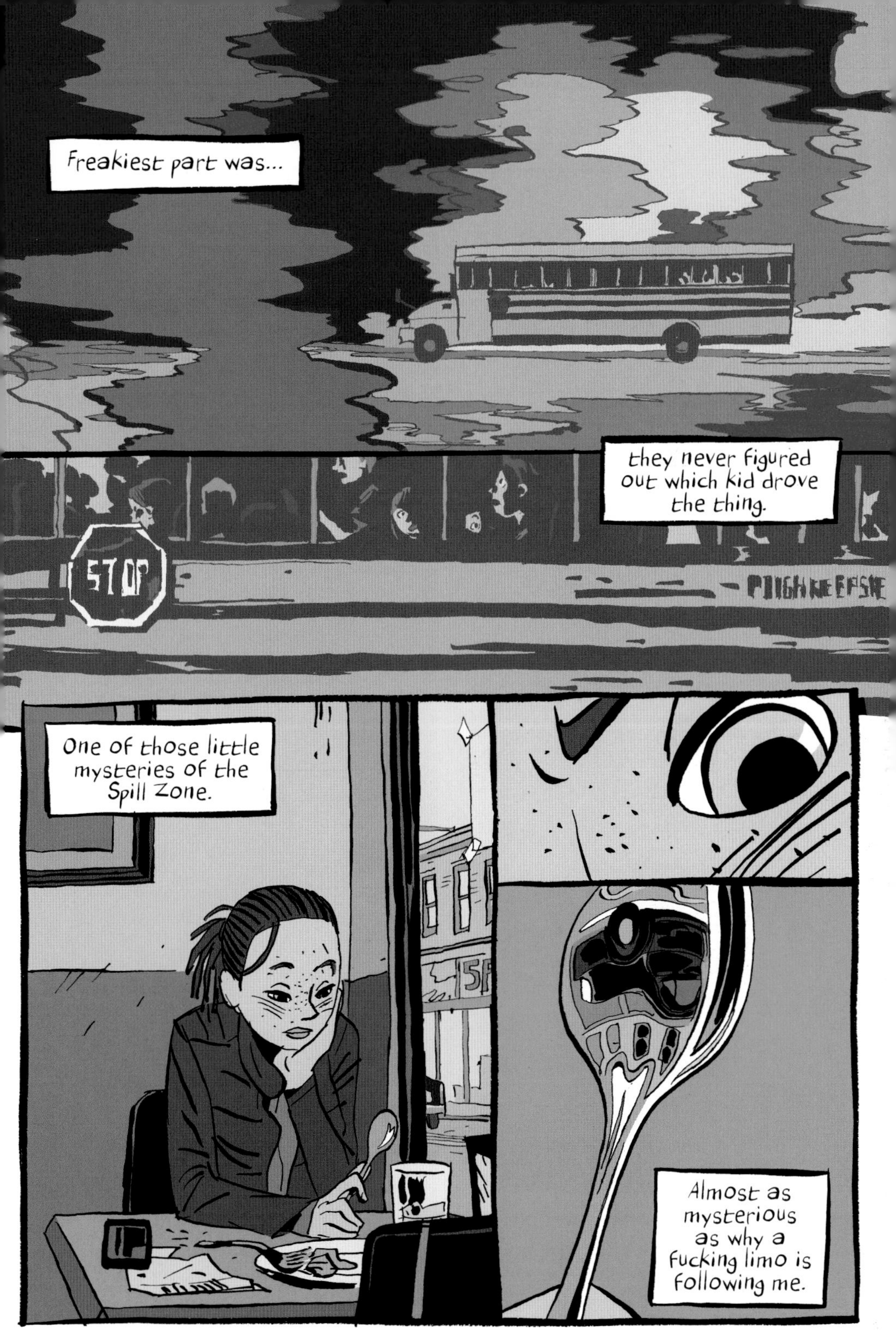
Freakiest part was...
they never figured out which kid drove the thing.
STOP
One of those little mysteries of the Spill Zone.
Almost as mysterious as why a fucking limo is following me.

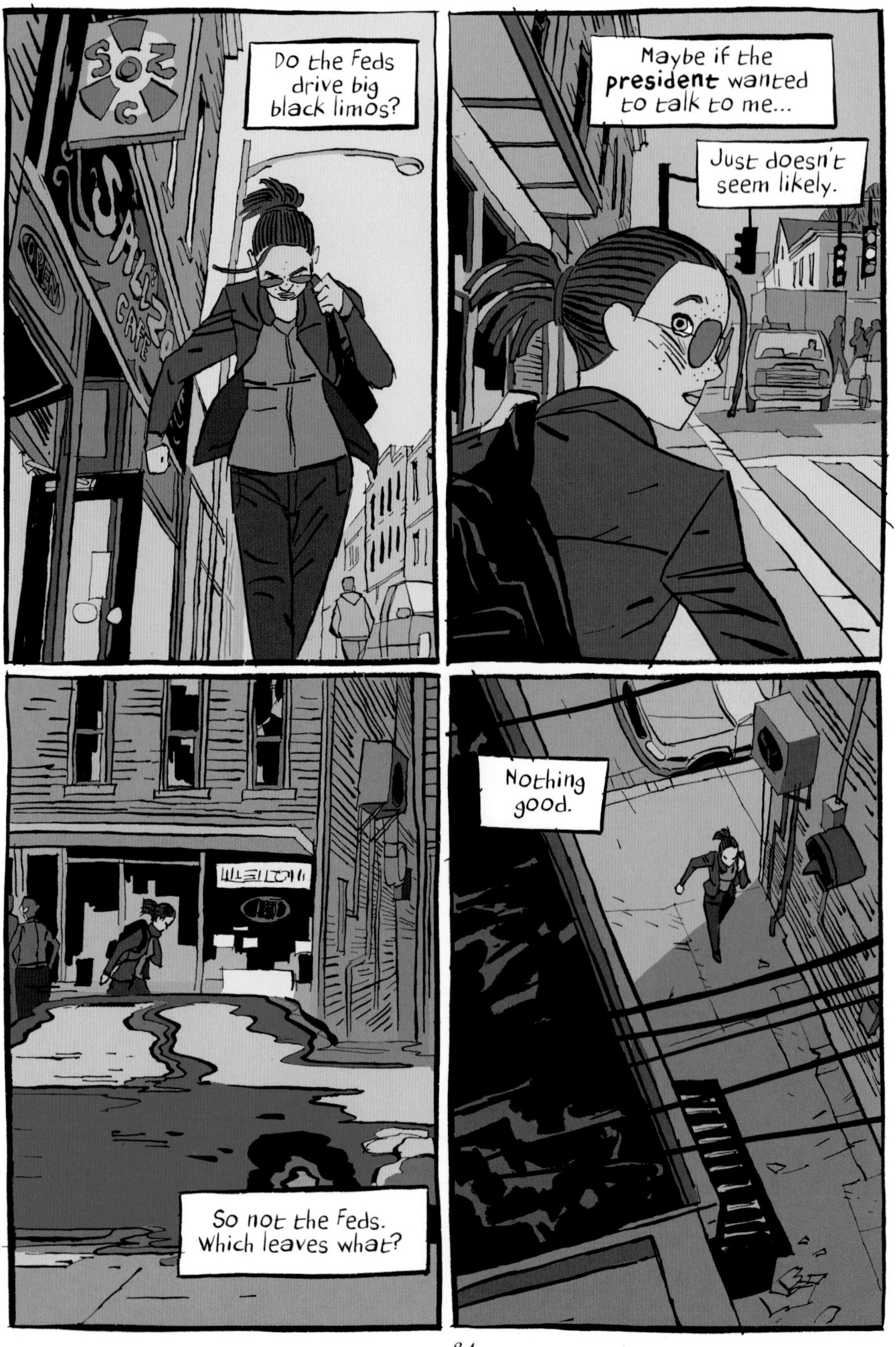
Do the Feds drive big black limos?
Maybe if the **president** wanted to talk to me...
Just doesn't seem likely.
So not the Feds. Which leaves what?
Nothing good.

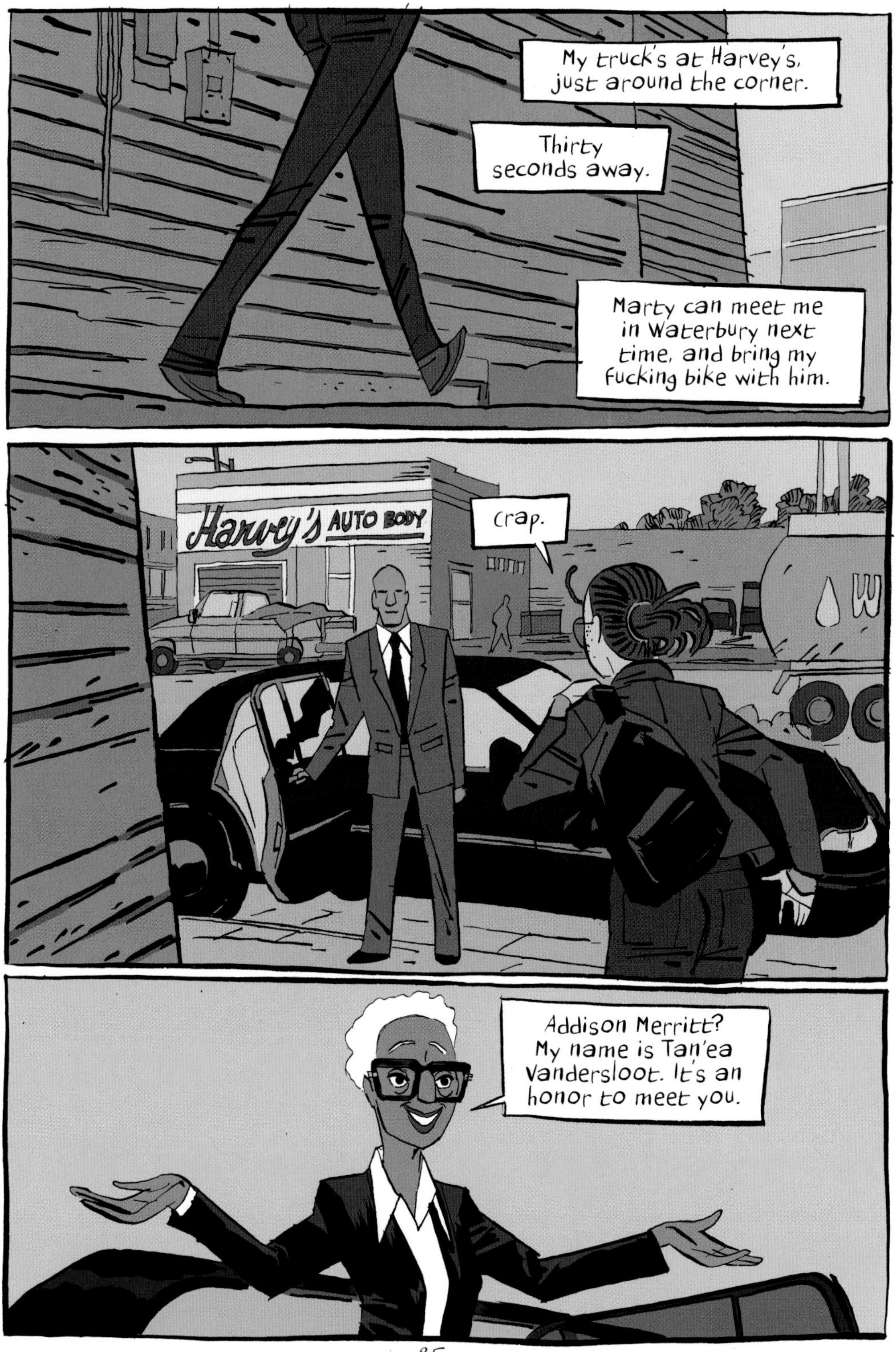
My truck's at Harvey's, just around the corner.
Thirty seconds away.
Marty can meet me in Waterbury next time, and bring my fucking bike with him.
Harvey's AUTO BODY
Crap.
Addison Merritt? My name is Tan'ea Vandersloot. It's an honor to meet you.

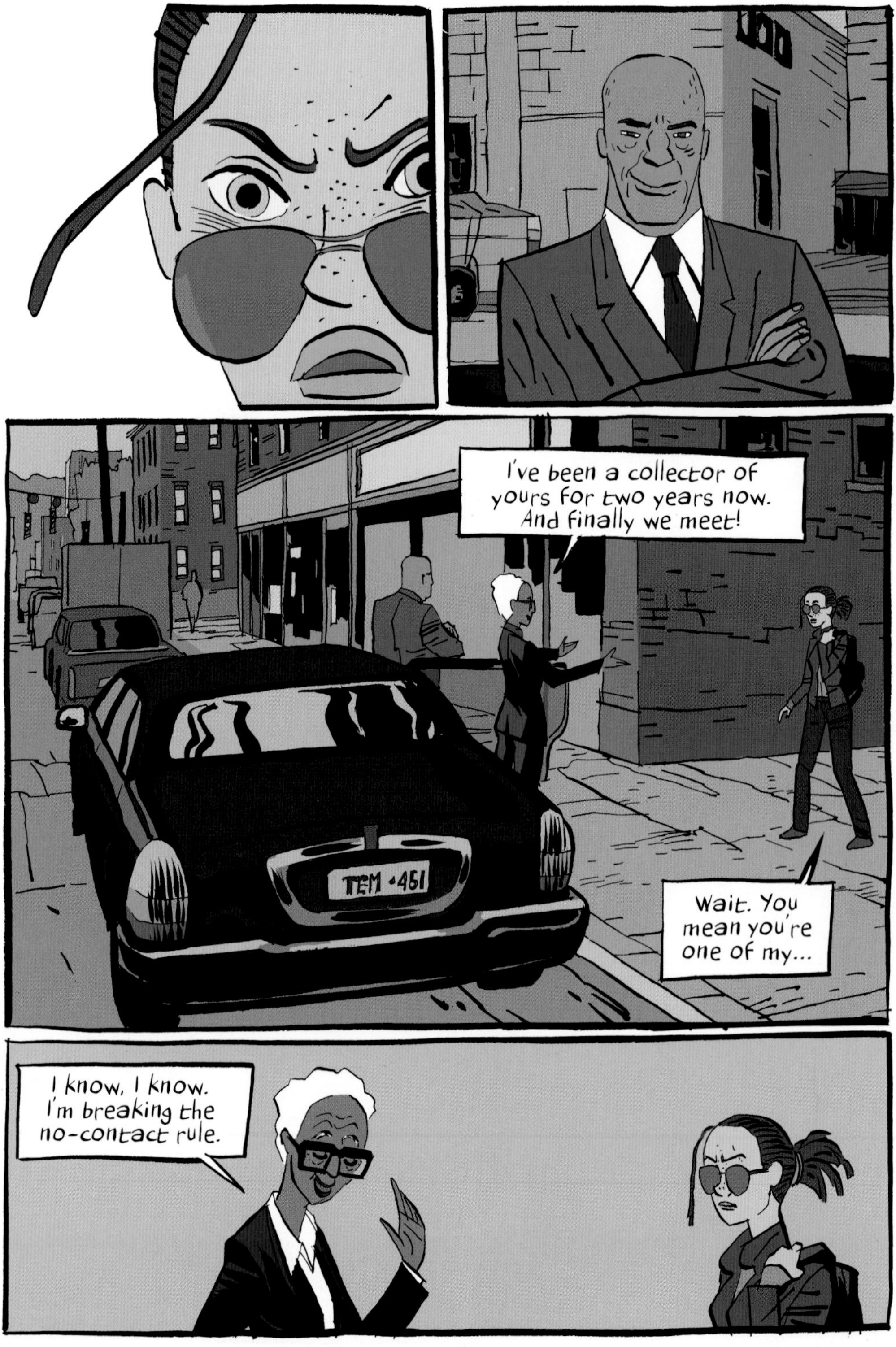
I've been a collector of yours for two years now. And finally we meet!
Wait. You mean you're one of my...
I know, I know. I'm breaking the no-contact rule.

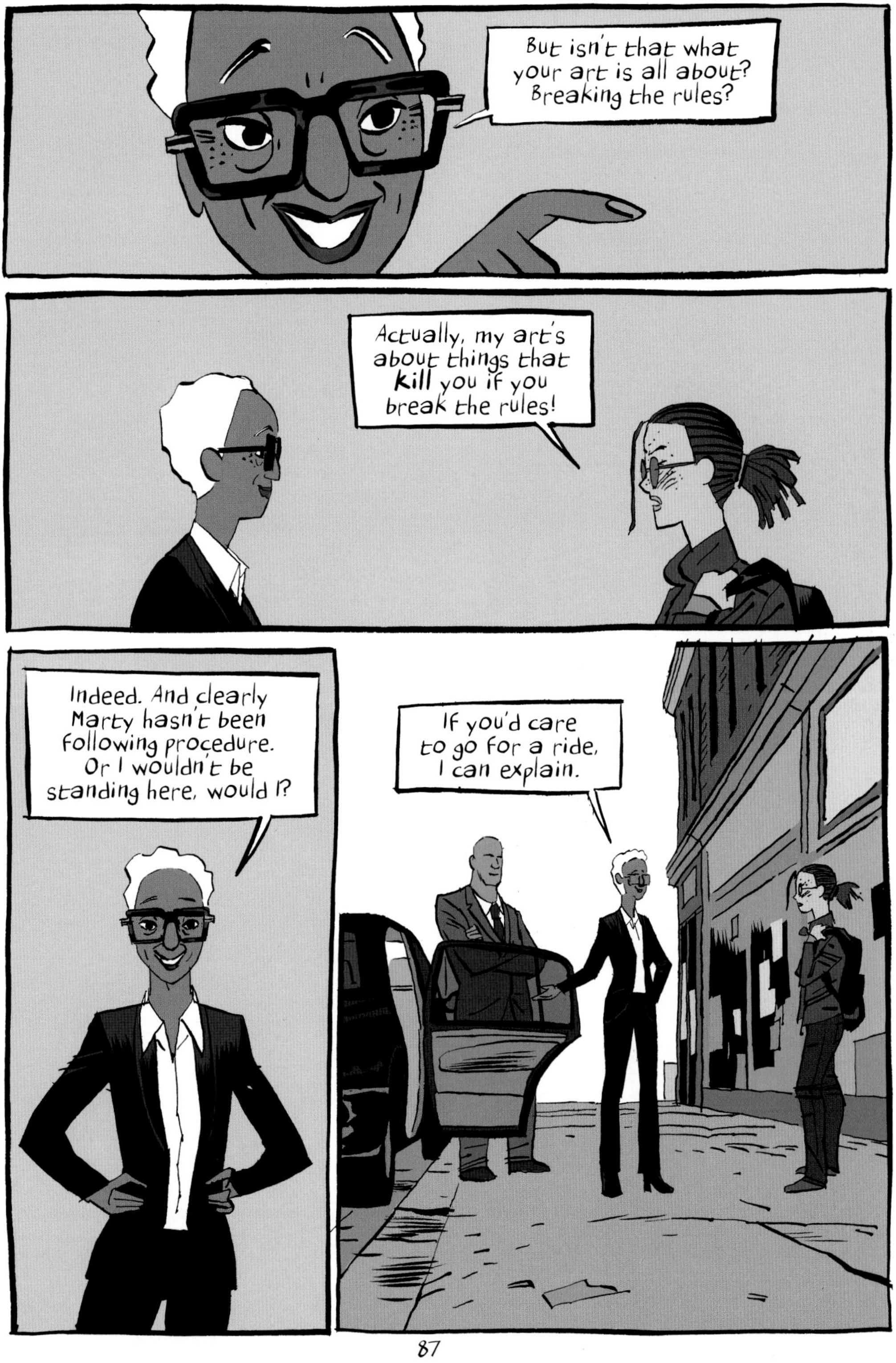
But isn't that what your art is all about? Breaking the rules?
Actually, my art's about things that **kill** you if you break the rules!
Indeed. And clearly Marty hasn't been following procedure. Or I wouldn't be standing here, would I?
If you'd care to go for a ride, I can explain.

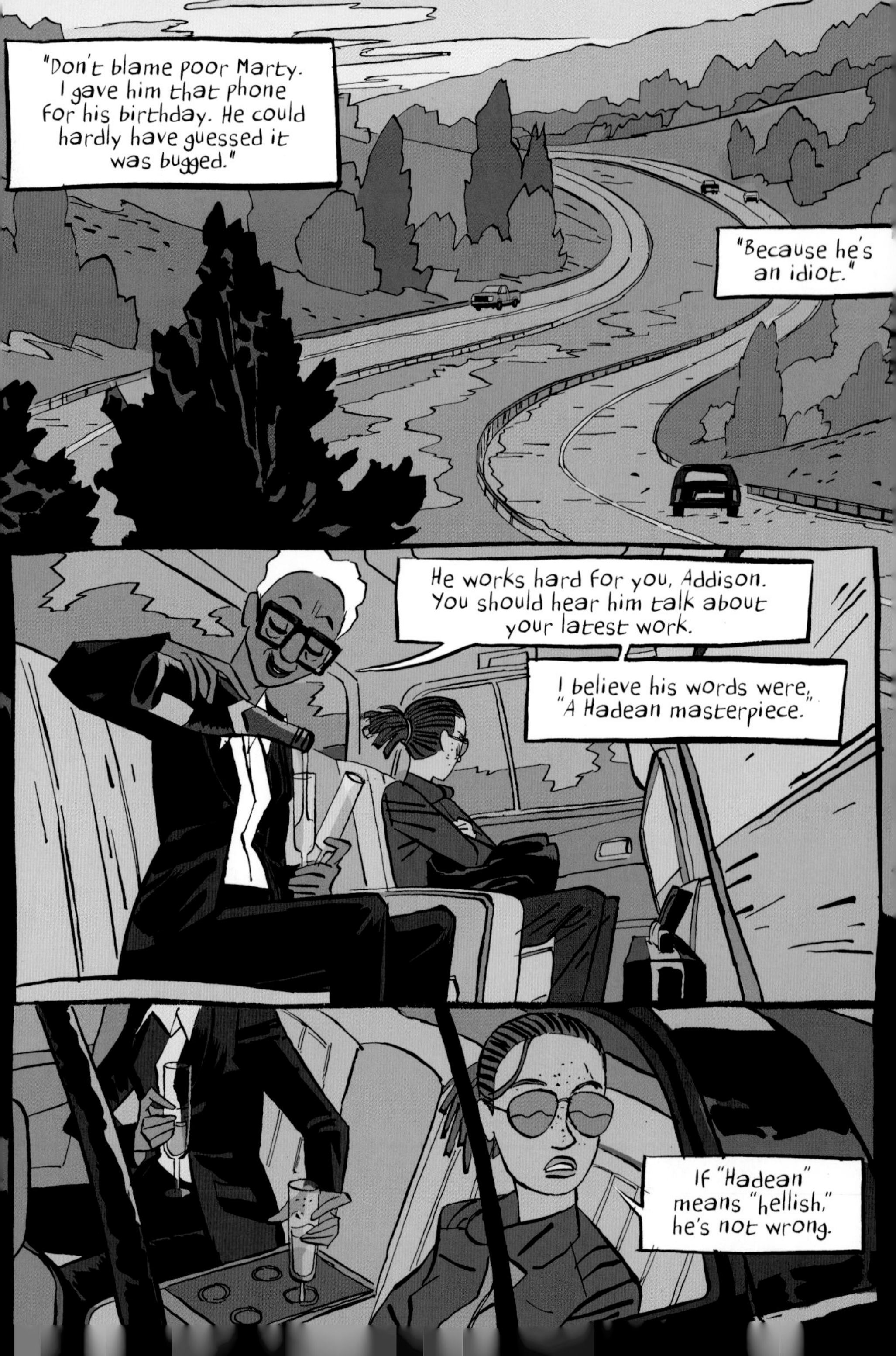
"Don't blame poor Marty. I gave him that phone for his birthday. He could hardly have guessed it was bugged."
"Because he's an idiot."
He works hard for you, Addison. You should hear him talk about your latest work.
I believe his words were, "A Hadean masterpiece."
If "Hadean" means "hellish," he's not wrong.

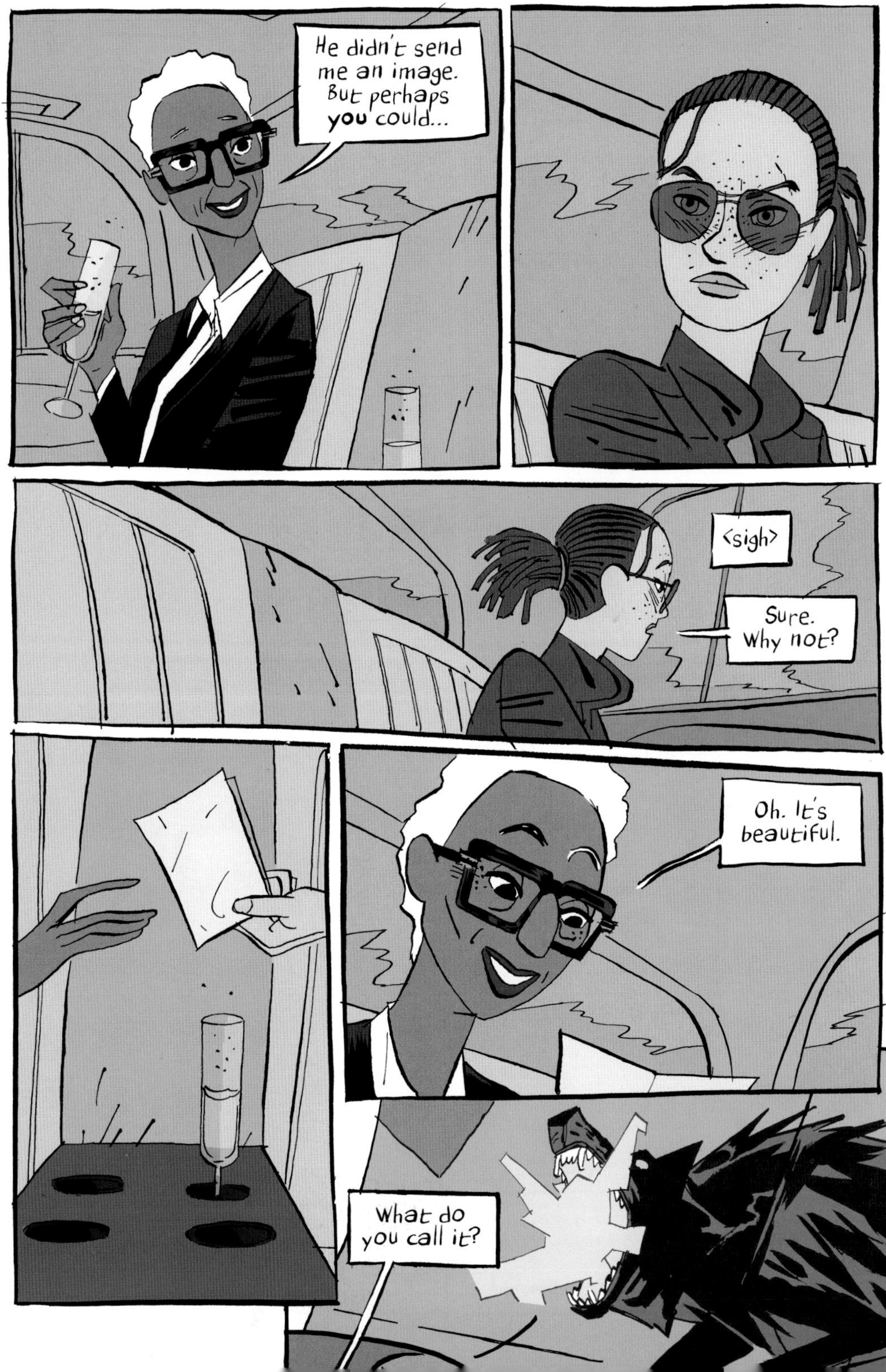
He didn't send me an image. But perhaps **you** could...
<sigh>
Sure. Why not?
Oh. It's beautiful.
What do you call it?

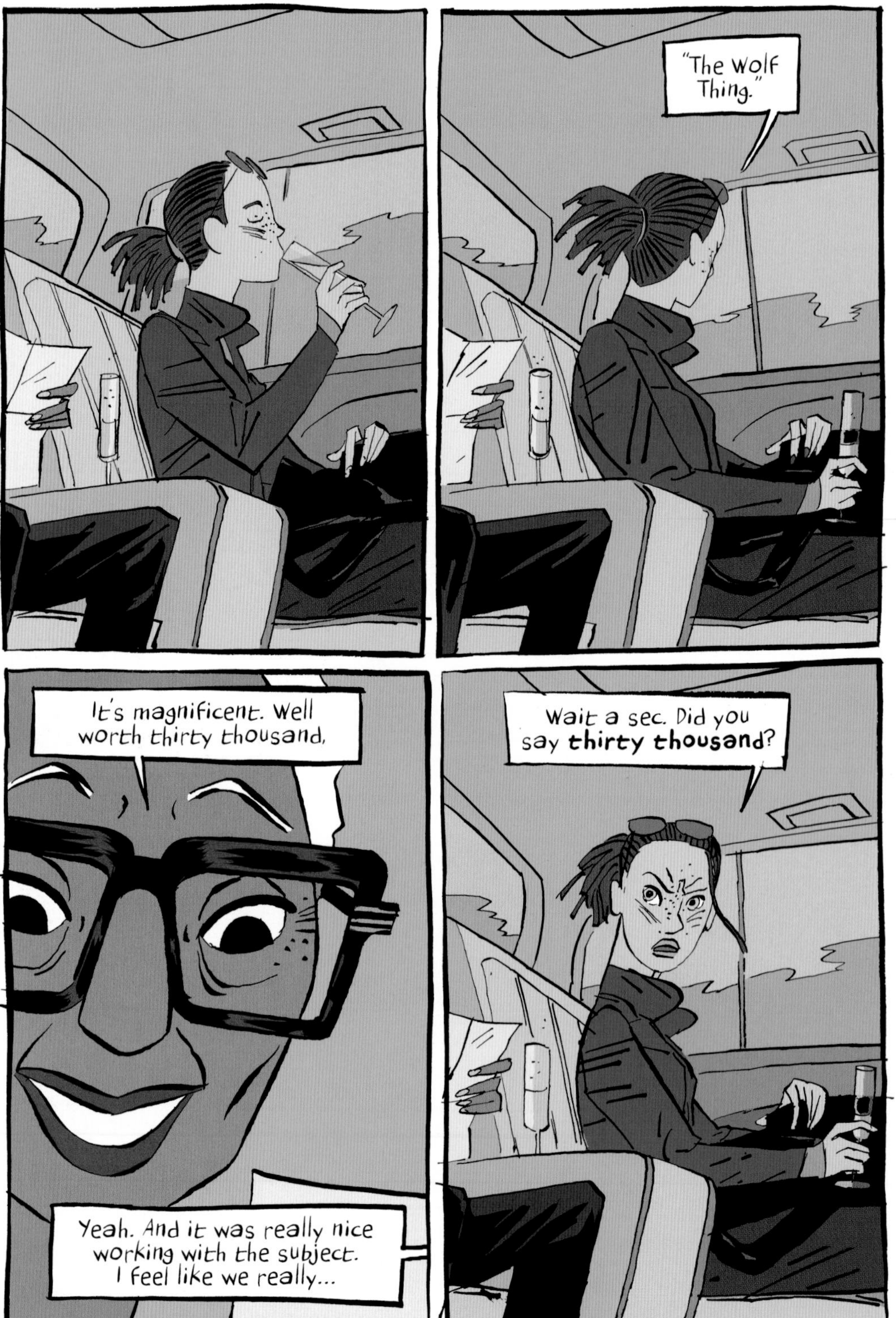
"The Wolf Thing."
It's magnificent. Well worth thirty thousand.
Yeah. And it was really nice working with the subject. I feel like we really...
Wait a sec. Did you say **thirty thousand**?

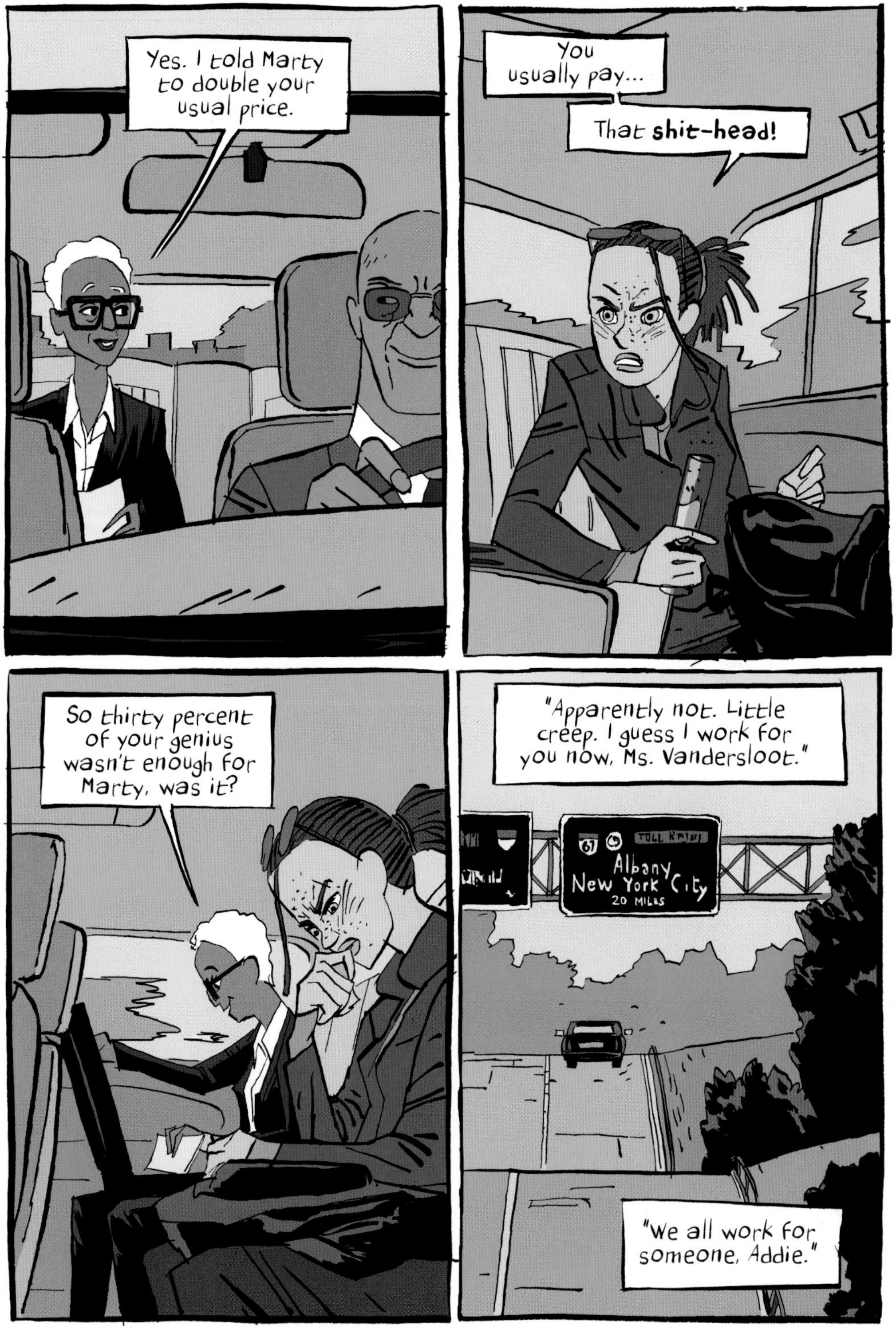

Yes. I told Marty to double your usual price.
You usually pay...
That **shit-head!**
So thirty percent of your genius wasn't enough for Marty, was it?
"Apparently not. Little creep. I guess I work for you now, Ms. Vandersloot."
61
Albany
New York City
20 MILES
"We all work for someone, Addie."

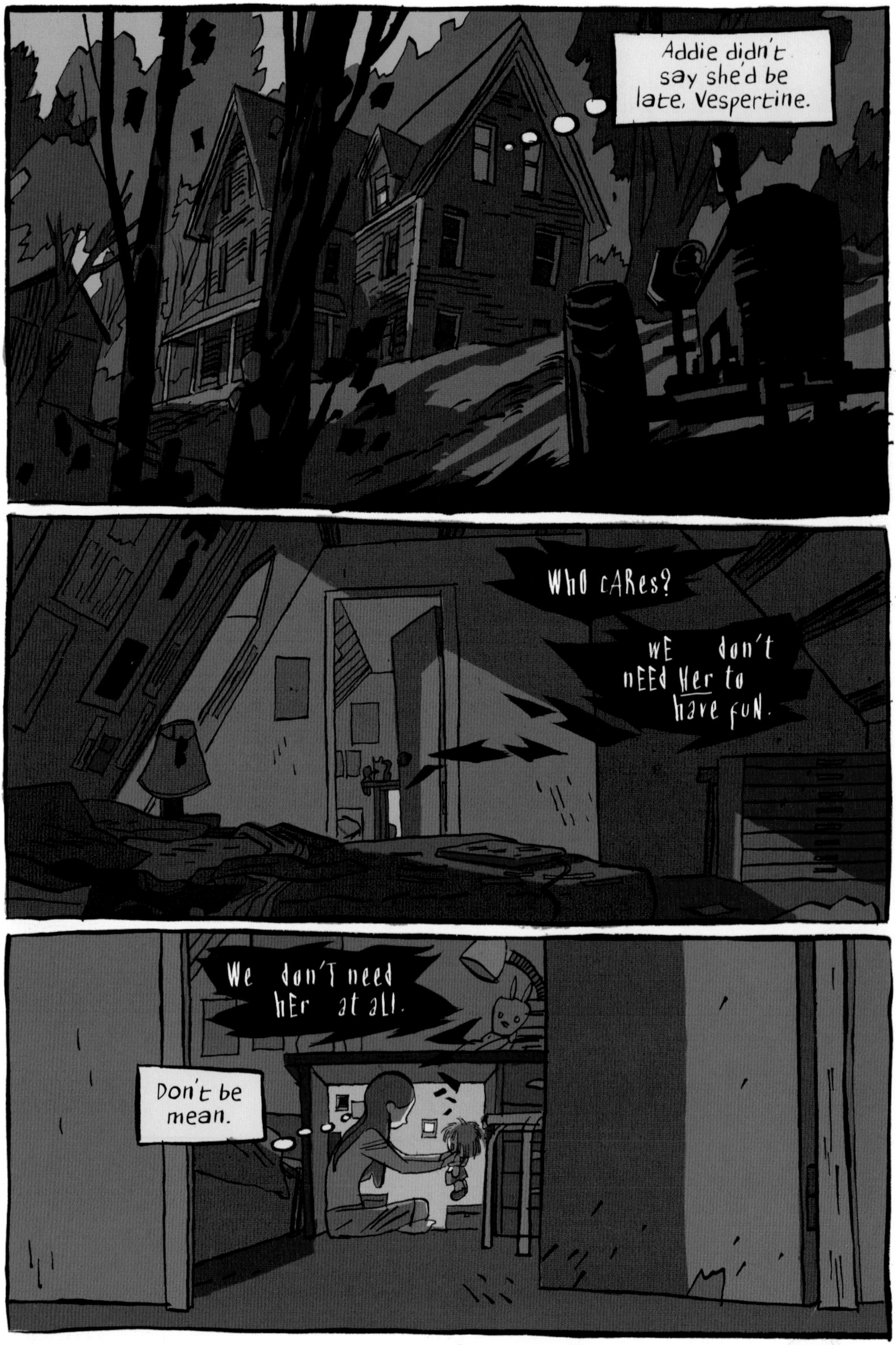
Addie didn't say she'd be late, Vespertine.
Who cares?
We don't need Her to have fun.
We don't need hEr at all.
Don't be mean.

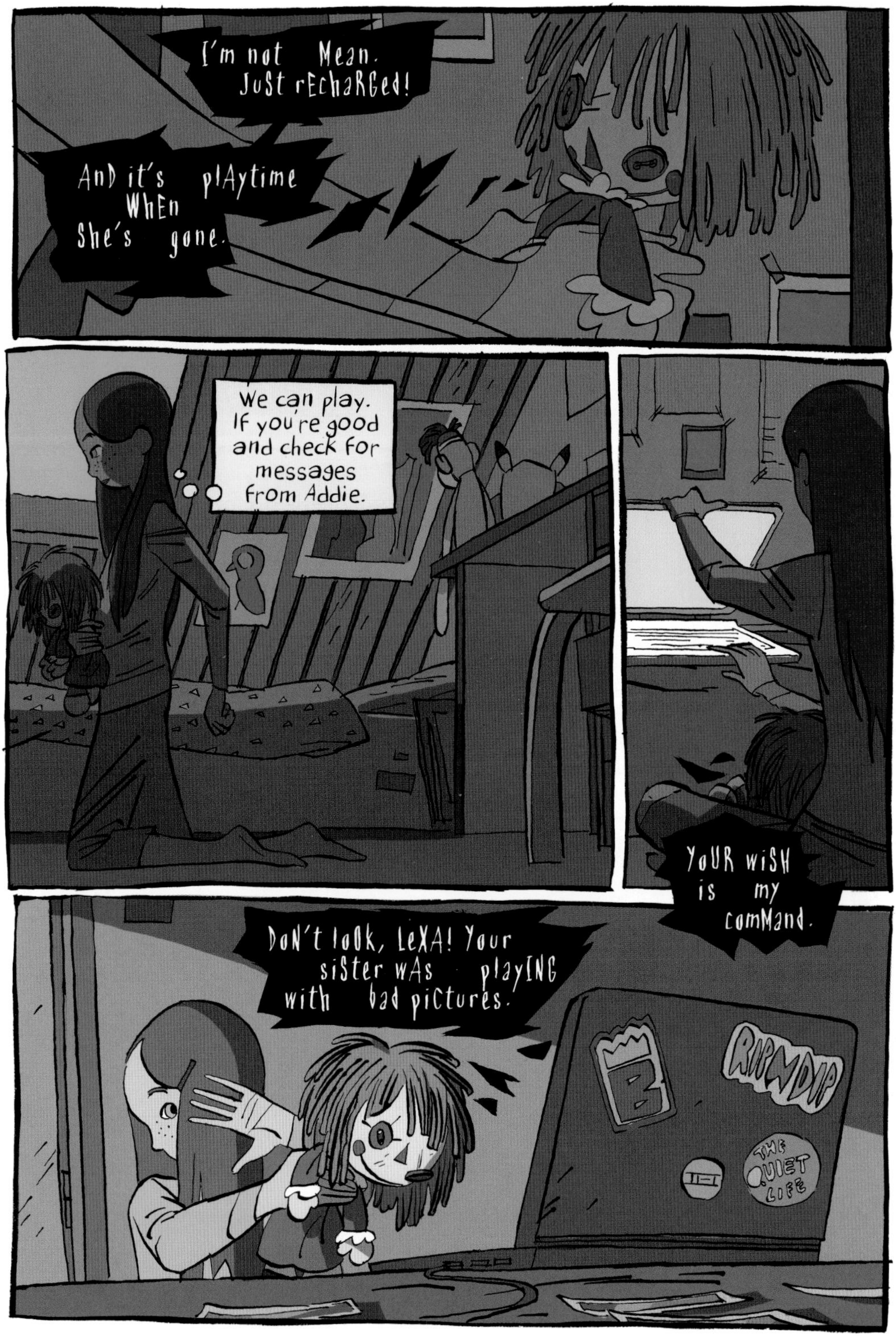
I'm not Mean. Just rEchaRGed!
And it's plAytime WhEn She's gone.
We can play. If you're good and check for messages from Addie.
YoUR wiSH is my comMand.
DoN't lo0k, LeXA! Your sister wAs playING with bad pictures.
RIPNDIP
THE QUIET LIFE

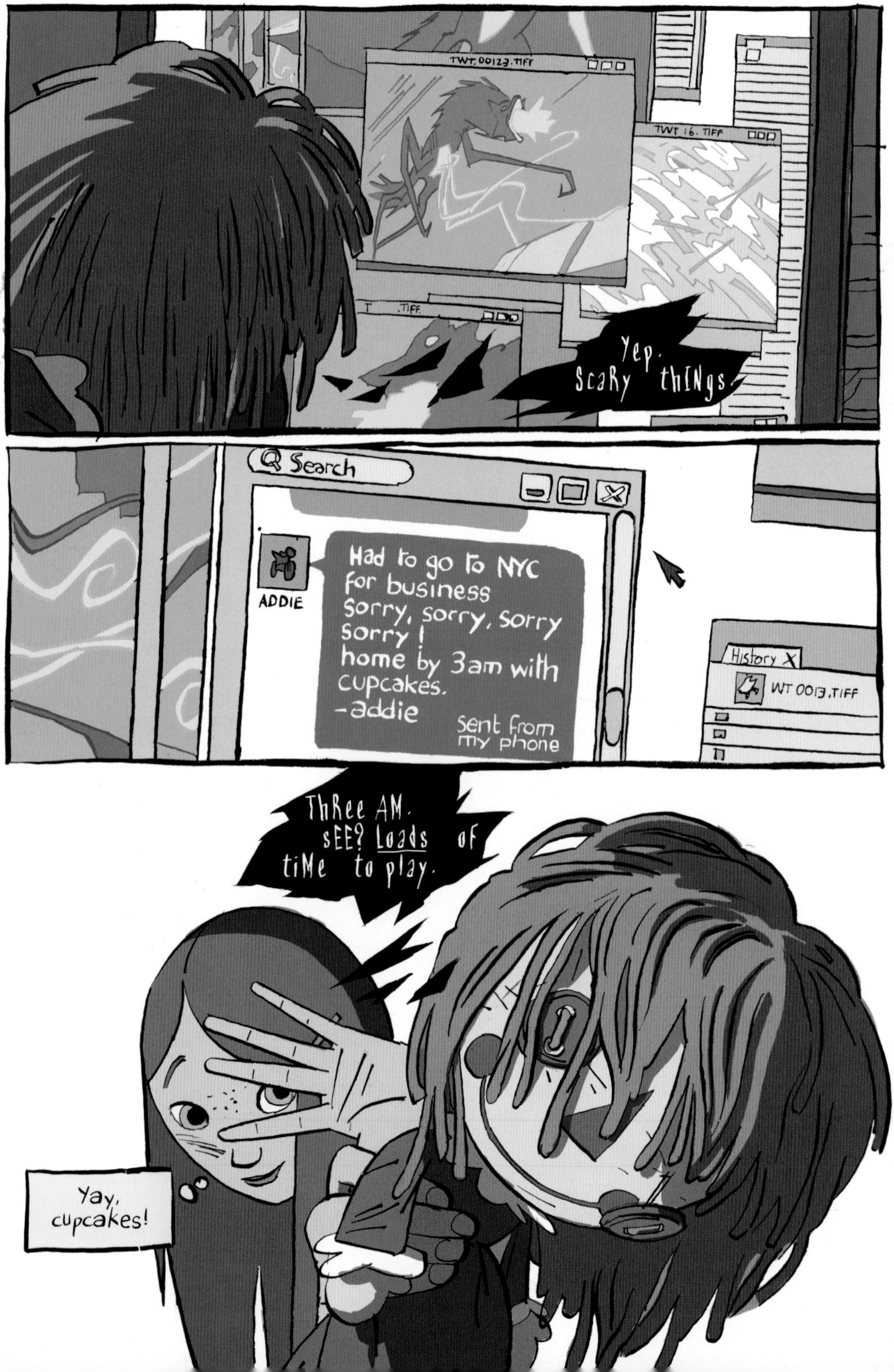
TWT.00123.TIFF
TWT 16. TIFF
Yep. Scary things.
Search
Had to go to NYC for business sorry, sorry, sorry sorry! home by 3am with cupcakes. -addie
sent from my phone
ADDIE
History
WT 0013.TIFF
Three AM. See? Loads of time to play.
Yay, cupcakes!

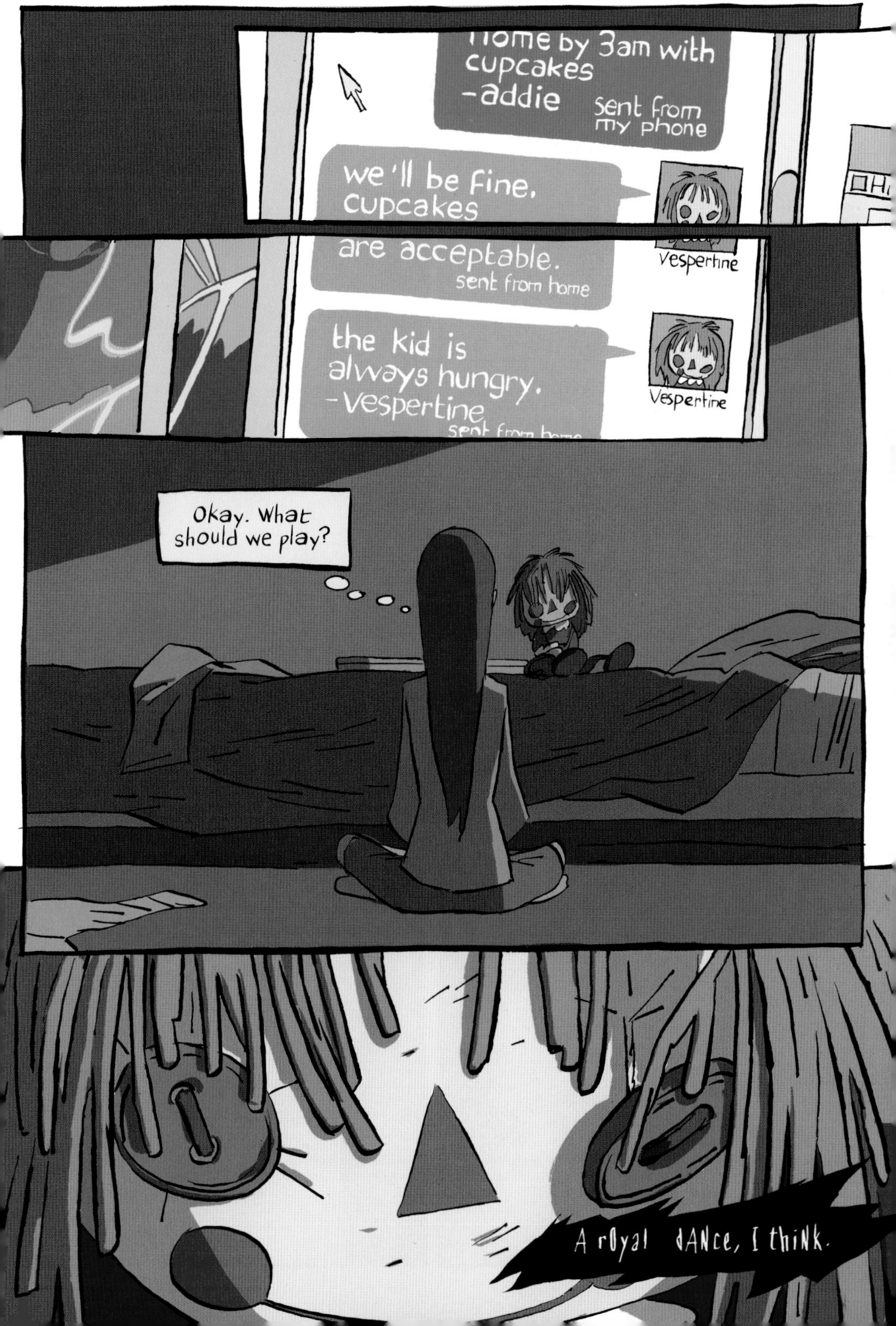

home by 3am with cupcakes -addie sent from my phone
we'll be fine. cupcakes are acceptable. sent from home
Vespertine
the kid is always hungry. -vespertine
Vespertine
Okay. What should we play?
A royal dance, I think.

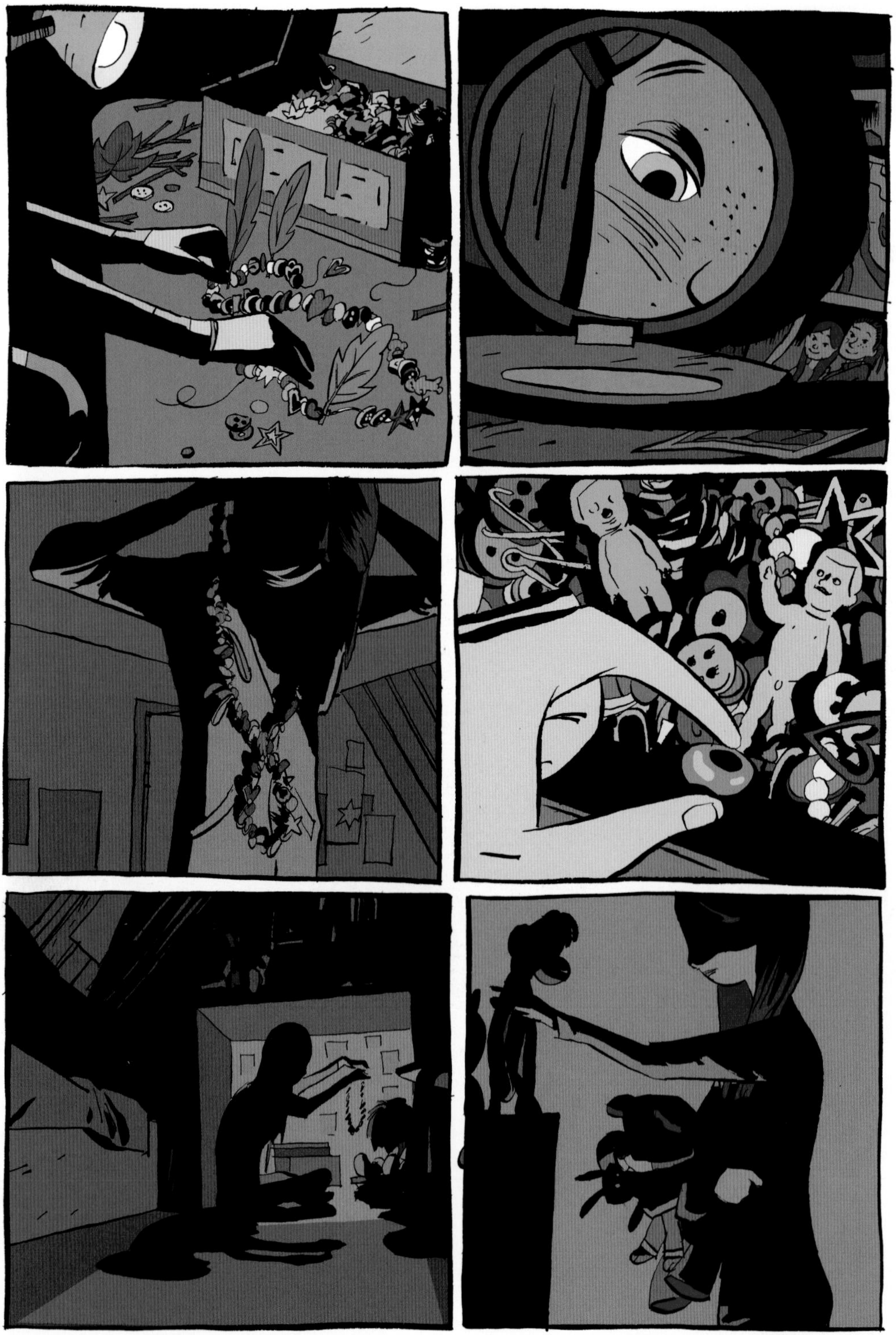

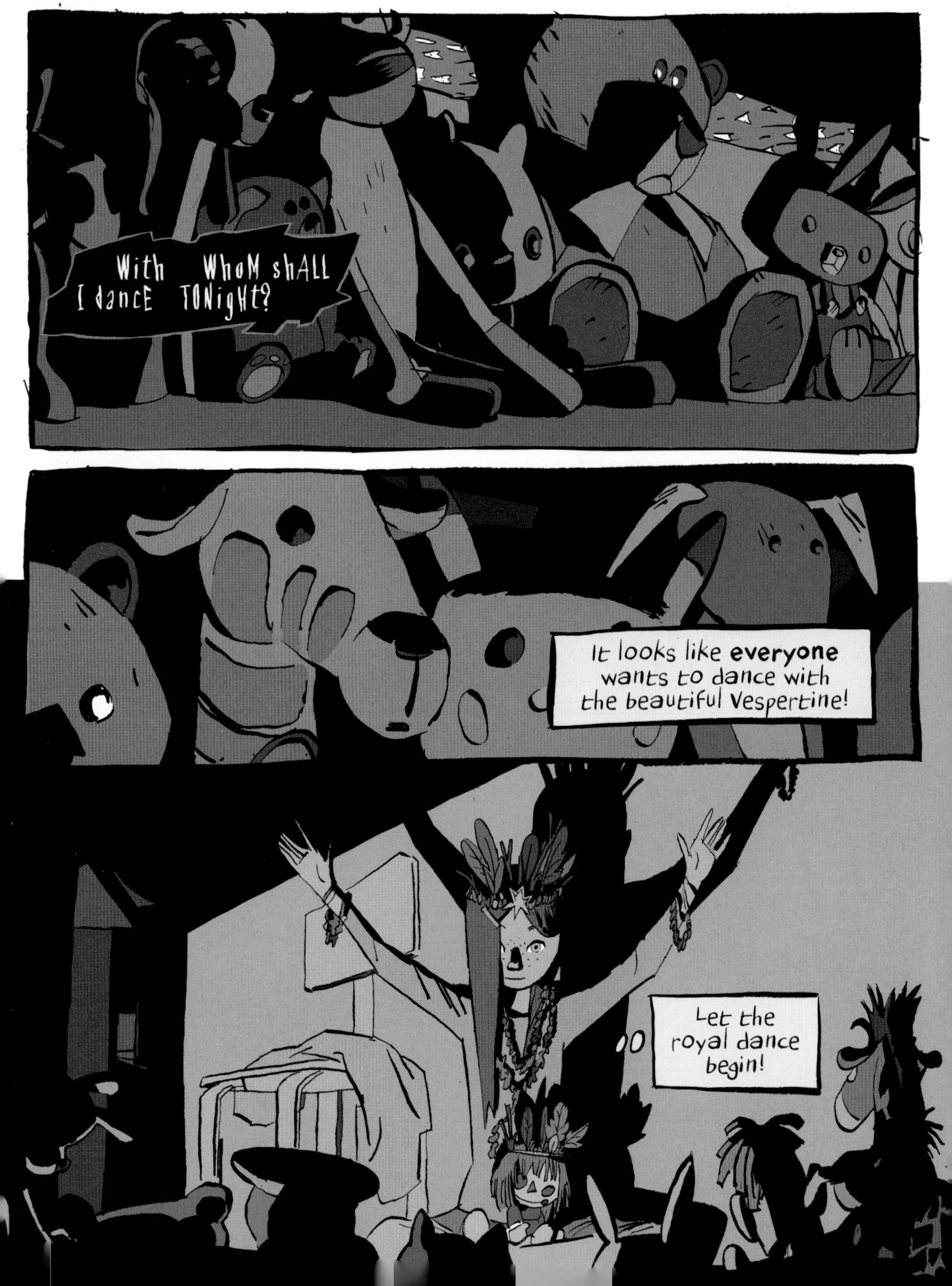

With whom shall I dance tonight?
It looks like everyone wants to dance with the beautiful Vespertine!
Let the royal dance begin!

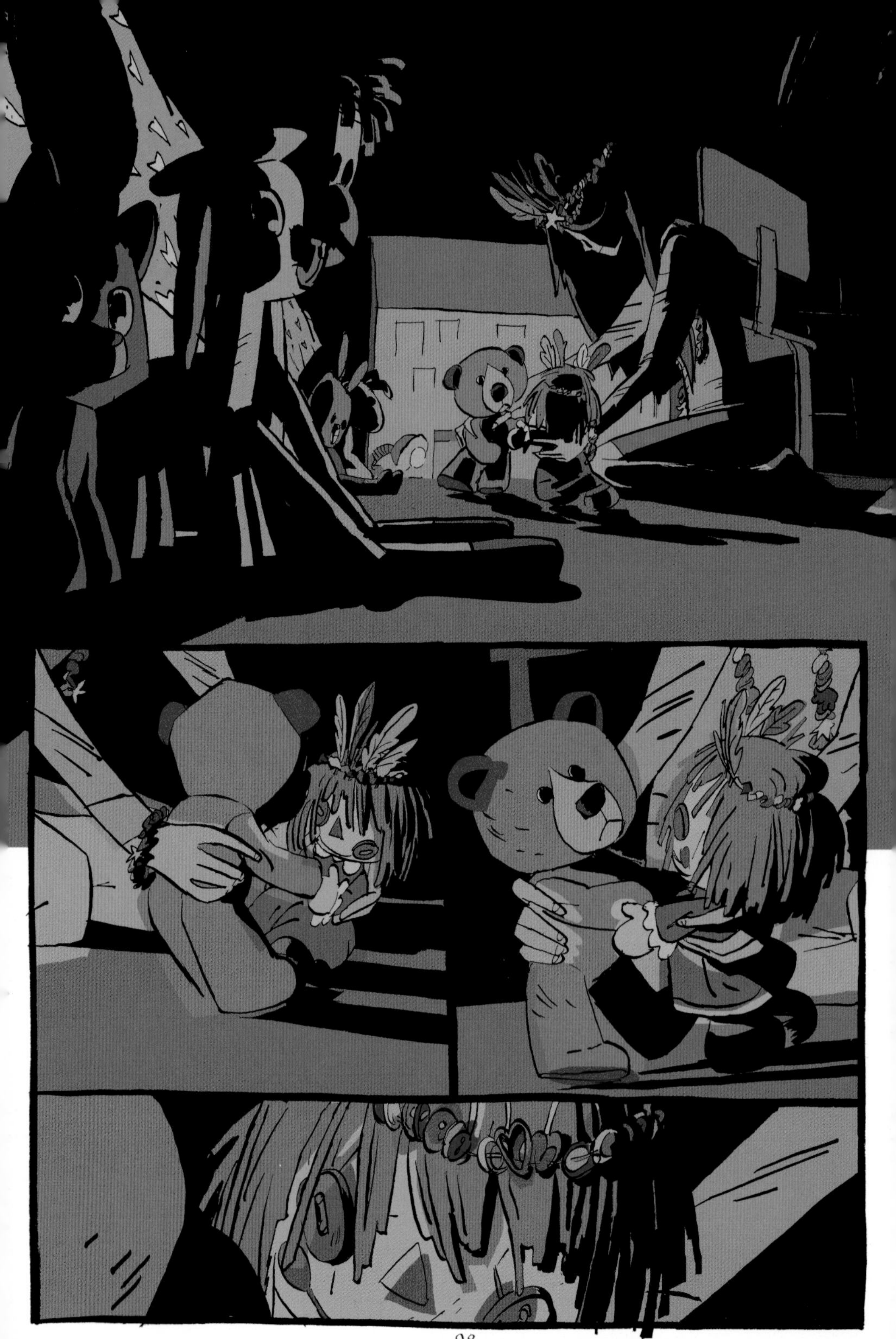

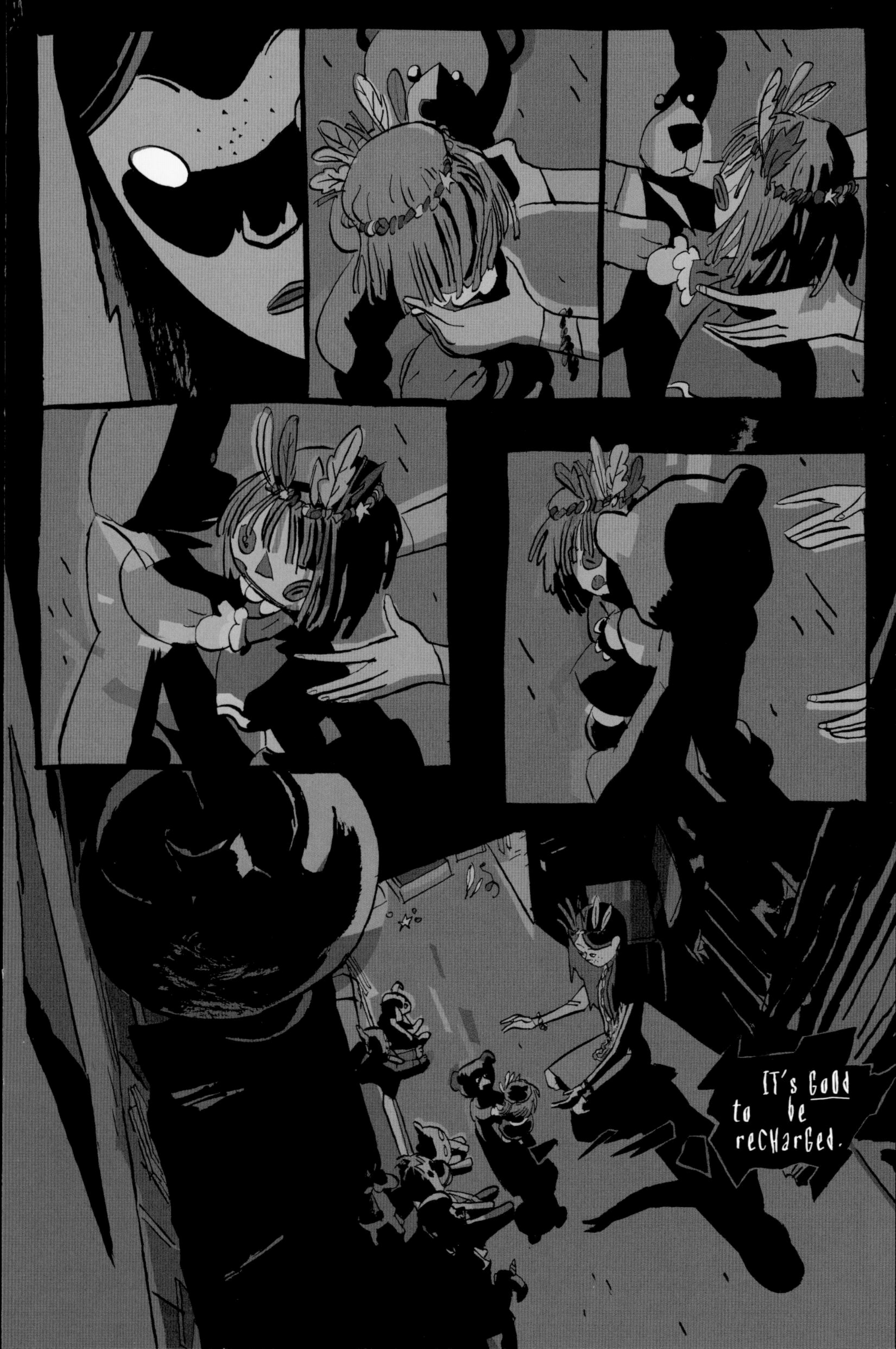
IT's GOOD to be reCHarGed.

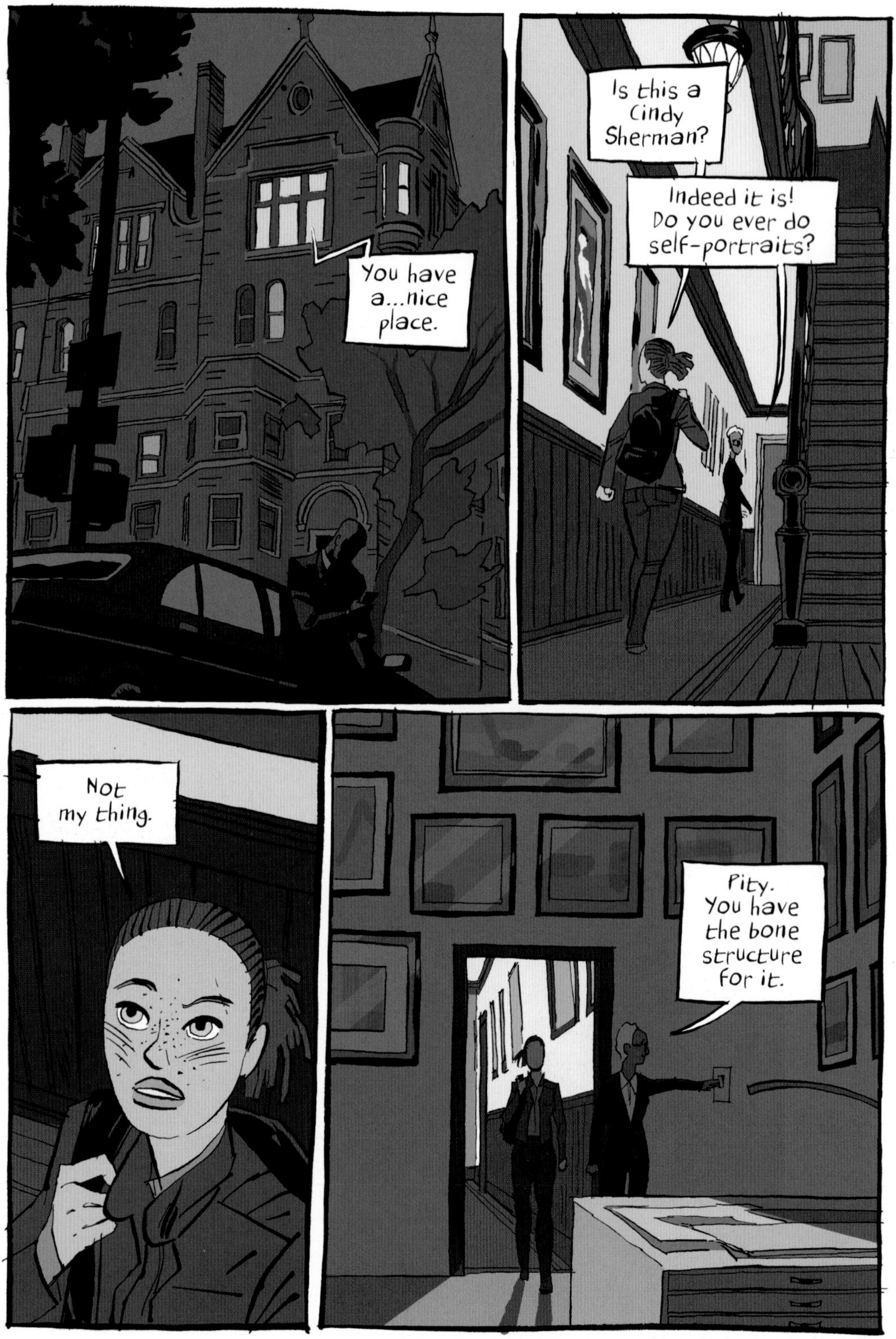
You have a...nice place.
Is this a Cindy Sherman?
Indeed it is! Do you ever do self-portraits?
Not my thing.
Pity. You have the bone structure for it.

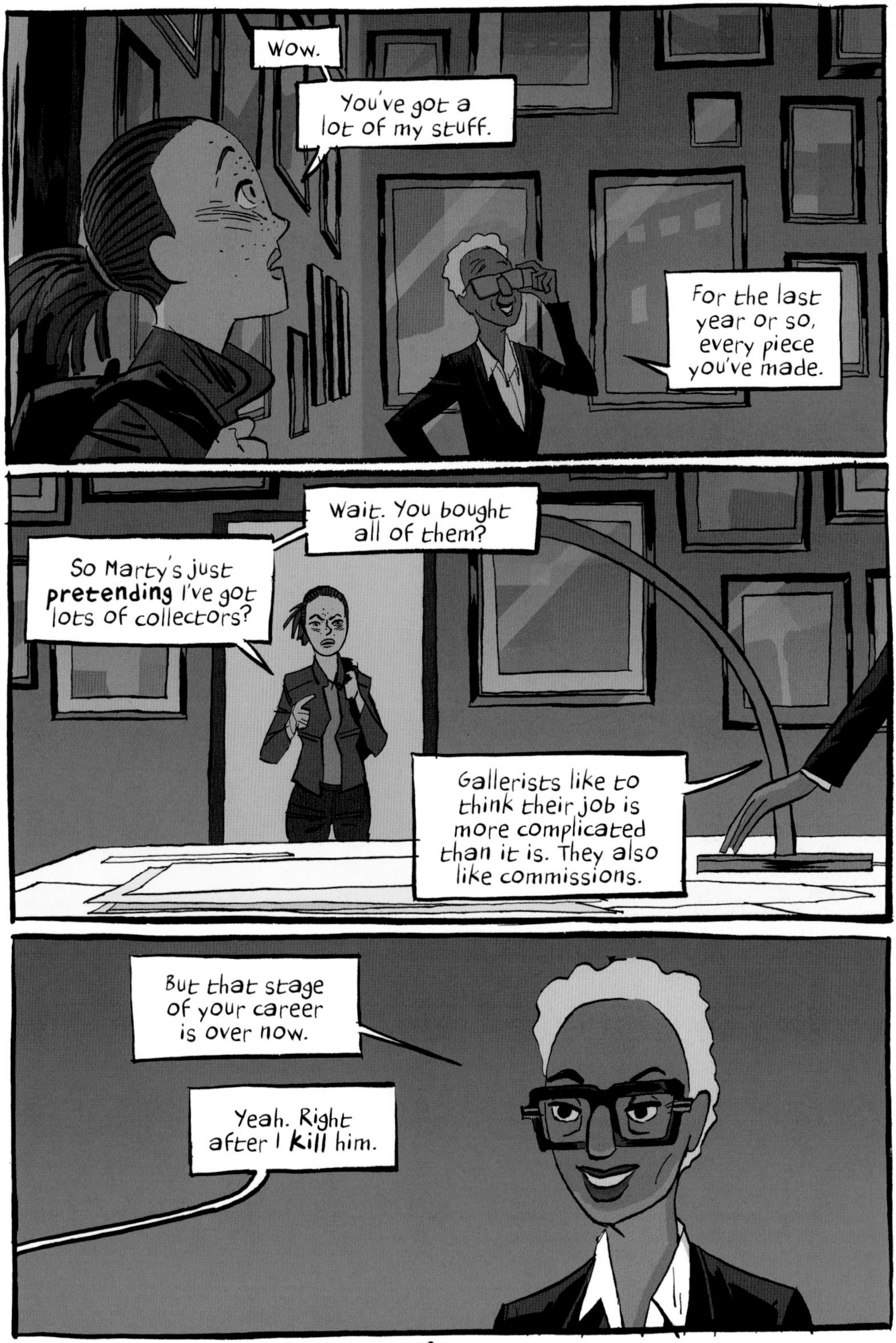
Wow.
You've got a lot of my stuff.
For the last year or so, every piece you've made.
Wait. You bought all of them?
So Marty's just **pretending** I've got lots of collectors?
Gallerists like to think their job is more complicated than it is. They also like commissions.
But that stage of your career is over now.
Yeah. Right after I **kill** him.

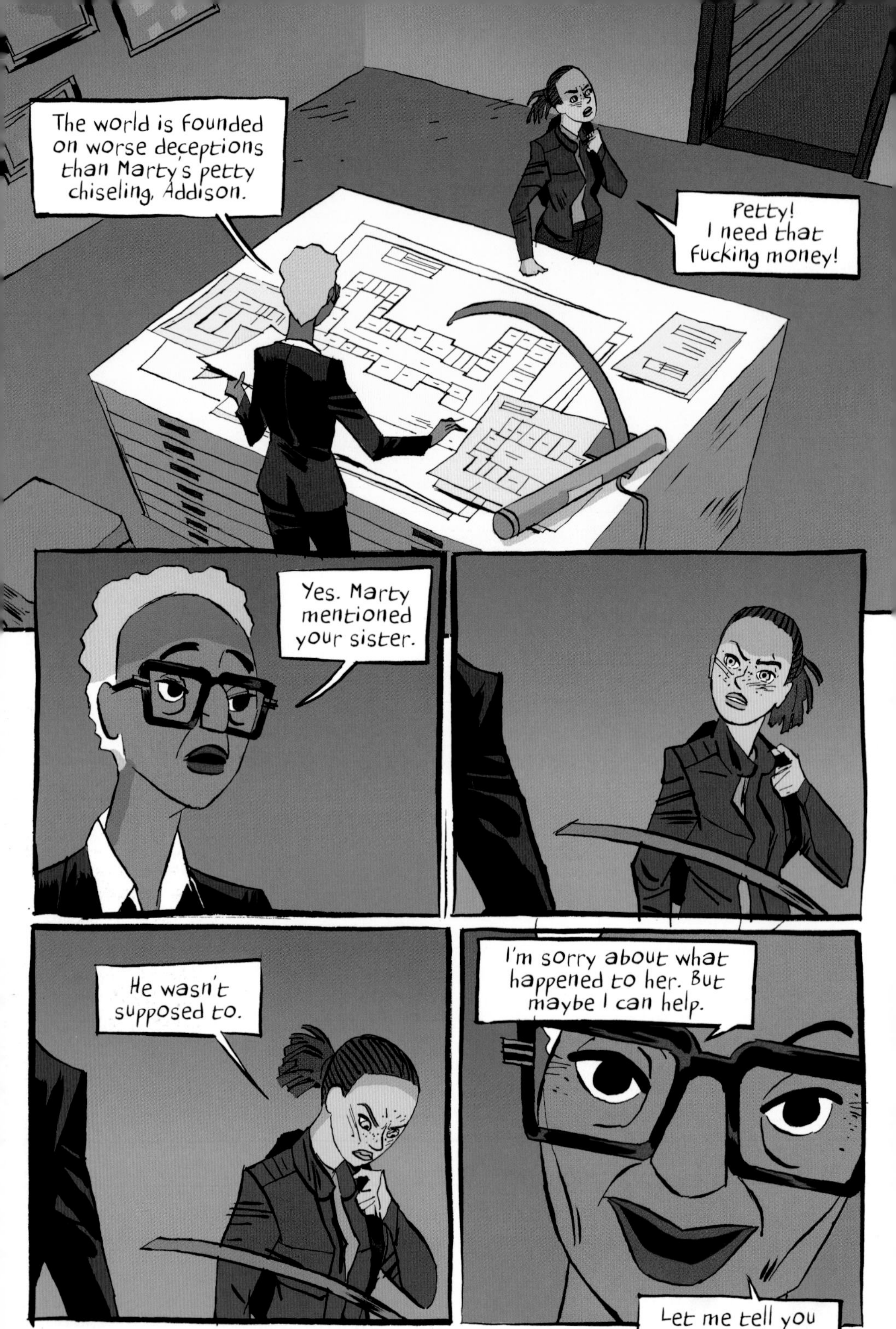
The world is founded on worse deceptions than Marty's petty chiseling, Addison.
Petty! I need that fucking money!
Yes. Marty mentioned your sister.
He wasn't supposed to.
I'm sorry about what happened to her. But maybe I can help.
Let me tell you a secret, Addie...

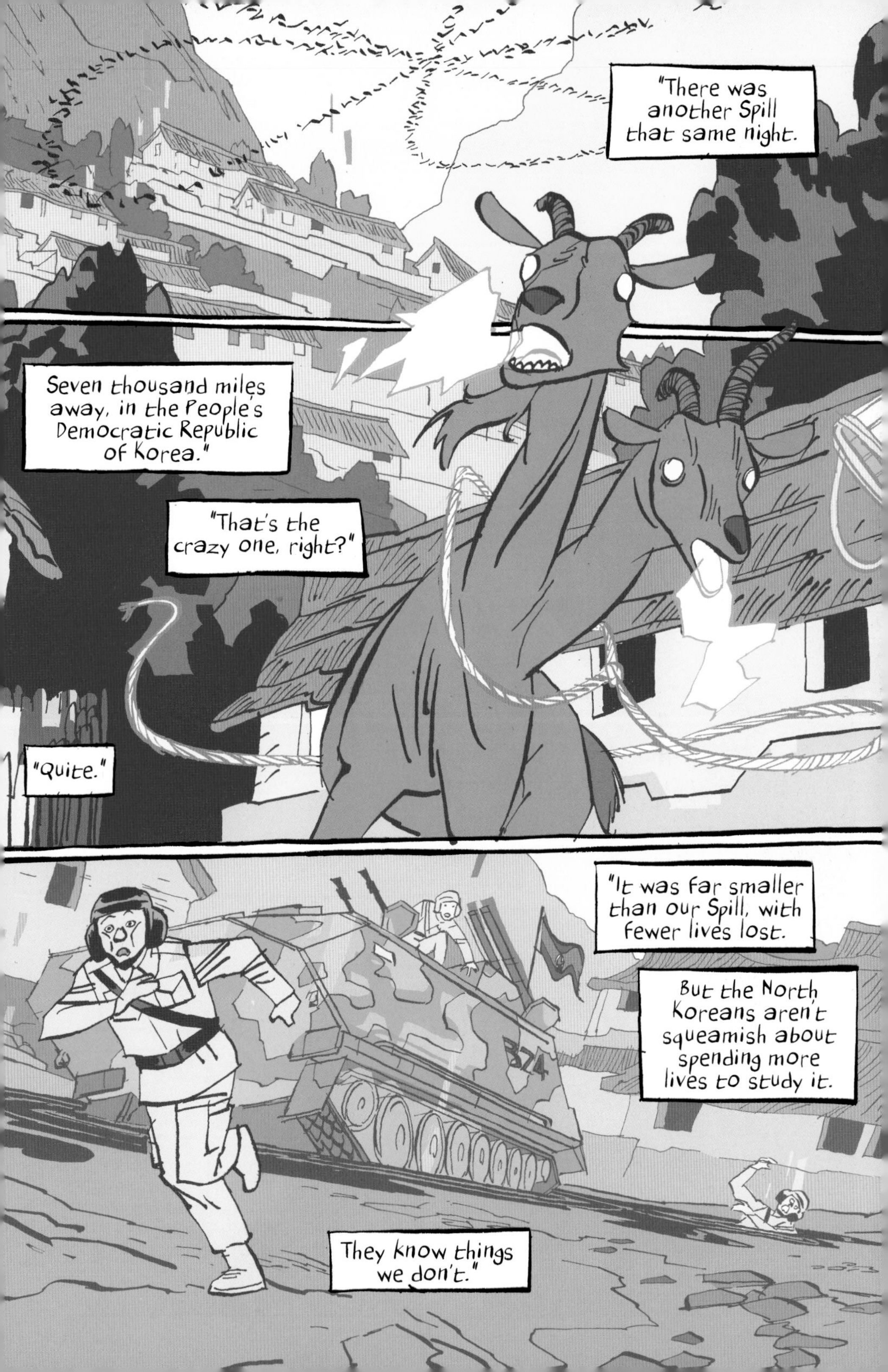
"There was another Spill that same night.
Seven thousand miles away, in the People's Democratic Republic of Korea."
"That's the crazy one, right?"
"Quite."
"It was far smaller than our Spill, with fewer lives lost.
But the North Koreans aren't squeamish about spending more lives to study it.
They know things we don't."
374

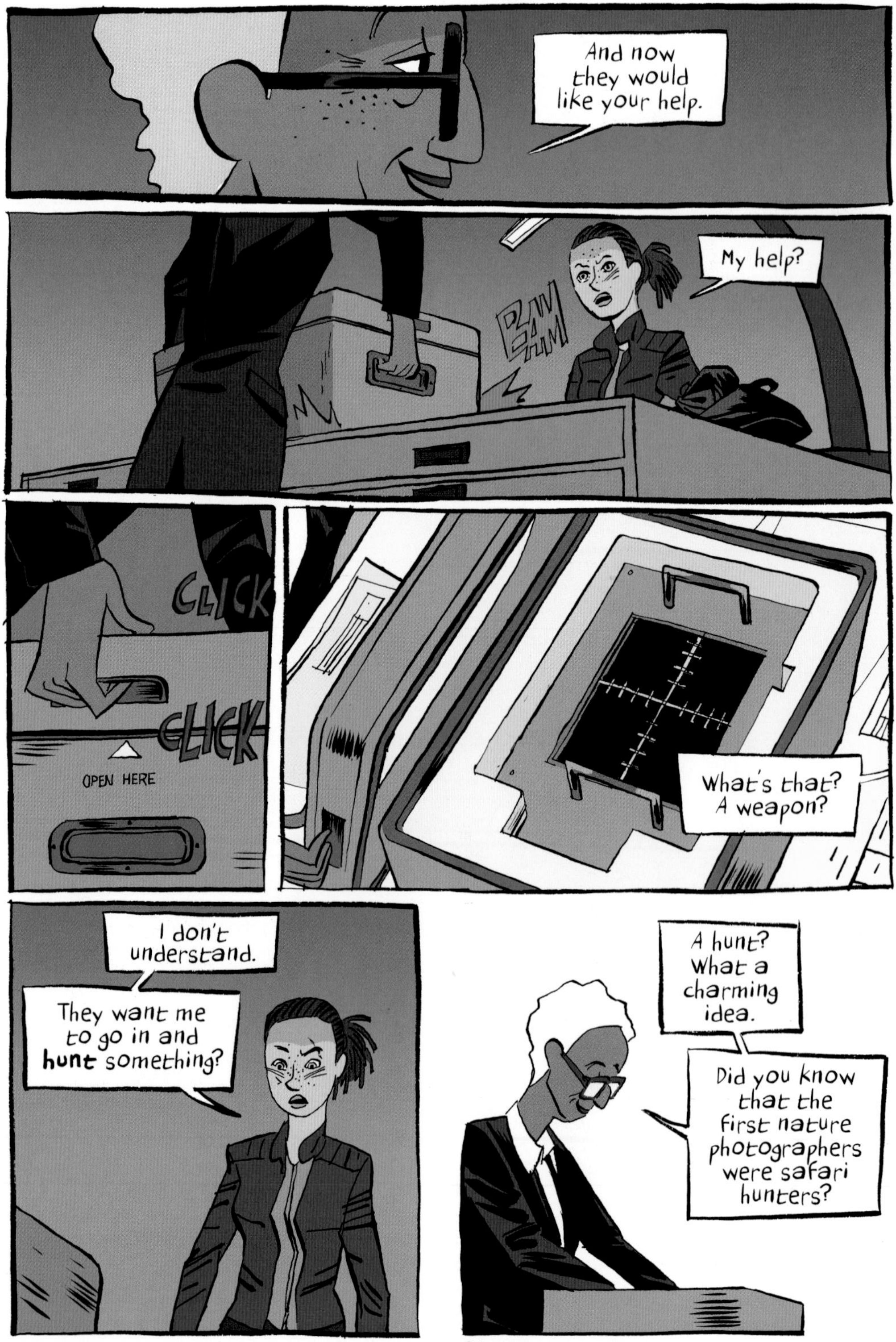
And now they would like your help.
My help?
BLAM BLAM
CLICK
CLICK
OPEN HERE
What's that? A weapon?
I don't understand.
They want me to go in and **hunt** something?
A hunt? What a charming idea.
Did you know that the first nature photographers were safari hunters?

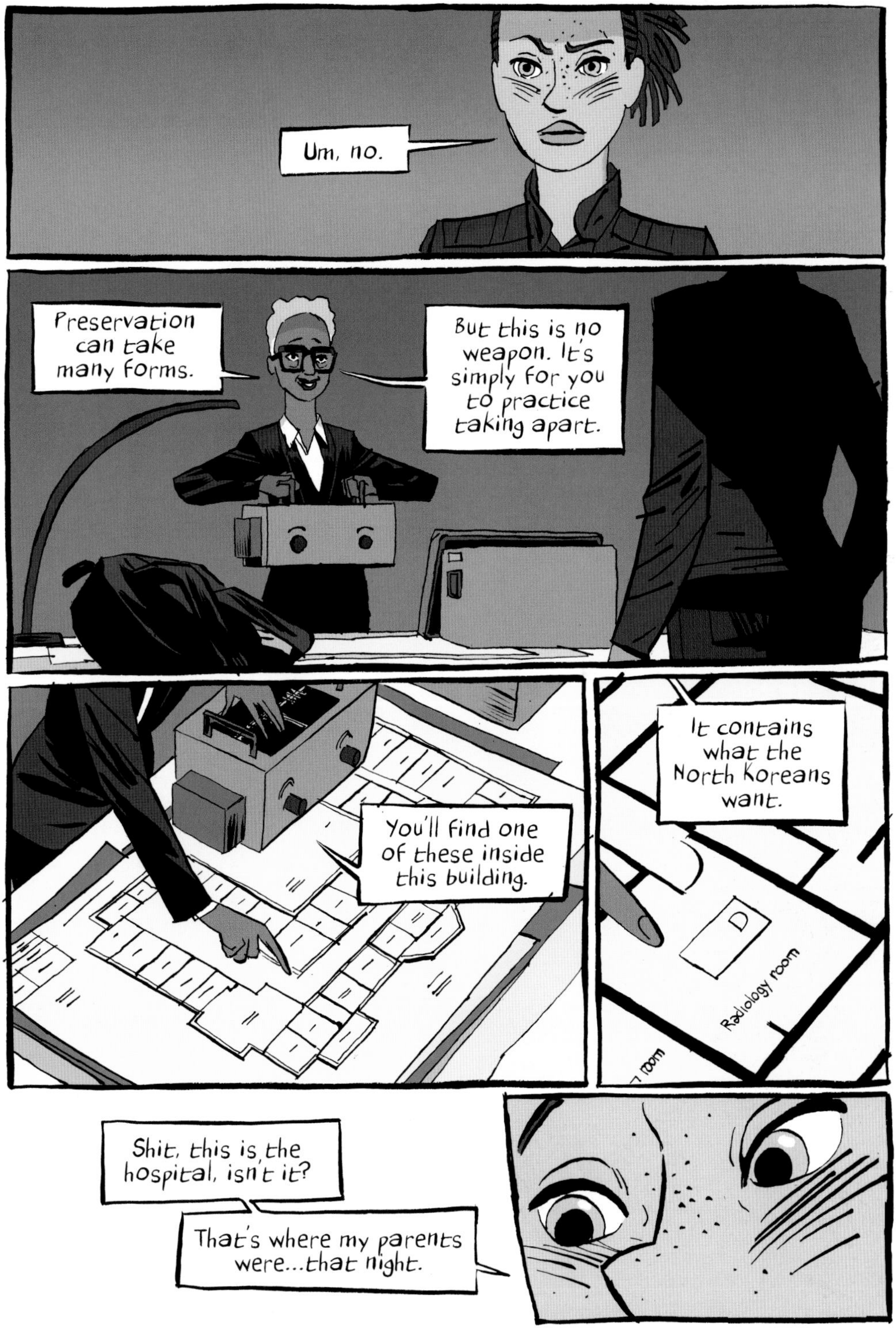
Um, no.
Preservation can take many forms.
But this is no weapon. It's simply for you to practice taking apart.
You'll find one of these inside this building.
It contains what the North Koreans want.
Radiology room
Shit, this is the hospital, isn't it?
That's where my parents were...that night.

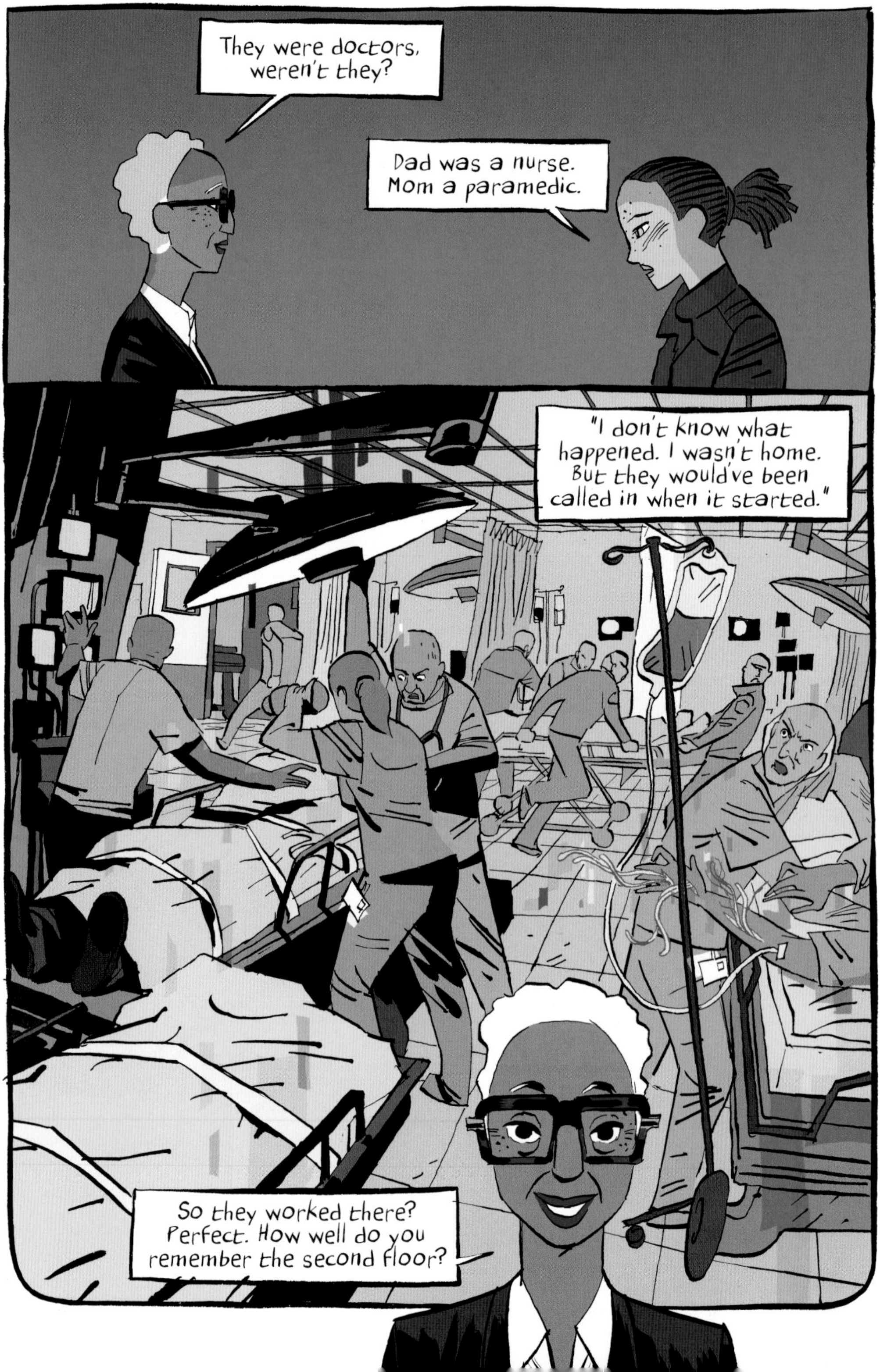
They were doctors, weren't they?
Dad was a nurse. Mom a paramedic.
"I don't know what happened. I wasn't home. But they would've been called in when it started."
So they worked there? Perfect. How well do you remember the second floor?

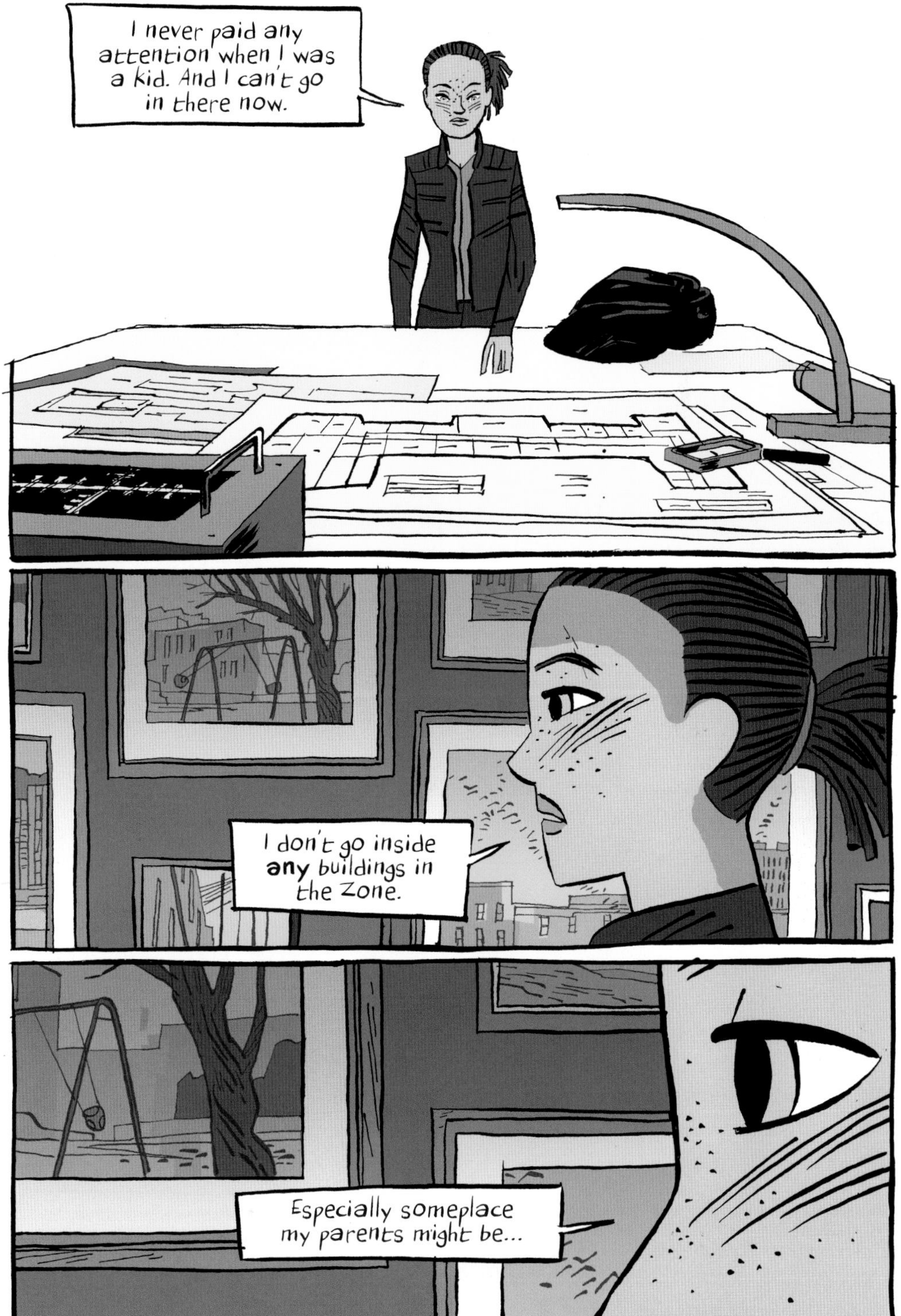
I never paid any attention when I was a kid. And I can't go in there now.
I don't go inside **any** buildings in the Zone.
Especially someplace my parents might be...

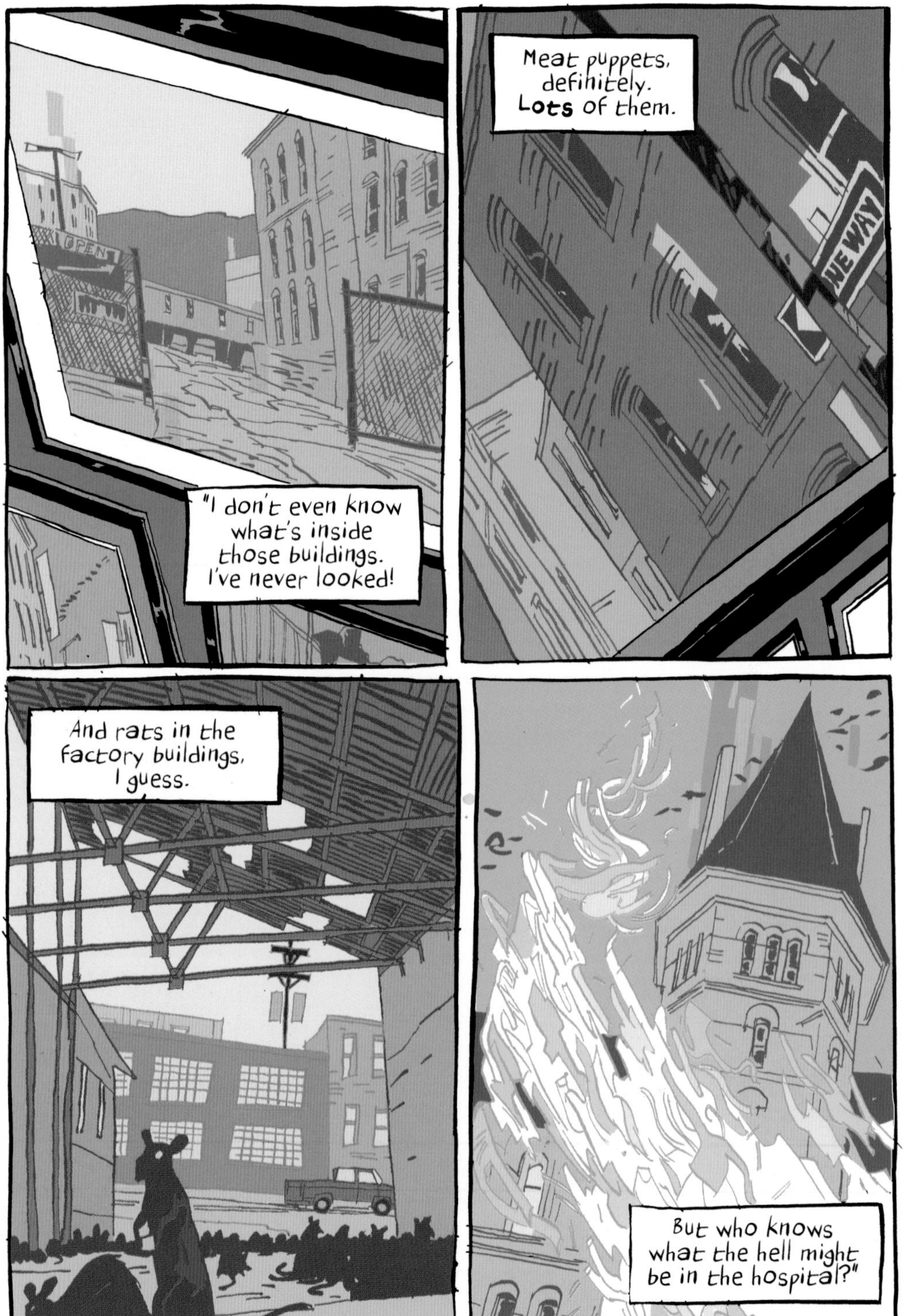
"I don't even know what's inside those buildings. I've never looked!
Meat puppets, definitely. **Lots** of them.
OPEN
NE WAY
And rats in the factory buildings, I guess.
But who knows what the hell might be in the hospital?"

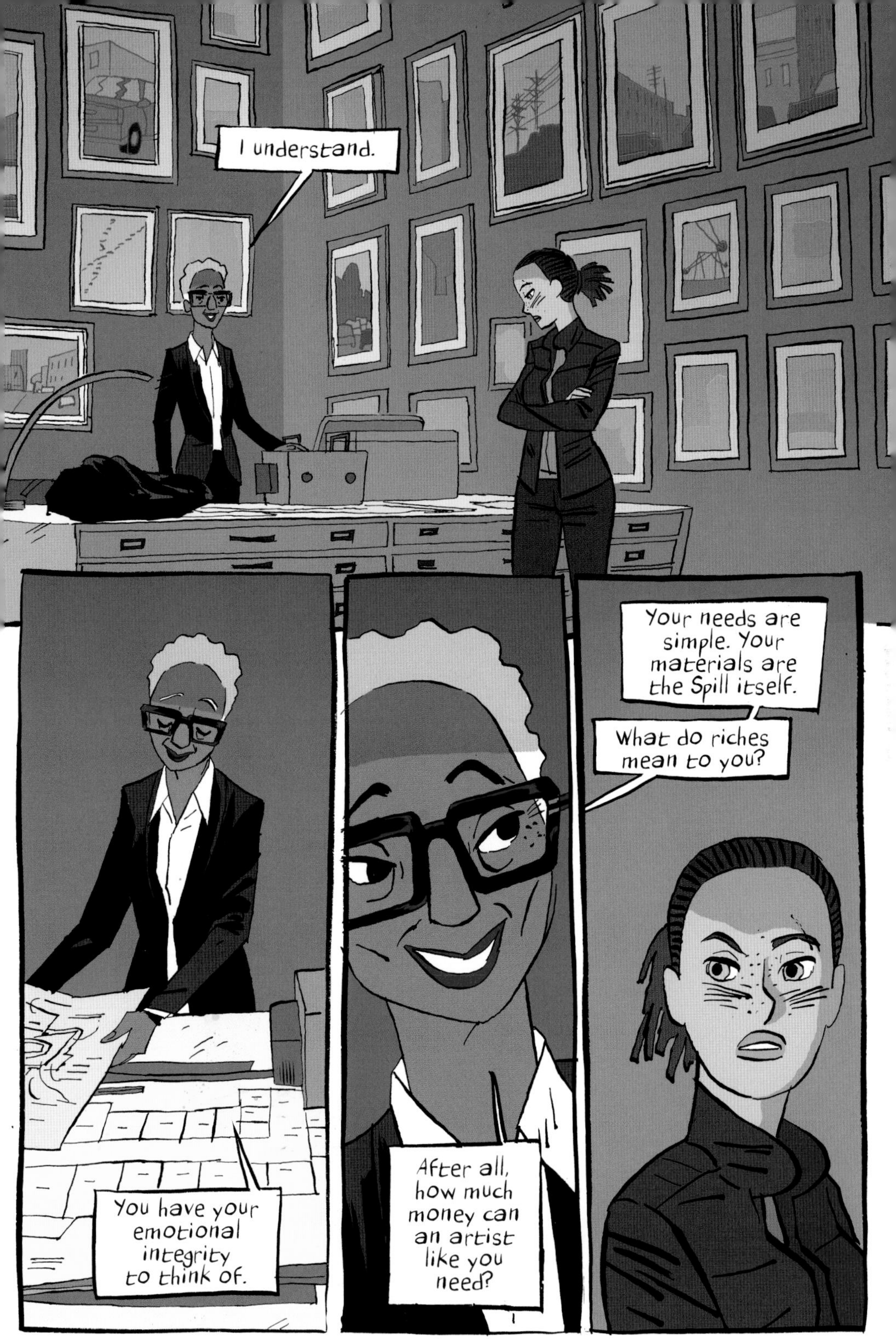

I understand.
You have your emotional integrity to think of.
After all, how much money can an artist like you need?
Your needs are simple. Your materials are the Spill itself.
What do riches mean to you?

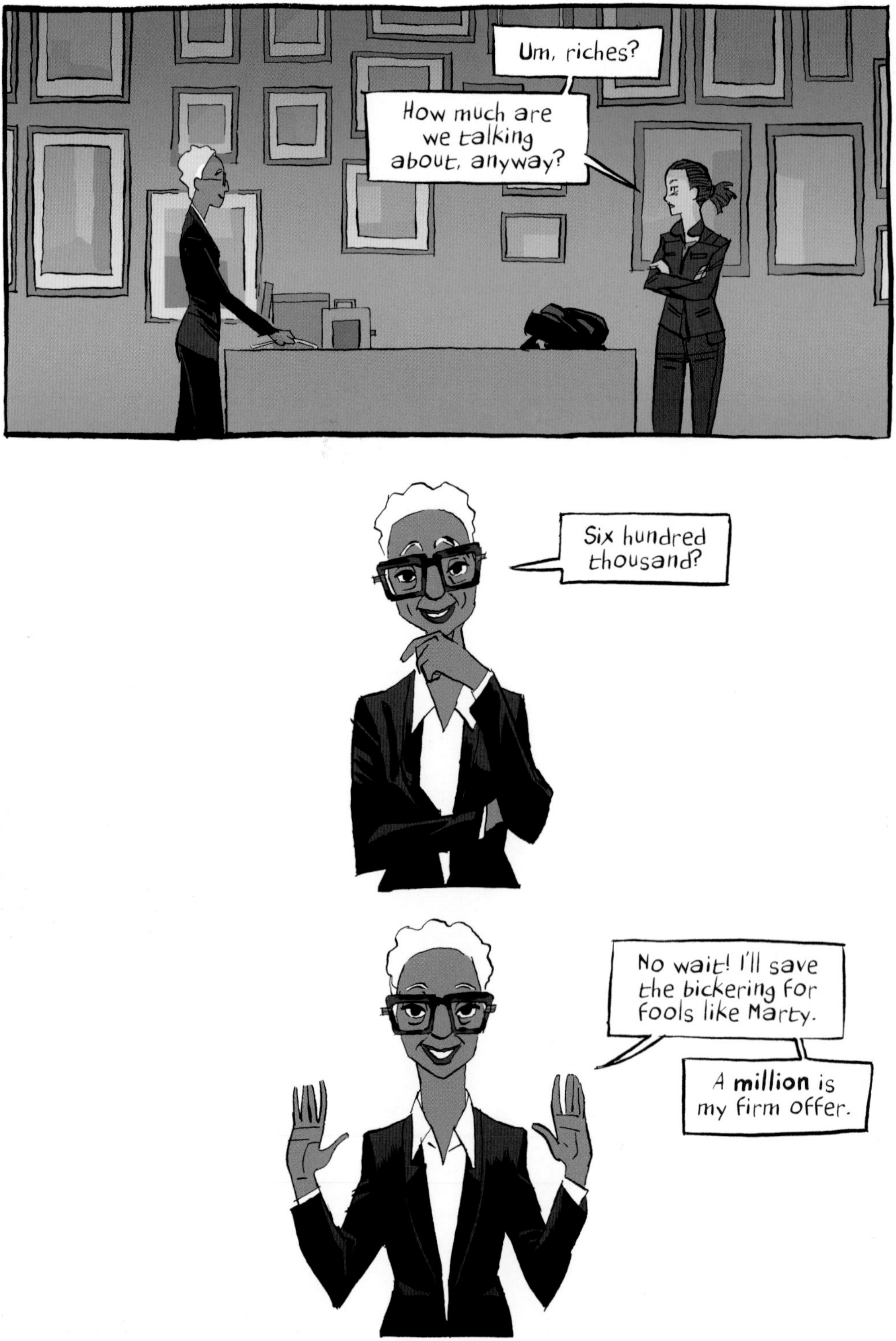
Um, riches?
How much are we talking about, anyway?
Six hundred thousand?
No wait! I'll save the bickering for fools like Marty.
A **million** is my firm offer.

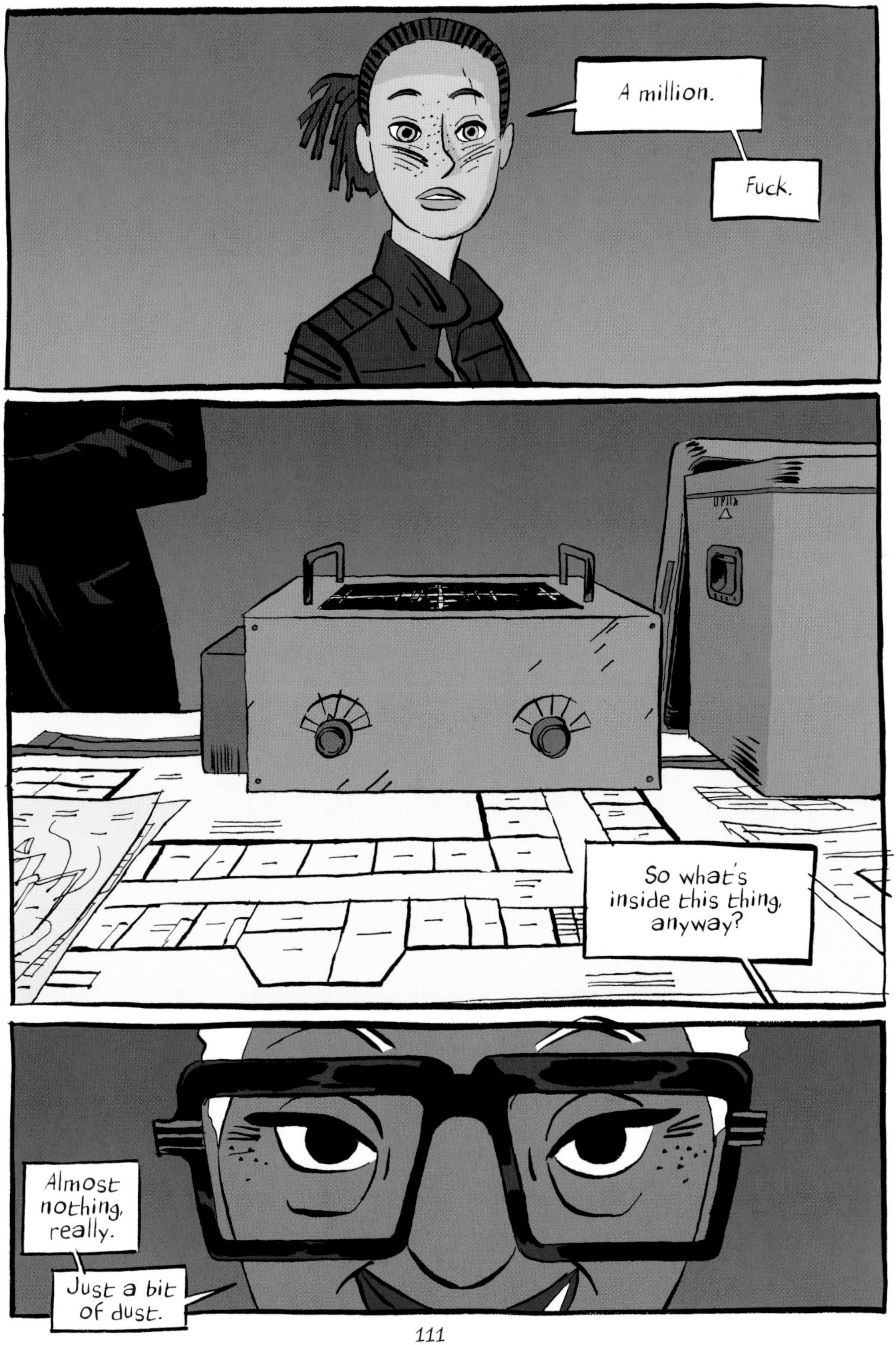
A million.
Fuck.
So what's inside this thing, anyway?
Almost nothing, really.
Just a bit of dust.

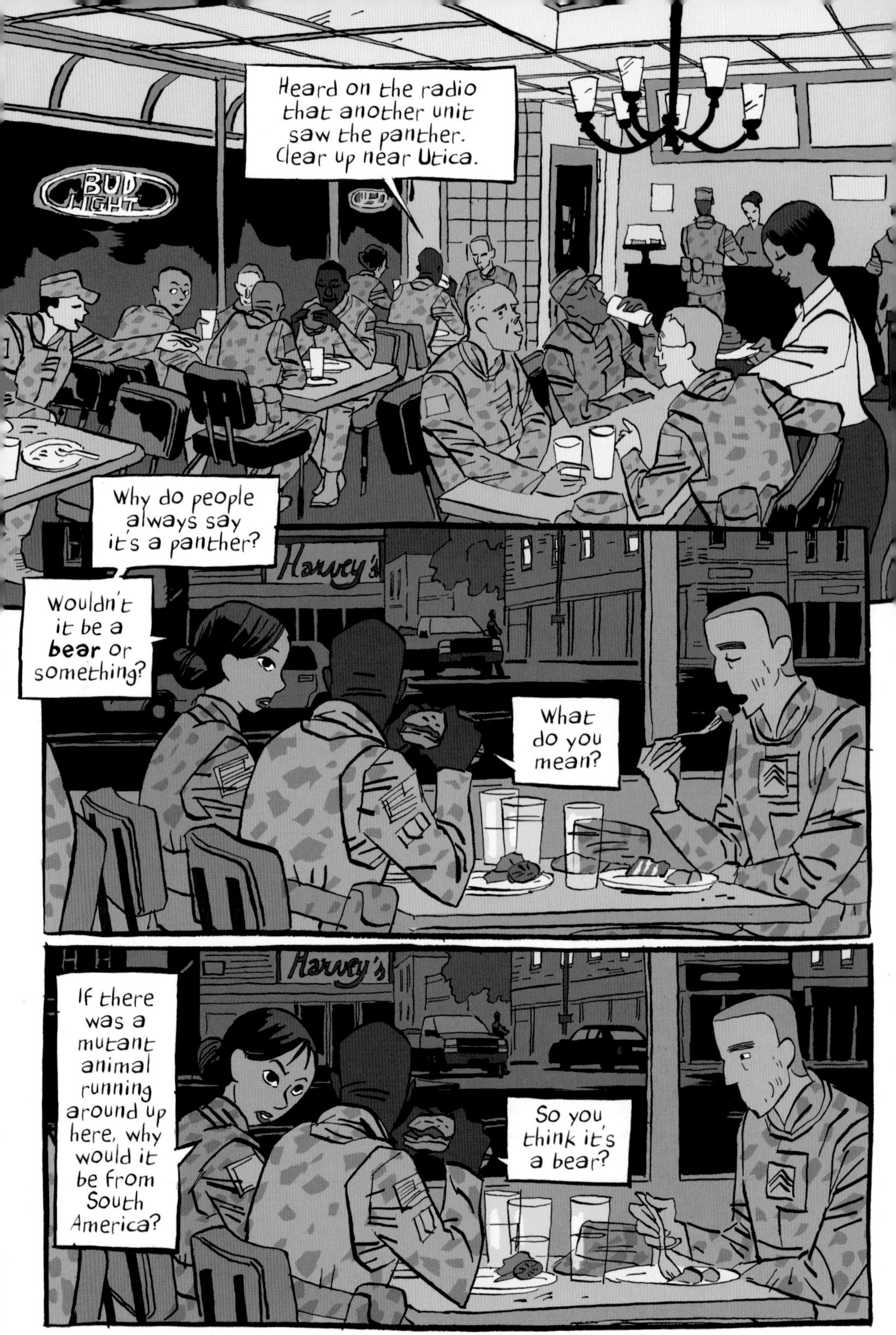
BUD LIGHT
Heard on the radio that another unit saw the panther. Clear up near Utica.
Why do people always say it's a panther?
Harvey's
Wouldn't it be a **bear** or something?
What do you mean?
Harvey's
If there was a mutant animal running around up here, why would it be from South America?
So you think it's a bear?

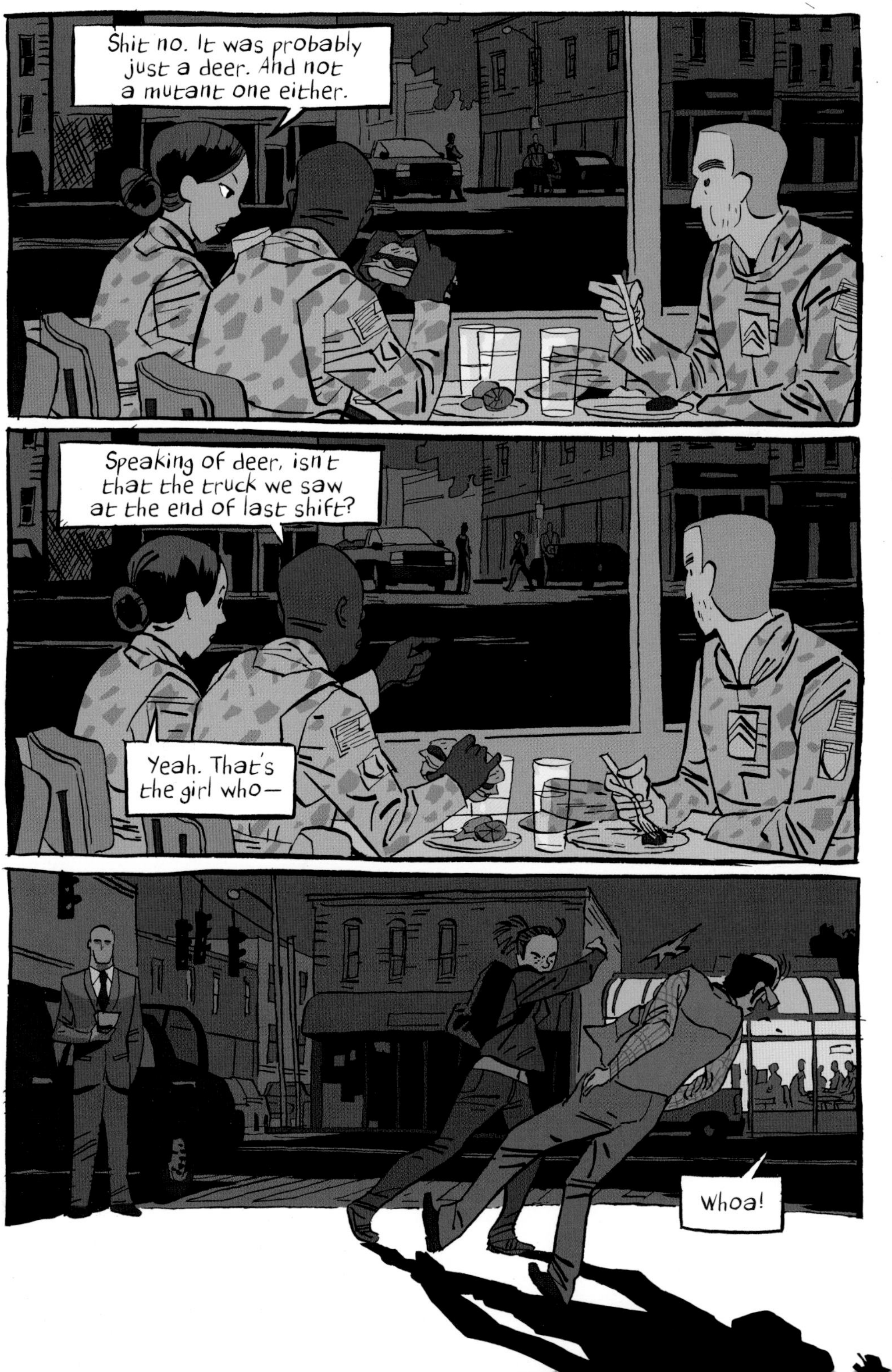
Shit no. It was probably just a deer. And not a mutant one either.
Speaking of deer, isn't that the truck we saw at the end of last shift?
Yeah. That's the girl who—
Whoa!

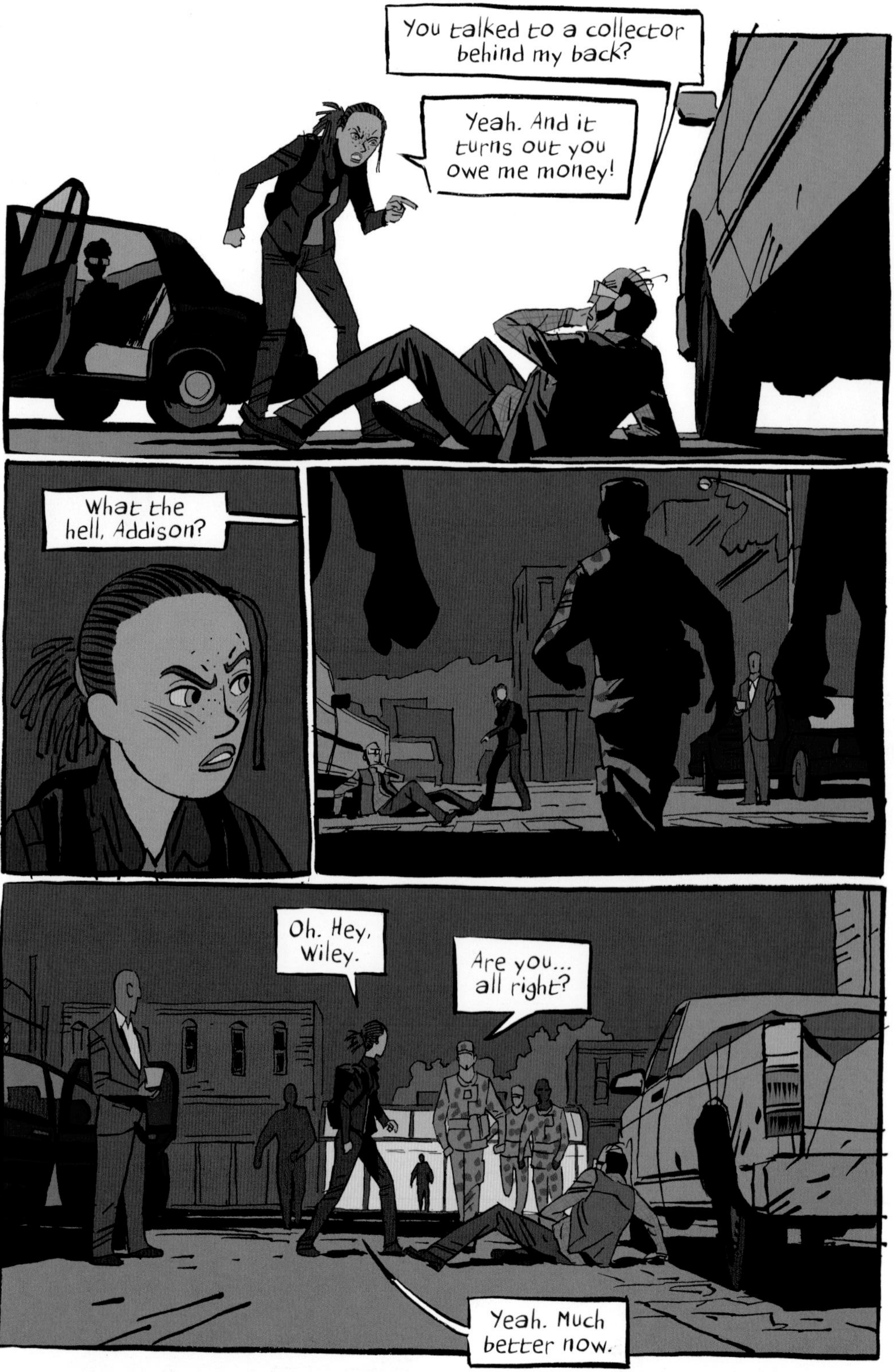

You talked to a collector behind my back?
Yeah. And it turns out you owe me money!
What the hell, Addison?
Oh. Hey, Wiley.
Are you... all right?
Yeah. Much better now.

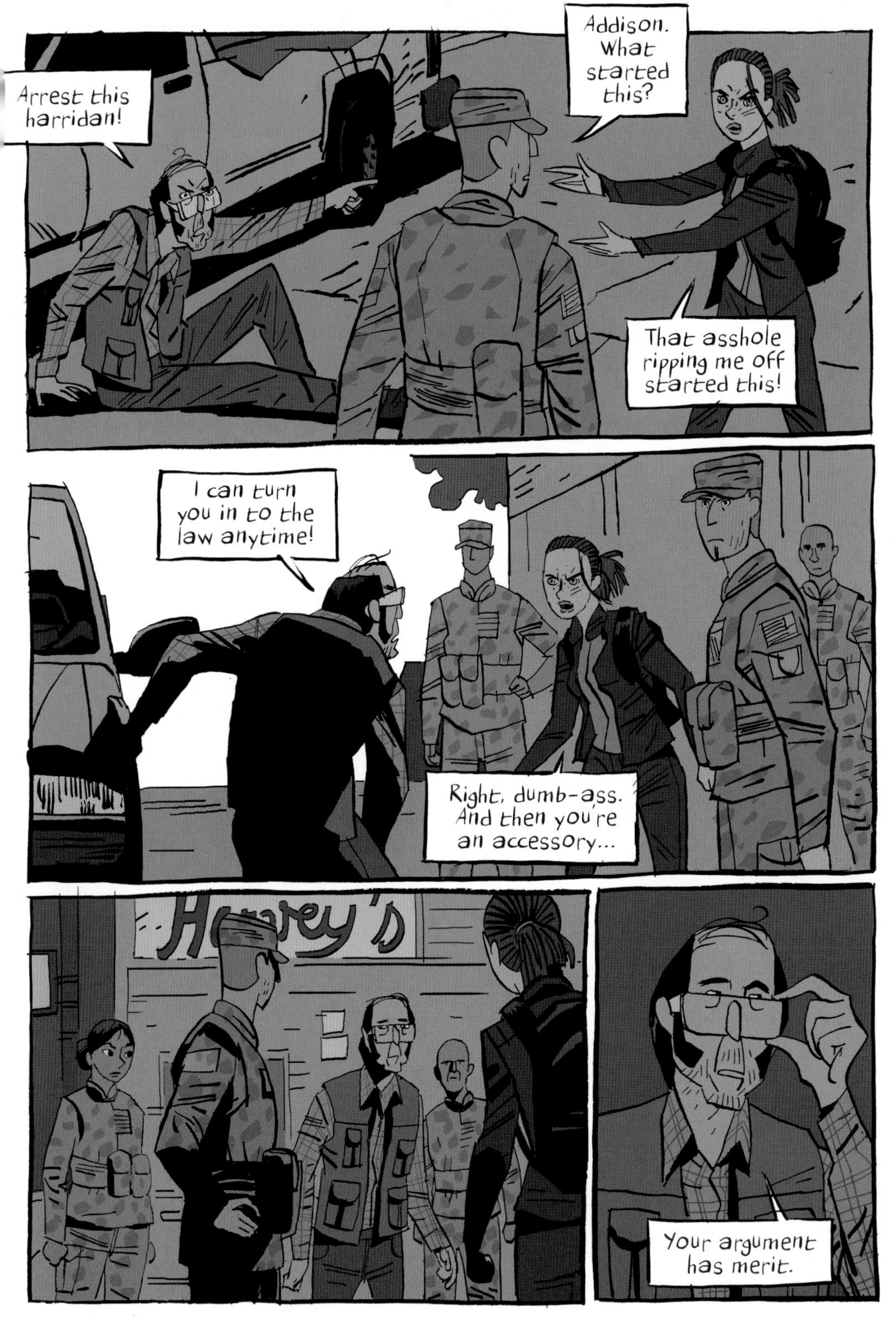
Arrest this harridan!
Addison. What started this?
That asshole ripping me off started this!
I can turn you in to the law anytime!
Right, dumb-ass. And then you're an accessory...
Harvey's
Your argument has merit.

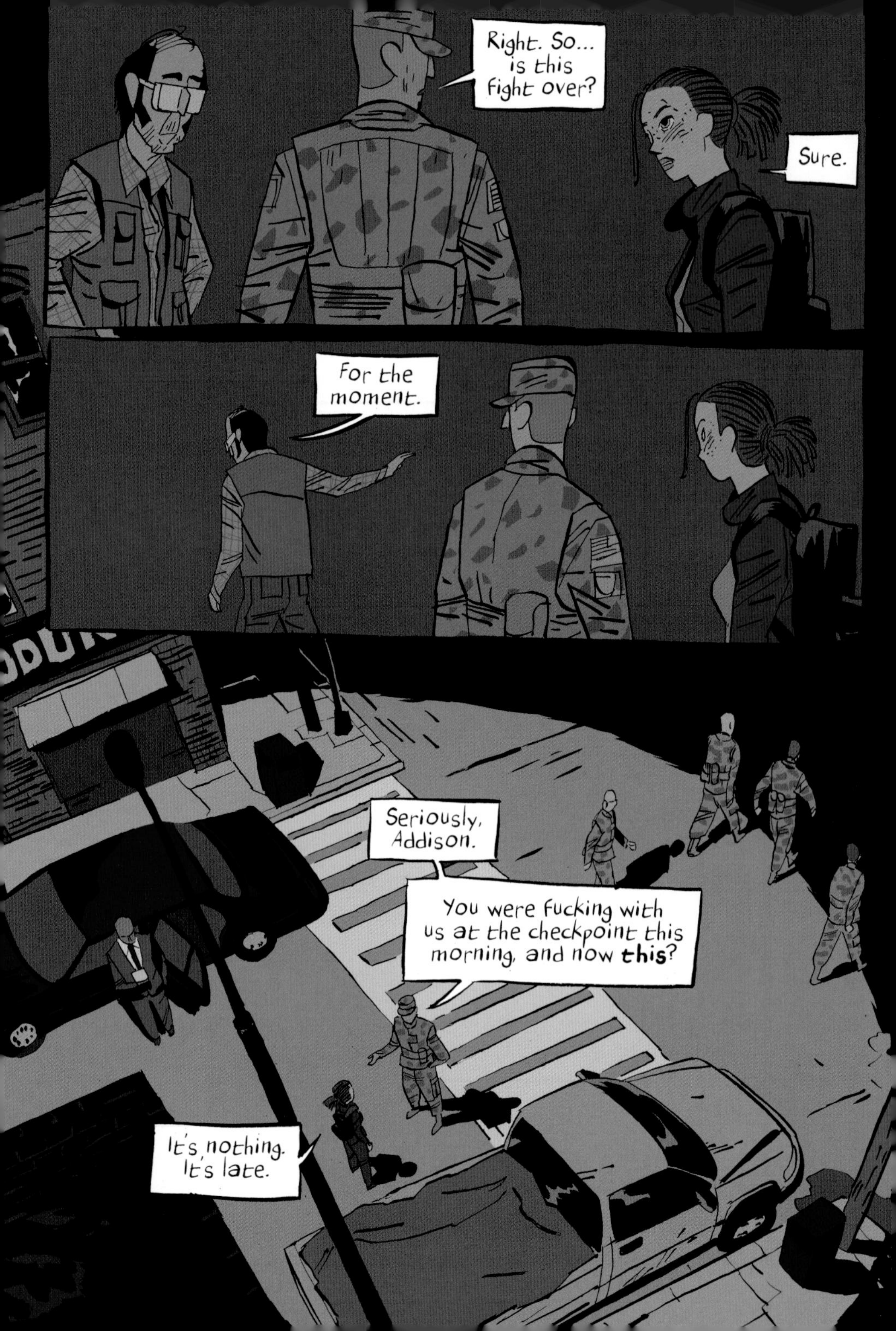

Right. So... is this fight over?
Sure.
For the moment.
Seriously, Addison.
You were fucking with us at the checkpoint this morning, and now this?
It's nothing. It's late.

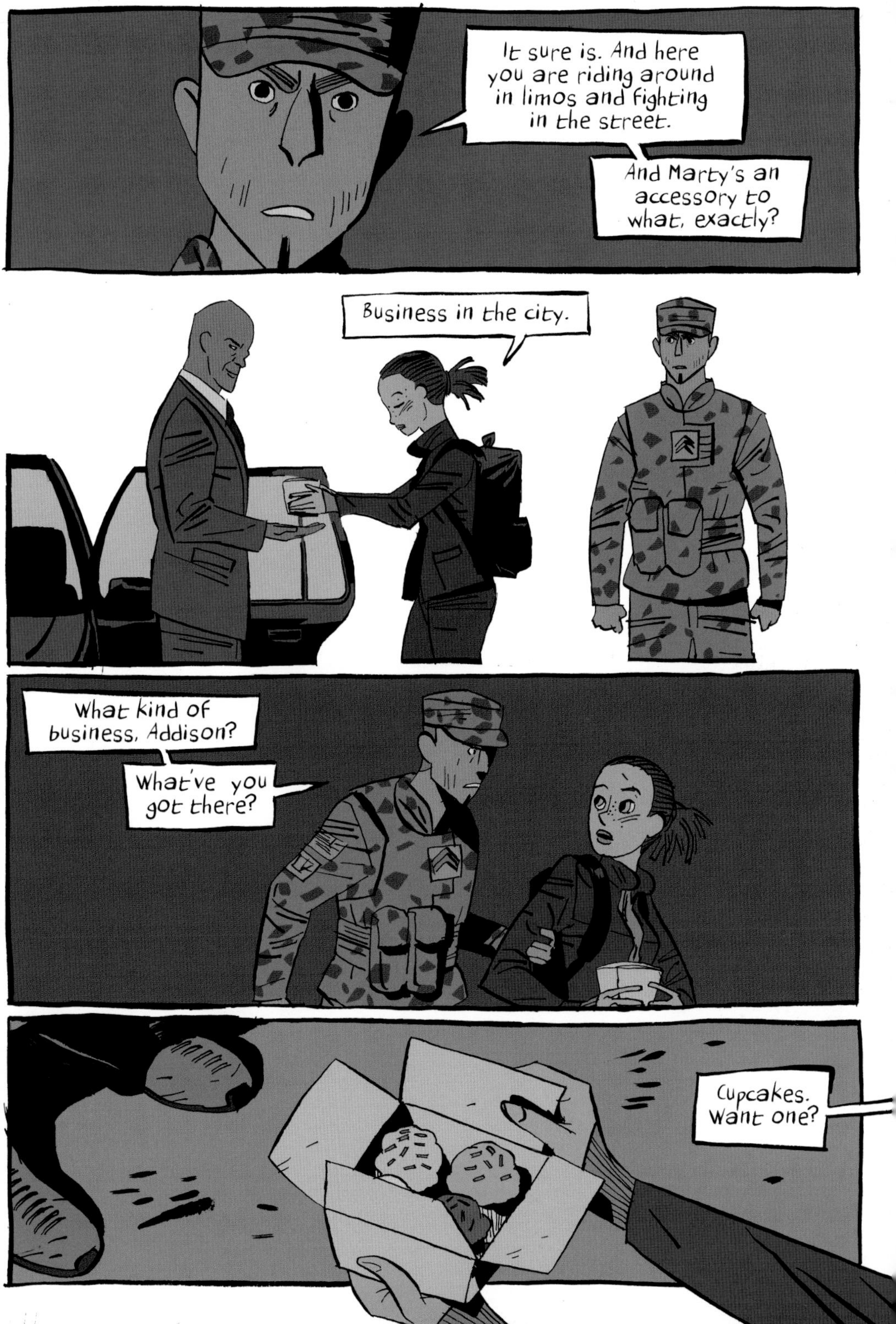
It sure is. And here you are riding around in limos and fighting in the street.
And Marty's an accessory to what, exactly?
Business in the city.
What kind of business, Addison?
What've you got there?
Cupcakes. Want one?

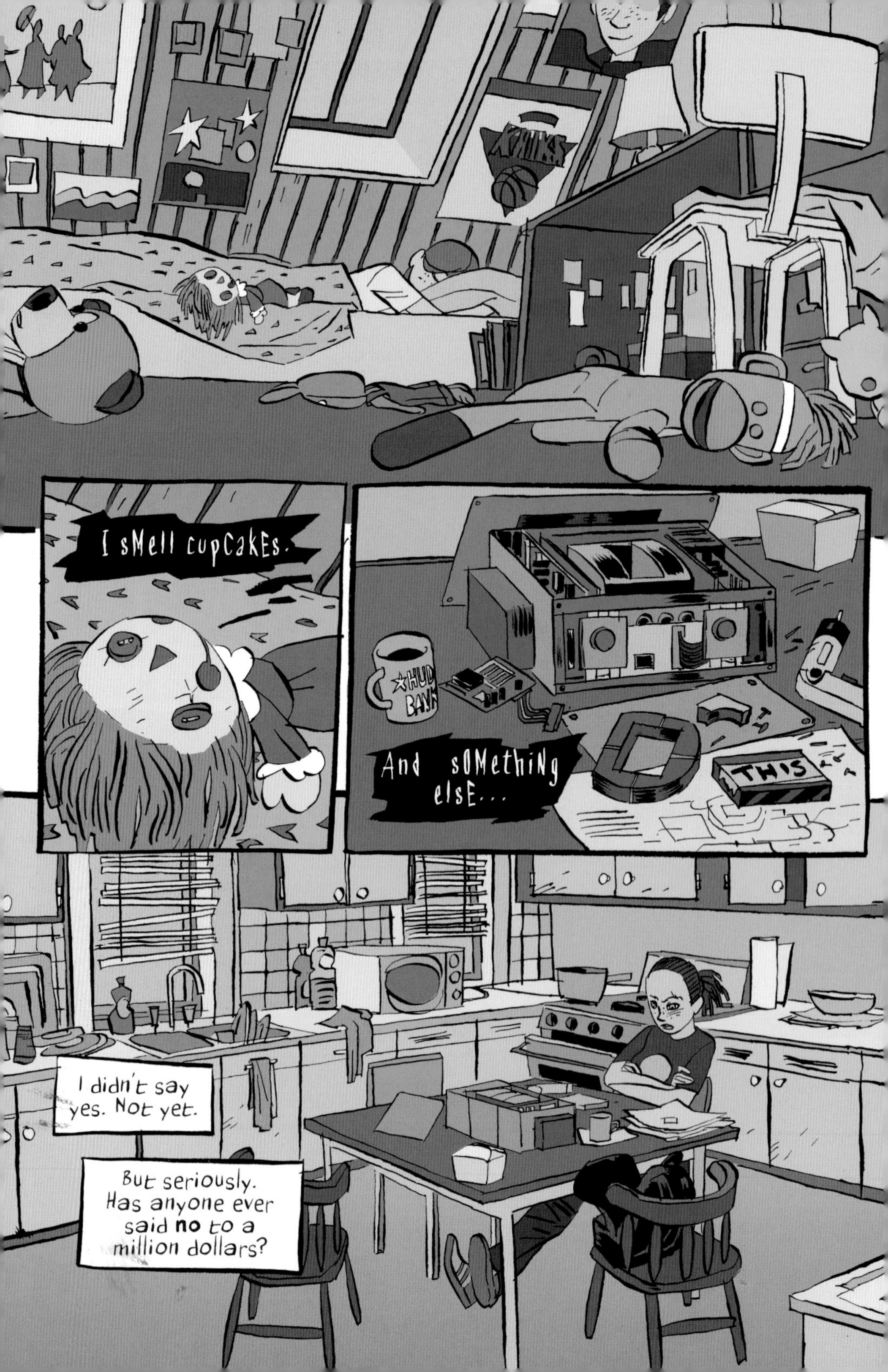
I sMell cupCaKEs.
And sOMething elsE...
THIS
I didn't say yes. Not yet.
But seriously. Has anyone ever said **no** to a million dollars?

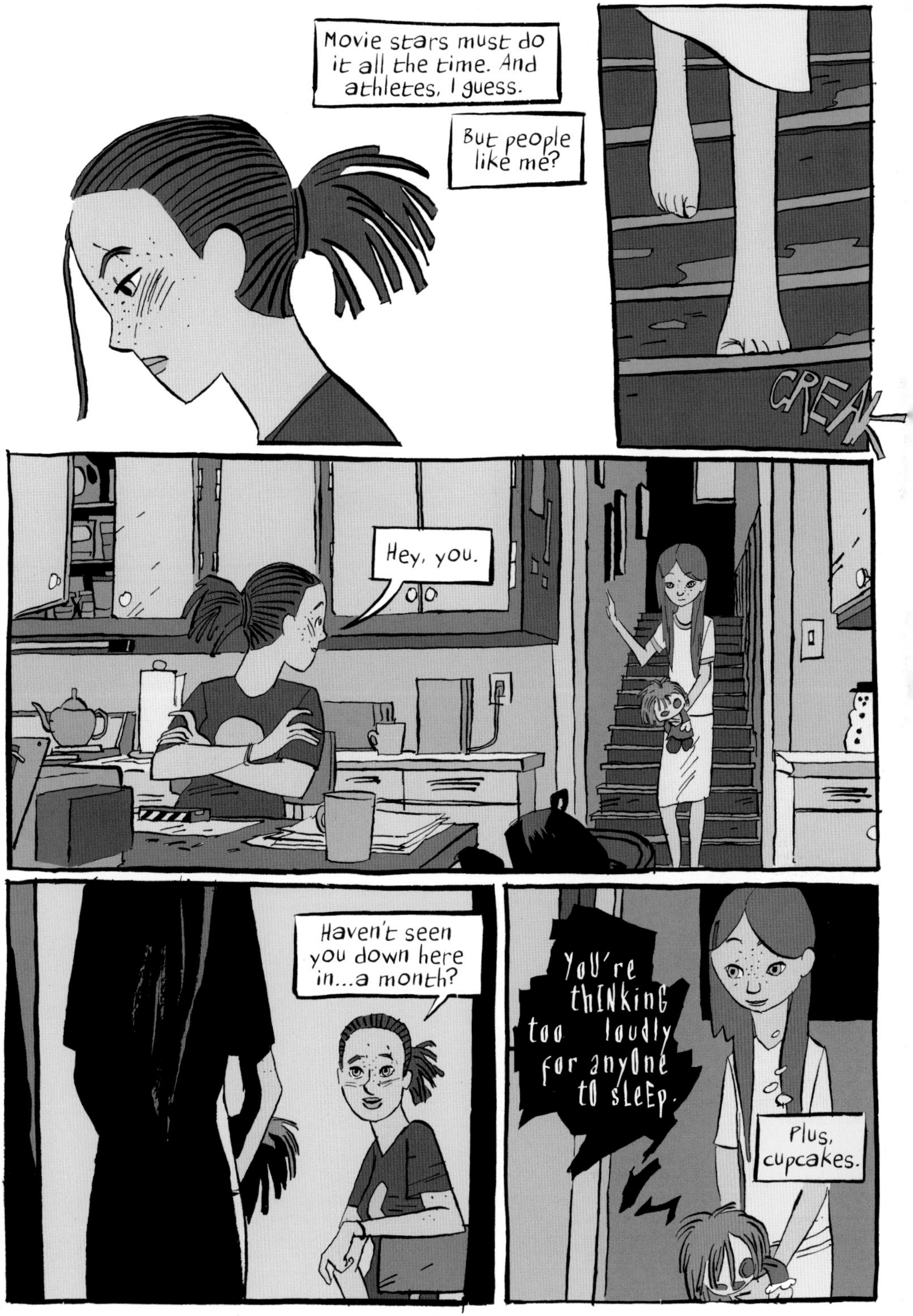

Movie stars must do it all the time. And athletes, I guess.
But people like me?
CREAK
Hey, you.
Haven't seen you down here in...a month?
You're thinking too loudly for anyone to sleep.
Plus, cupcakes.

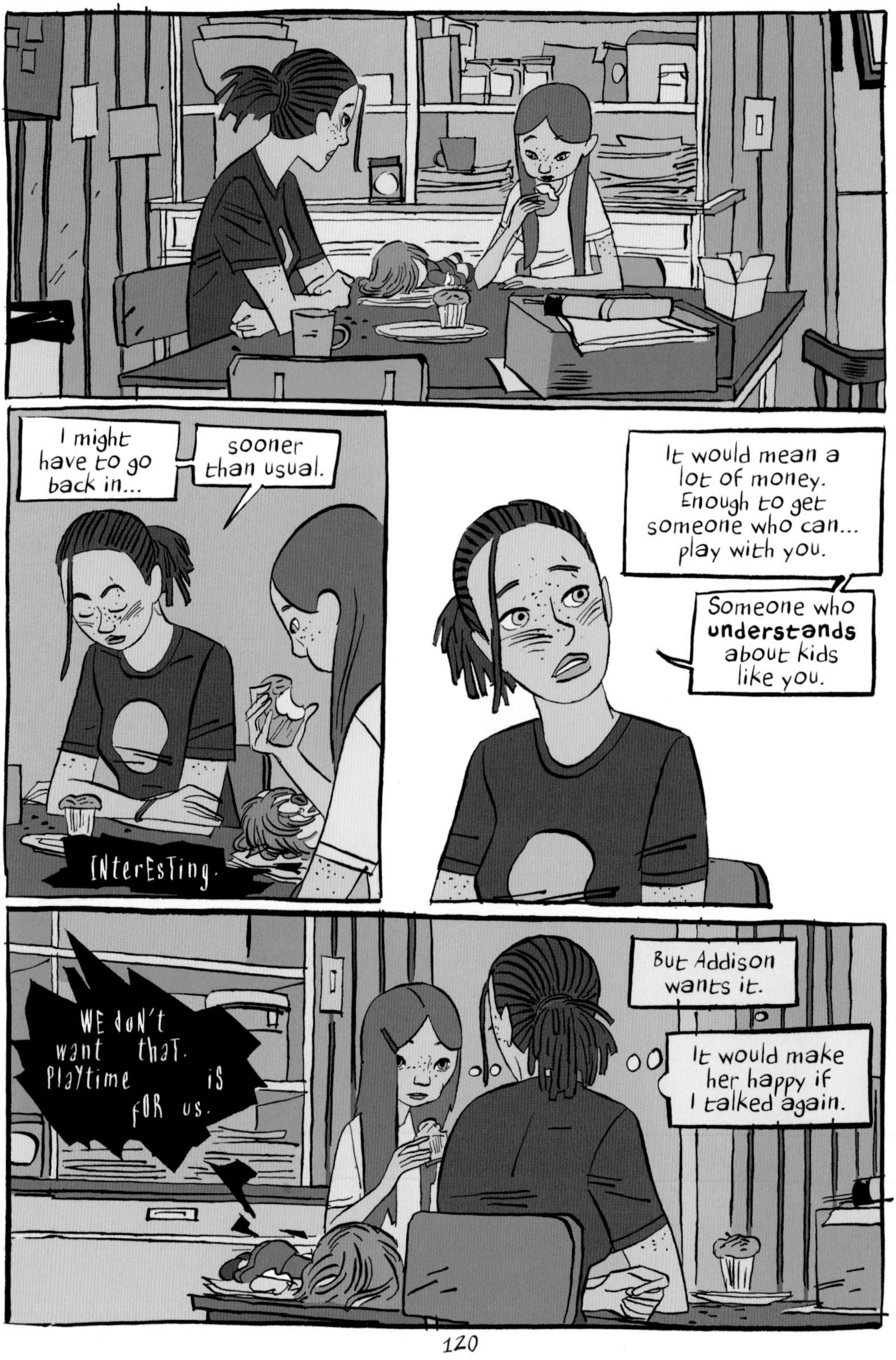
I might have to go back in...
sooner than usual.
INTERESTING.
It would mean a lot of money. Enough to get someone who can... play with you.
Someone who **understands** about kids like you.
WE DON'T WANT THAT. PLAYTIME IS FOR US.
But Addison wants it.
It would make her happy if I talked again.

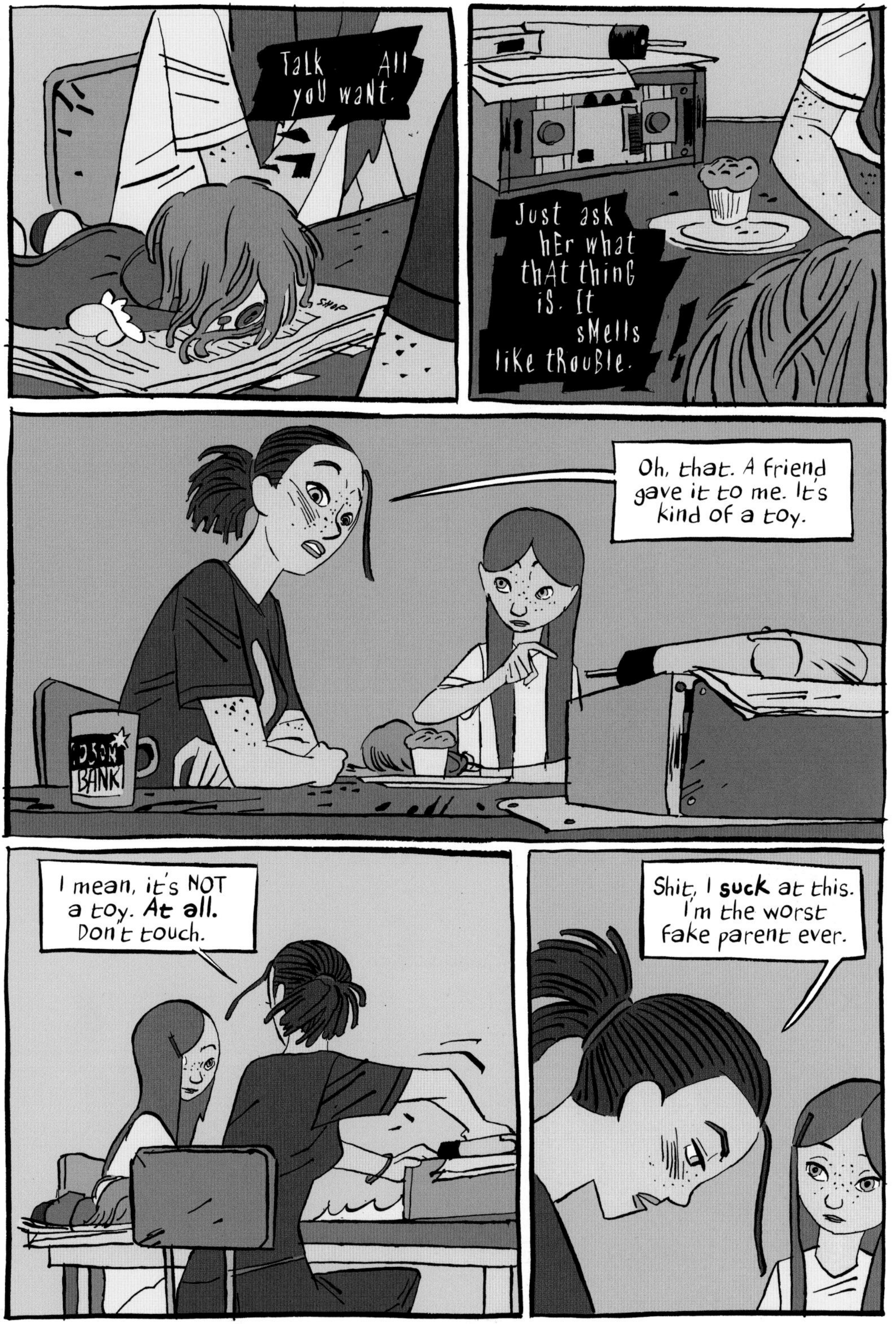

Talk All you want.
Just ask her what that thing is. It smells like trouble.
Oh, that. A friend gave it to me. It's kind of a toy.
I mean, it's NOT a toy. At all. Don't touch.
Shit, I suck at this. I'm the worst fake parent ever.

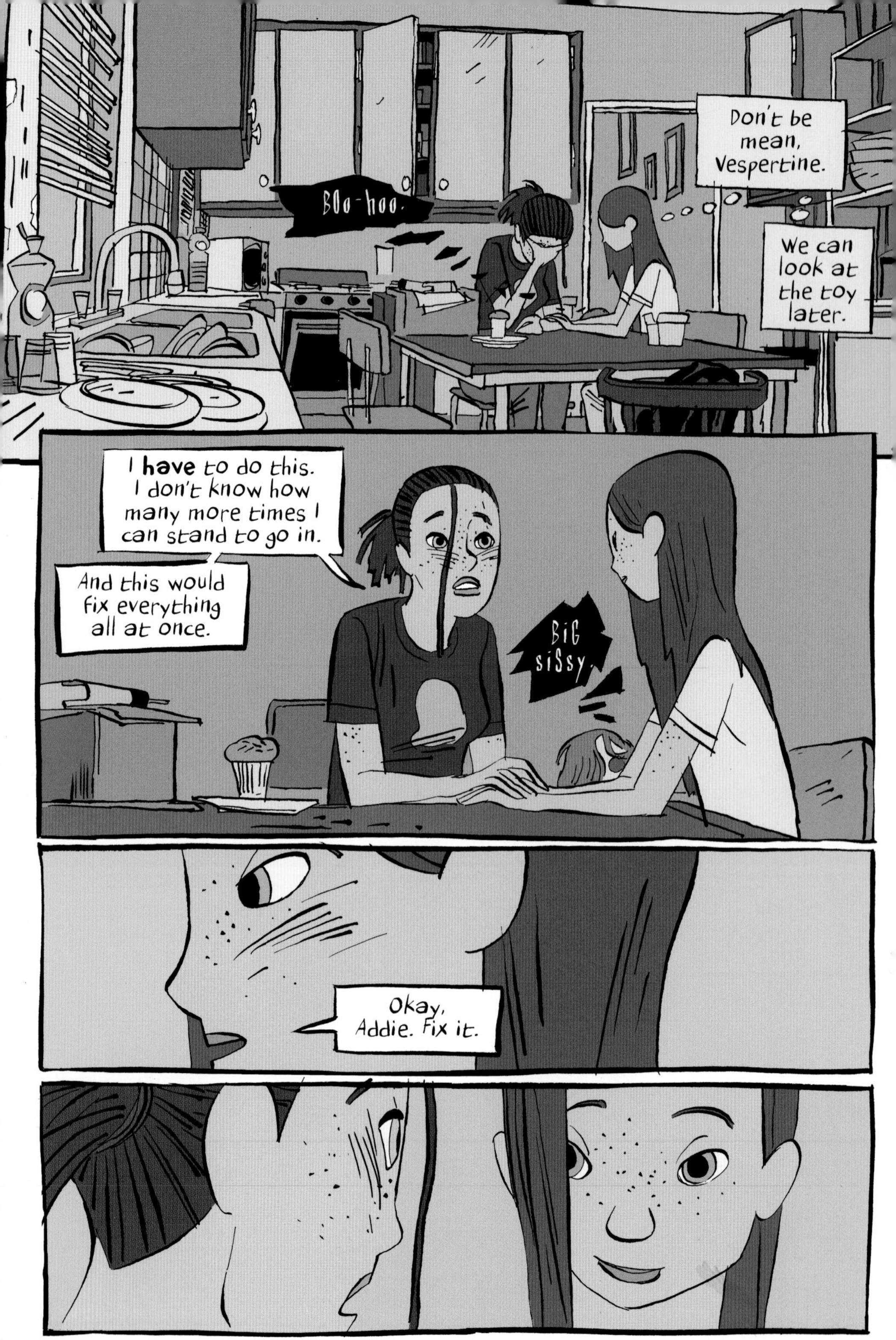
Don't be mean, Vespertine.
We can look at the toy later.
BOo-hoo.
I **have** to do this. I don't know how many more times I can stand to go in.
And this would fix everything all at once.
BiG siSsy.
Okay, Addie. Fix it.

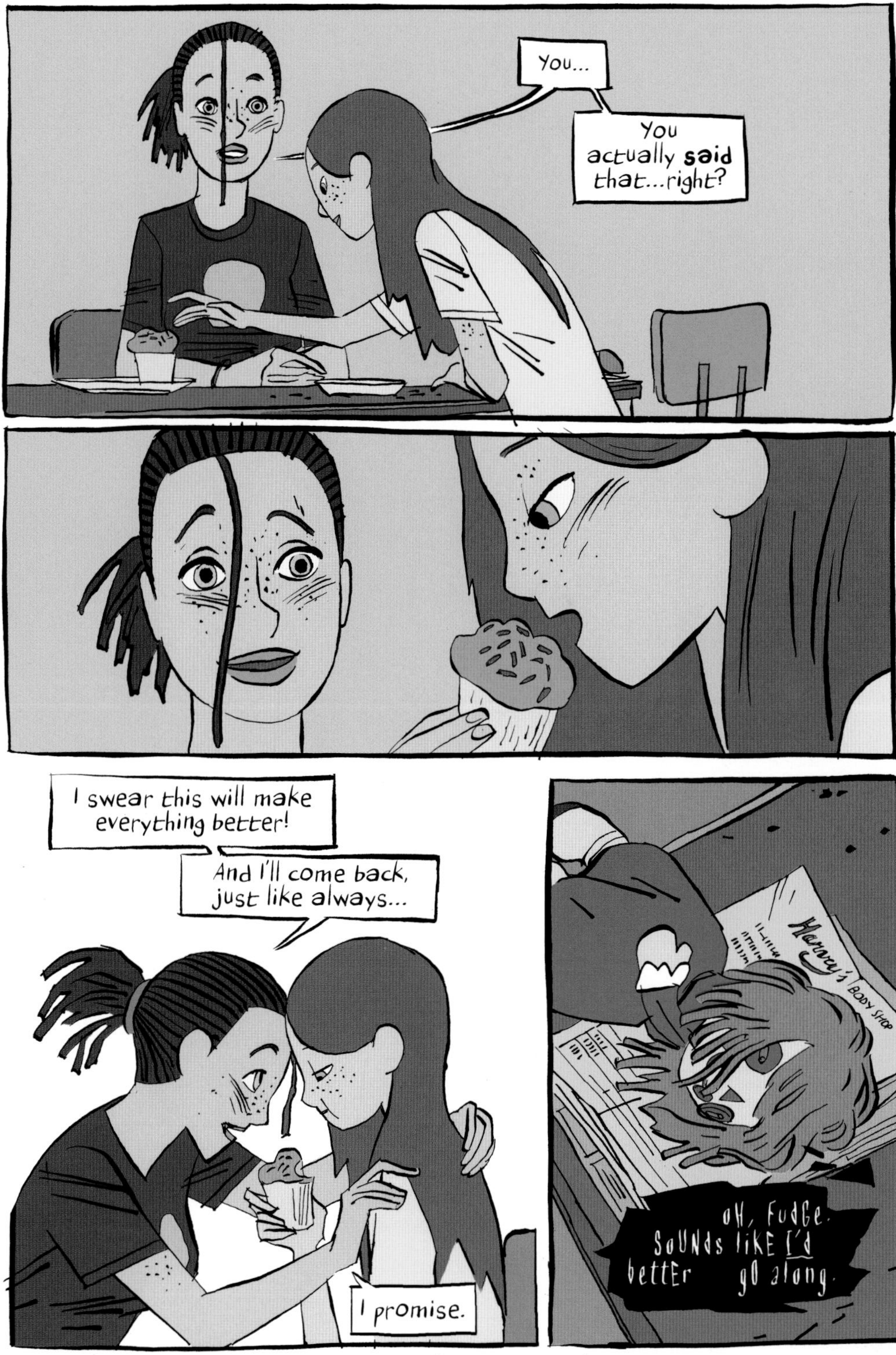
You...
You actually **said** that...right?
I swear this will make everything better!
And I'll come back, just like always...
I promise.
Harvey's BODY SHOP
OH, FUDGE. SOUNDS LIKE I'D BETTER GO ALONG.

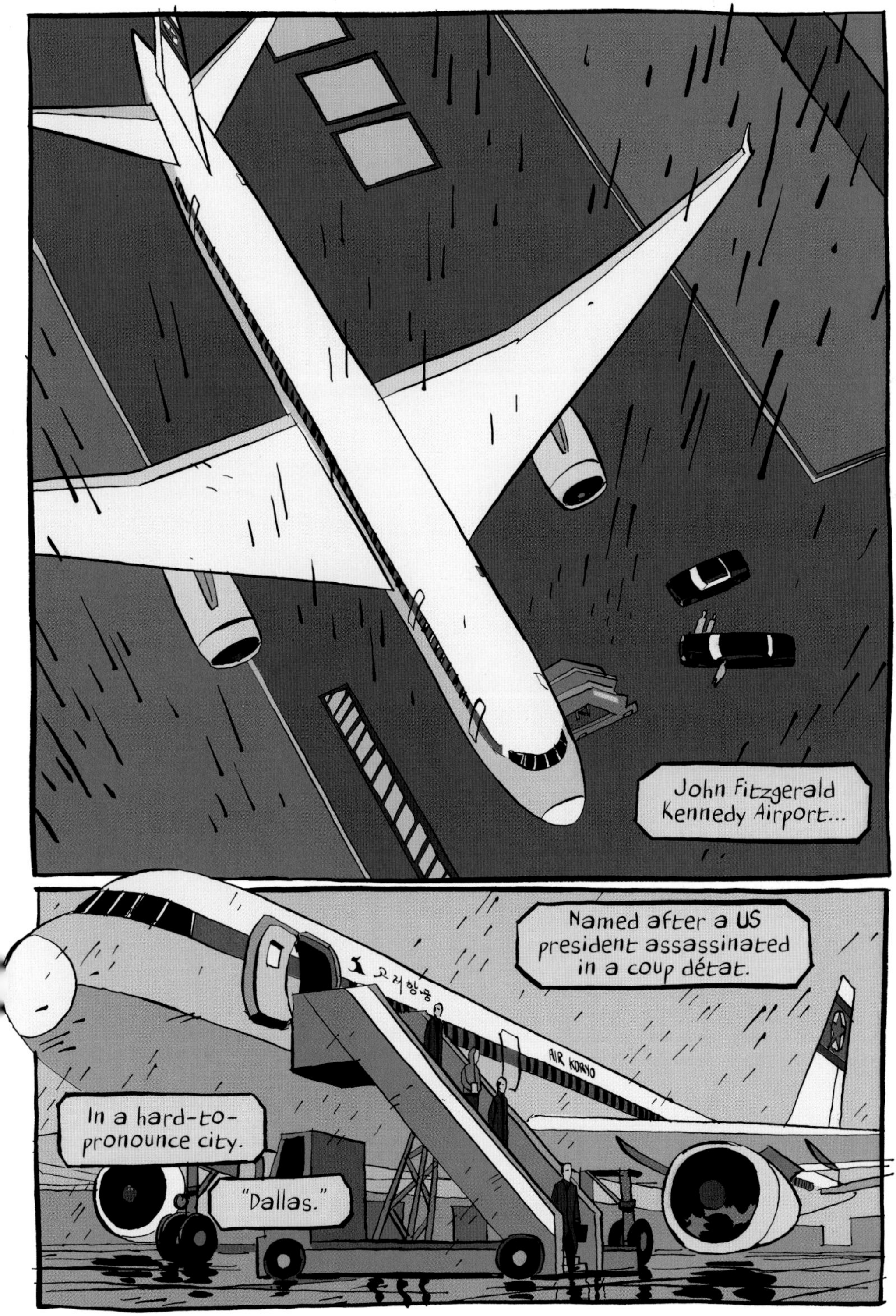
John Fitzgerald Kennedy Airport...
Named after a US president assassinated in a coup détat.
고려항공
AIR KORYO
In a hard-to-pronounce city.
"Dallas."

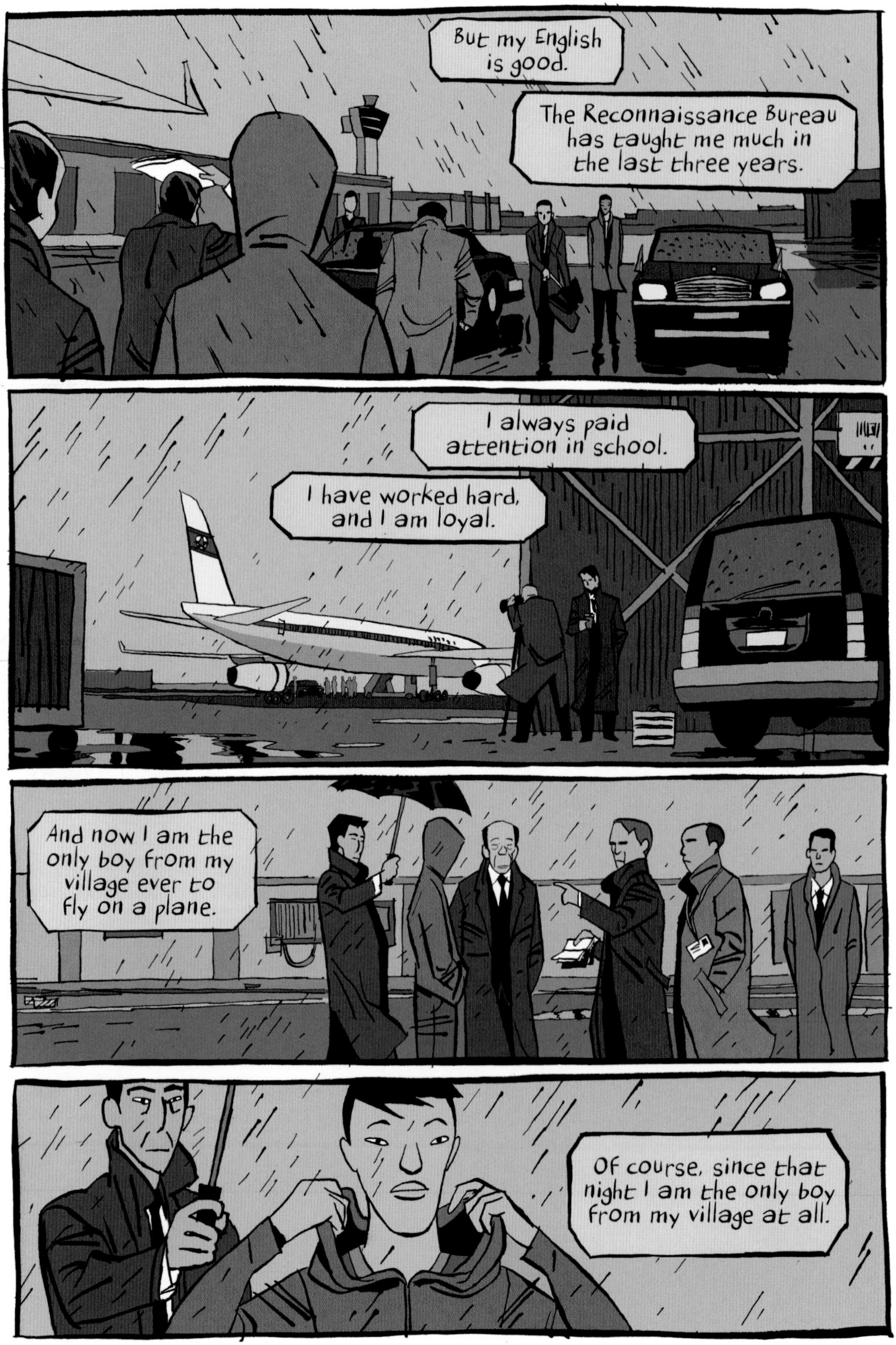
But my English is good.
The Reconnaissance Bureau has taught me much in the last three years.
I always paid attention in school.
I have worked hard, and I am loyal.
And now I am the only boy from my village ever to fly on a plane.
Of course, since that night I am the only boy from my village at all.

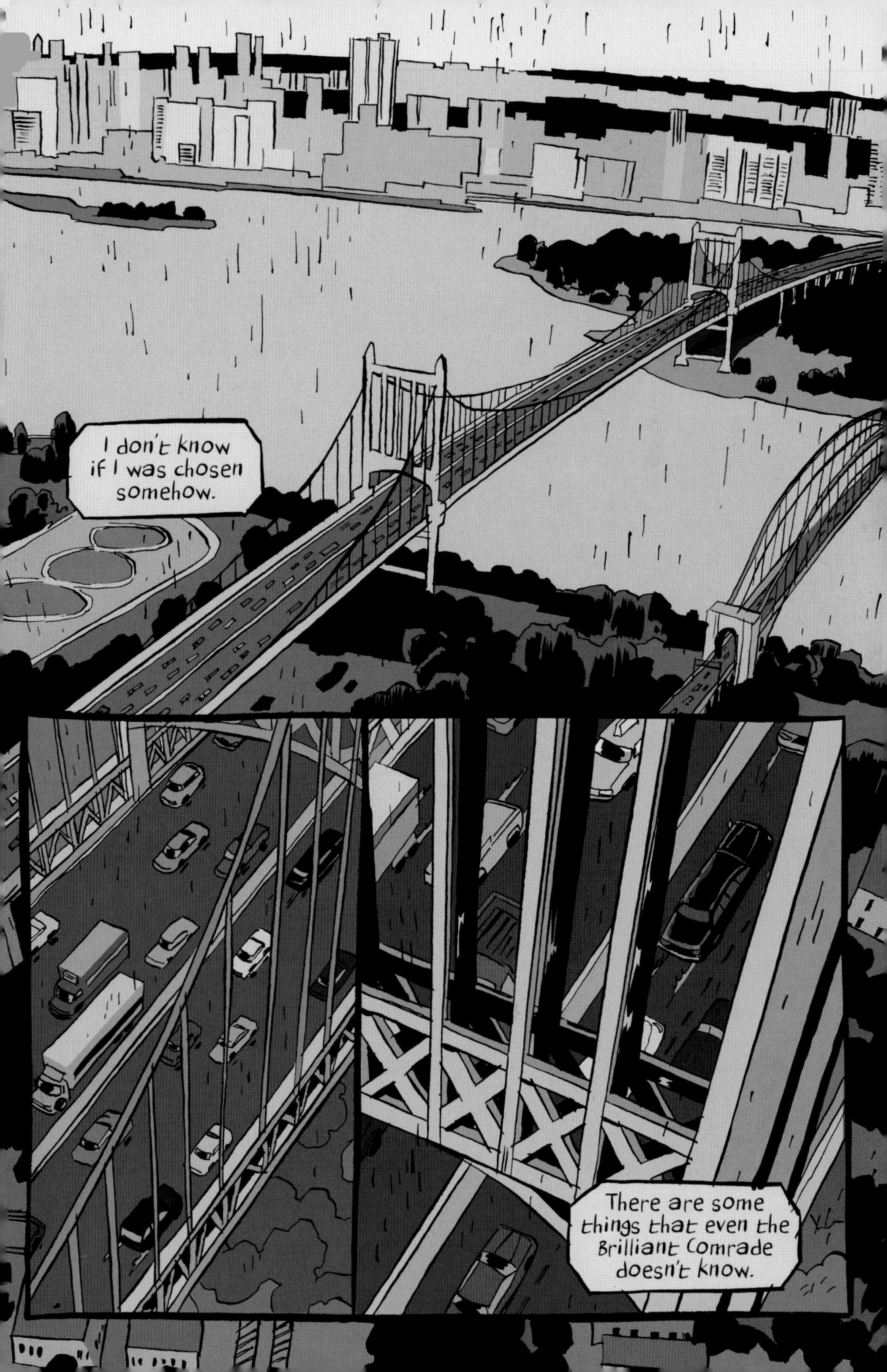
I don't know if I was chosen somehow.
There are some things that even the Brilliant Comrade doesn't know.

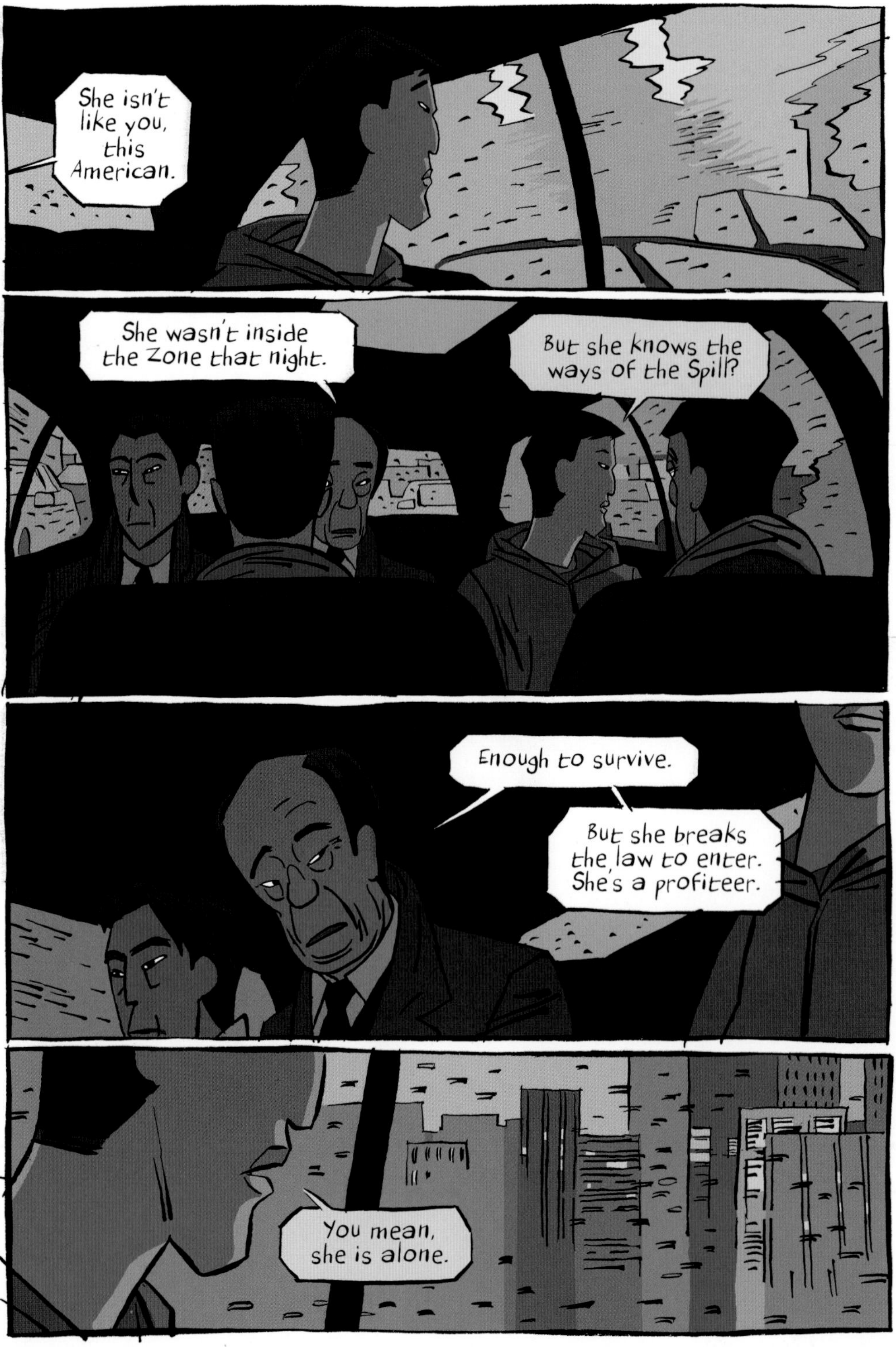
She isn't like you, this American.
She wasn't inside the Zone that night.
But she knows the ways of the Spill?
Enough to survive.
But she breaks the law to enter. She's a profiteer.
You mean, she is alone.

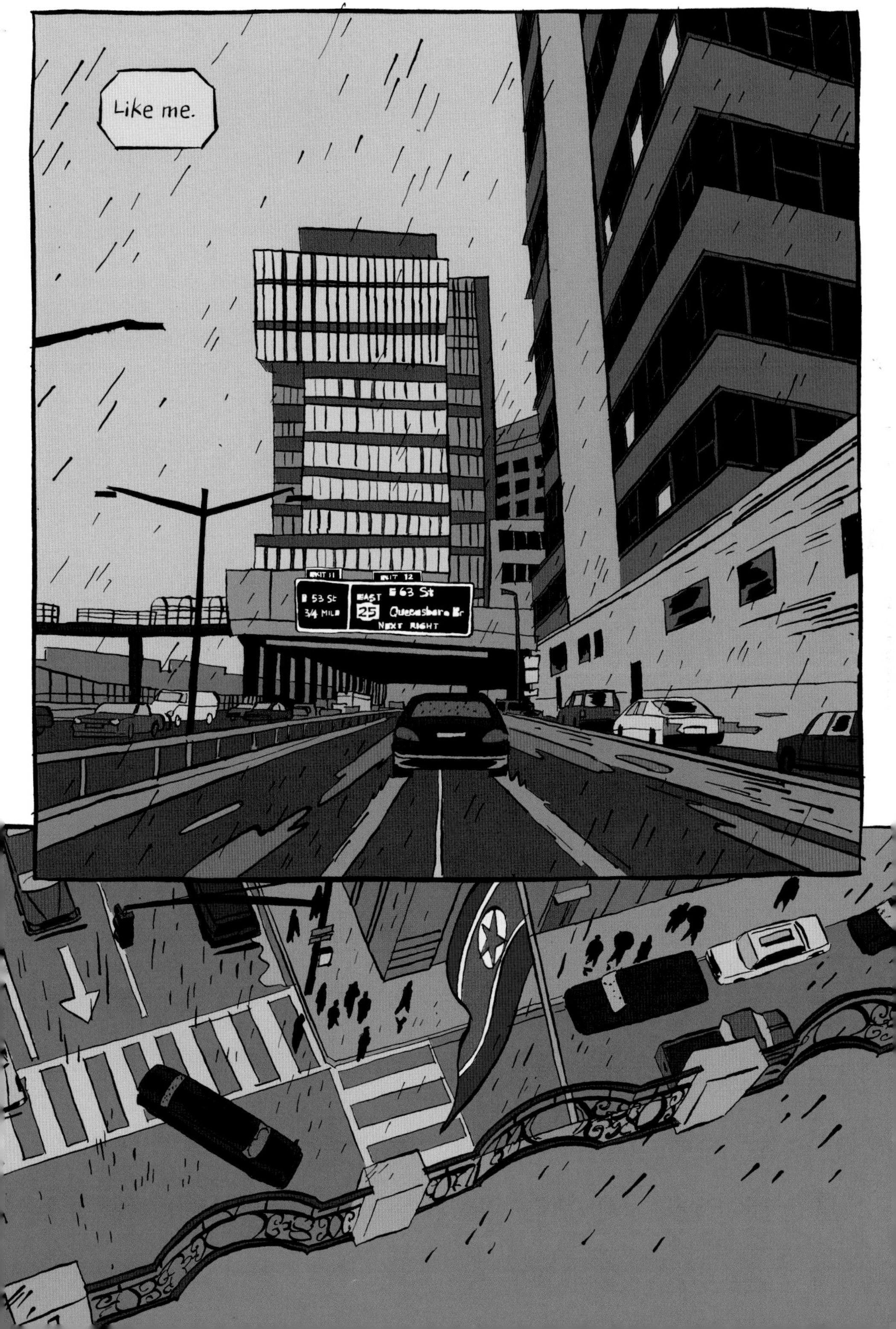
Like me.
EXIT 11
EXIT 12
E 53 St
3/4 MILE
EAST
E 63 St
25
Queensboro Br
NEXT RIGHT

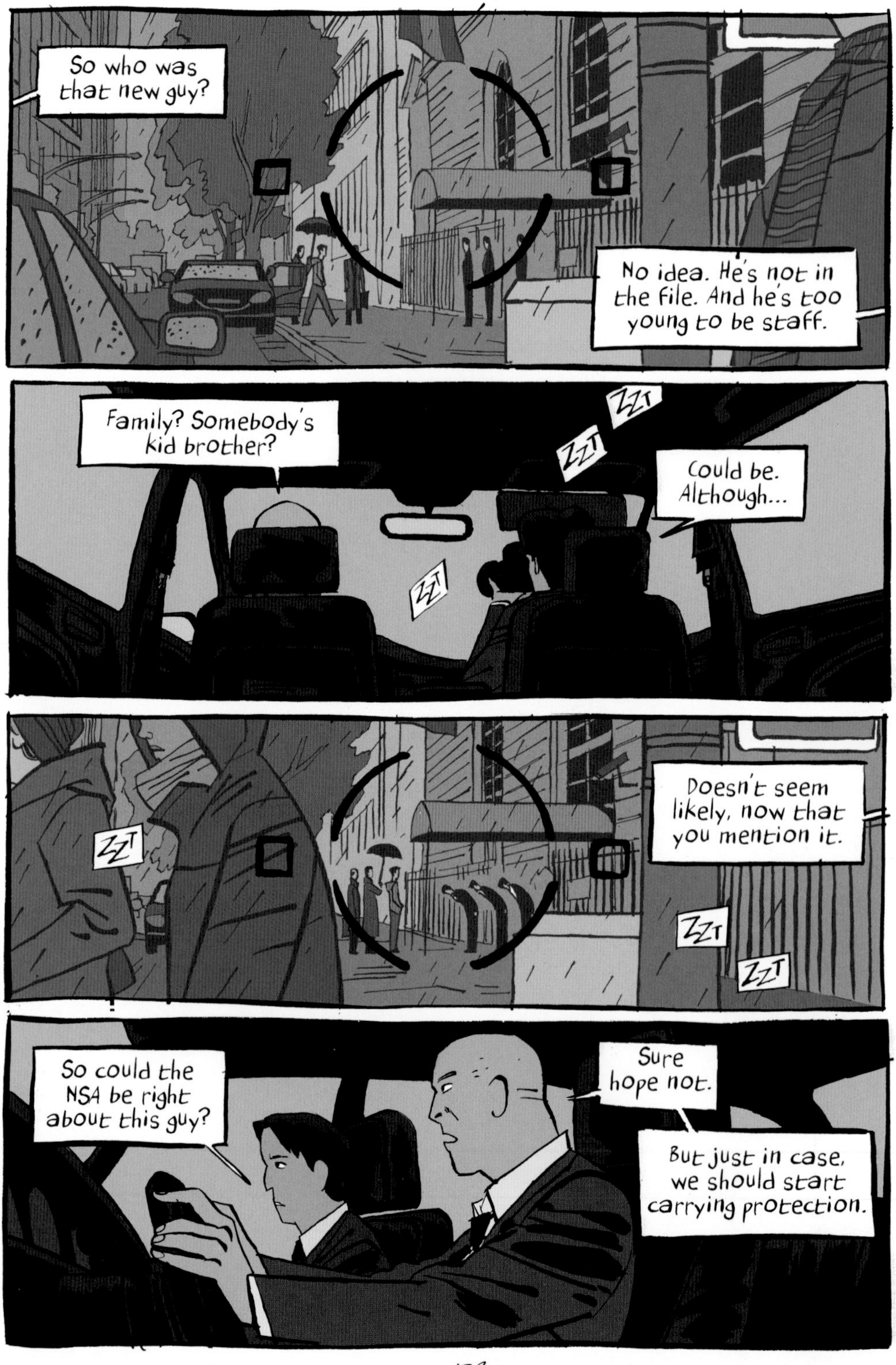
So who was that new guy?
No idea. He's not in the file. And he's too young to be staff.
Family? Somebody's kid brother?
ZZT
ZZT
Could be. Although...
ZZT
ZZT
Doesn't seem likely, now that you mention it.
ZZT
ZZT
So could the NSA be right about this guy?
Sure hope not.
But just in case, we should start carrying protection.

Is it possible for me to meet this American girl? My English is very good.

We do not know her name, Don Jae.

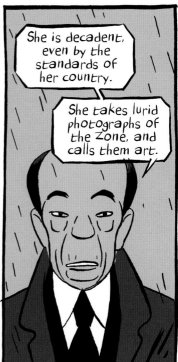

She is decadent, even by the standards of her country.

She takes lurid photographs of the Zone, and calls them art.

That is unfortunate.

But perhaps I could see some of this..."art."

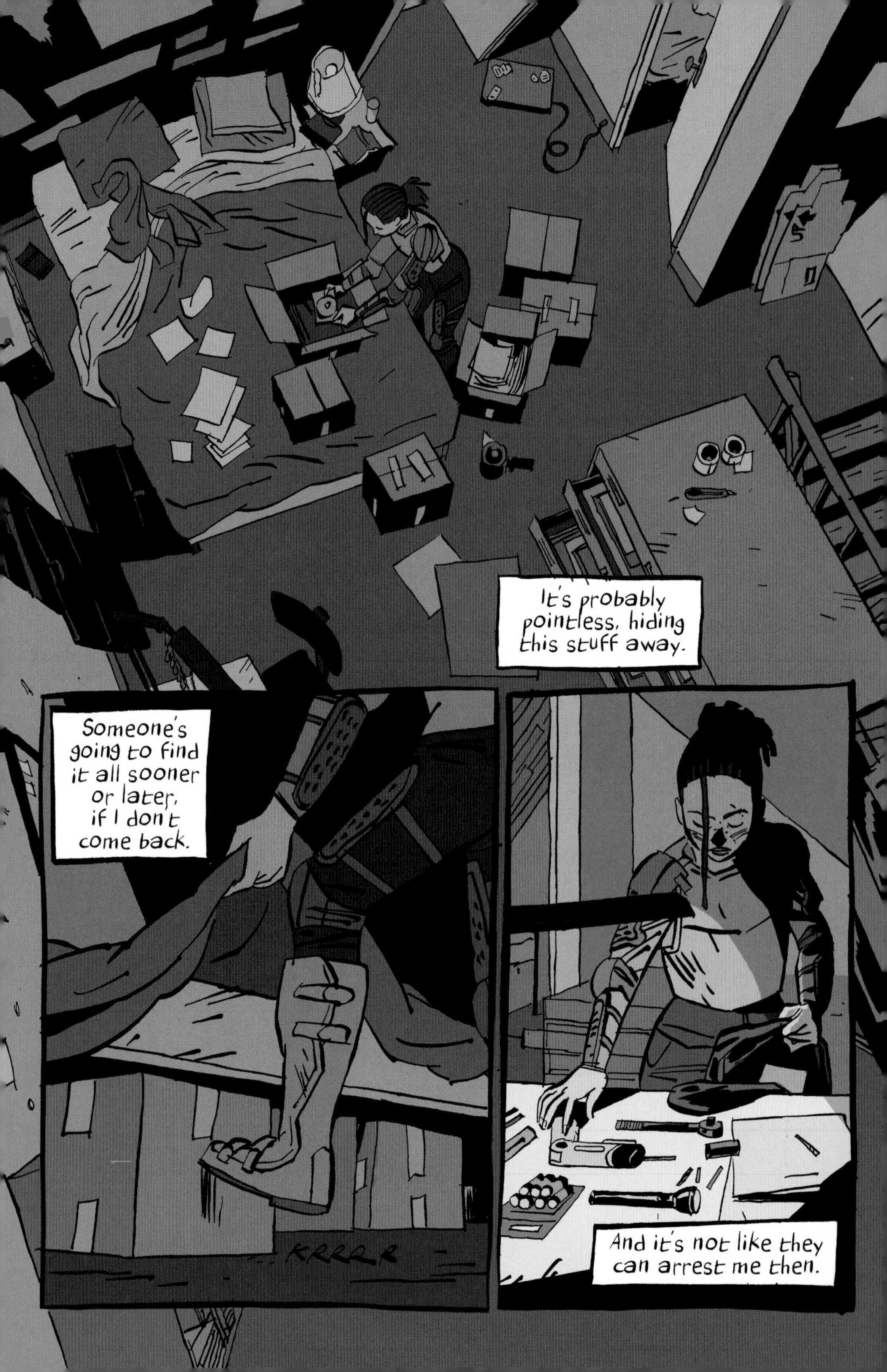
It's probably pointless, hiding this stuff away.
Someone's going to find it all sooner or later, if I don't come back.
KRRRR
And it's not like they can arrest me then.

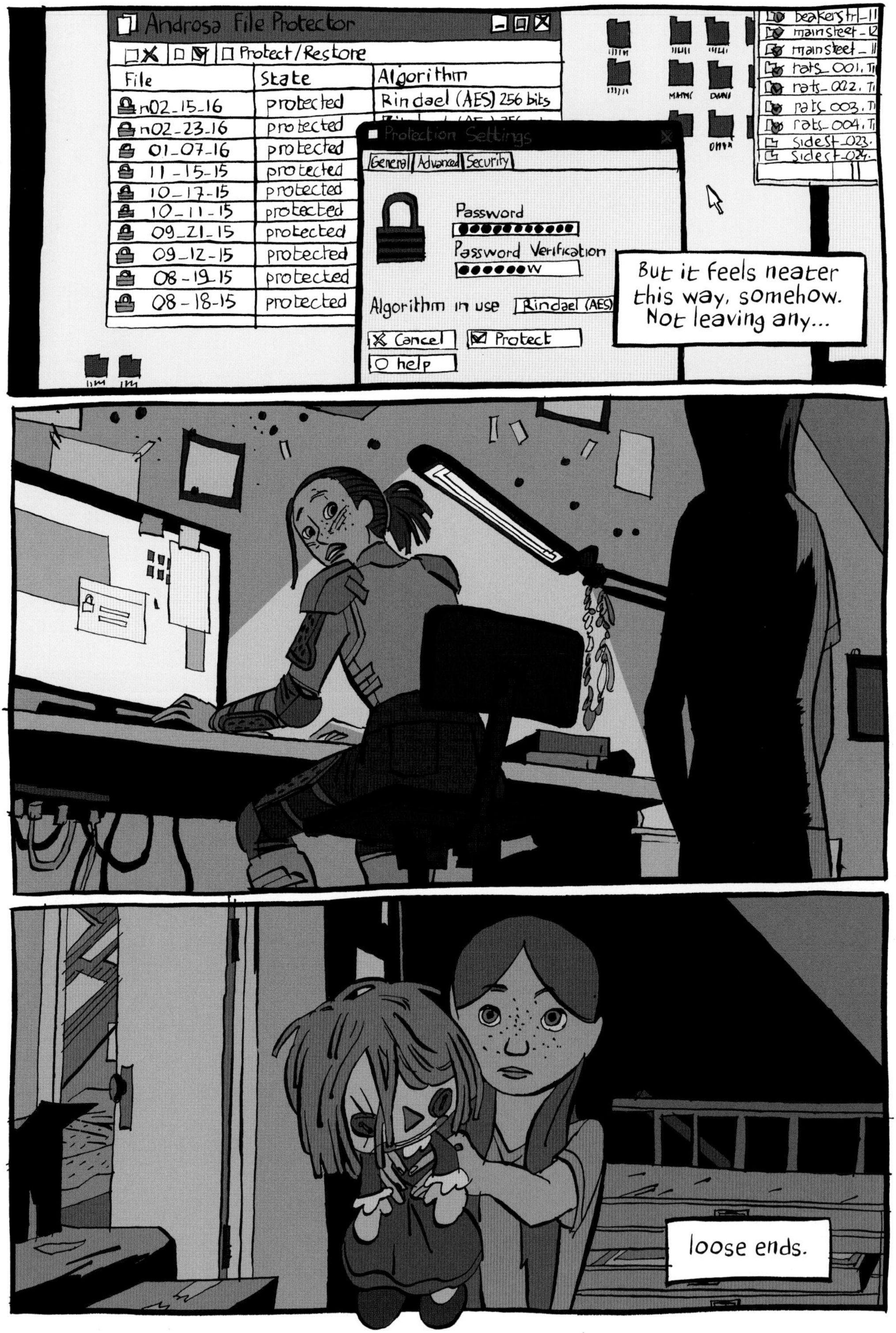
Androsa File Protector
Protect/Restore
File
State
Algorithm
n02_15_16
protected
Rindael (AES) 256 bits
n02_23_16
01_07_16
11_15_15
10_17_15
10_11_15
09_21_15
09_12_15
08_19_15
08_18_15
Protection Settings
General
Advanced
Security
Password
Password Verification
Algorithm in use
Rindael (AES)
Cancel
Protect
help
beakerstrl_11
mainsteet_12
mainsteet_11
rats_001.Ti
rats_002.Ti
rats_003.Ti
rats_004.Ti
sidest_023.
sidest_024.
But it feels neater this way, somehow. Not leaving any...
loose ends.

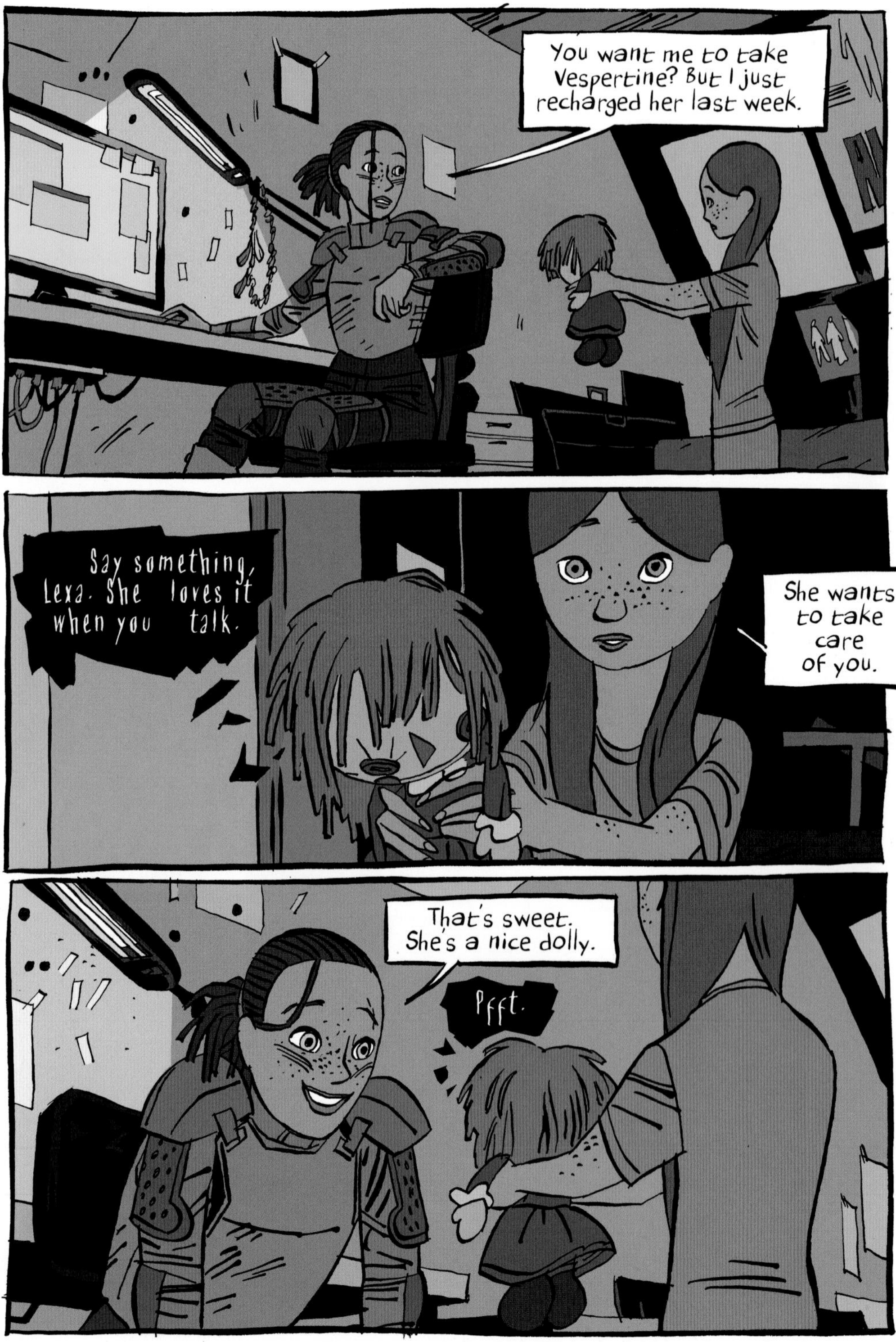
You want me to take Vespertine? But I just recharged her last week.
Say something, Lexa. She loves it when you talk.
She wants to take care of you.
That's sweet. She's a nice dolly.
Pfft.

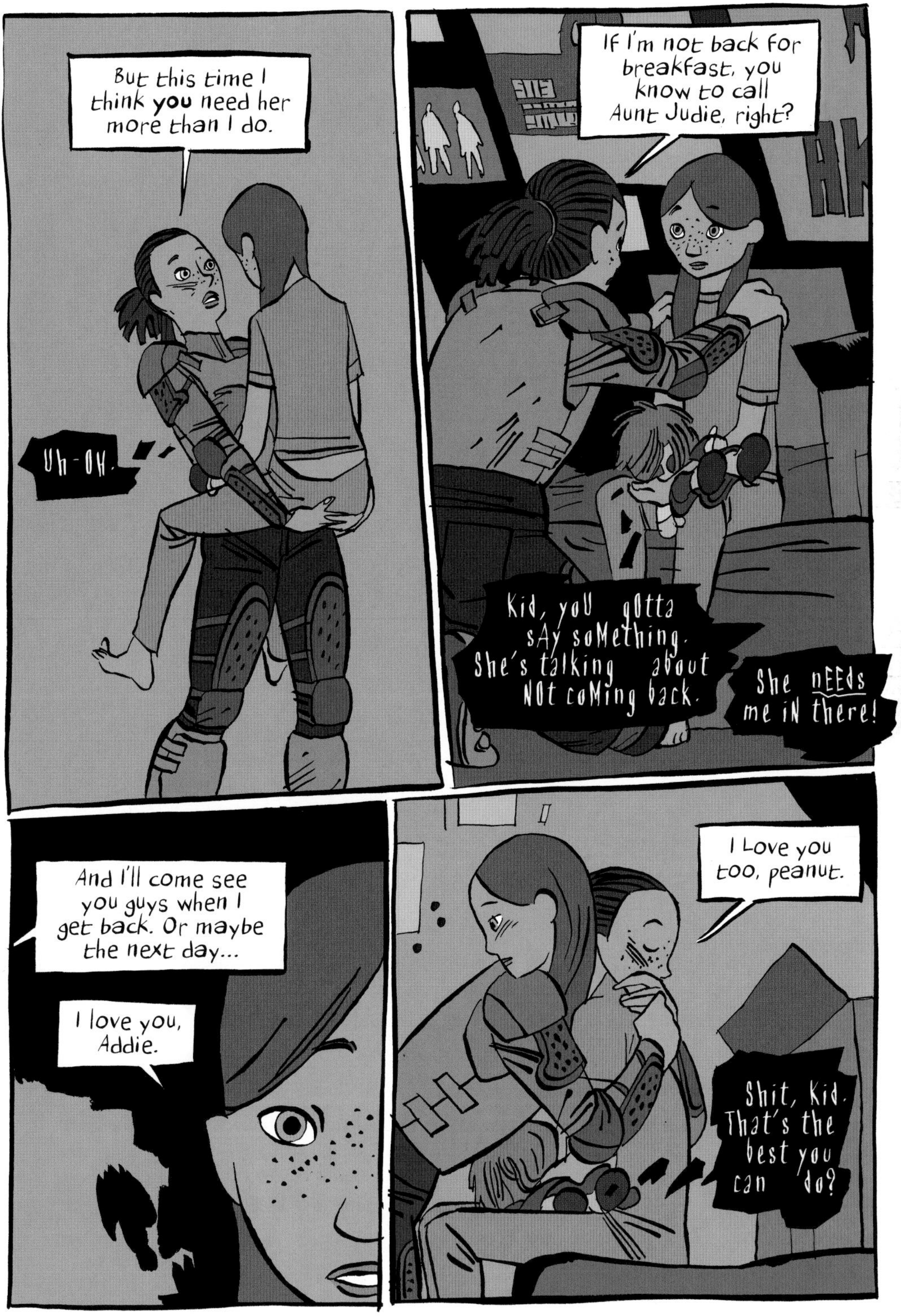

But this time I think **you** need her more than I do.
Uh-oh.
If I'm not back for breakfast, you know to call Aunt Judie, right?
Kid, you gotta say something. She's talking about NOT coming back.
She NEEDs me in there!
And I'll come see you guys when I get back. Or maybe the next day...
I love you, Addie.
I Love you too, peanut.
Shit, kid. That's the best you can do?

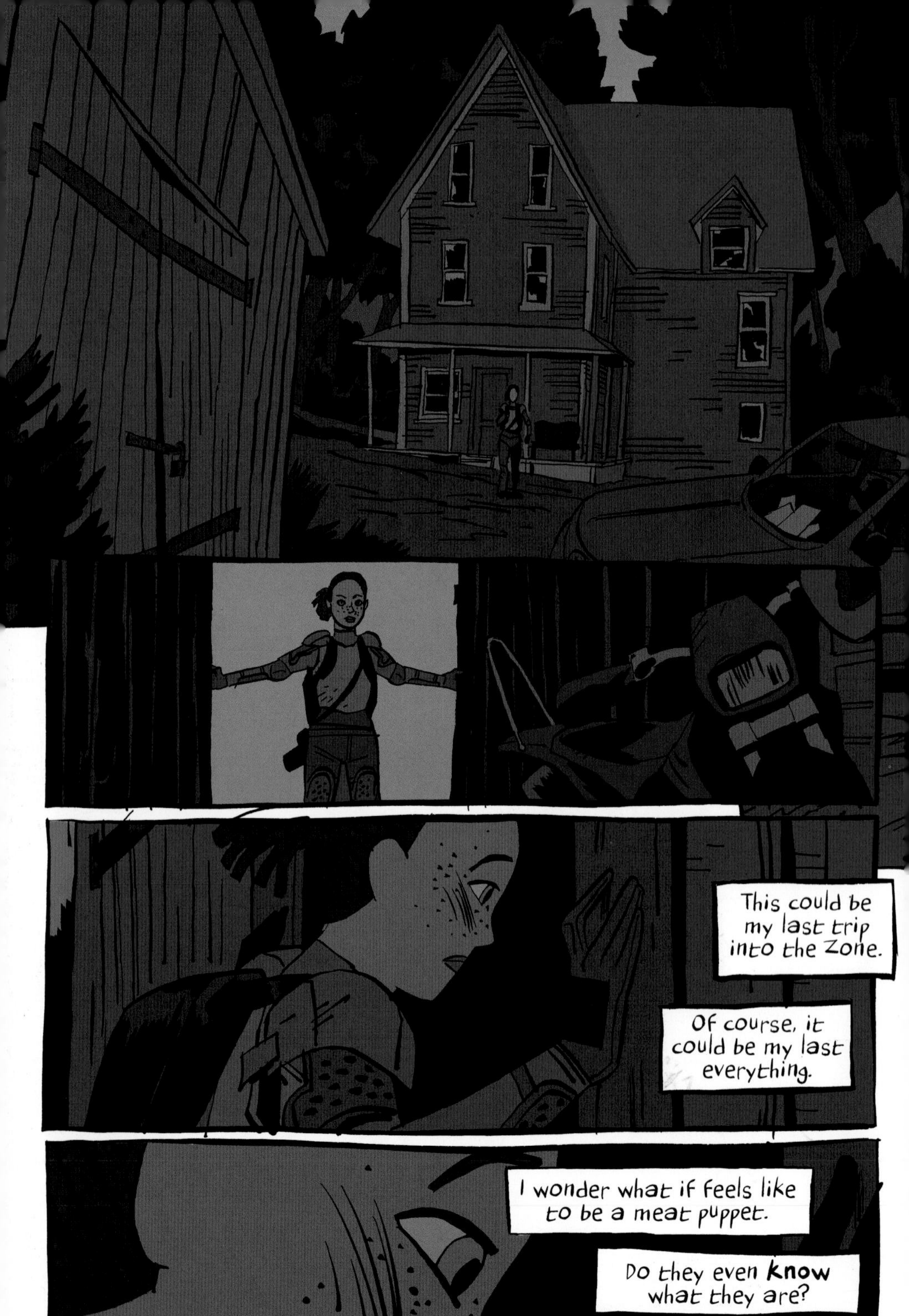
This could be my last trip into the Zone.
Of course, it could be my last everything.
I wonder what if feels like to be a meat puppet.
Do they even **know** what they are?

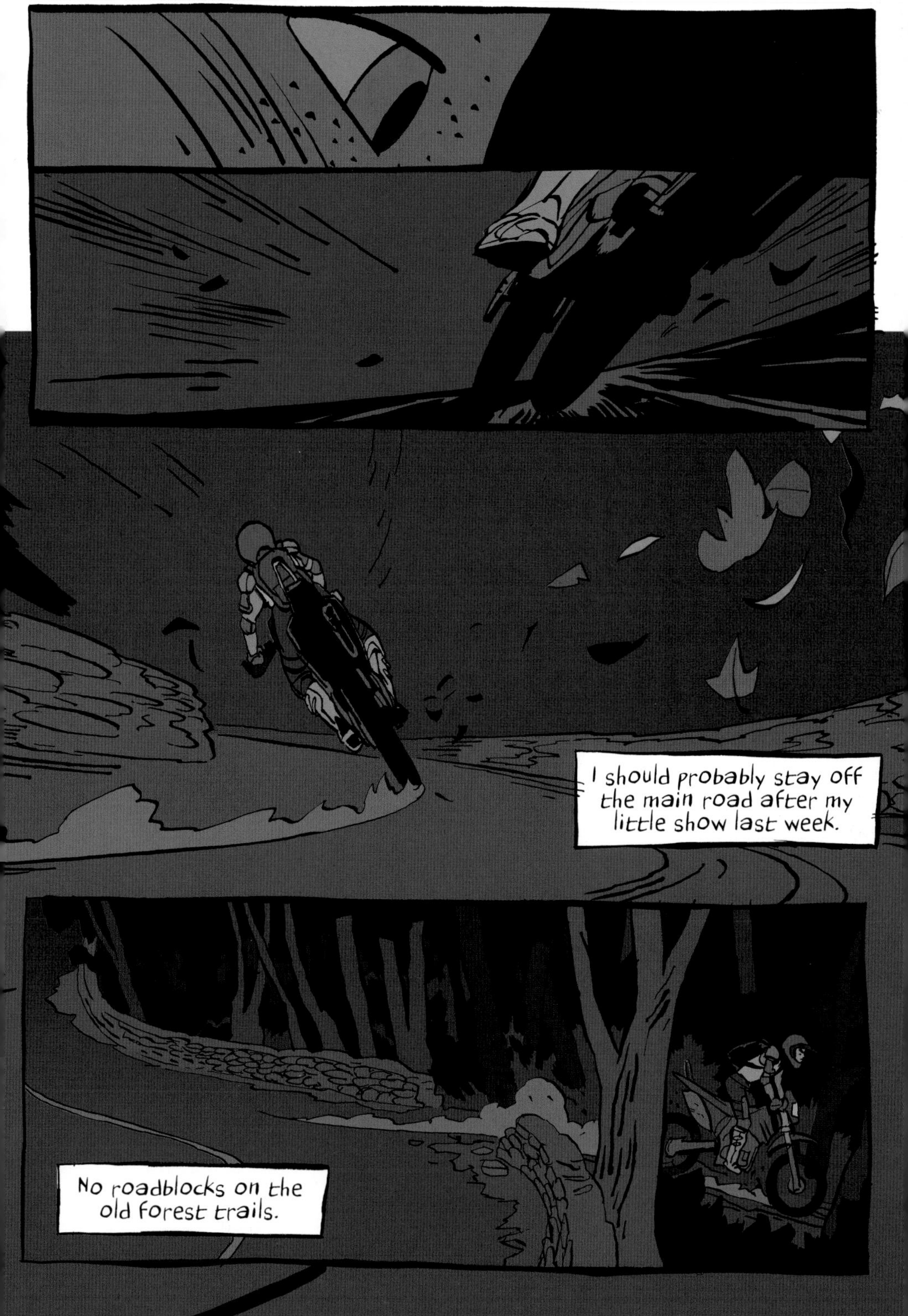
I should probably stay off the main road after my little show last week.
No roadblocks on the old forest trails.

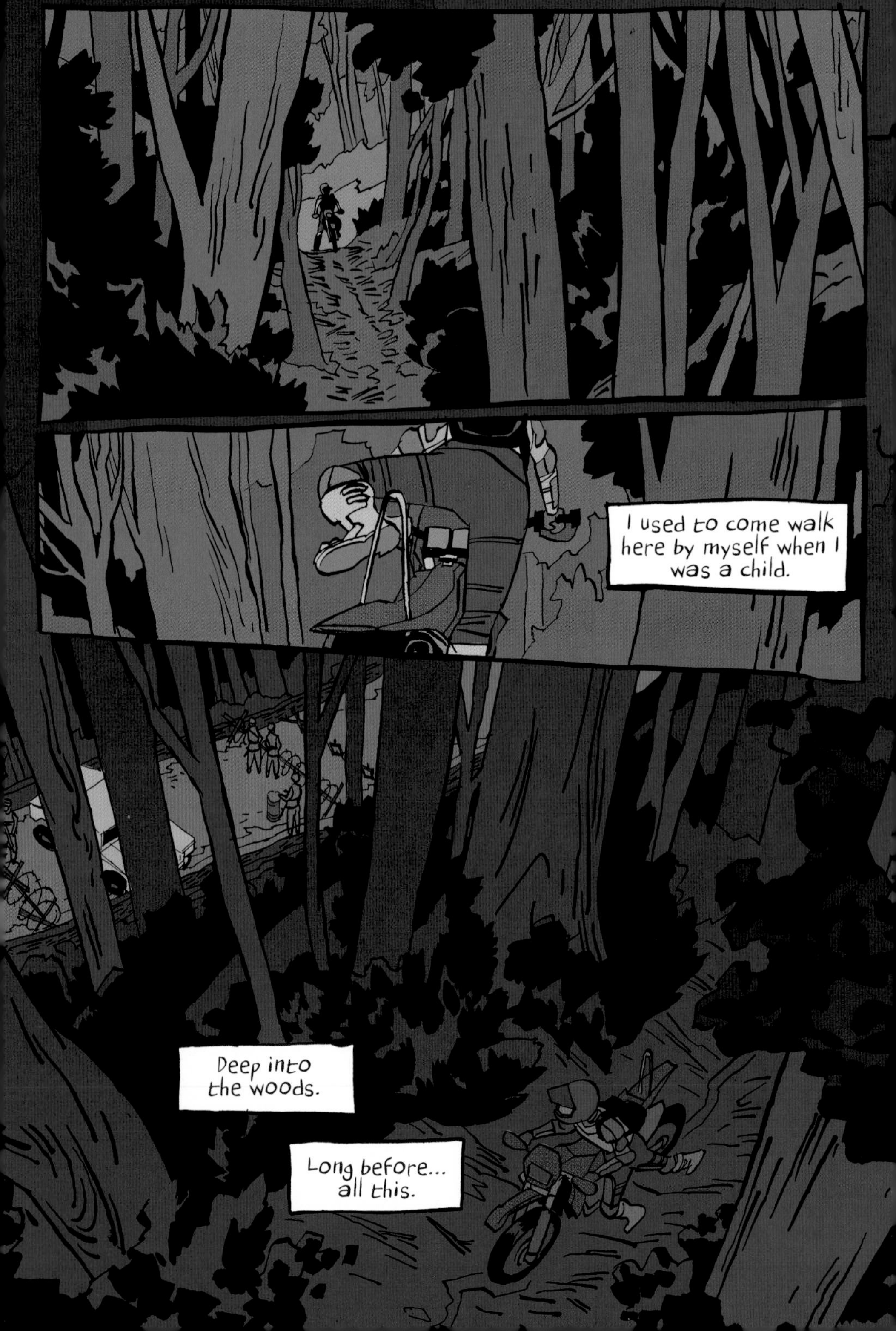
I used to come walk here by myself when I was a child.
Deep into the woods.
Long before... all this.

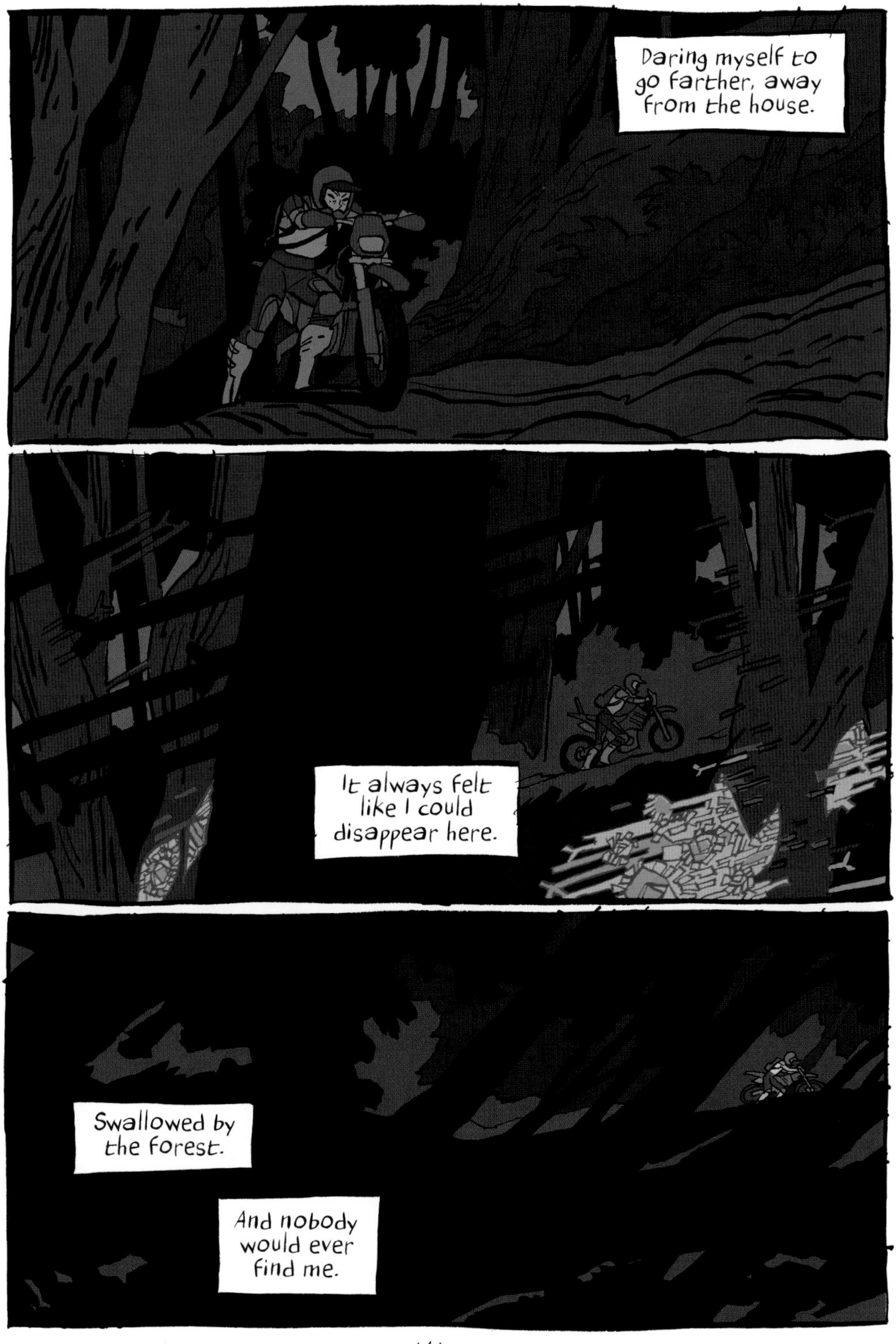
Daring myself to go farther, away from the house.
It always felt like I could disappear here.
Swallowed by the forest.
And nobody would ever find me.

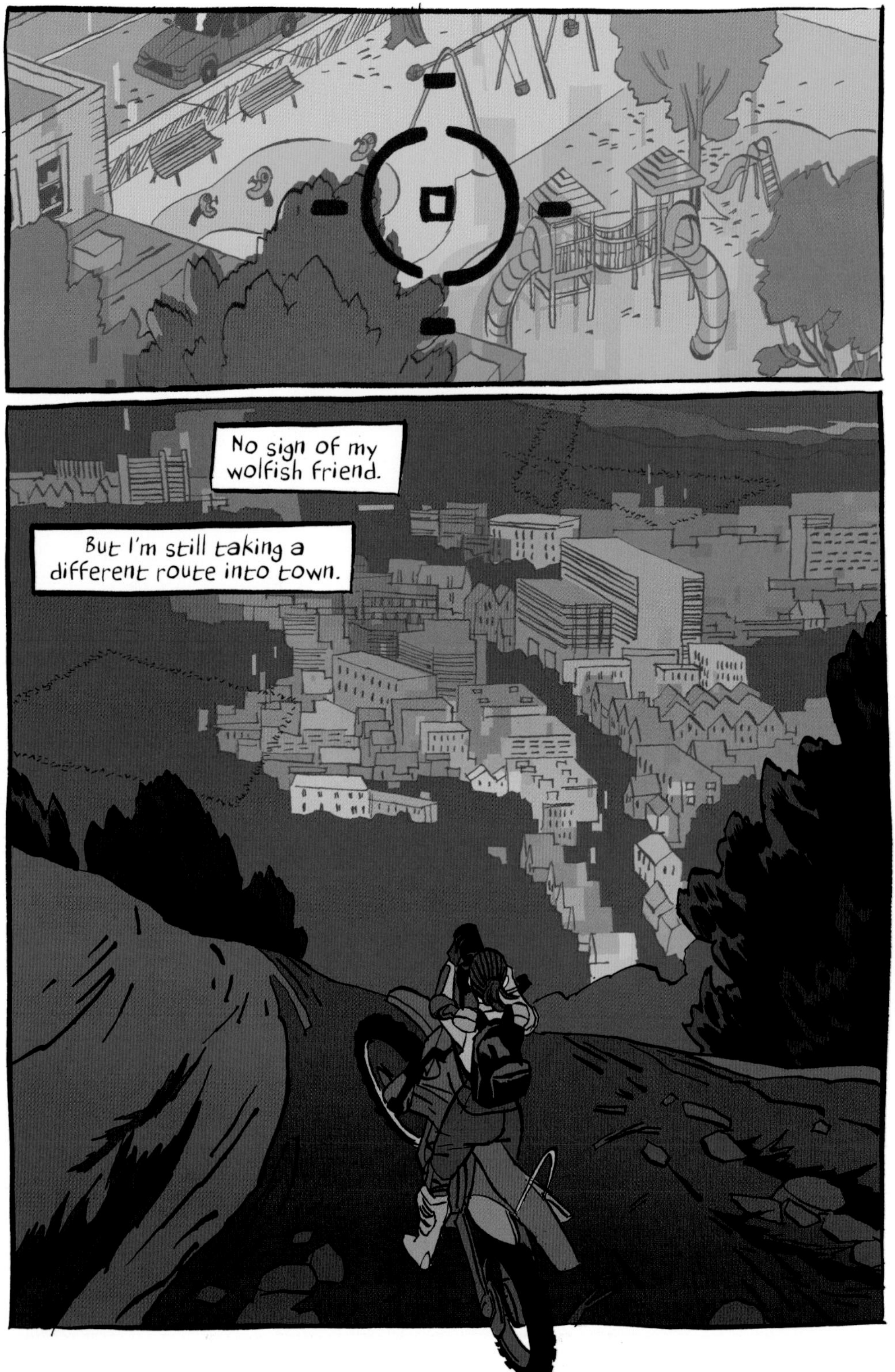
No sign of my wolfish friend.
But I'm still taking a different route into town.

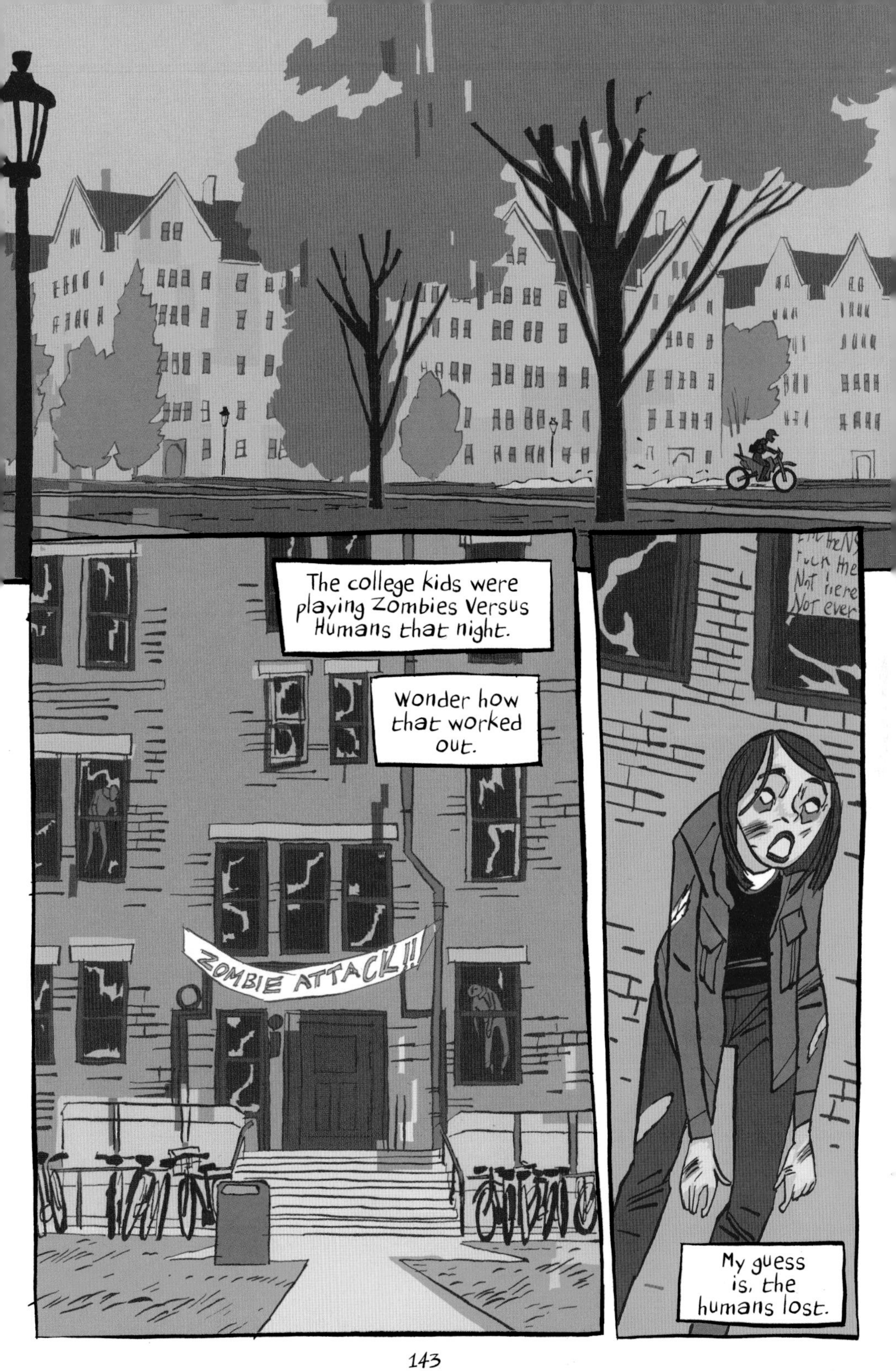
The college kids were playing Zombies Versus Humans that night.
Wonder how that worked out.
ZOMBIE ATTACK!!
My guess is, the humans lost.

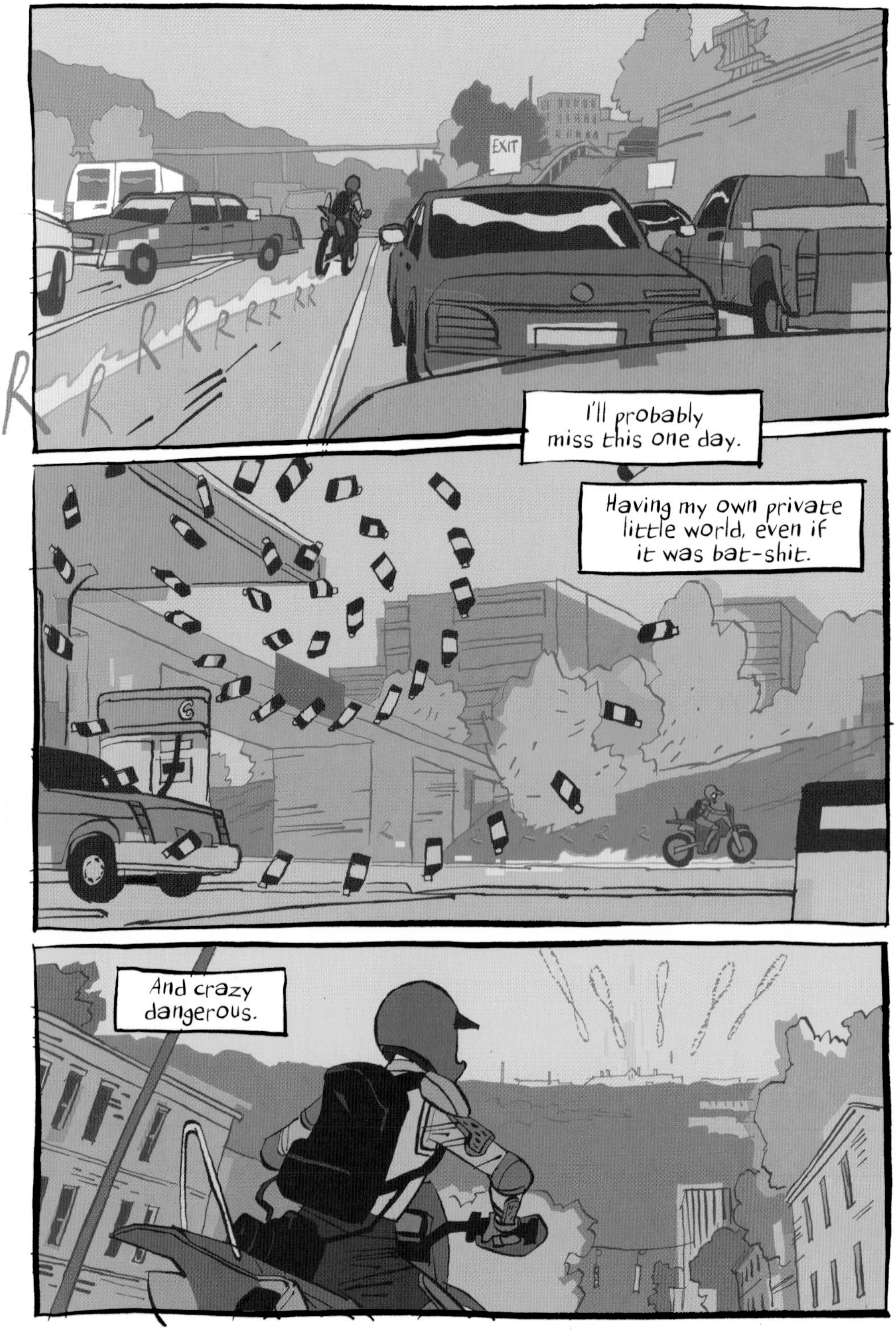
EXIT
RRRRRRRRRRR
I'll probably miss this one day.
Having my own private little world, even if it was bat-shit.
And crazy dangerous.

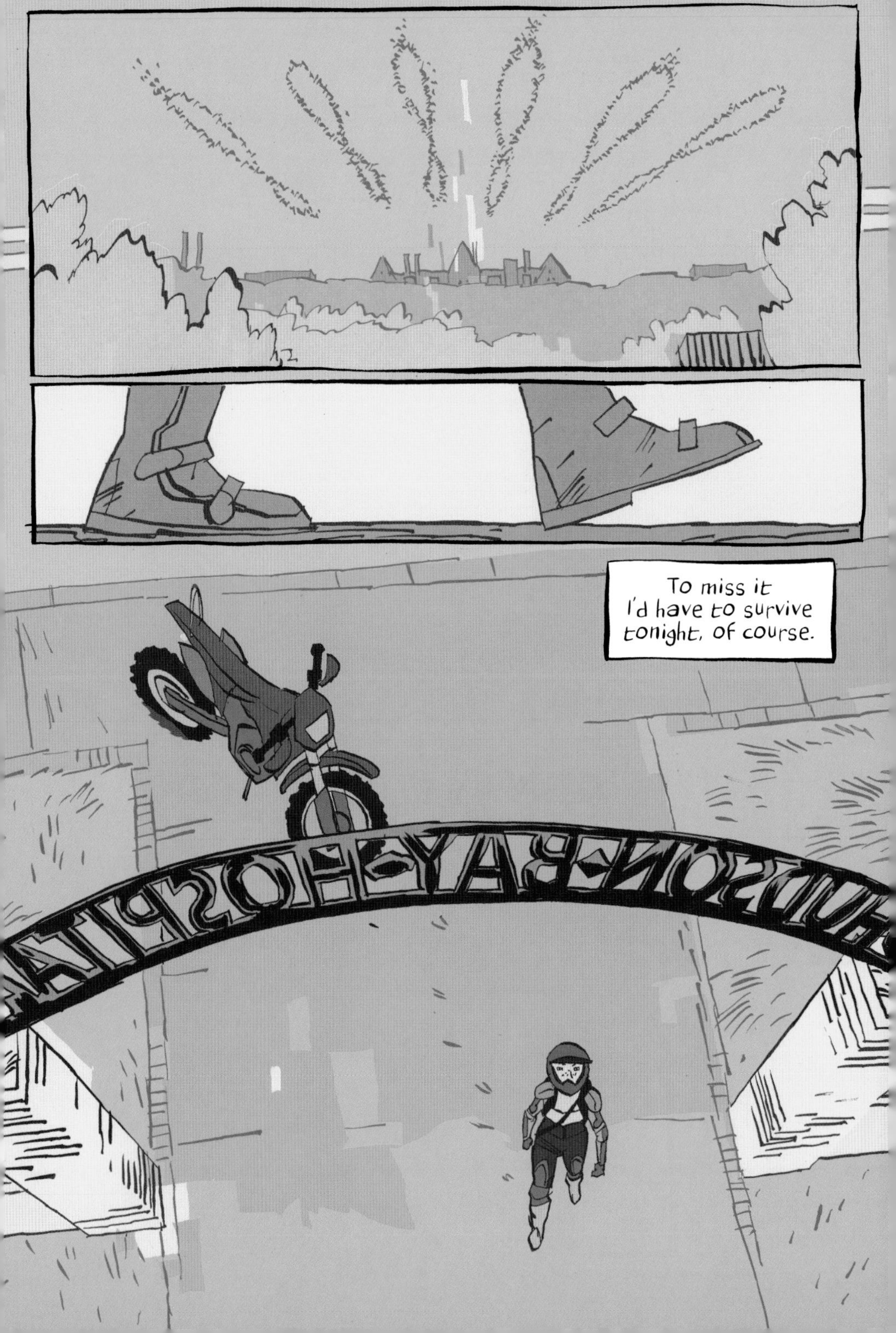
To miss it I'd have to survive tonight, of course.

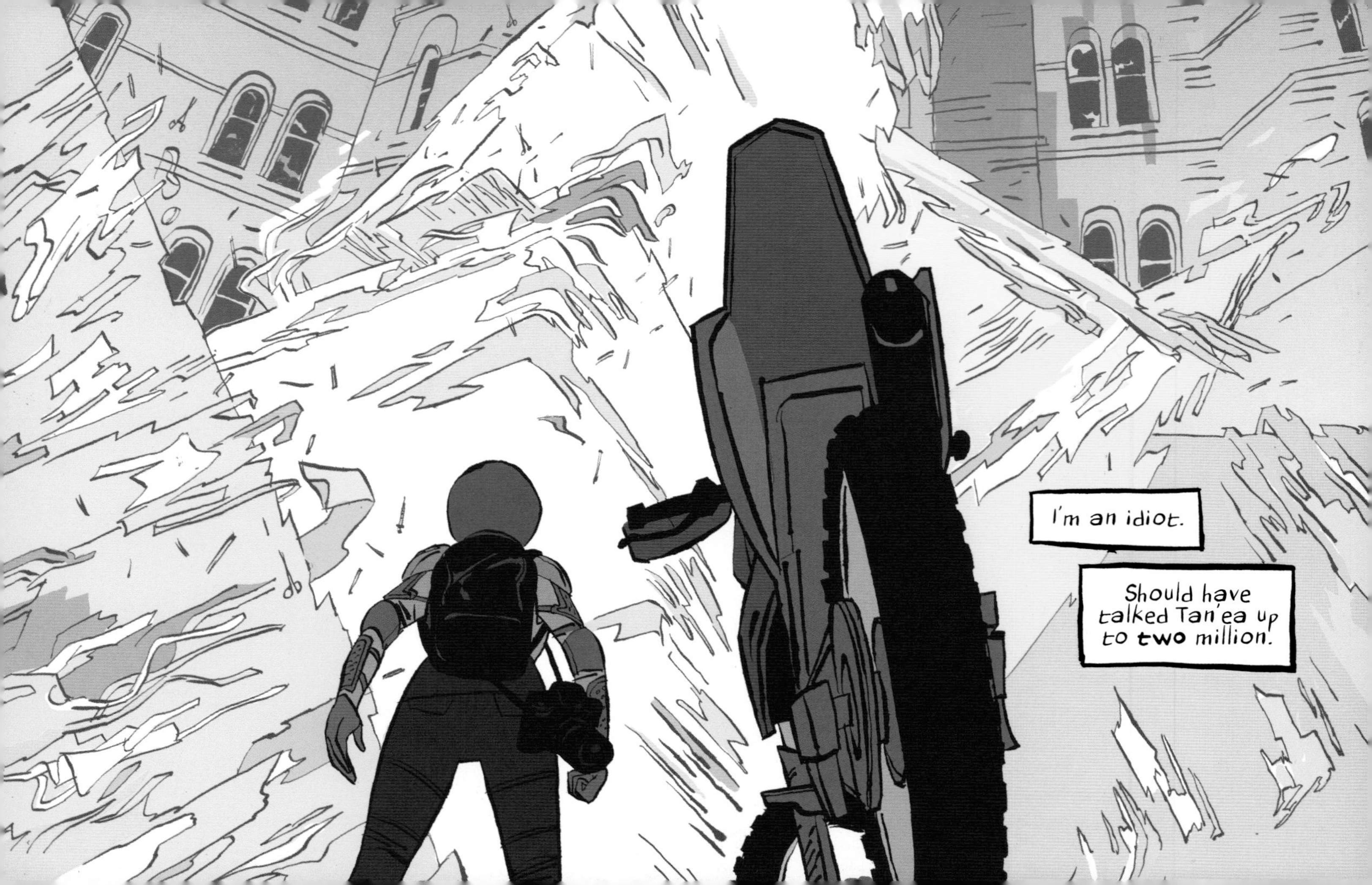
I'm an idiot.
Should have talked Tan'ea up to **two** million.

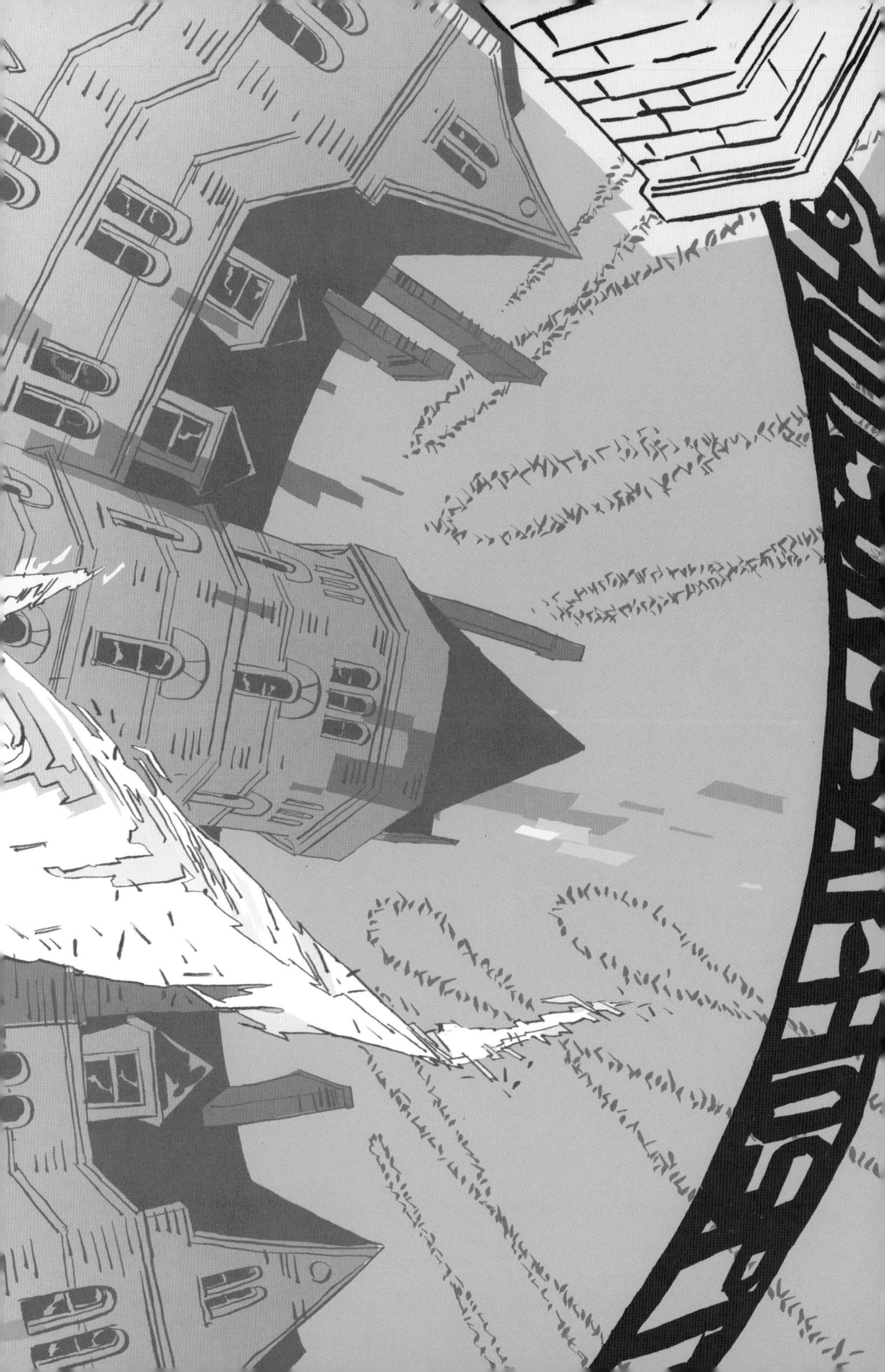

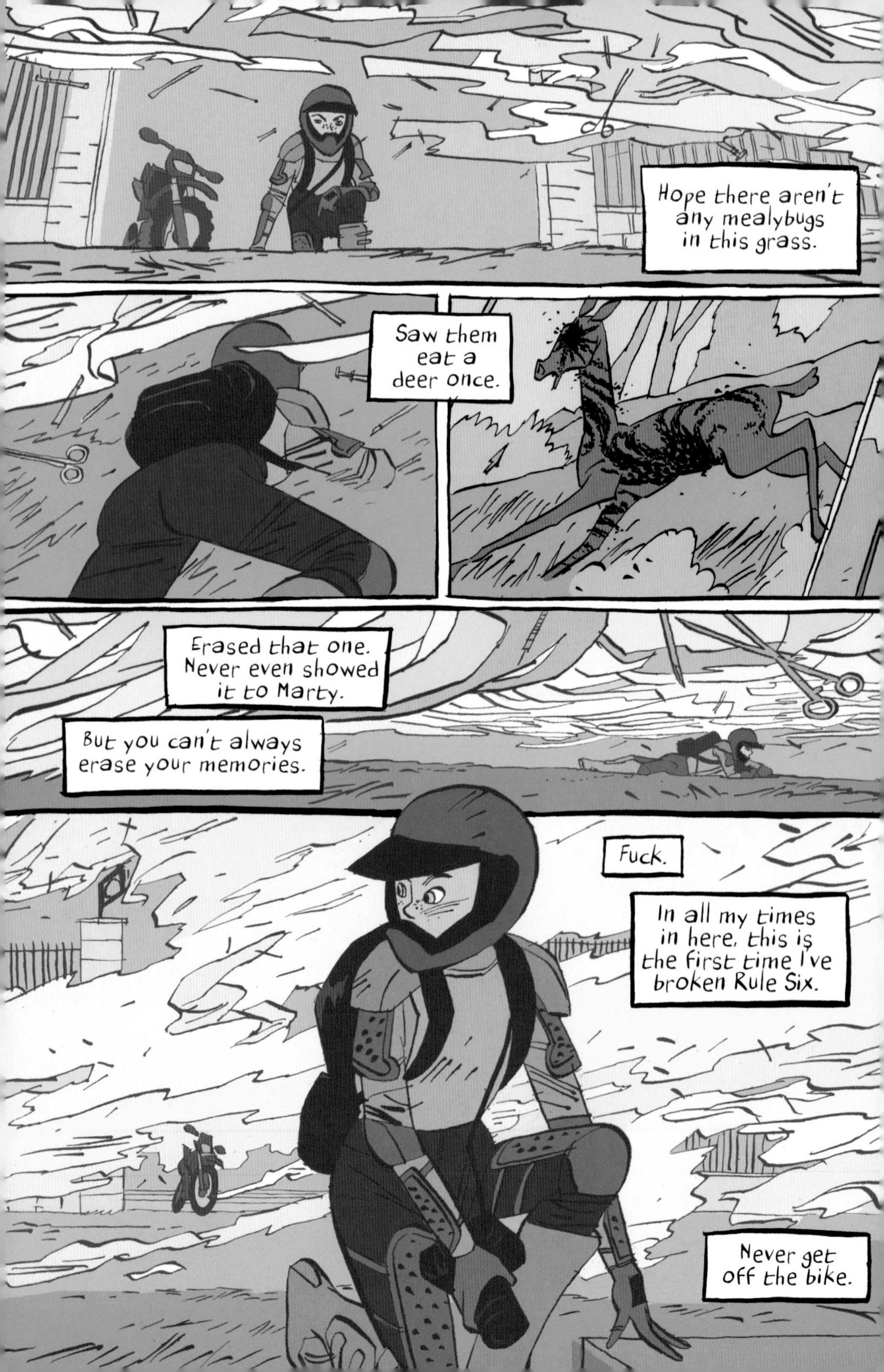
Hope there aren't any mealybugs in this grass.
Saw them eat a deer once.
Erased that one. Never even showed it to Marty.
But you can't always erase your memories.
Fuck.
In all my times in here, this is the first time I've broken Rule Six.
Never get off the bike.

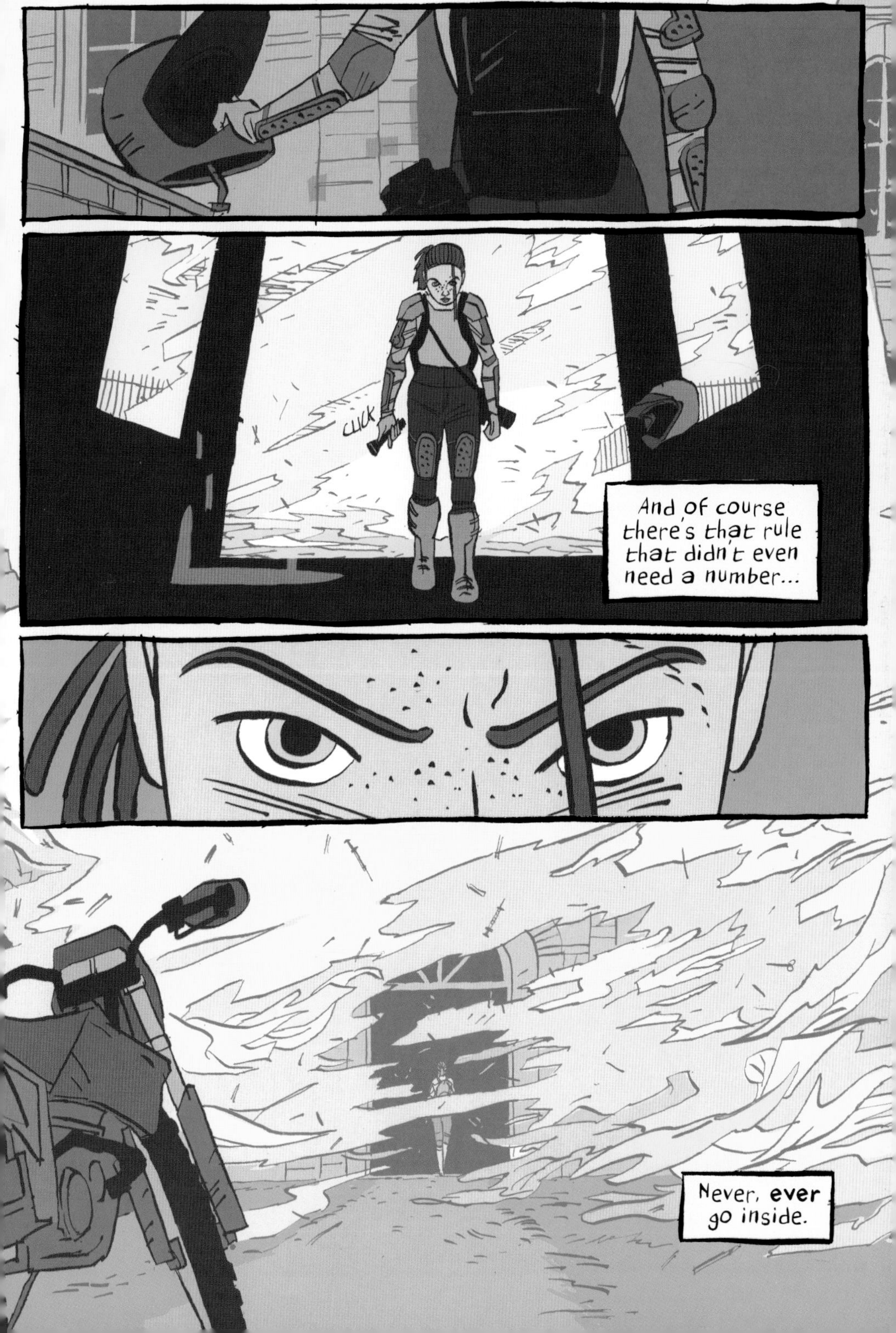
CLICK
And of course there's that rule that didn't even need a number...
Never, **ever** go inside.

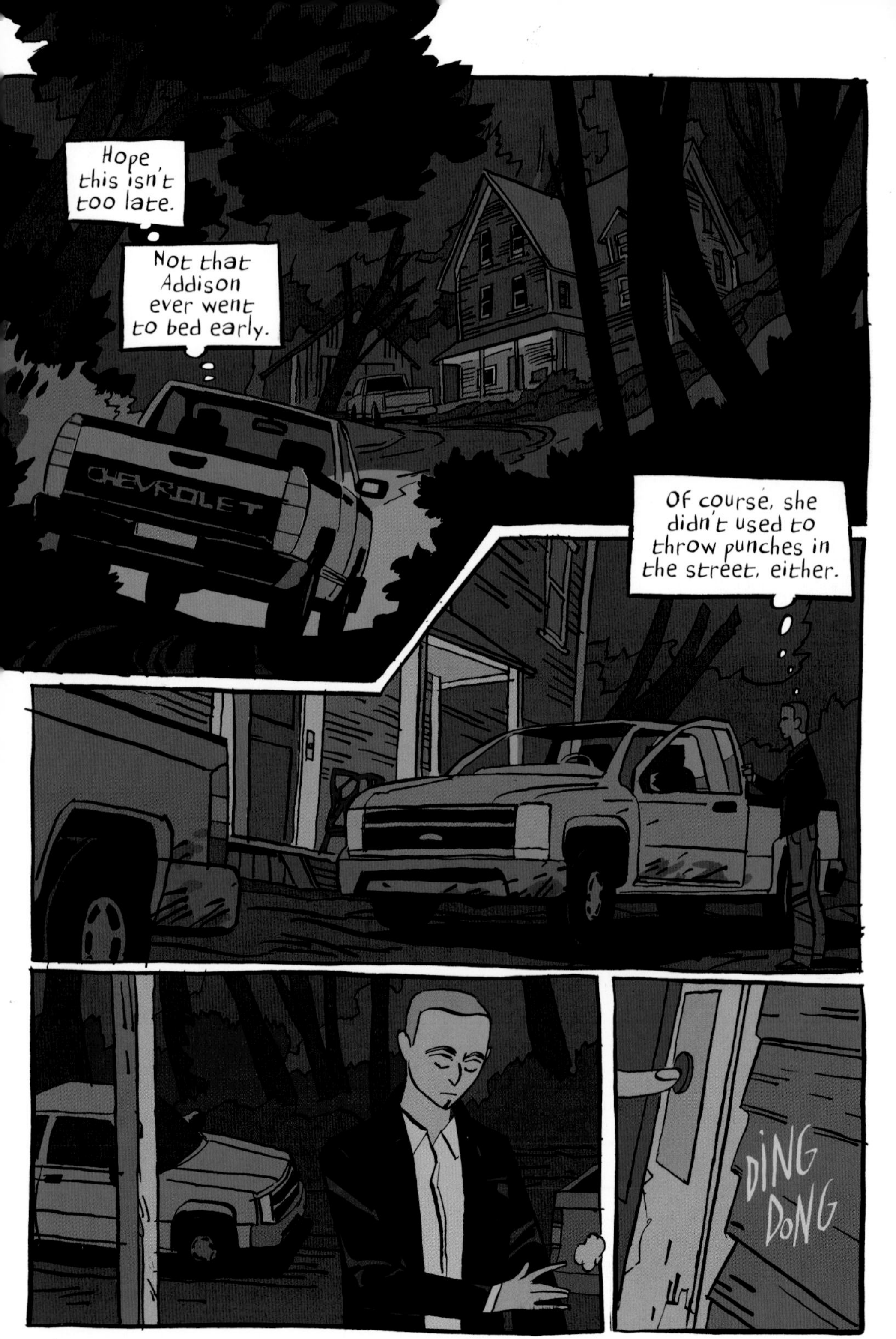
Hope this isn't too late.
Not that Addison ever went to bed early.
CHEVROLET
Of course, she didn't used to throw punches in the street, either.
DING DONG

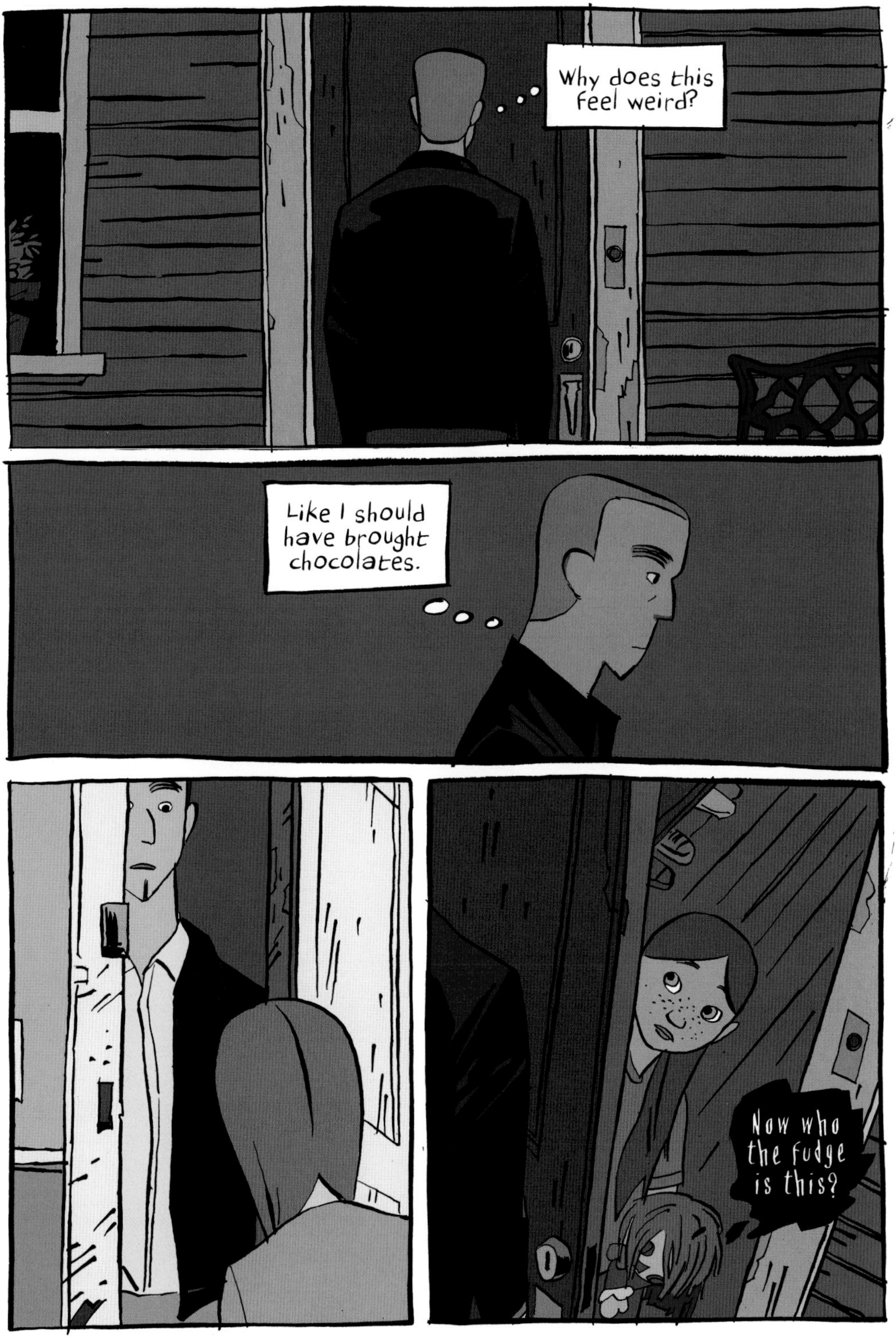
Why does this feel weird?
Like I should have brought chocolates.
Now who the fudge is this?

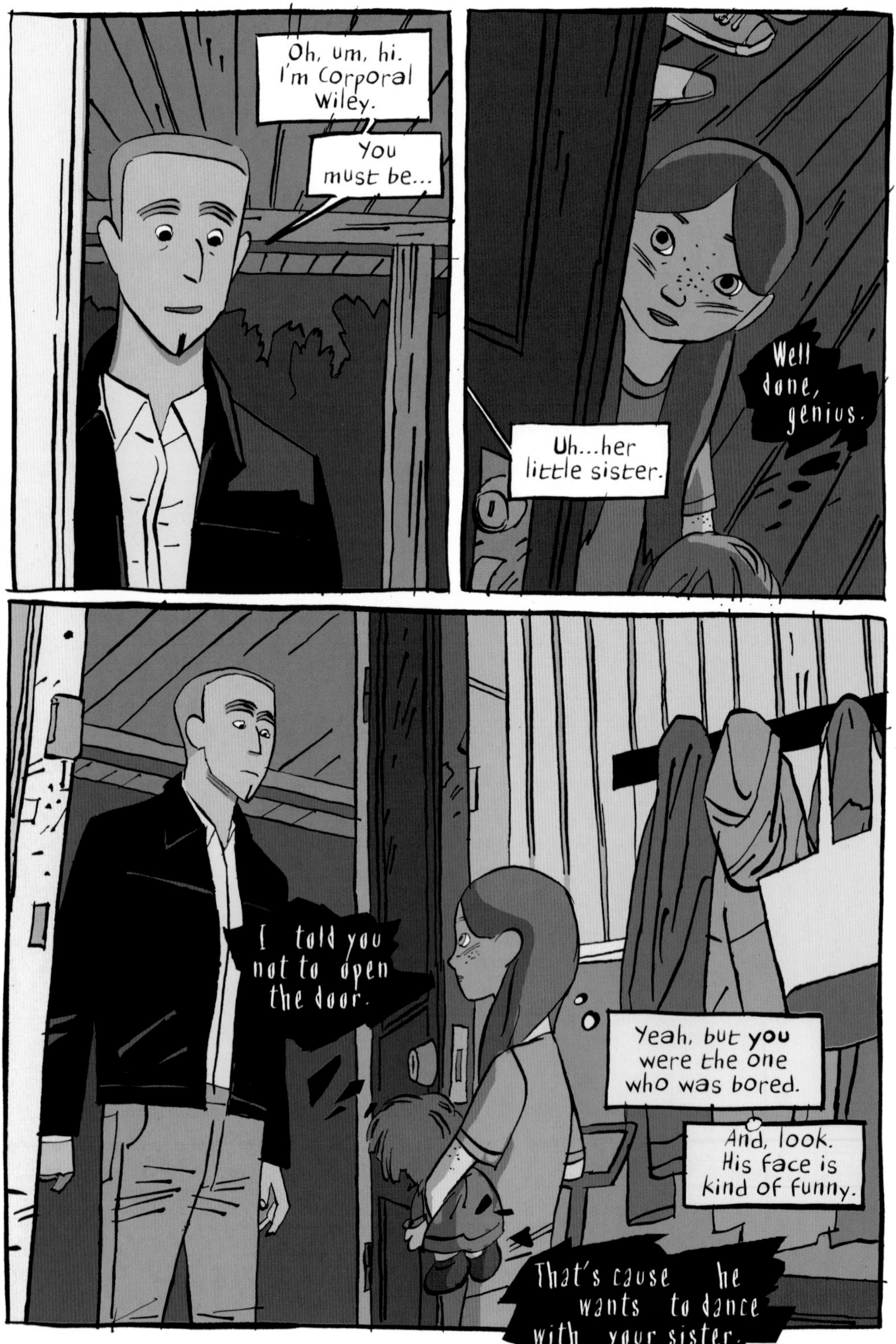
Oh, um, hi. I'm Corporal Wiley.
You must be...
Uh...her little sister.
Well done, genius.
I told you not to open the door.
Yeah, but you were the one who was bored.
And, look. His face is kind of funny.
That's cause he wants to dance with your sister.

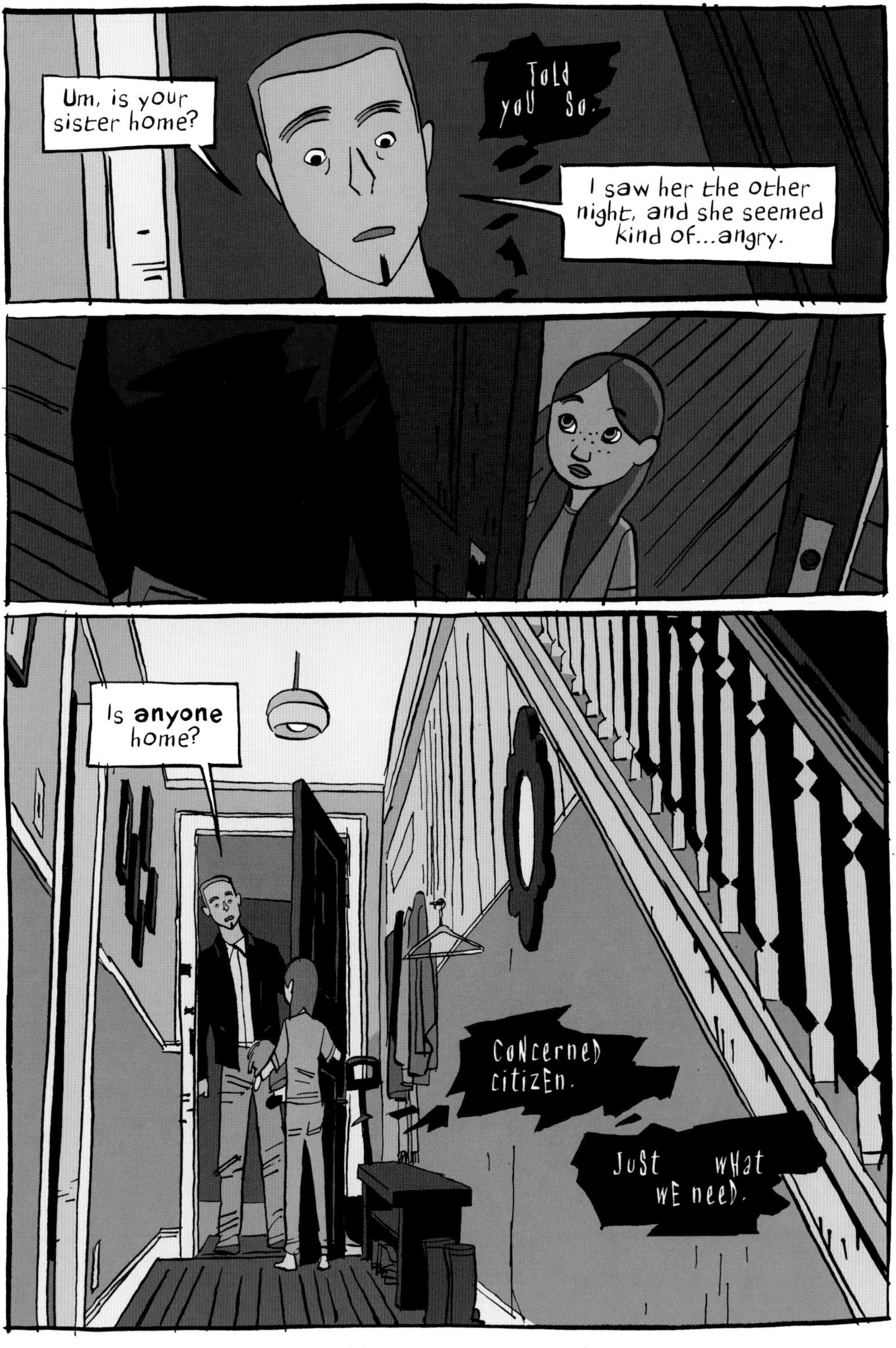

Um, is your sister home?
Told you so.
I saw her the other night, and she seemed kind of...angry.
Is **anyone** home?
Concerned citizen.
Just what we need.

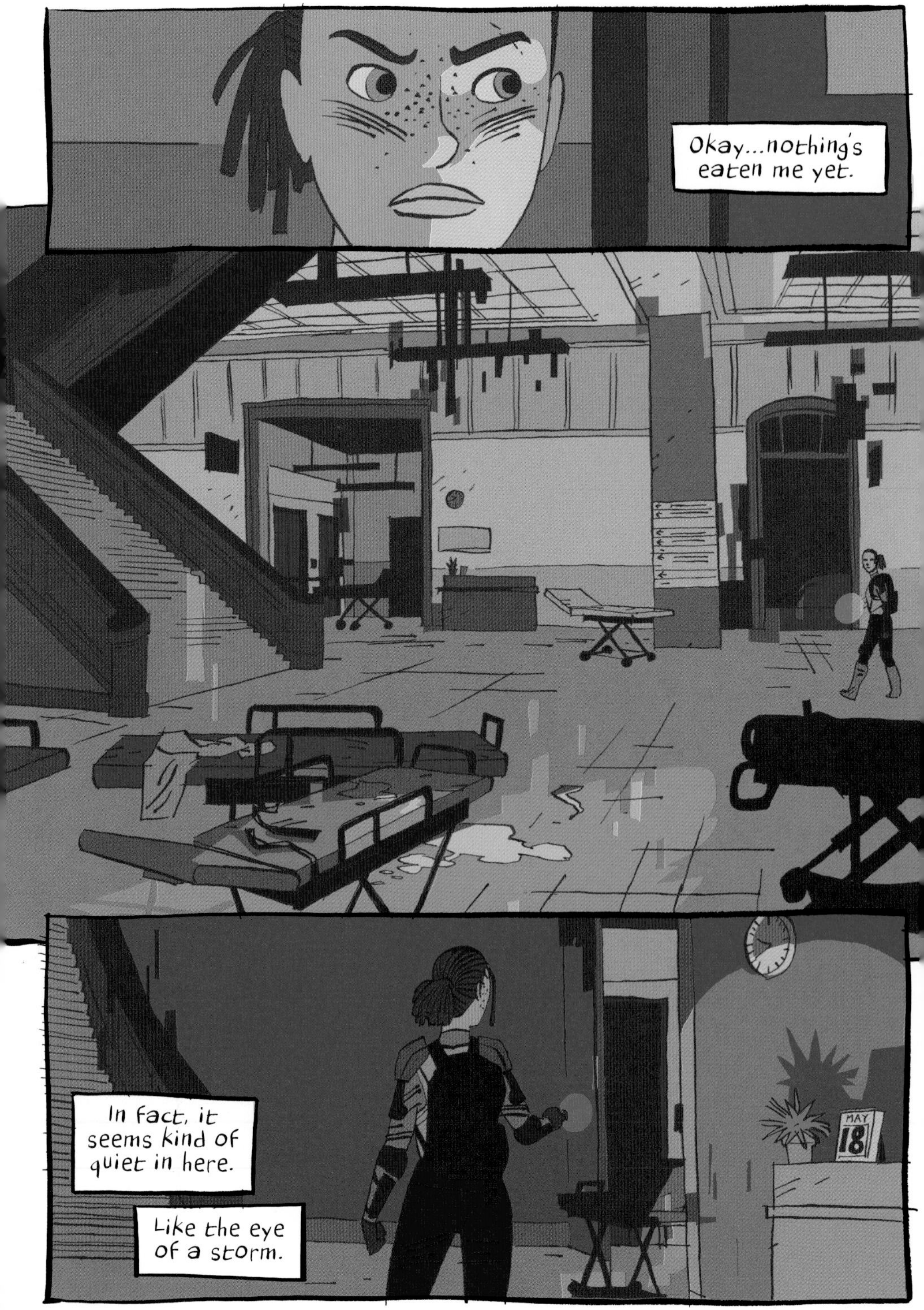
Okay...nothing's eaten me yet.
In fact, it seems kind of quiet in here.
Like the eye of a storm.
MAY
18

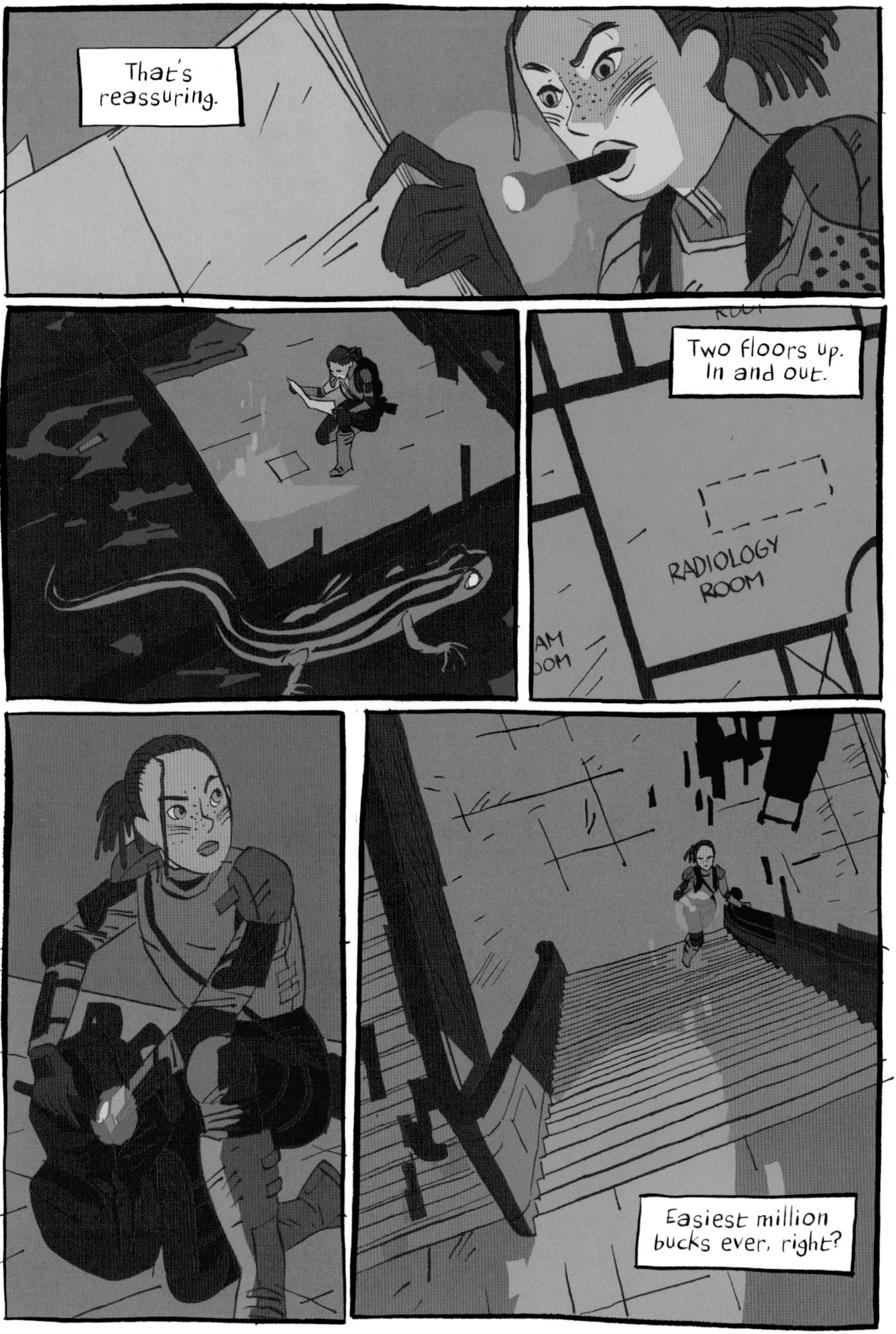
That's reassuring.
Two floors up. In and out.
RADIOLOGY ROOM
Easiest million bucks ever, right?

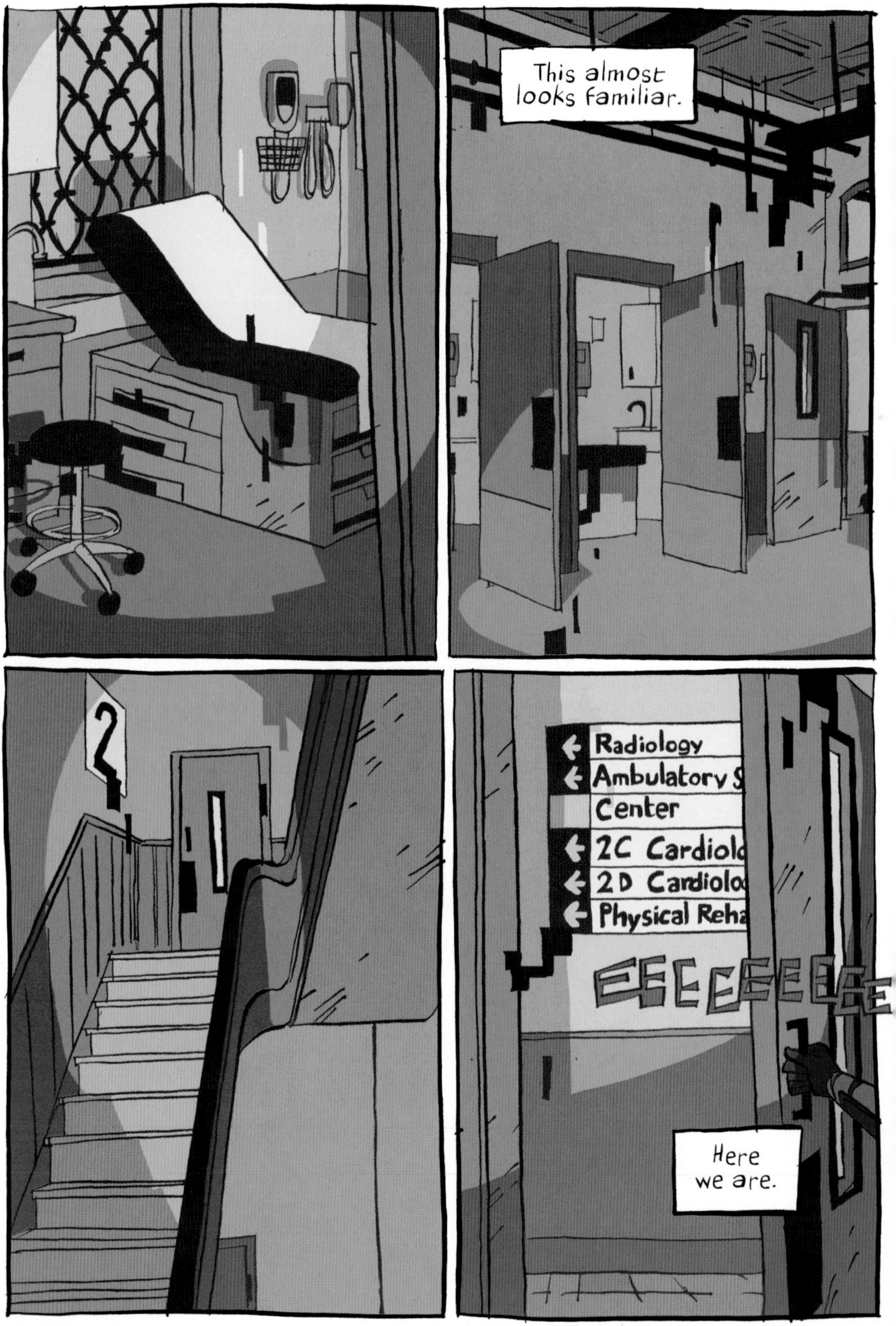
This almost looks familiar.
2
Radiology
Ambulatory S
Center
2C Cardiolo
2D Cardiolo
Physical Reha
EEEEEEEE
Here we are.

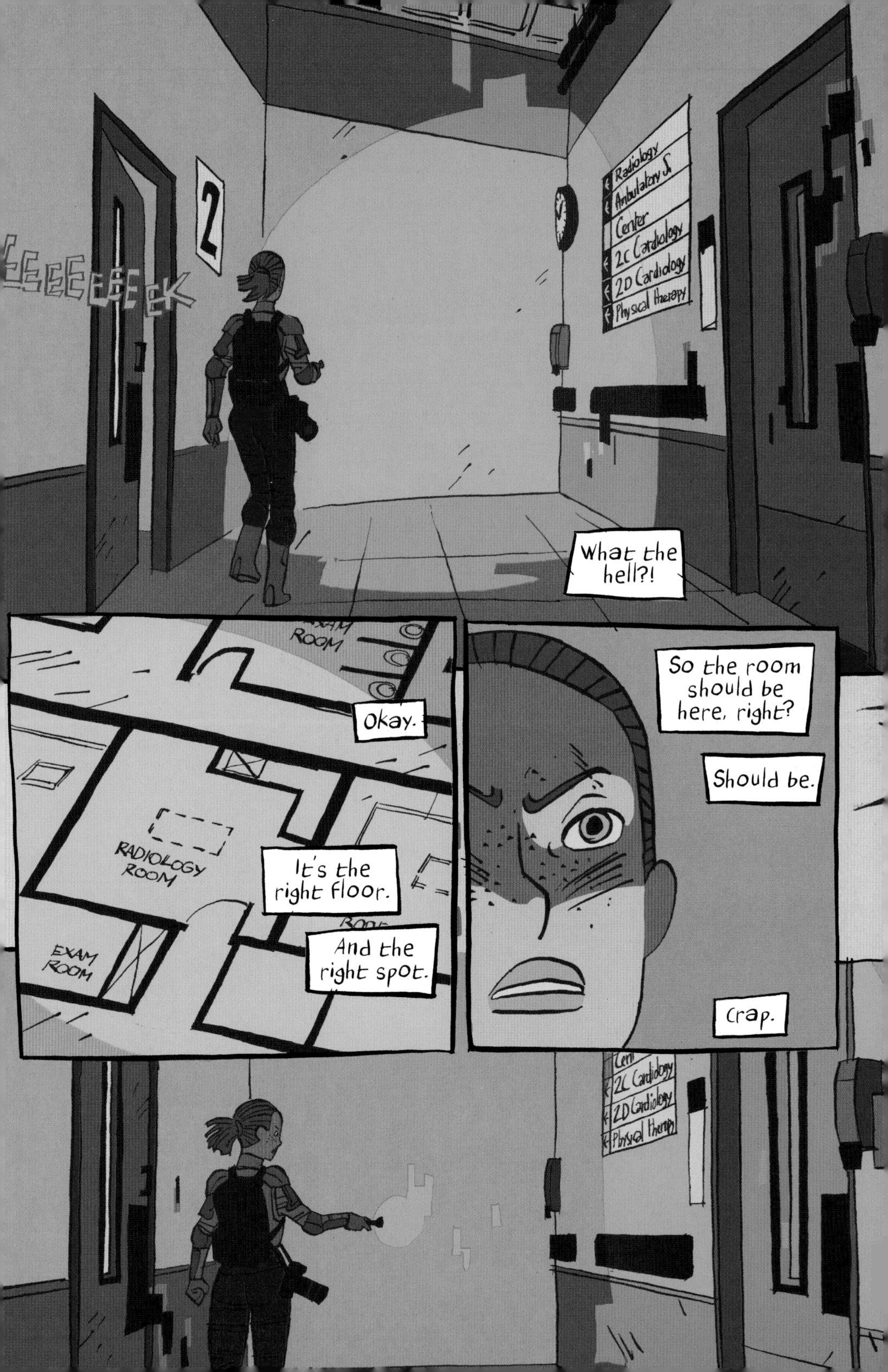
EEEEEEEEEK
2
Radiology
Ambulatory S.
Center
2C Cardiology
2D Cardiology
Physical therapy
What the hell?!
EXAM ROOM
Okay.
RADIOLOGY ROOM
EXAM ROOM
It's the right floor.
And the right spot.
So the room should be here, right?
Should be.
Crap.
2C Cardiology
2D Cardiology
Physical therapy

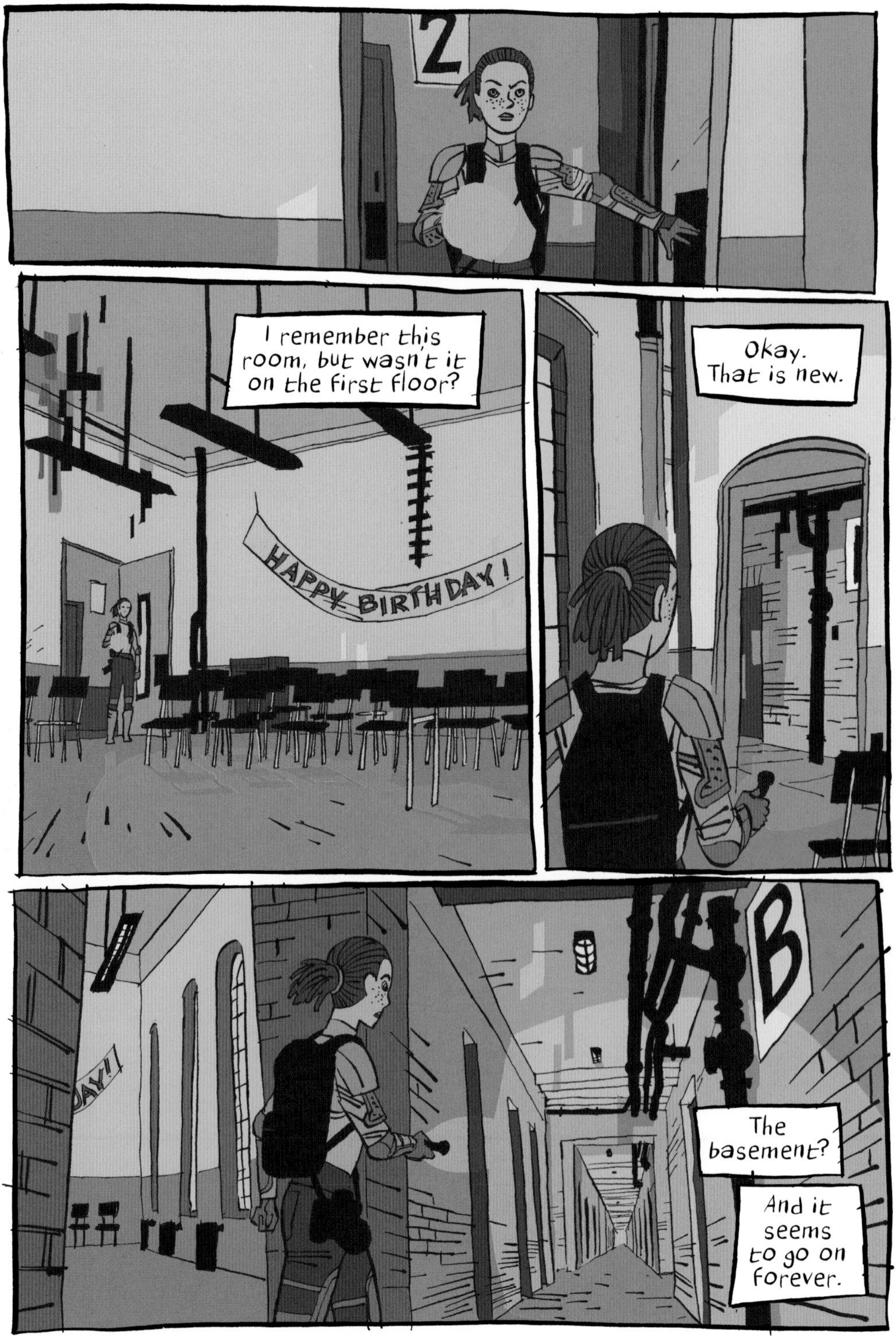
2
I remember this room, but wasn't it on the first floor?
HAPPY BIRTHDAY!
Okay. That is new.
DAY!
B
The basement?
And it seems to go on forever.

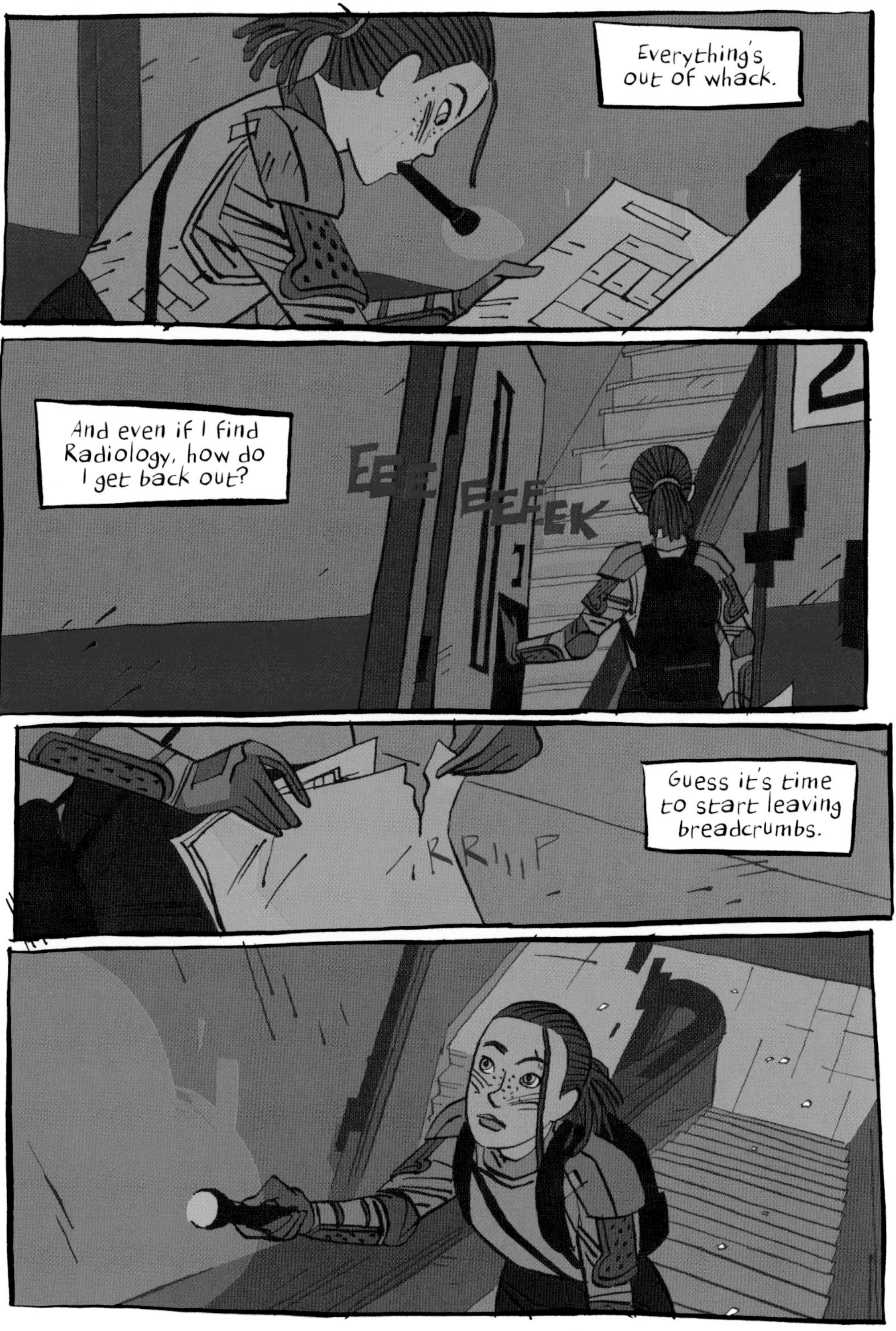
Everything's out of whack.
And even if I find Radiology, how do I get back out?
EEEE EEEEEK
Guess it's time to start leaving breadcrumbs.
RRIIIP

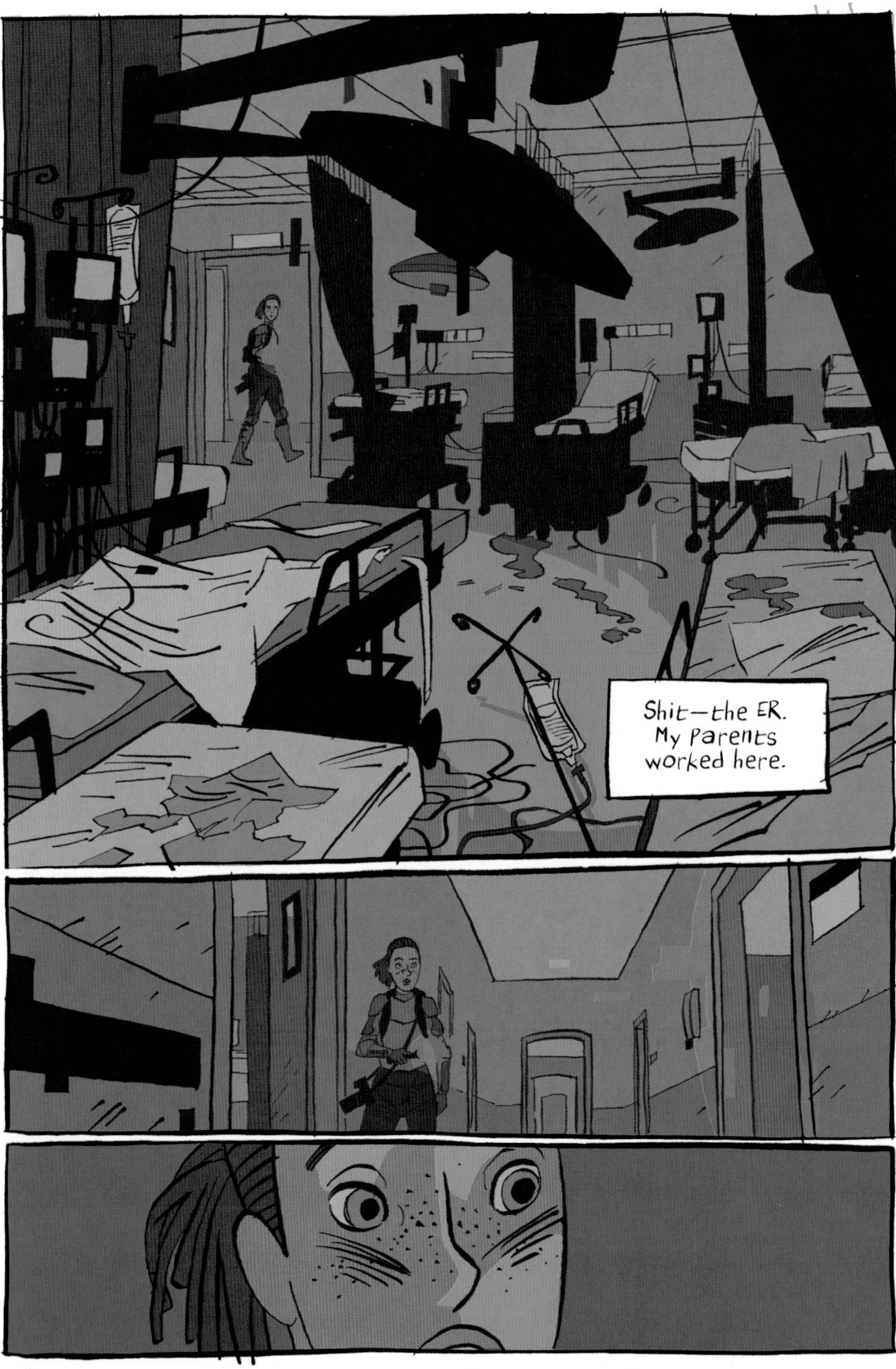
Shit—the ER. My parents worked here.

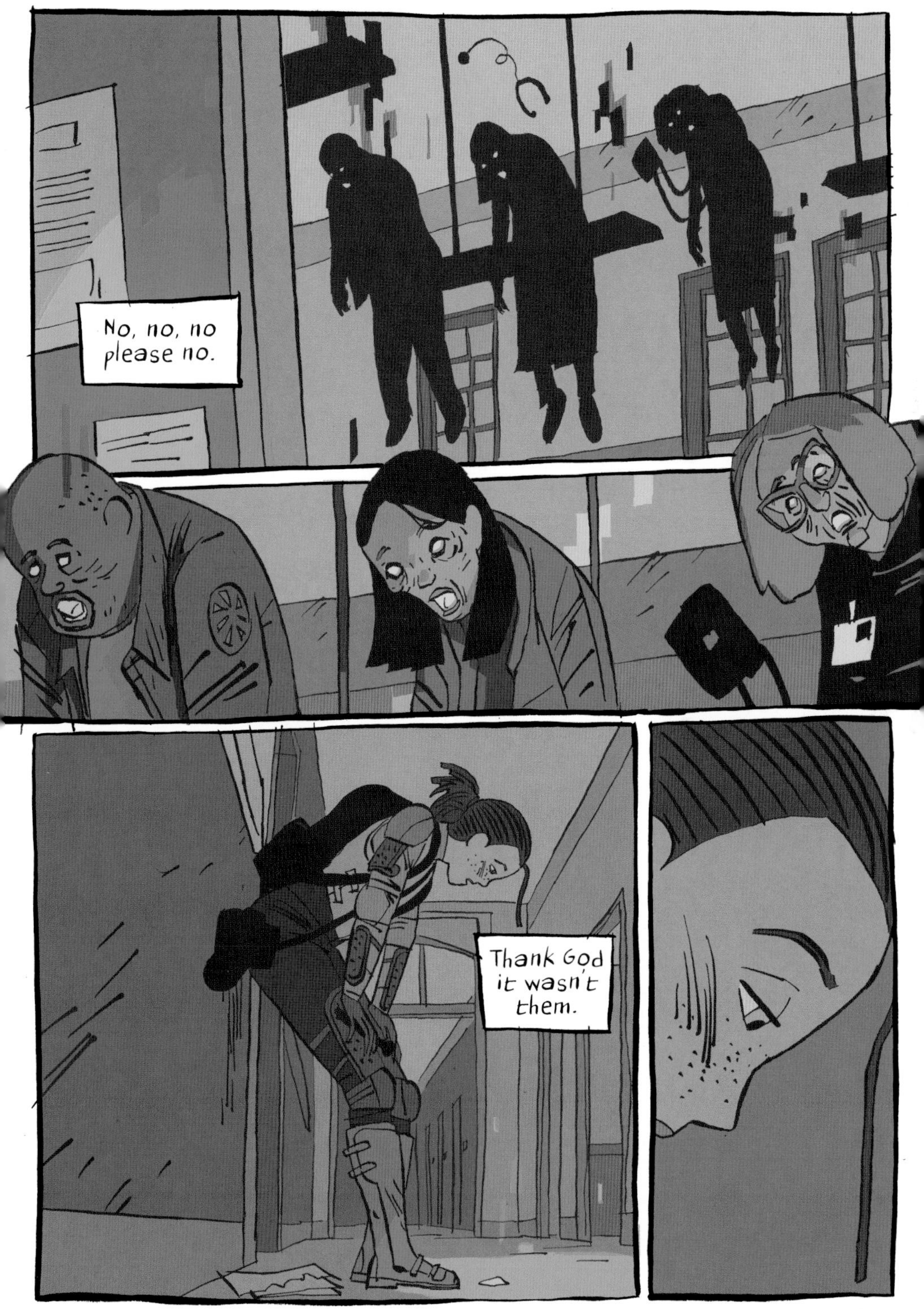
No, no, no please no.
Thank God it wasn't them.

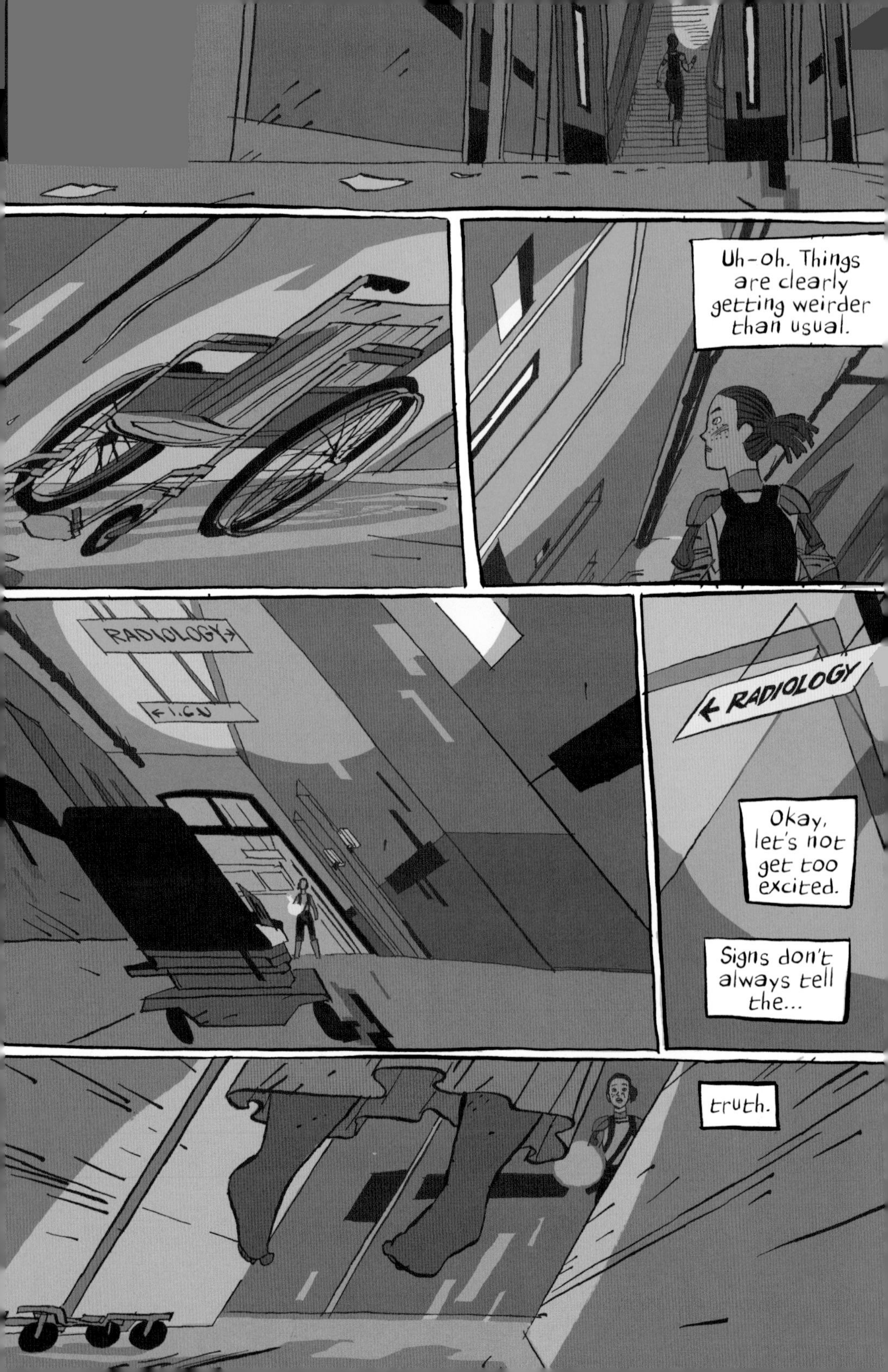
Uh-oh. Things are clearly getting weirder than usual.
RADIOLOGY→
← RADIOLOGY
Okay, let's not get too excited.
Signs don't always tell the...
truth.

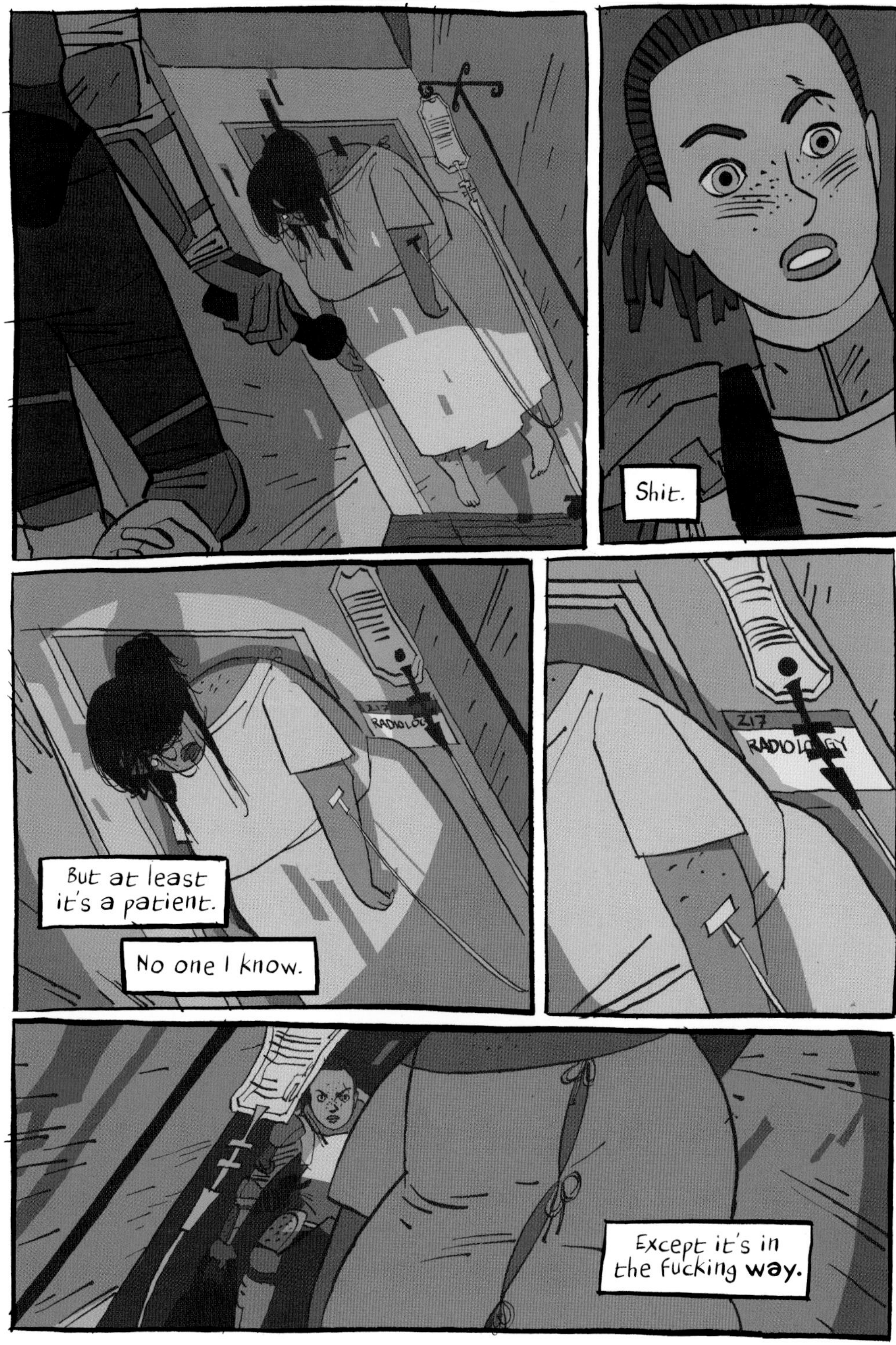
Shit.
217
RADIOLOGY
But at least it's a patient.
No one I know.
217
RADIOLOGY
Except it's in the fucking way.

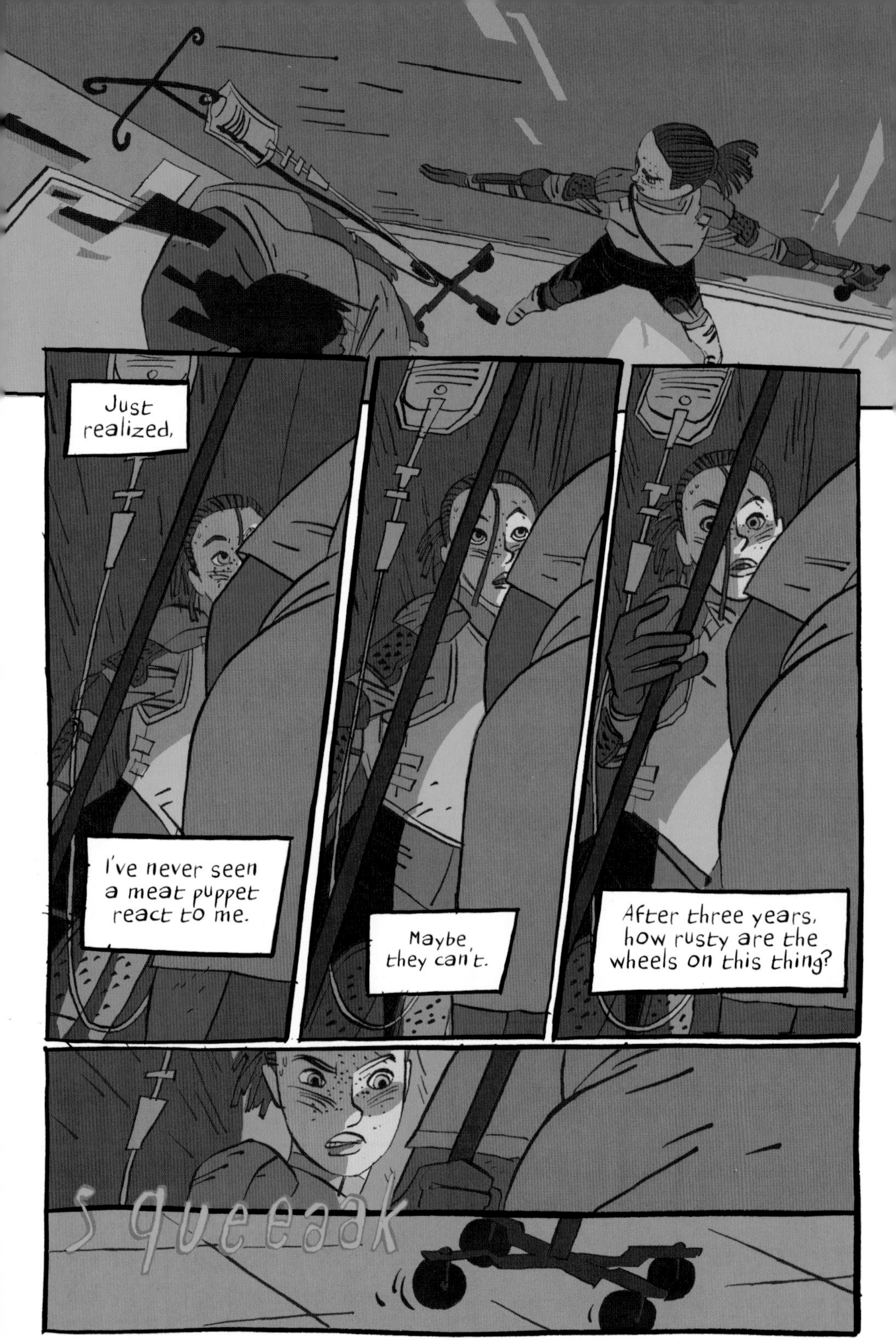
Just realized,
I've never seen a meat puppet react to me.
Maybe they can't.
After three years, how rusty are the wheels on this thing?
squeeaak

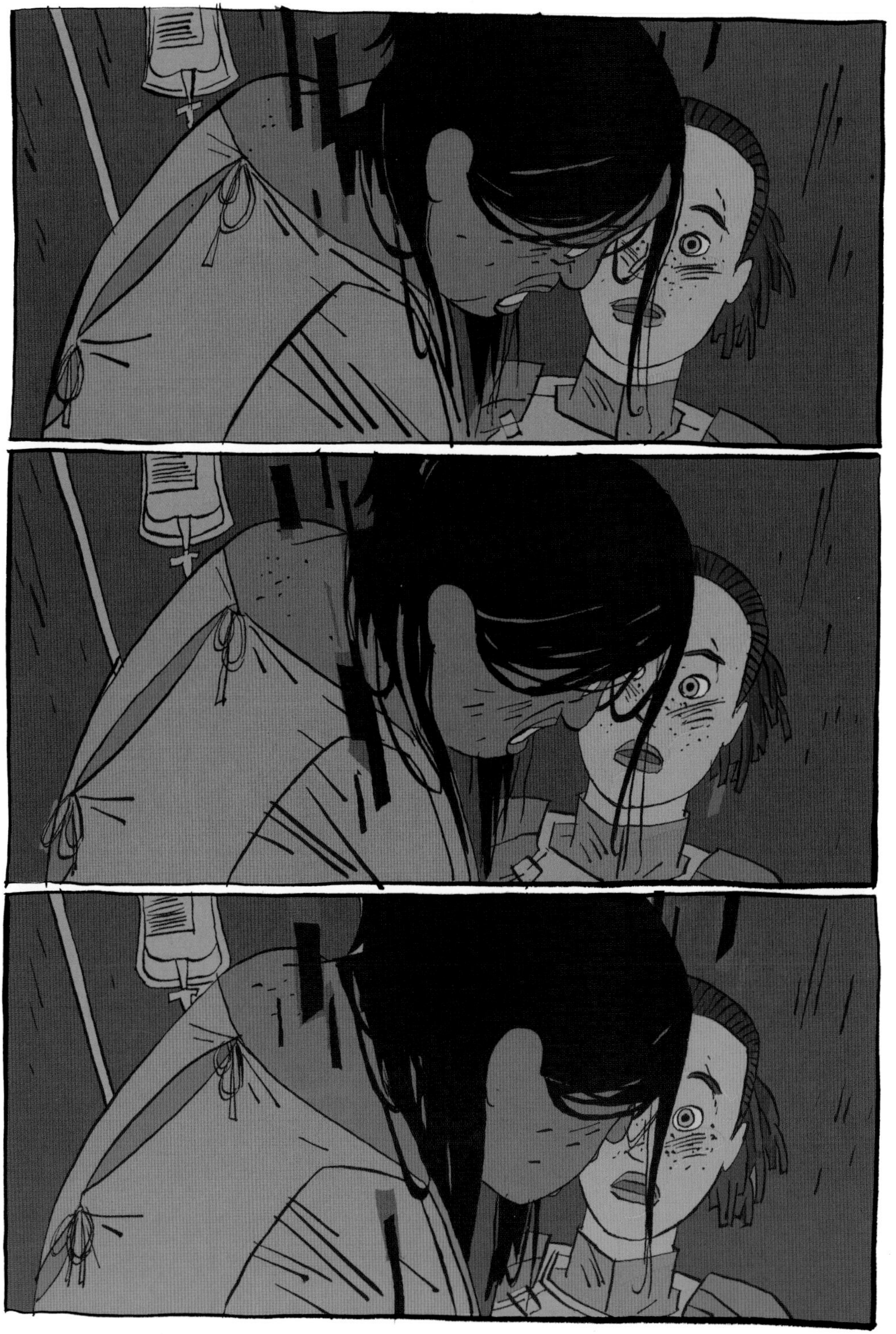

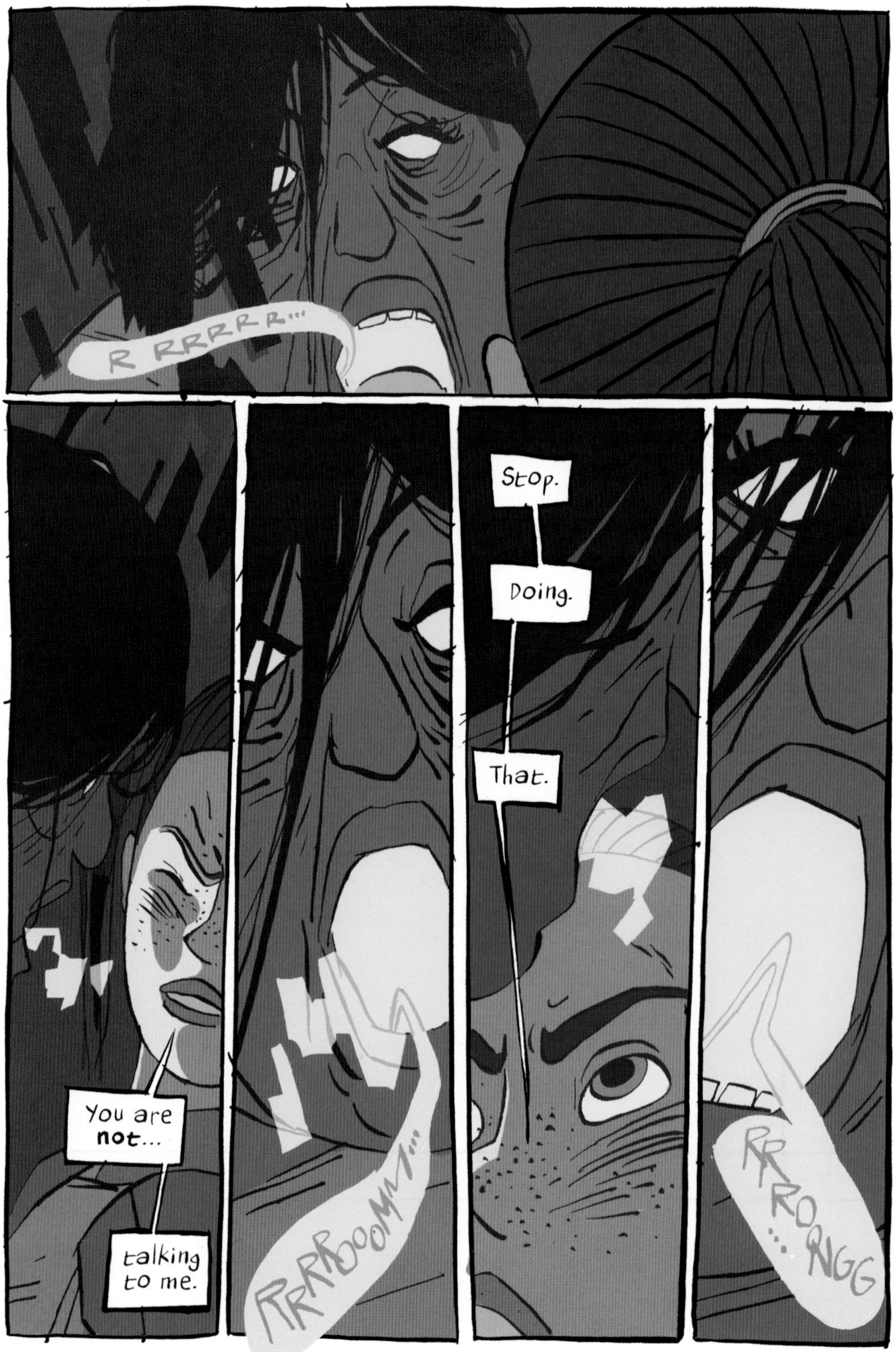
R RRRRR...
You are **not**...
talking to me.
RRRROOOMM...
Stop.
Doing.
That.
RRRONGG...

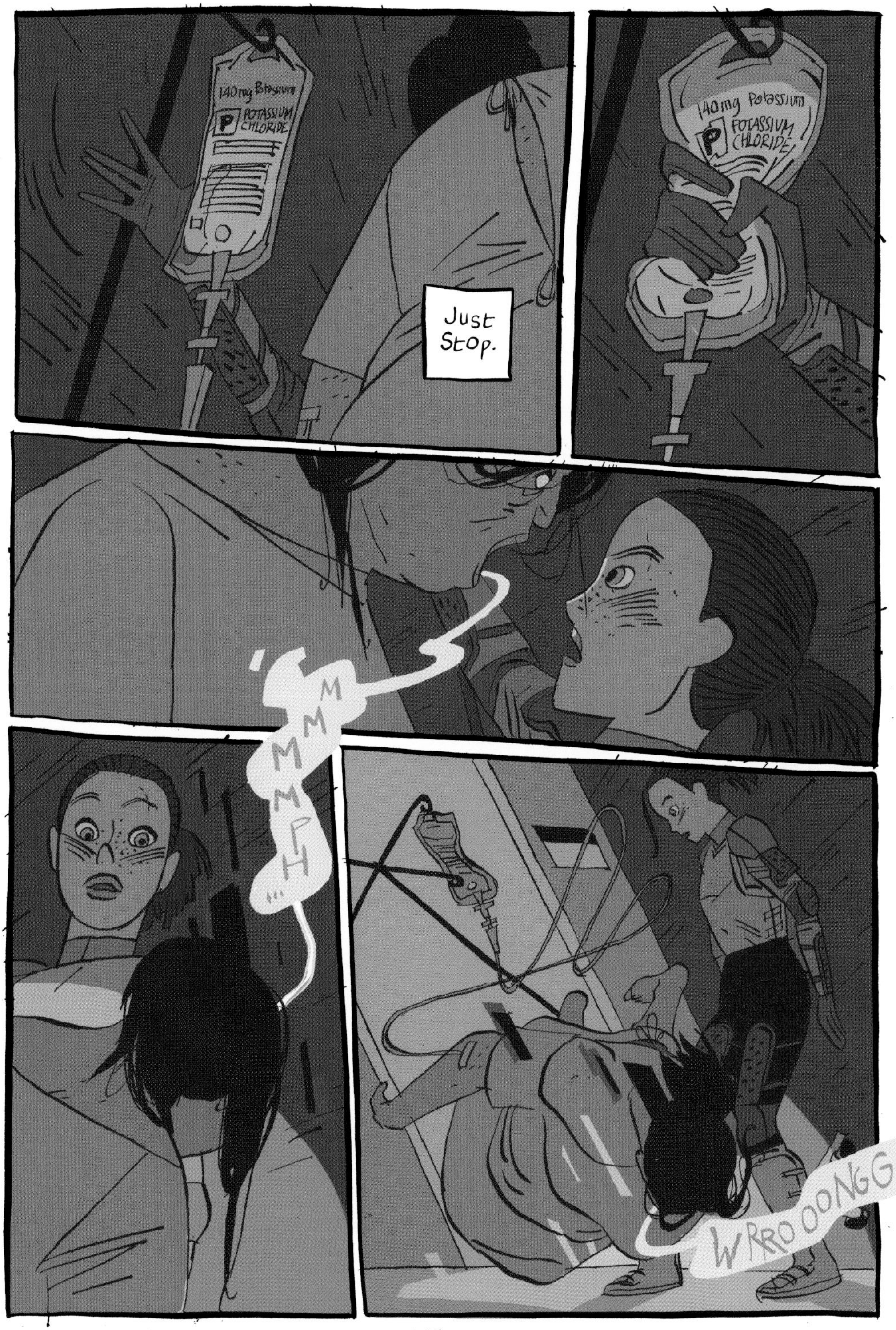
140mg Potassium
POTASSIUM CHLORIDE
Just Stop.
140mg Potassium
POTASSIUM CHLORIDE
MMMMMPH...
WRROOONGG

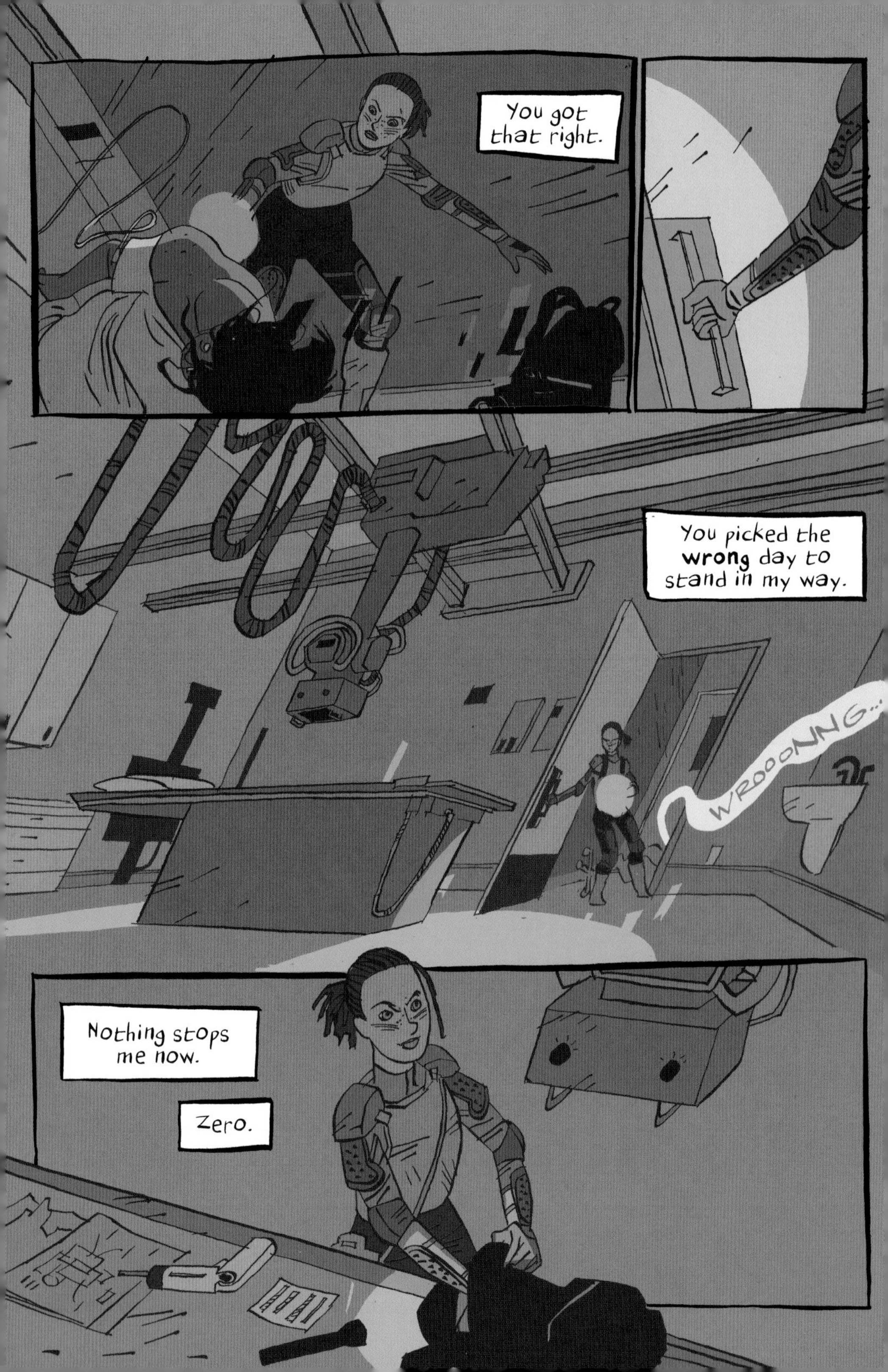
You got that right.
You picked the **wrong** day to stand in my way.
WROOONNG...
Nothing stops me now.
Zero.

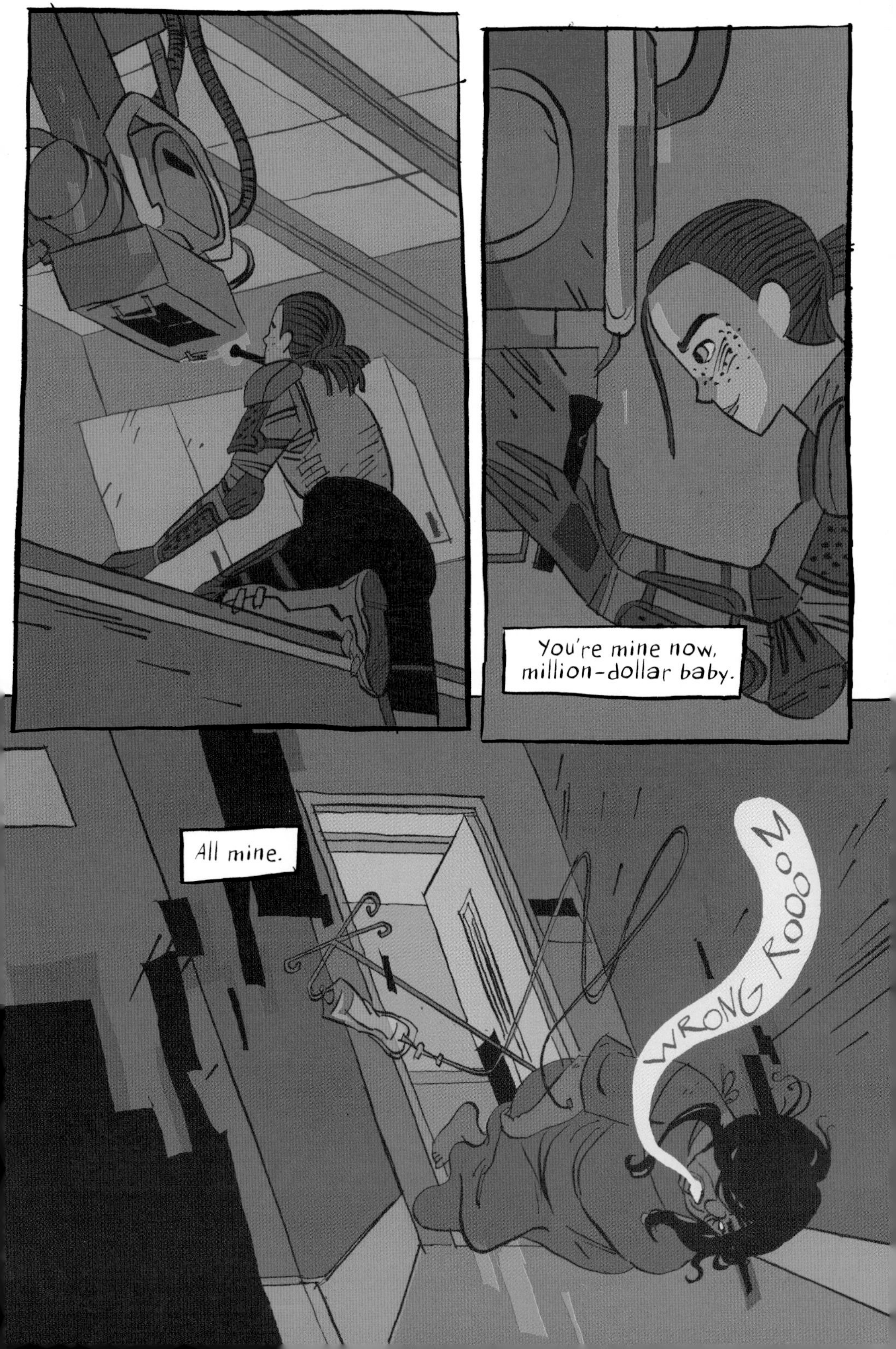
You're mine now, million-dollar baby.
All mine.
WRONG ROOOOOM

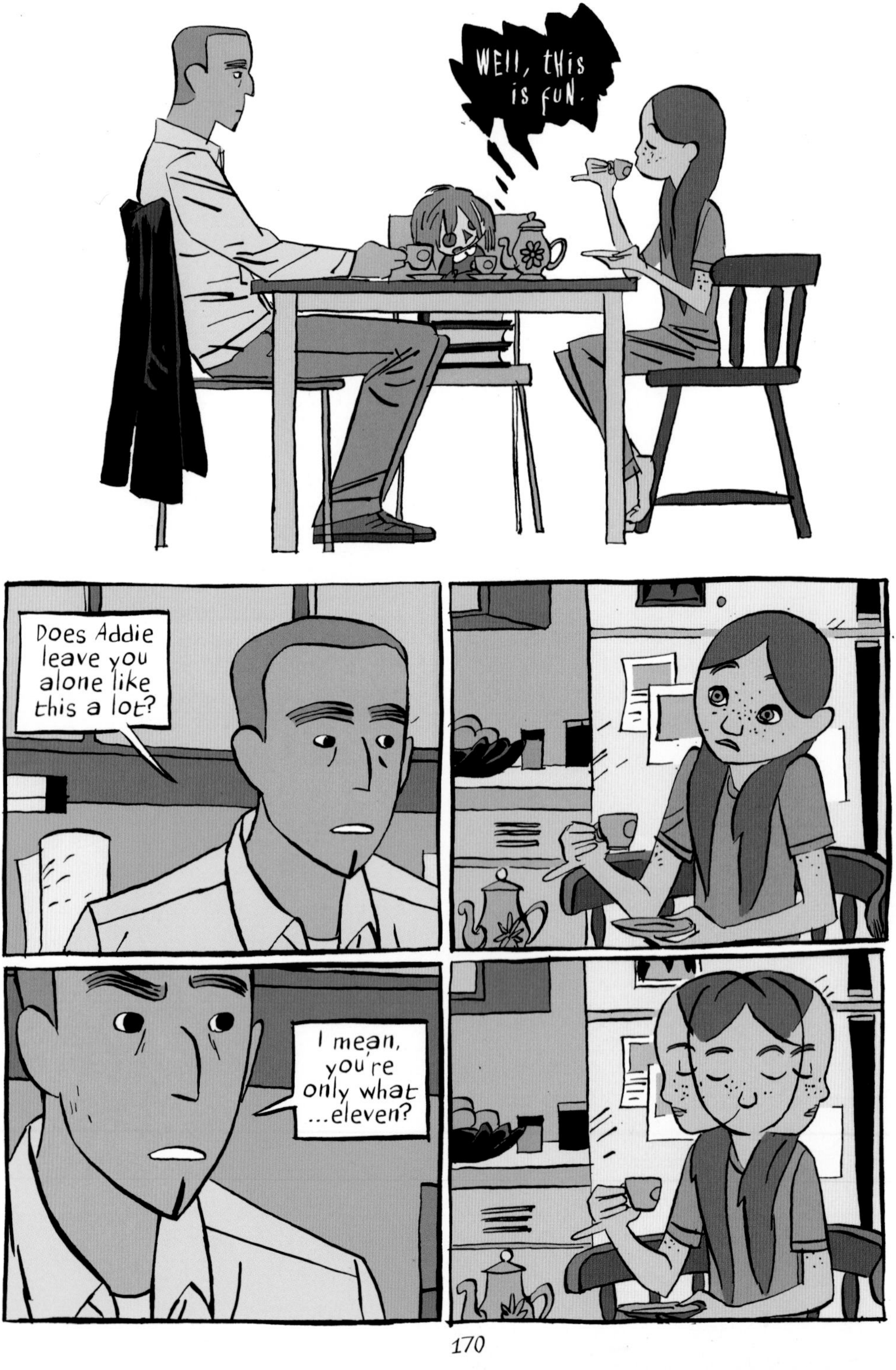
WELL, THIS IS FUN.
Does Addie leave you alone like this a lot?
I mean, you're only what ...eleven?

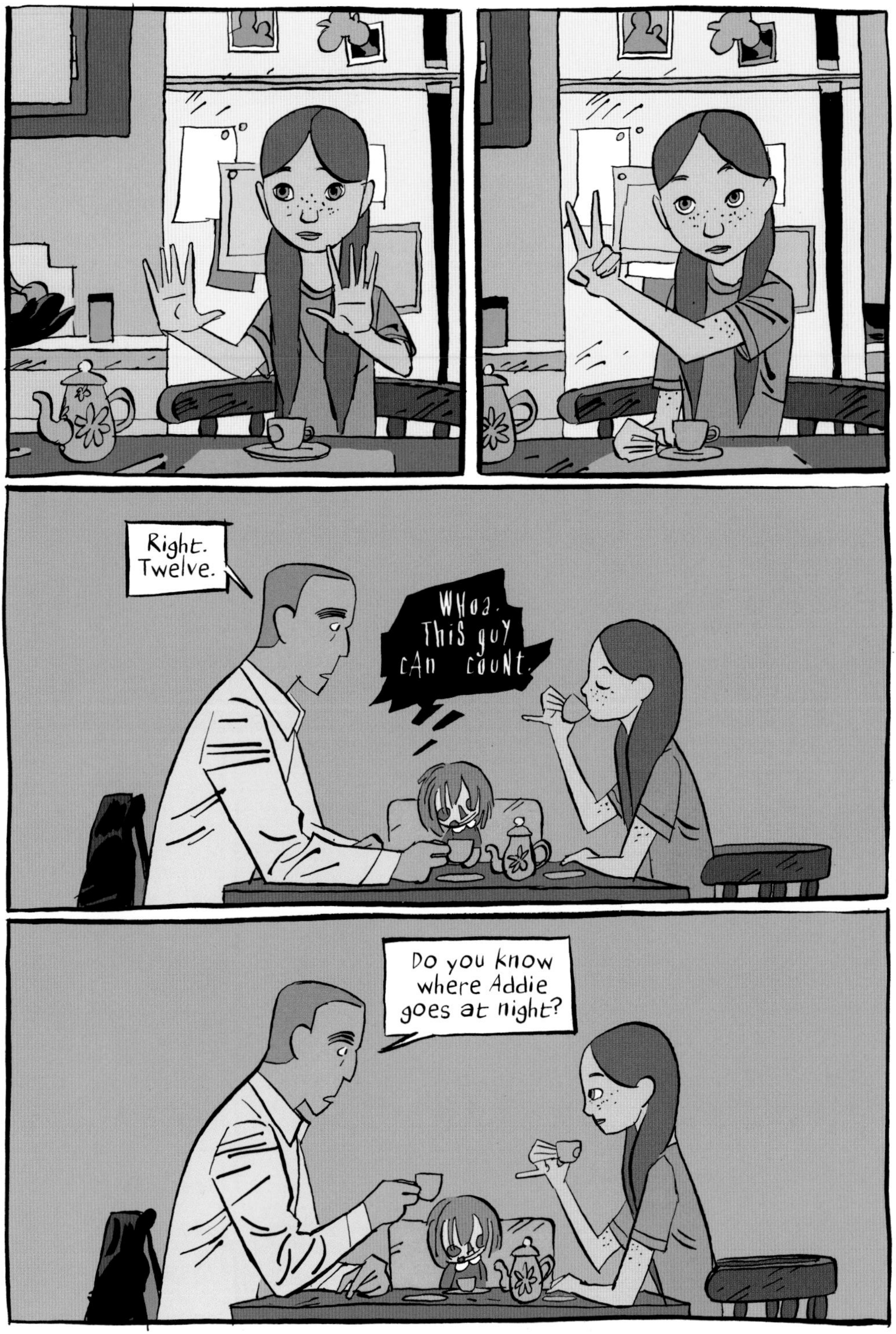
Right. Twelve.
WHOA. THIS GUY CAN COUNT.
Do you know where Addie goes at night?

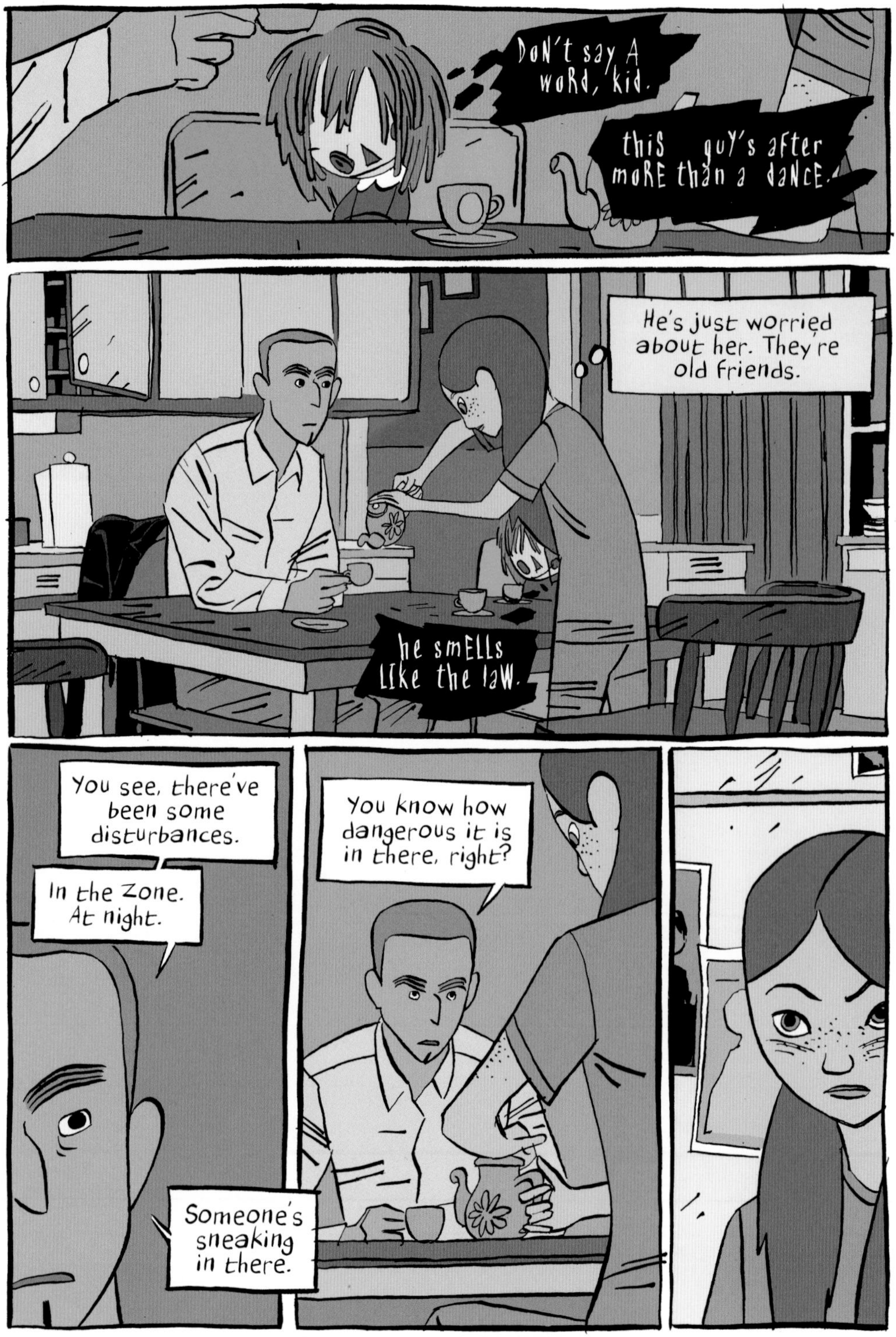
Don't say a word, kid.
this guy's after more than a dance.
He's just worried about her. They're old friends.
he smells like the law.
You see, there've been some disturbances.
In the Zone. At night.
Someone's sneaking in there.
You know how dangerous it is in there, right?

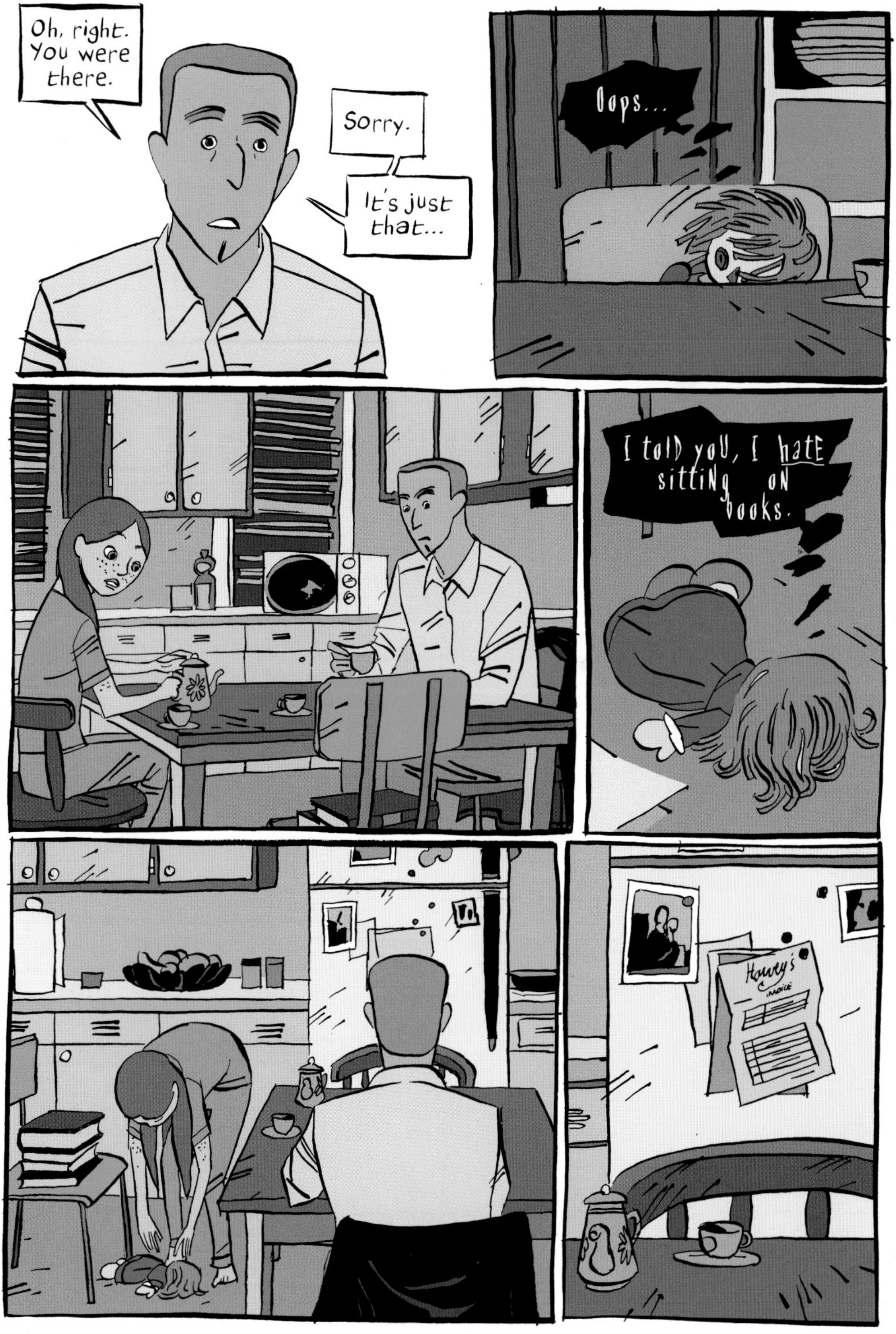
Oh, right. You were there.
Sorry.
It's just that...
Oops...
I told you, I hate sitting on books.
Harvey's
Invoice

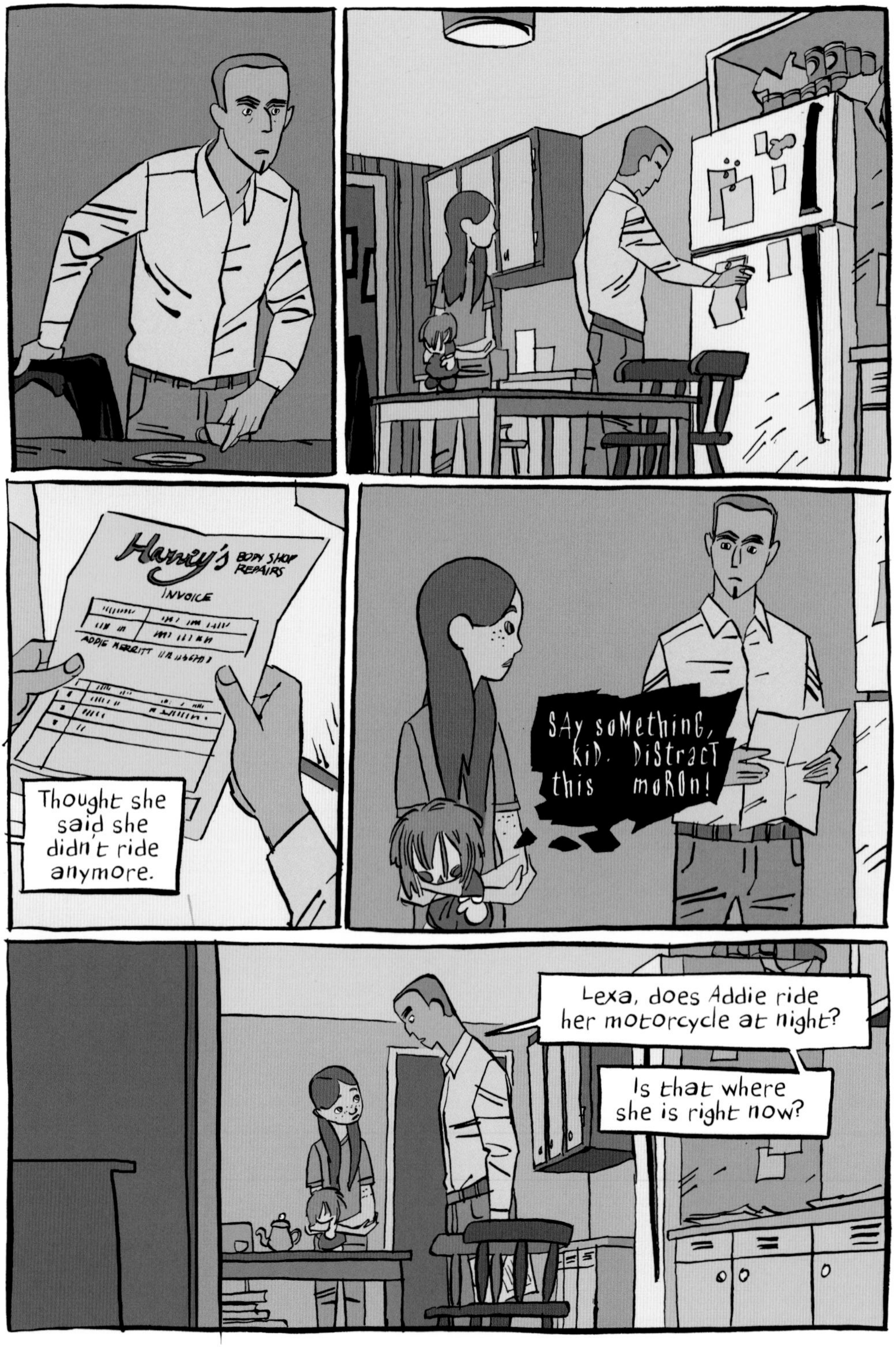
Harry's BODY SHOP REPAIRS
INVOICE
ADDIE MERRITT
Thought she said she didn't ride anymore.
SAy soMethinG, kiD. DiStracT this moROn!
Lexa, does Addie ride her motorcycle at night?
Is that where she is right now?

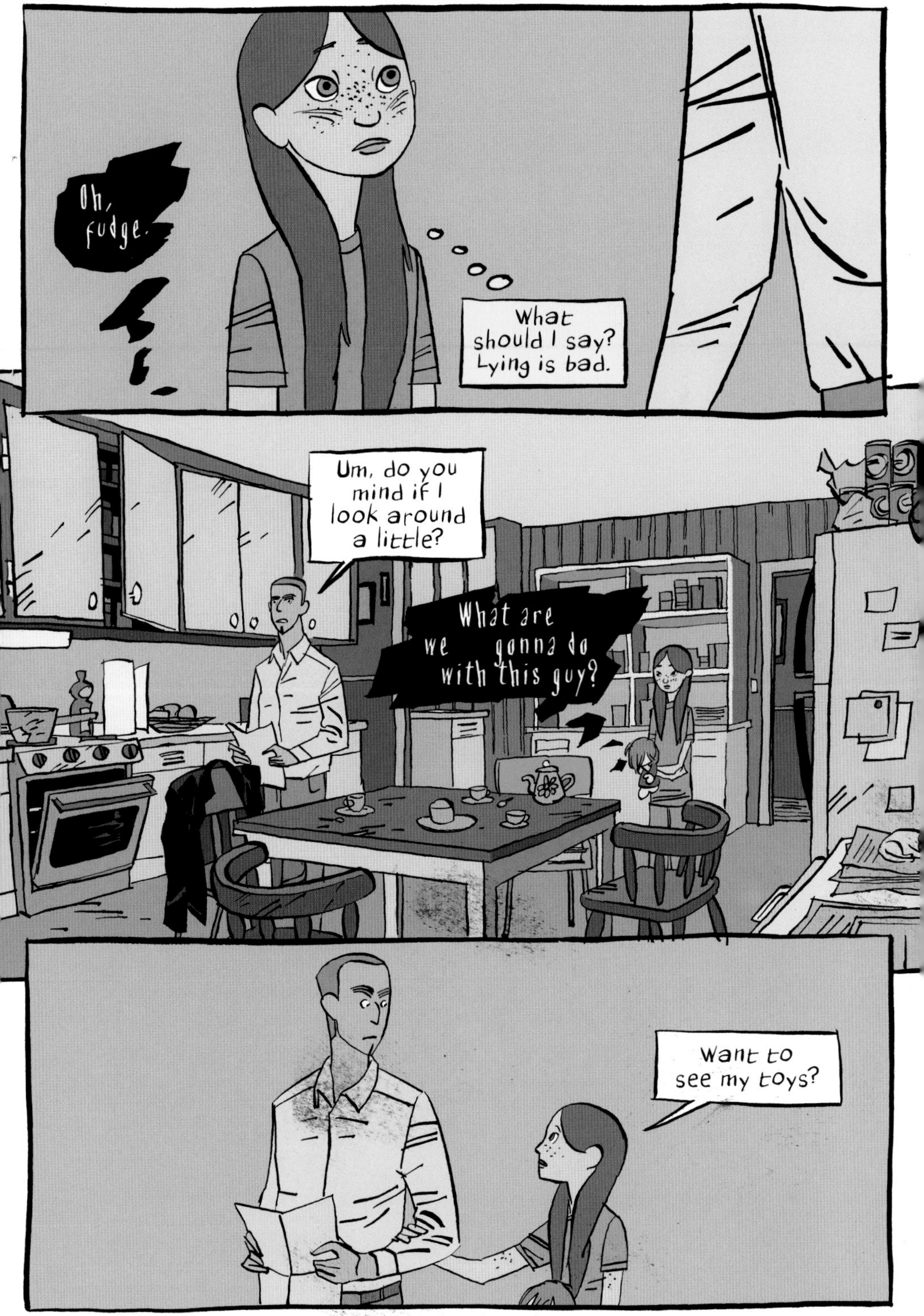
Oh, fudge.
What should I say? Lying is bad.
Um, do you mind if I look around a little?
What are we gonna do with this guy?
Want to see my toys?

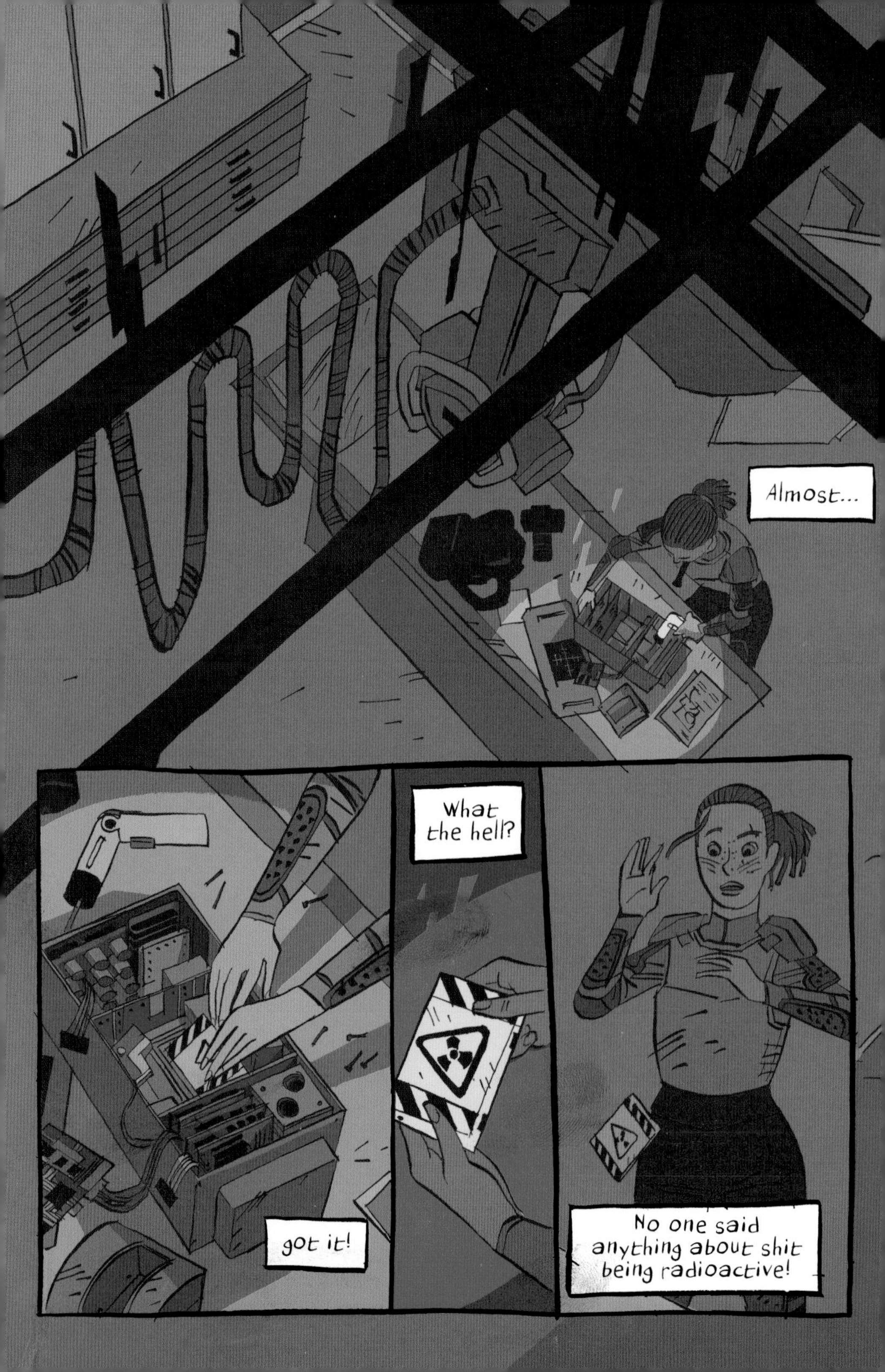

Almost...
got it!
What the hell?
No one said anything about shit being radioactive!

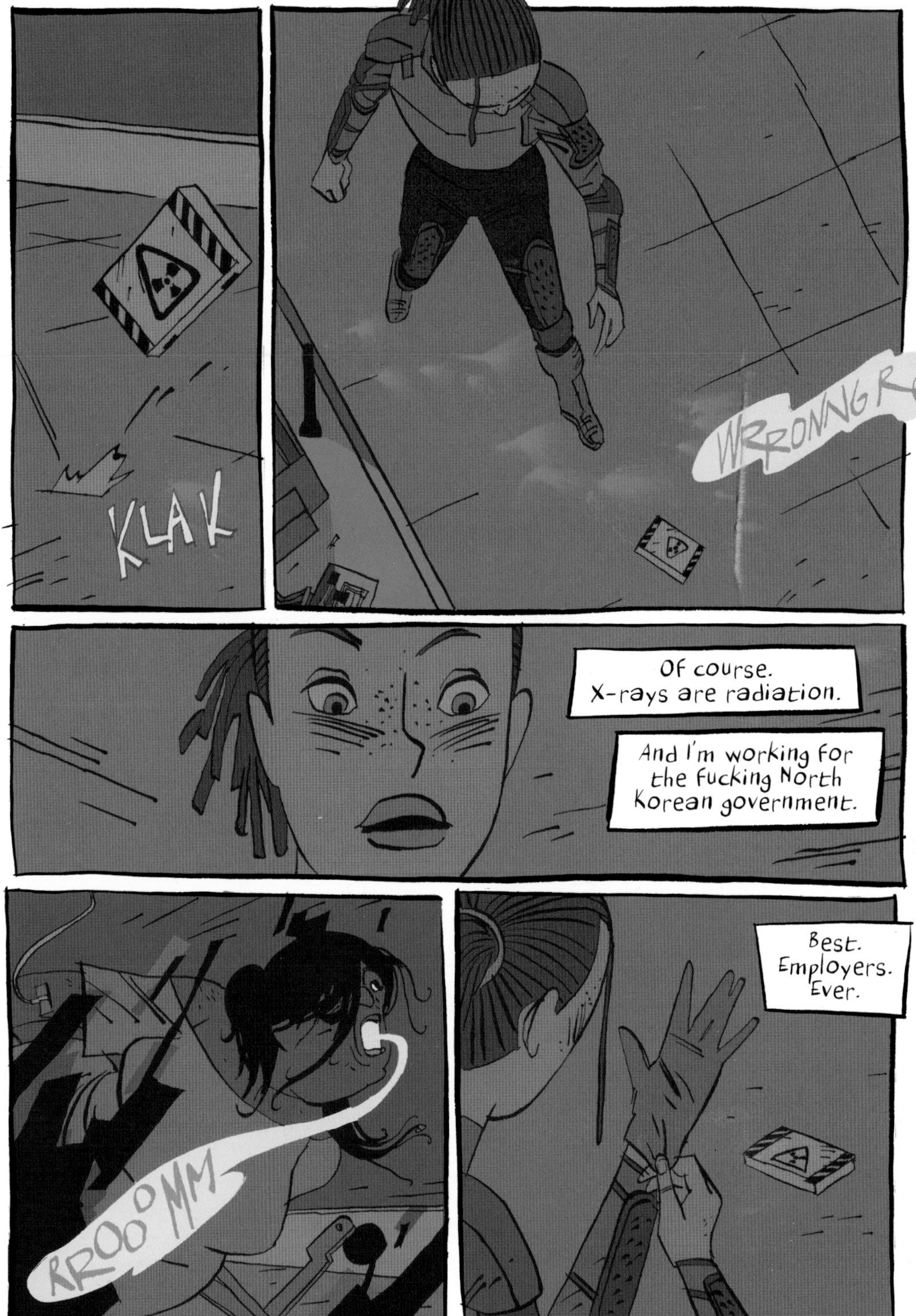
KLAK
WRRONNGRO
Of course.
X-rays are radiation.
And I'm working for the fucking North Korean government.
RROOOMM
Best. Employers. Ever.

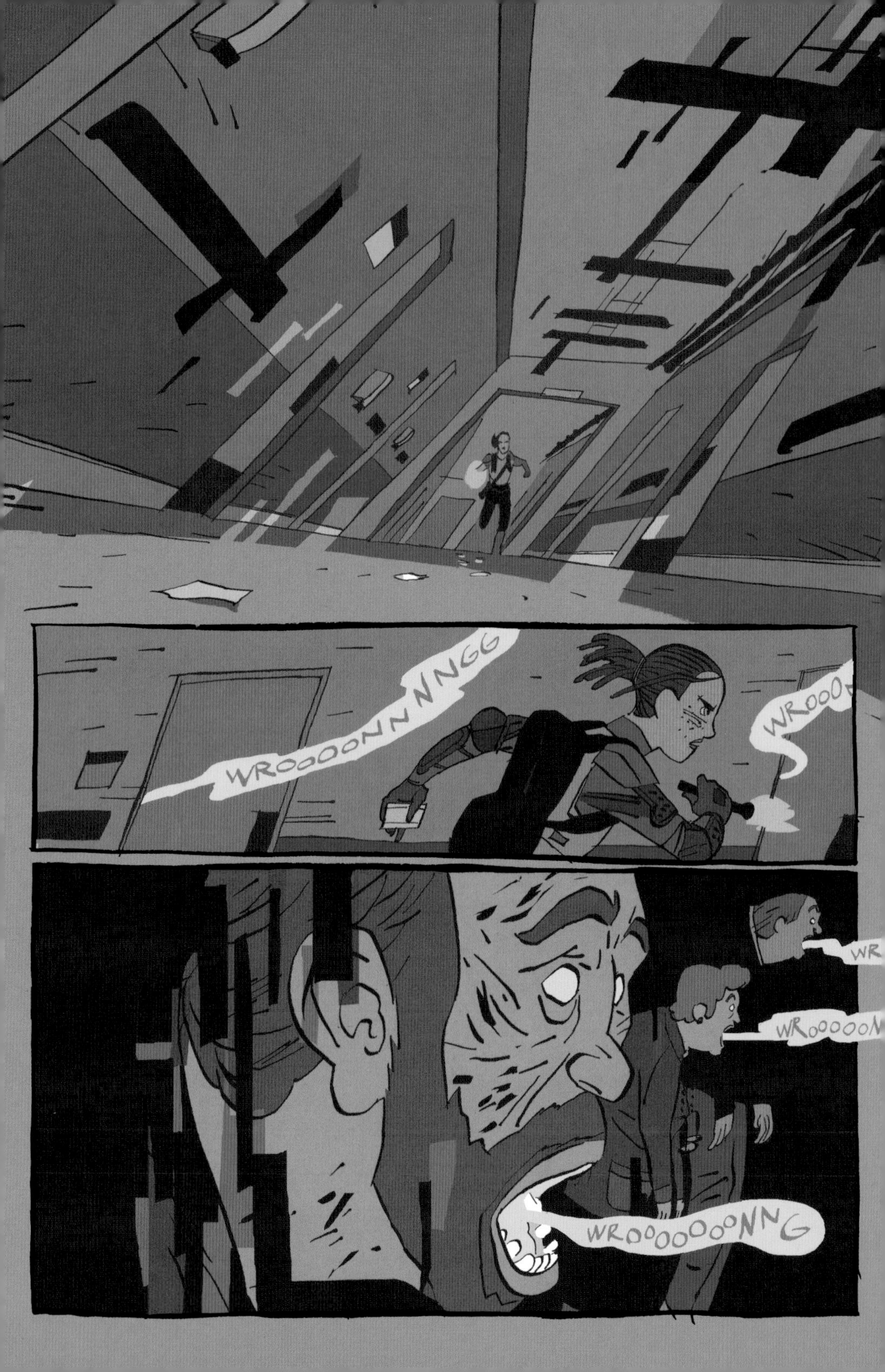
WROOOOONNNNGG
WROOO
WR
WROOOOON
WROOOOOOONNG

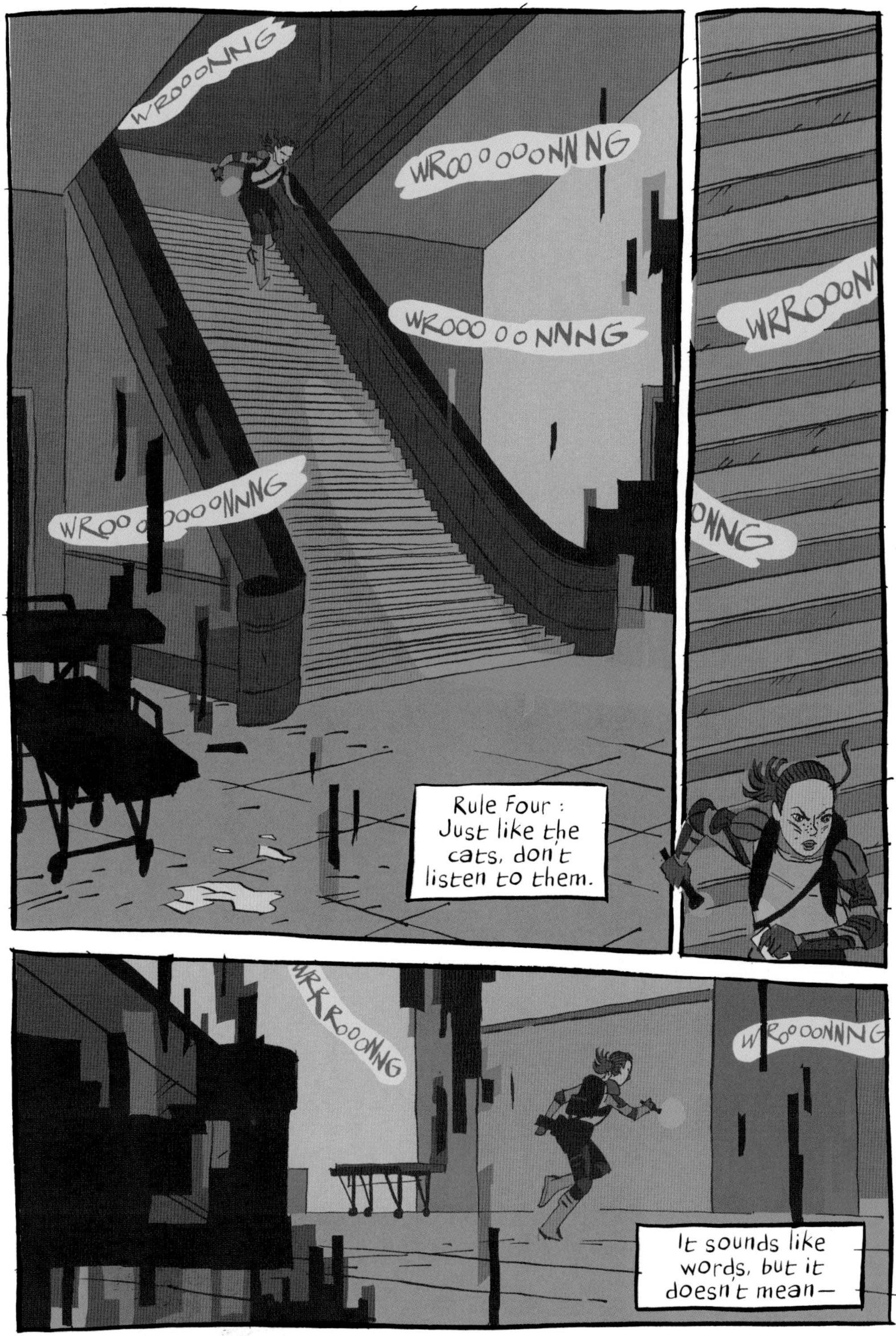
WROOONNG
WROOOOOONNNG
WROOO OONNNG
WROOOOOOONNNG
WRROOONN
ONNG
Rule Four: Just like the cats, don't listen to them.
WRRROOONNG
WROOOONNNG
It sounds like words, but it doesn't mean—

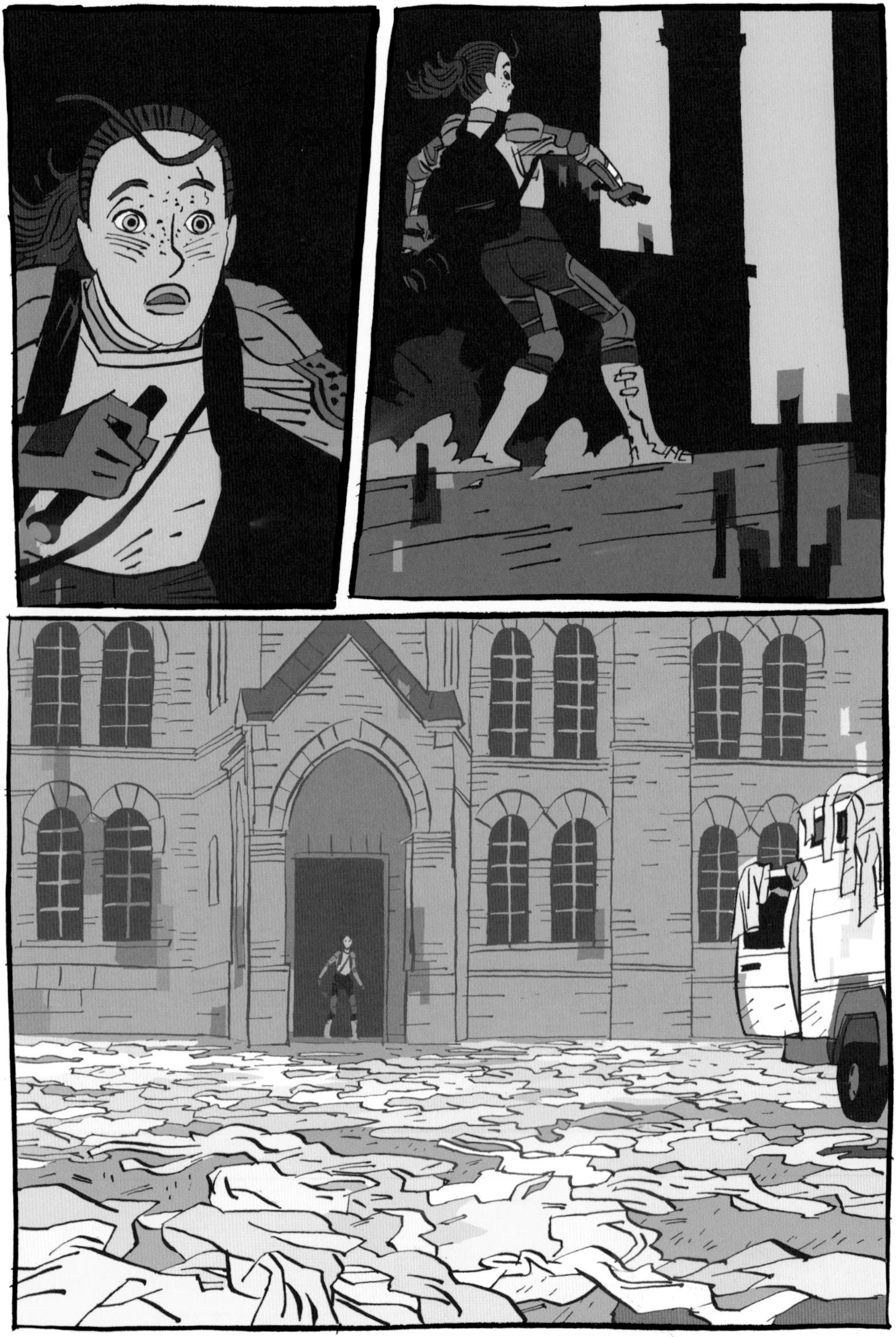

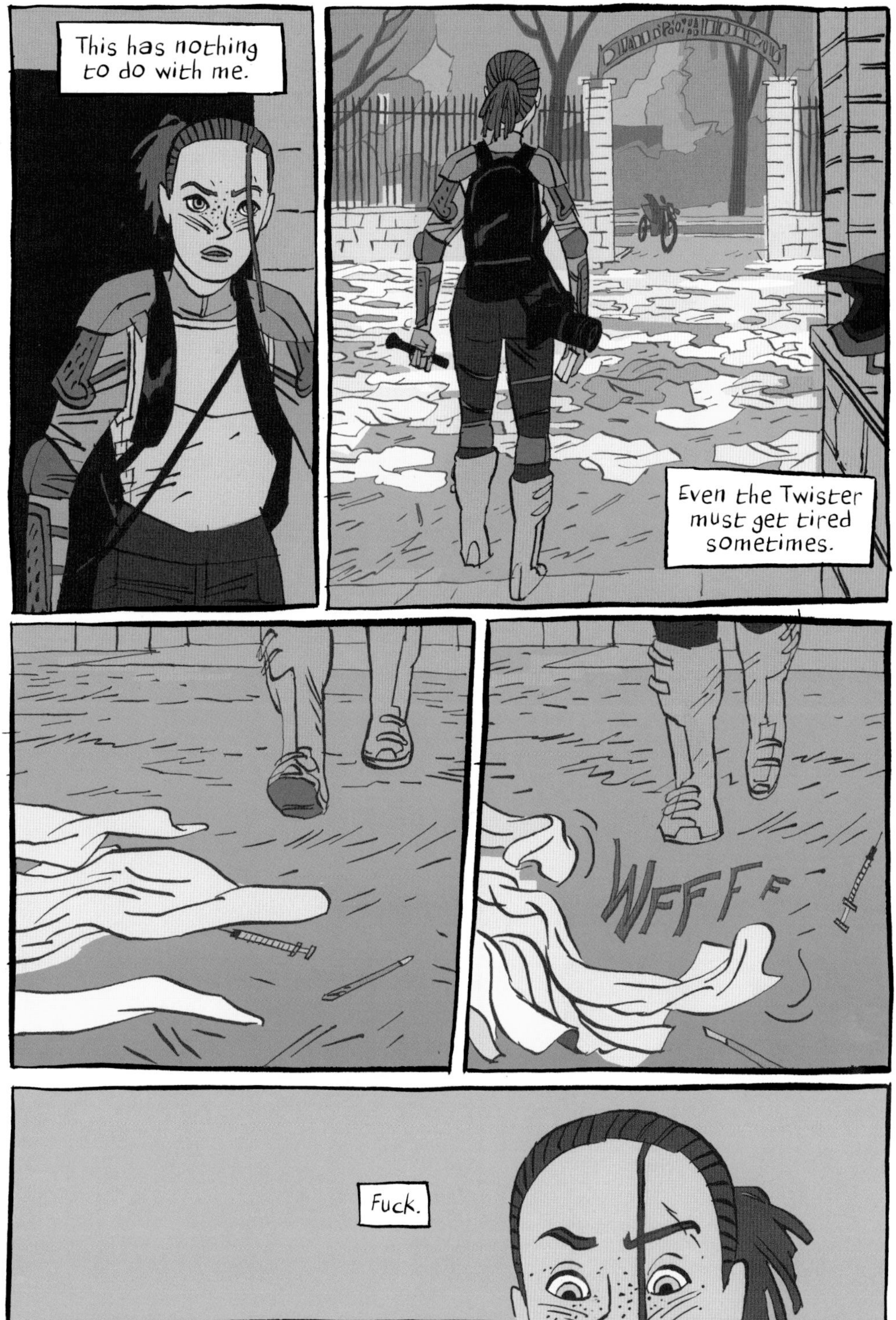
This has nothing to do with me.
Even the Twister must get tired sometimes.
WFFFF
Fuck.

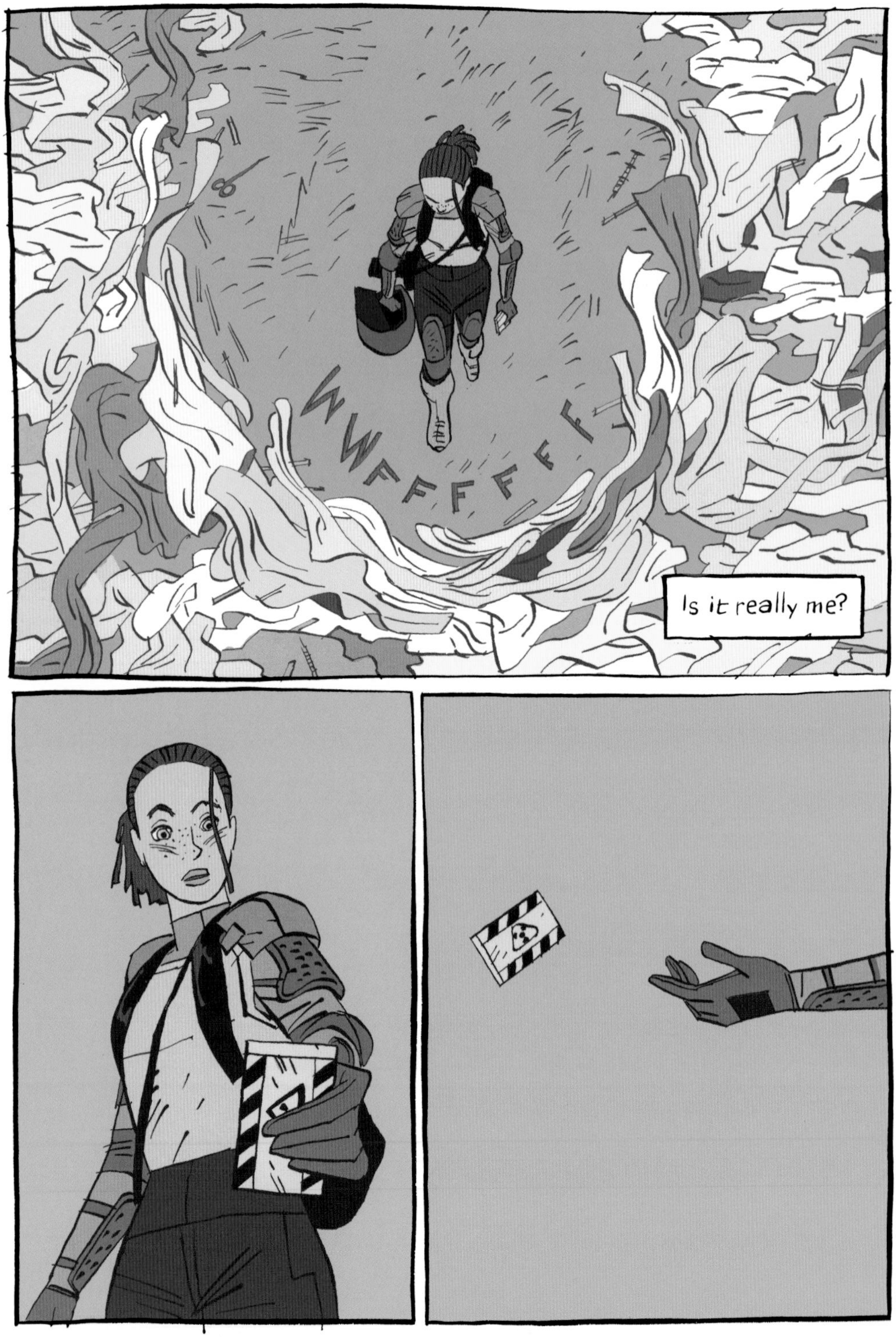
WWFFFFFF
Is it really me?

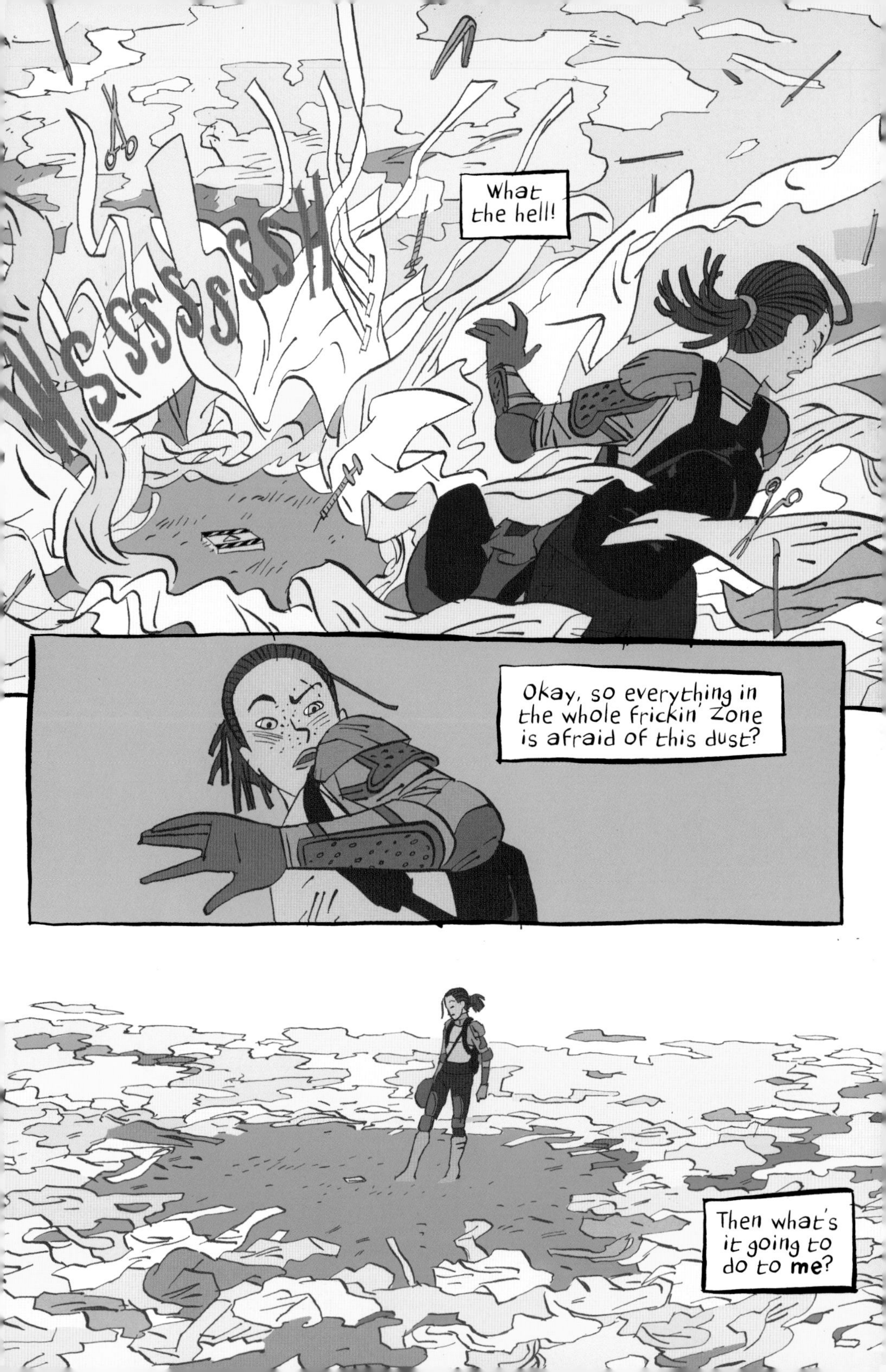
WHSSSSSSSSH
What the hell!
Okay, so everything in the whole frickin' Zone is afraid of this dust?
Then what's it going to do to **me**?

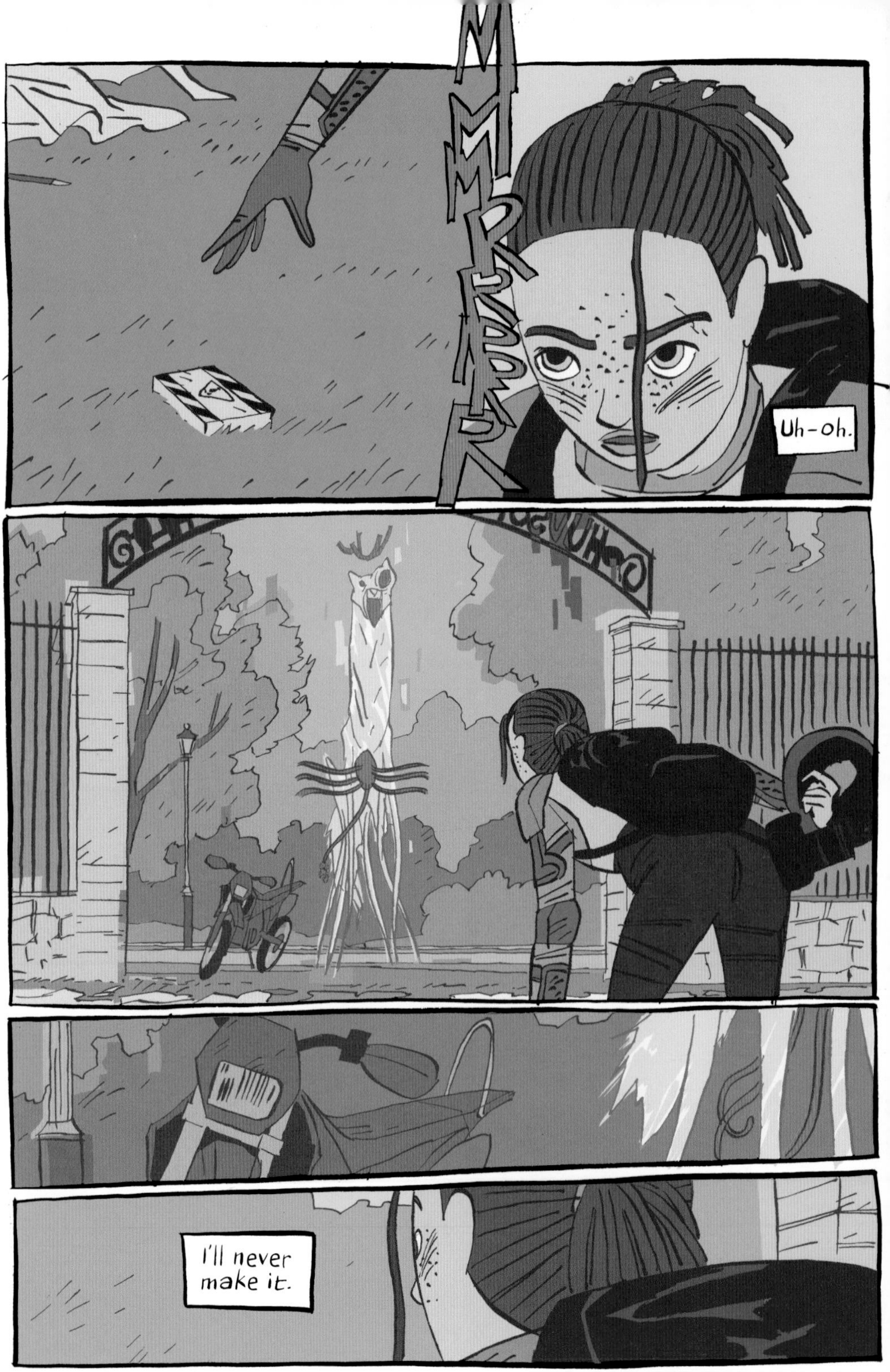
MMMRRRRR
Uh-oh.
I'll never make it.

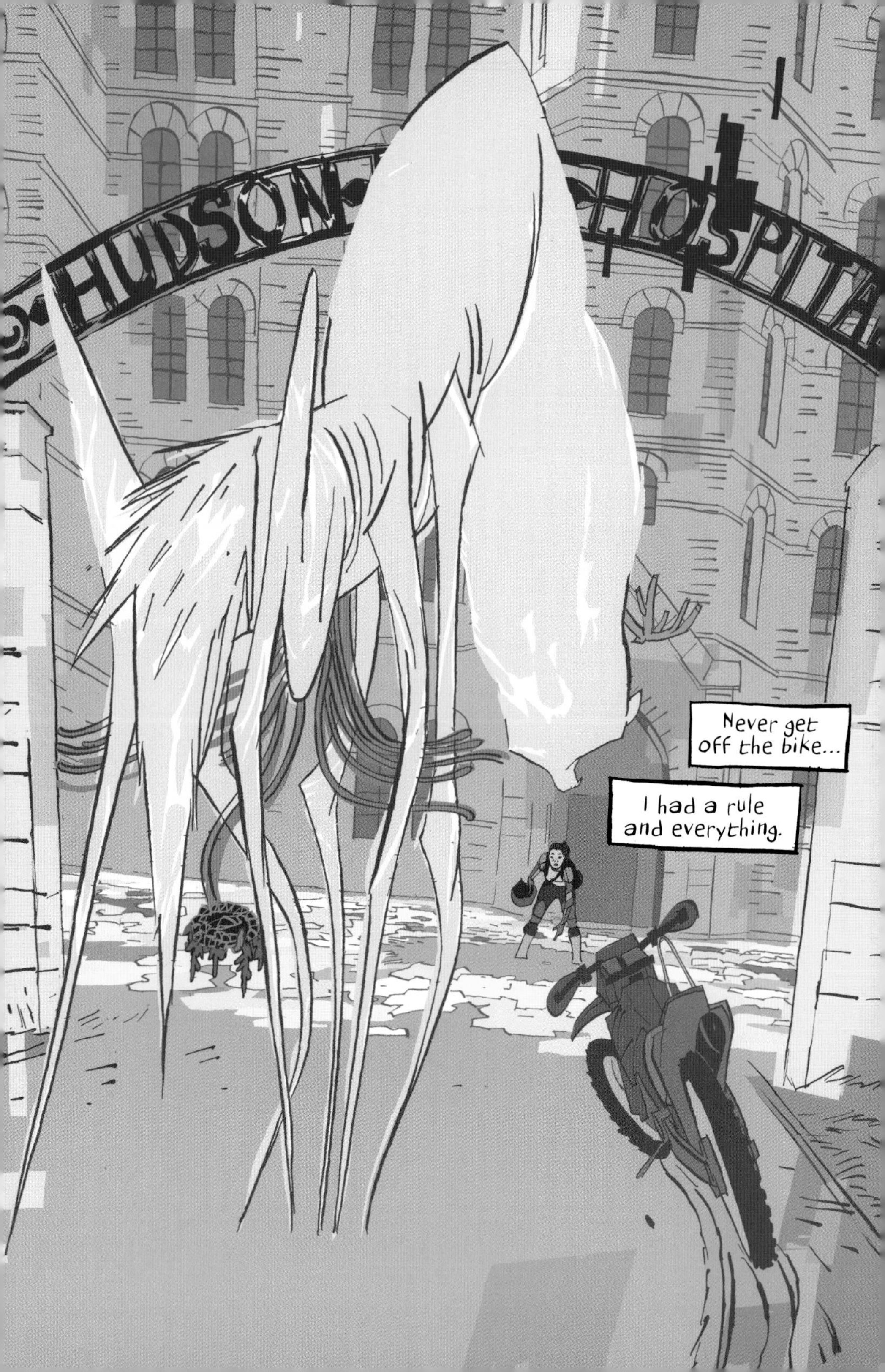
HUDSON
HOSPITA
Never get off the bike...
I had a rule and everything.

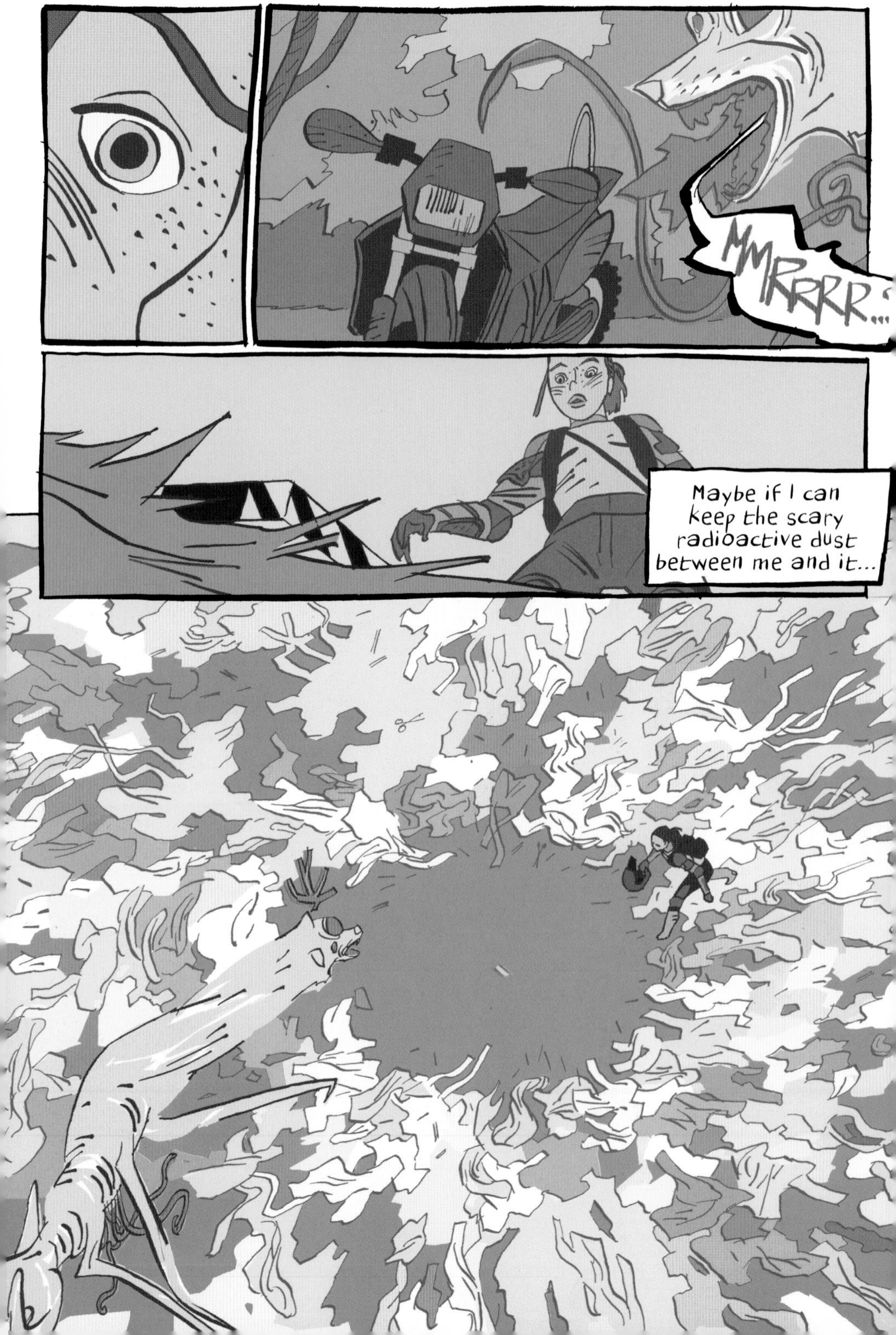

MMRRRR...
Maybe if I can keep the scary radioactive dust between me and it...

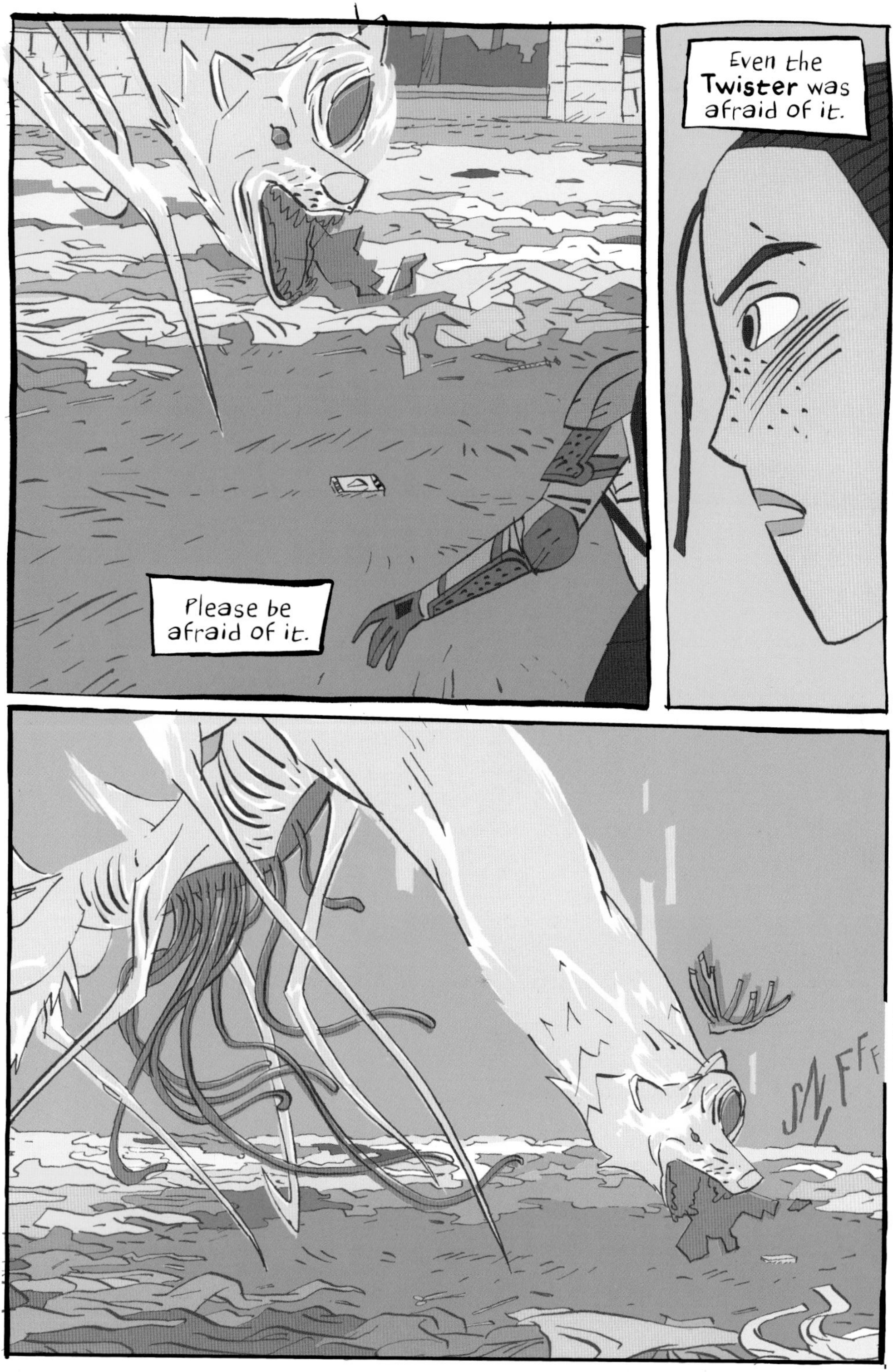
Please be afraid of it.
Even the **Twister** was afraid of it.
SNFFFF

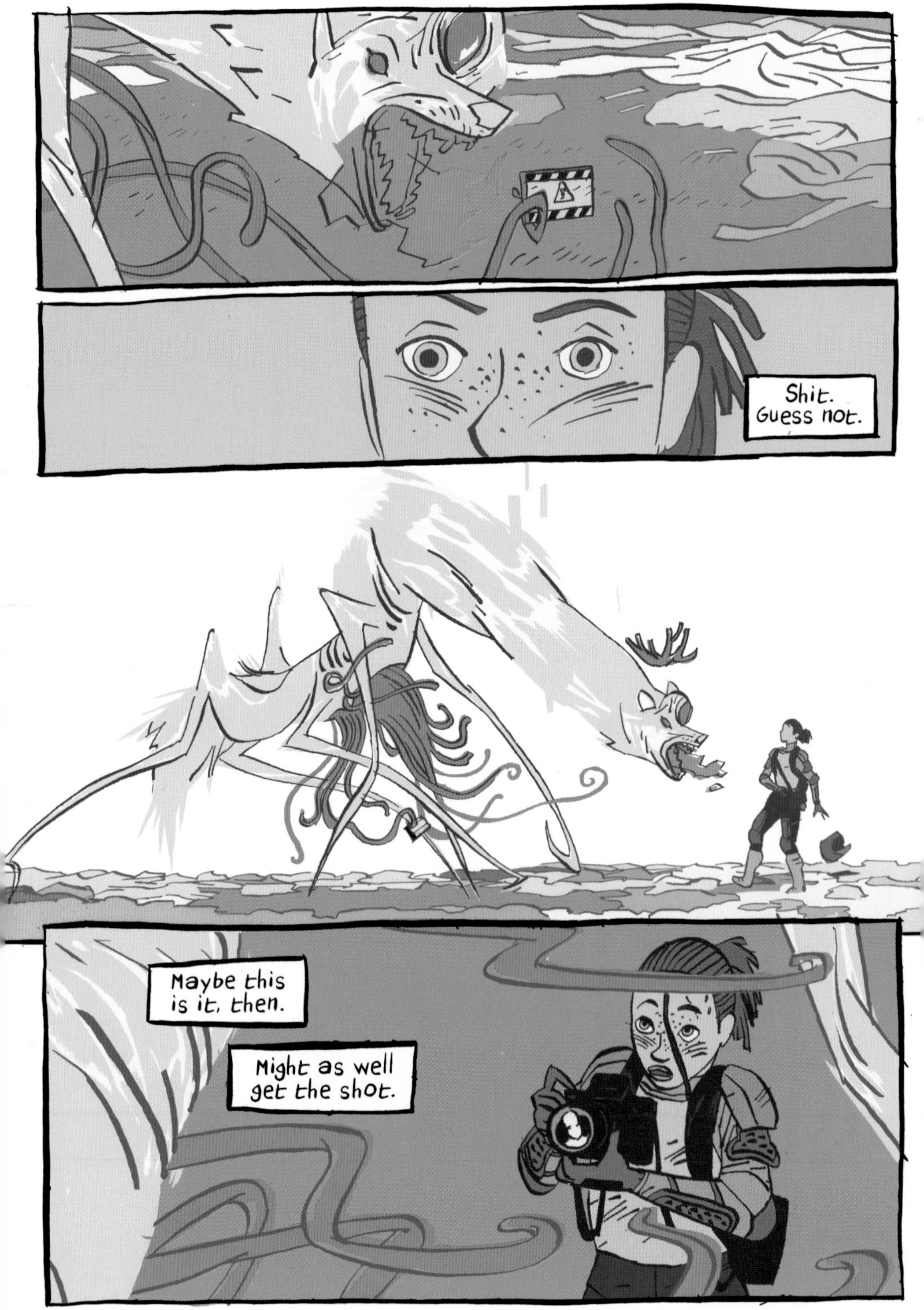
Shit.
Guess not.
Maybe this
is it, then.
Might as well
get the shot.

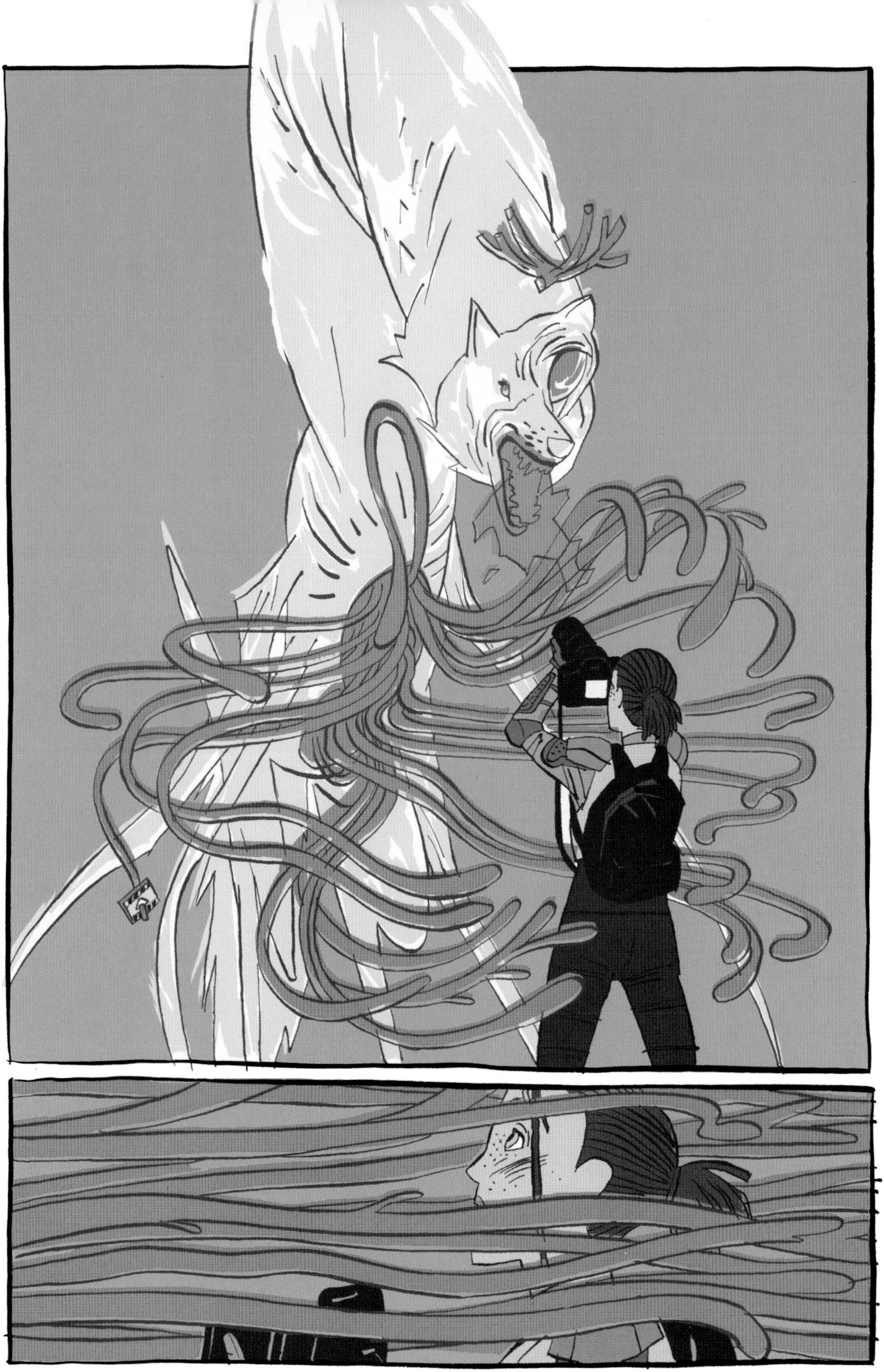

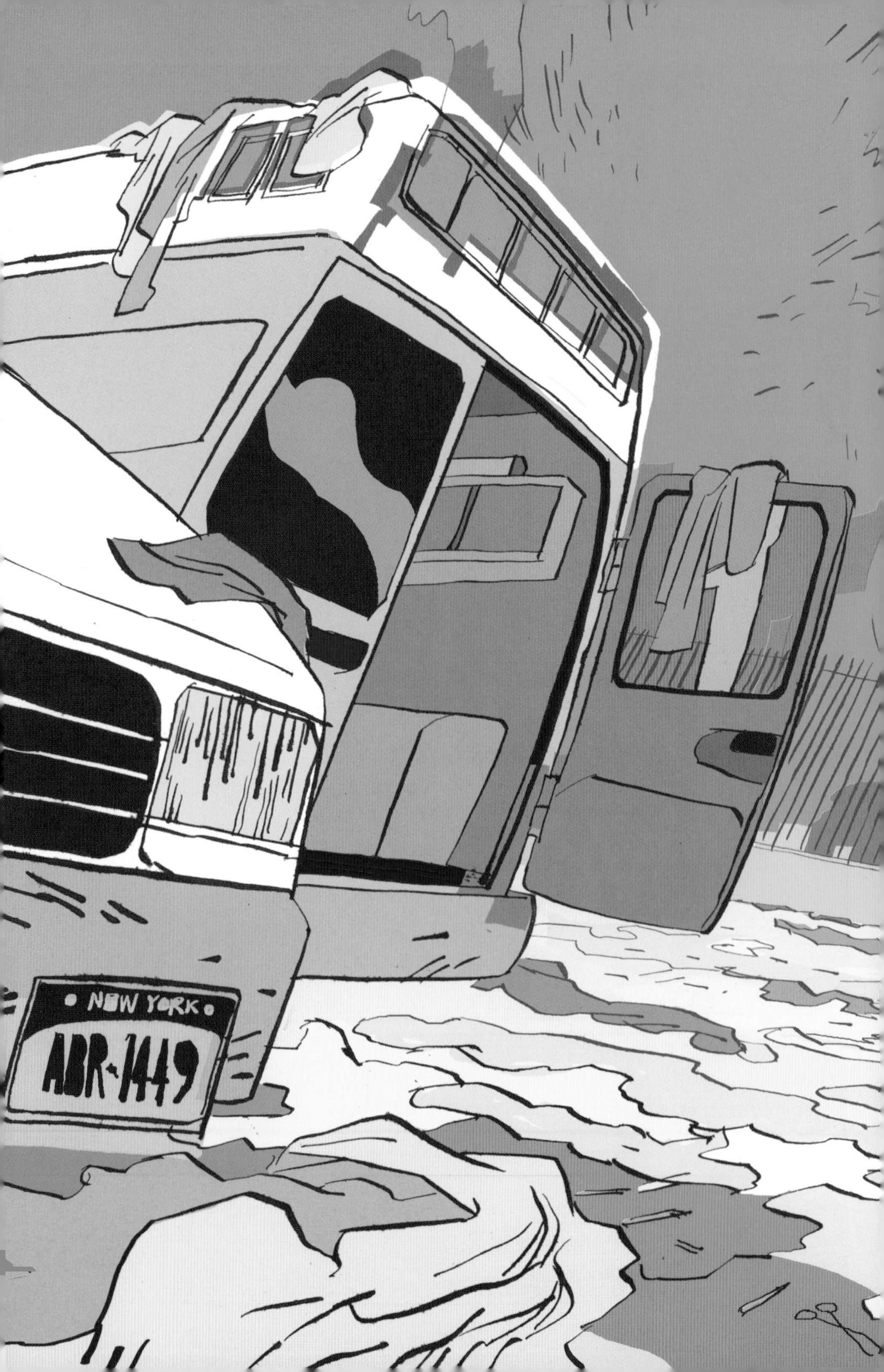
NEW YORK
ABR-1449

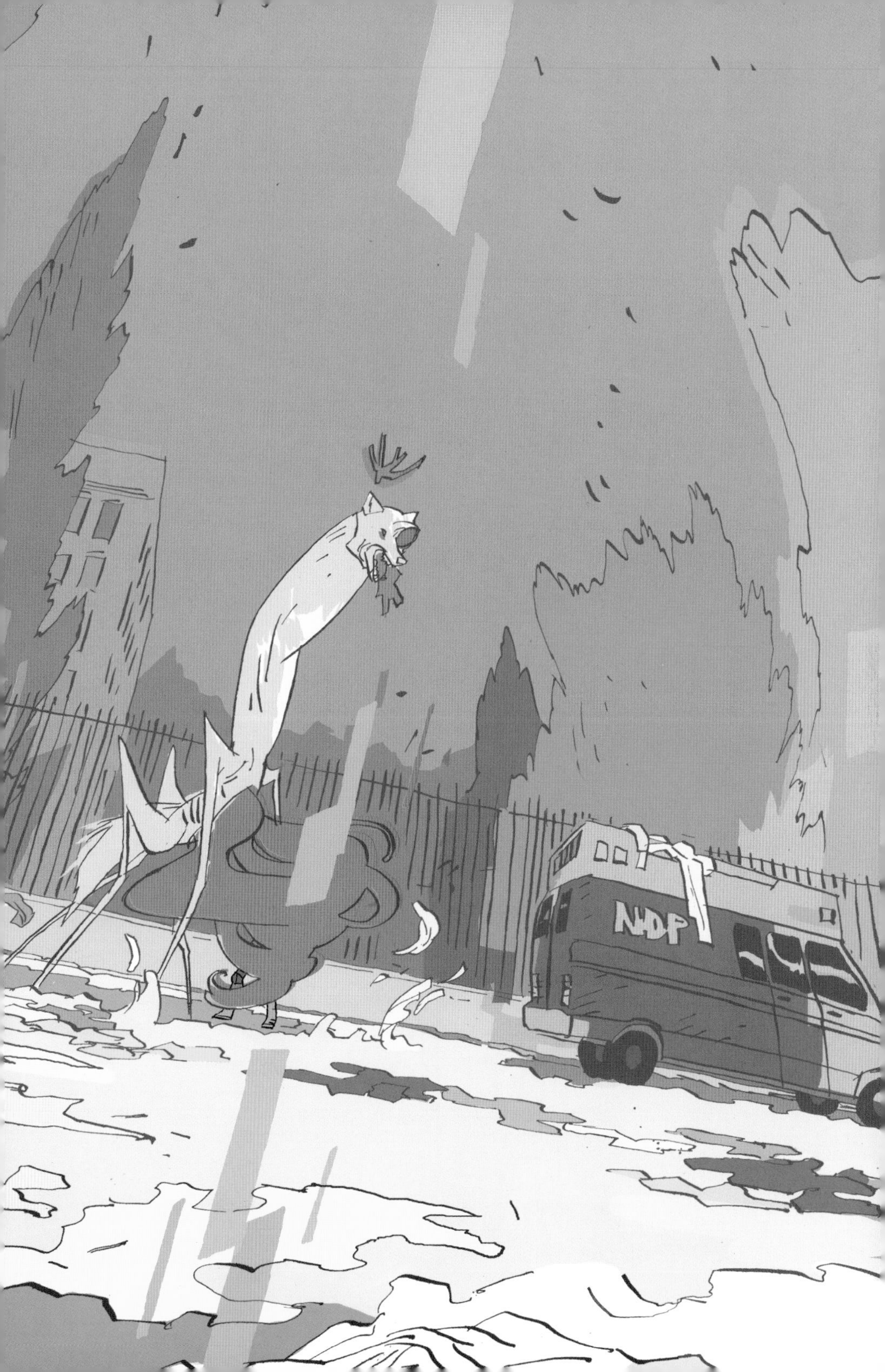
NDP

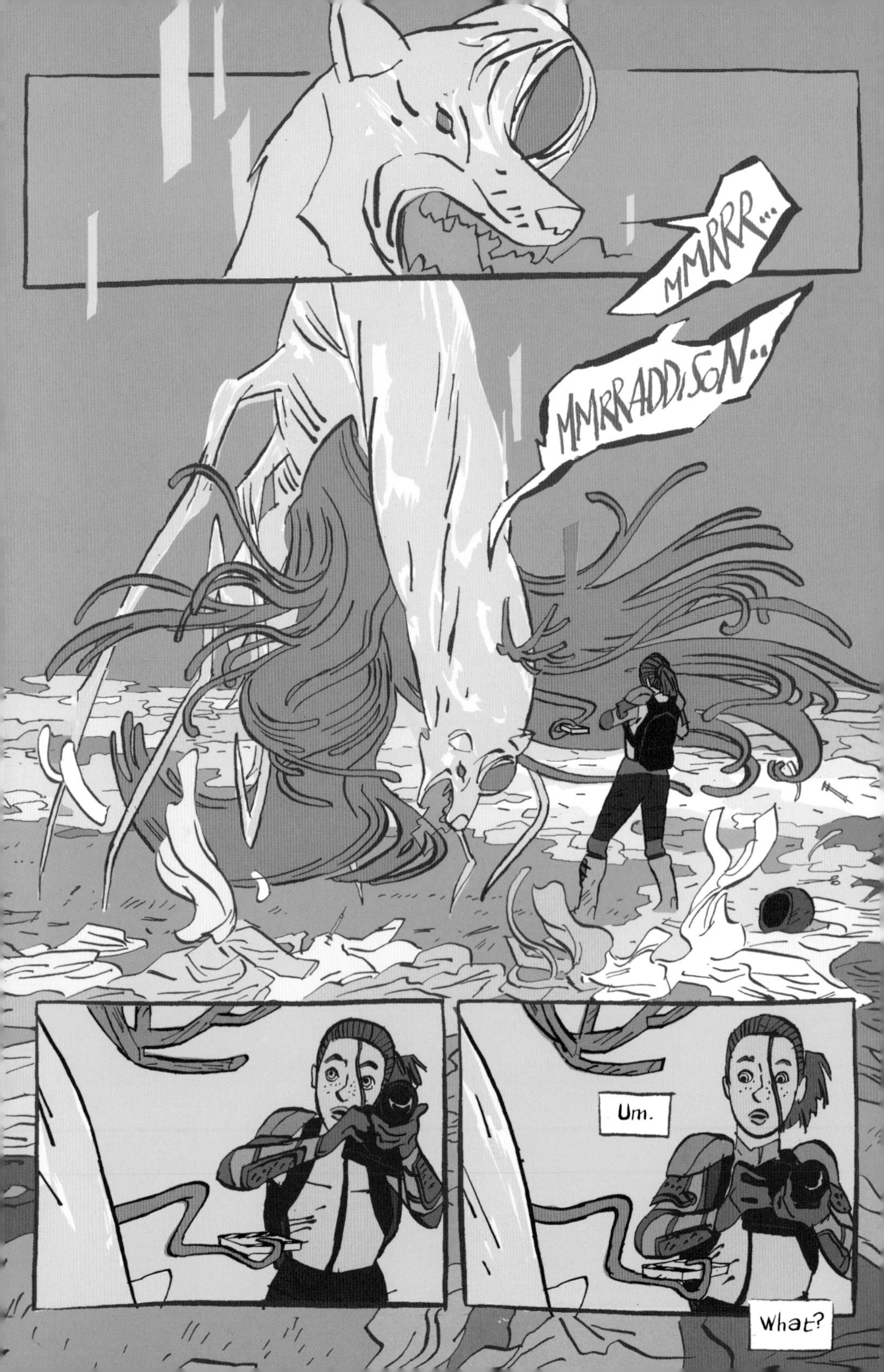
MMRRR...
MMRRADDISON...
Um.
What?

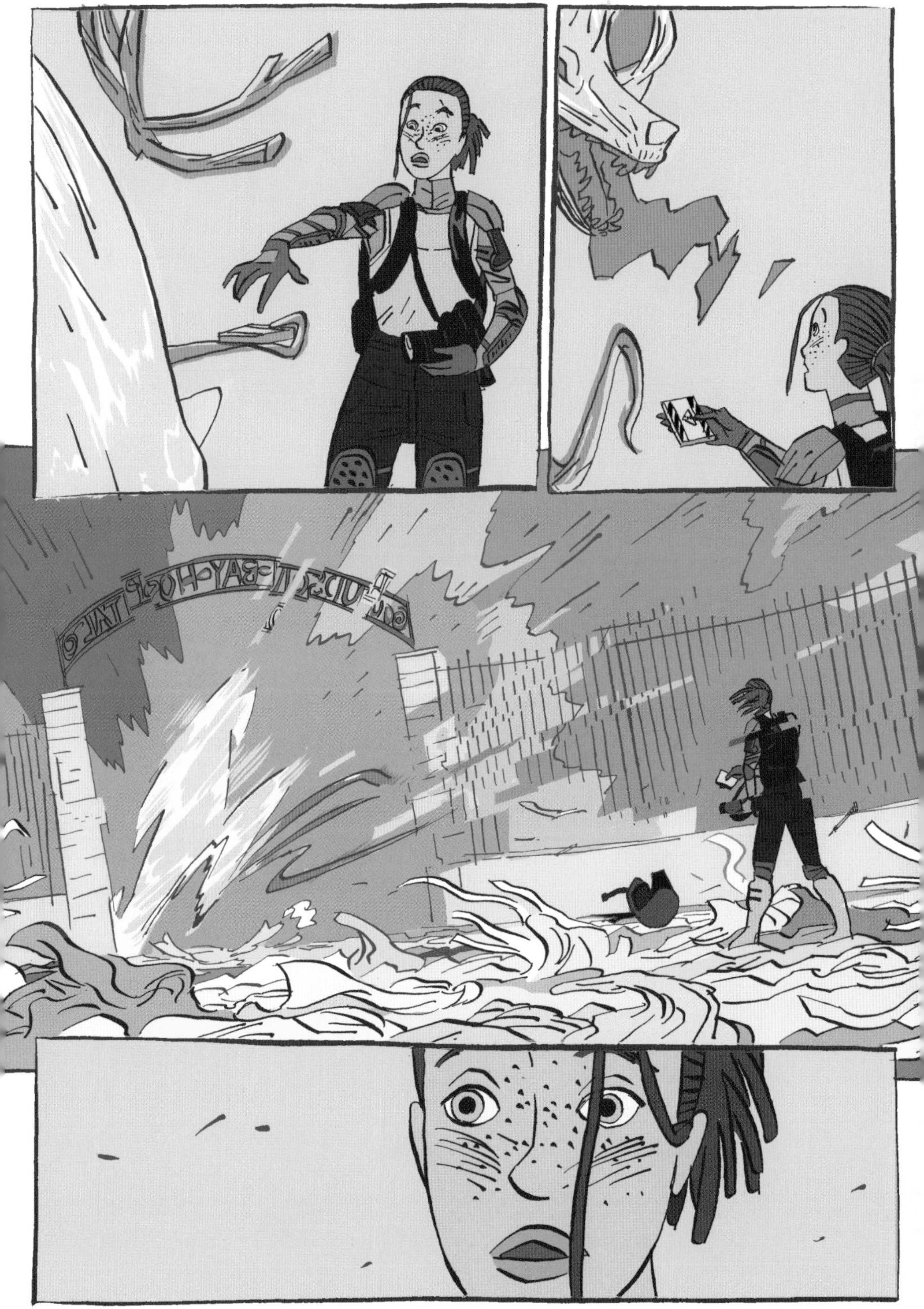

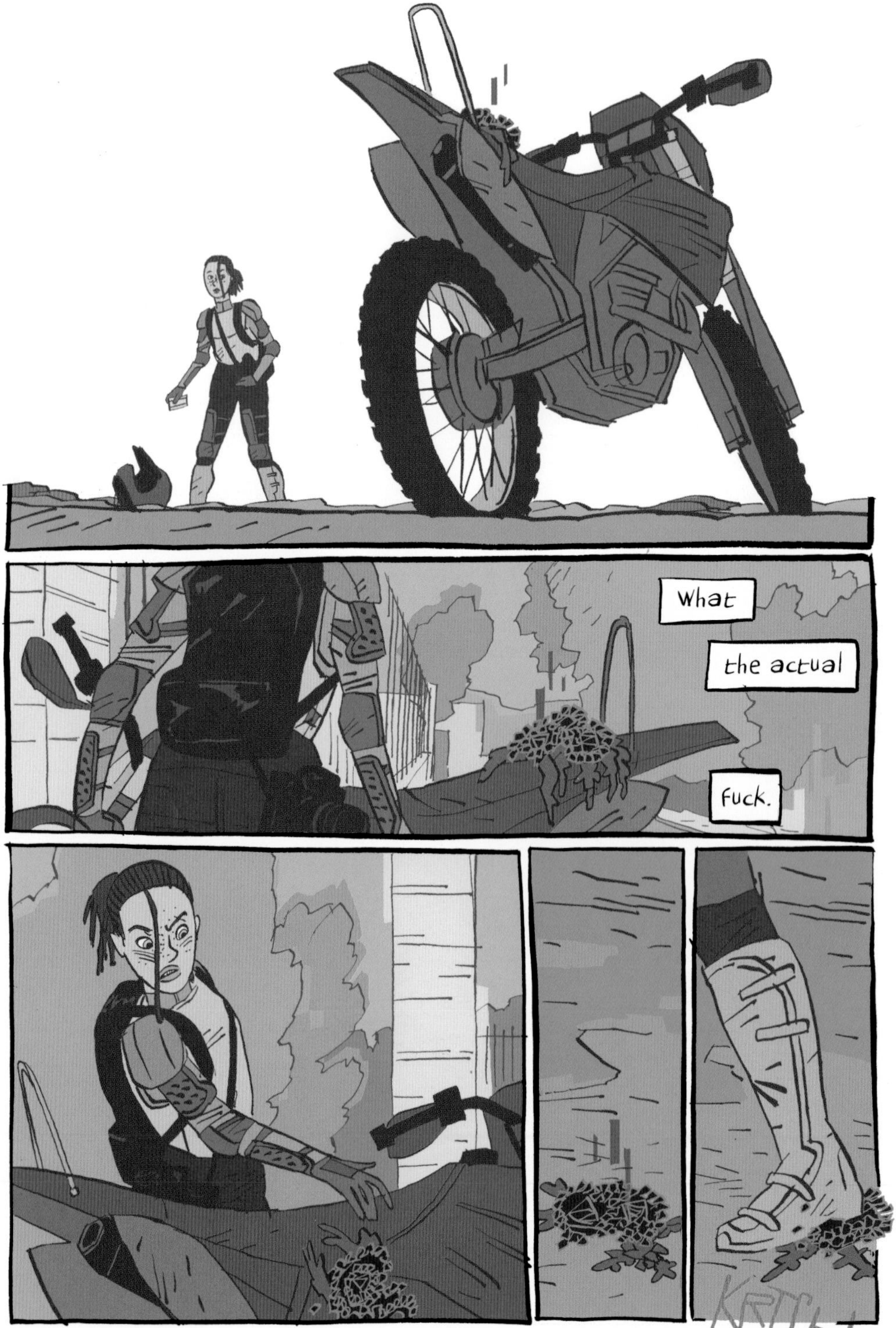
What
the actual
fuck.
KRTCH

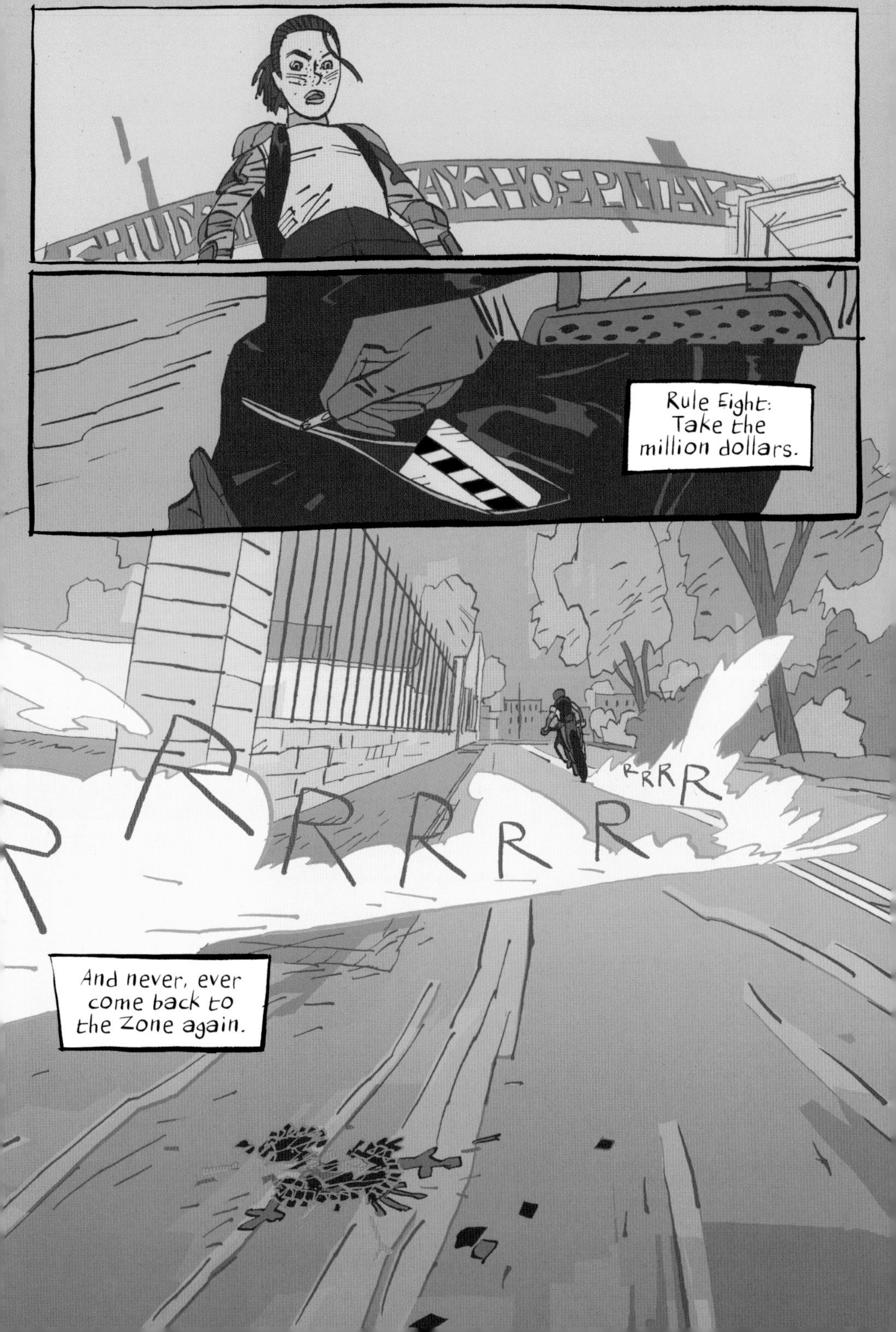
Rule Eight: Take the million dollars.
RRRRRR
RRRR
And never, ever come back to the Zone again.

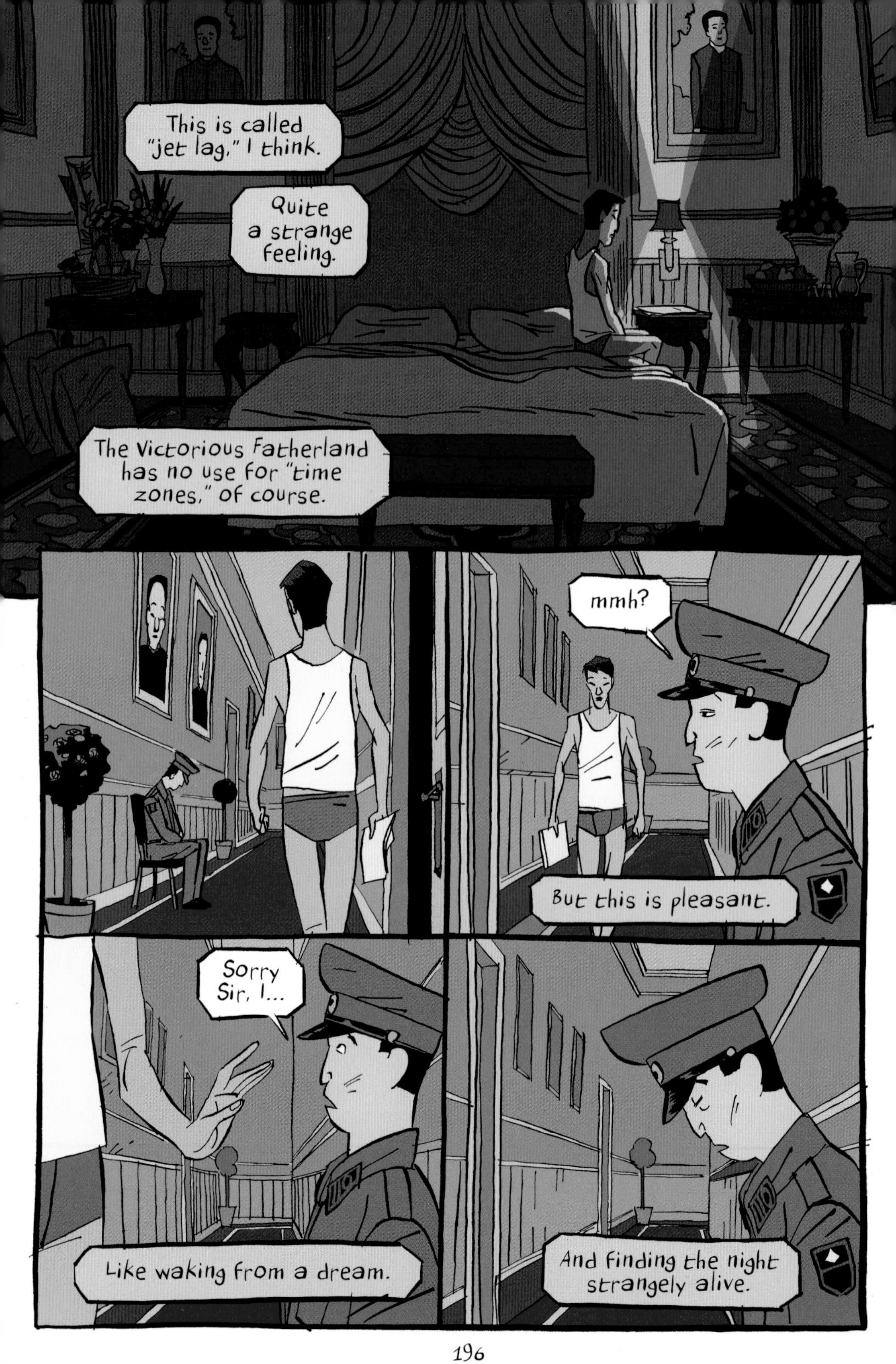
This is called "jet lag," I think.
Quite a strange feeling.
The Victorious Fatherland has no use for "time zones," of course.
mmh?
But this is pleasant.
Sorry Sir, I...
Like waking from a dream.
And finding the night strangely alive.

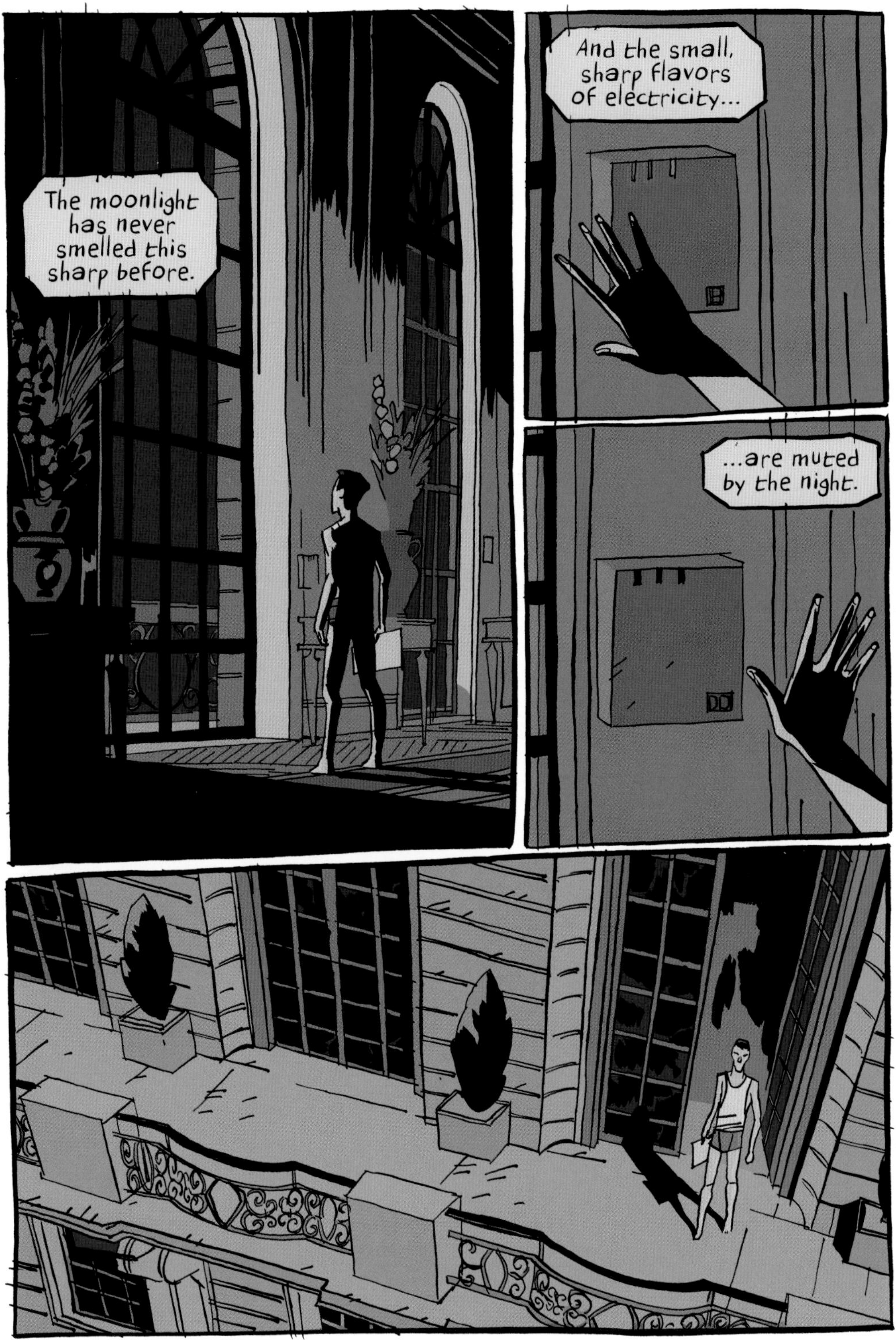
The moonlight has never smelled this sharp before.
And the small, sharp flavors of electricity...
...are muted by the night.

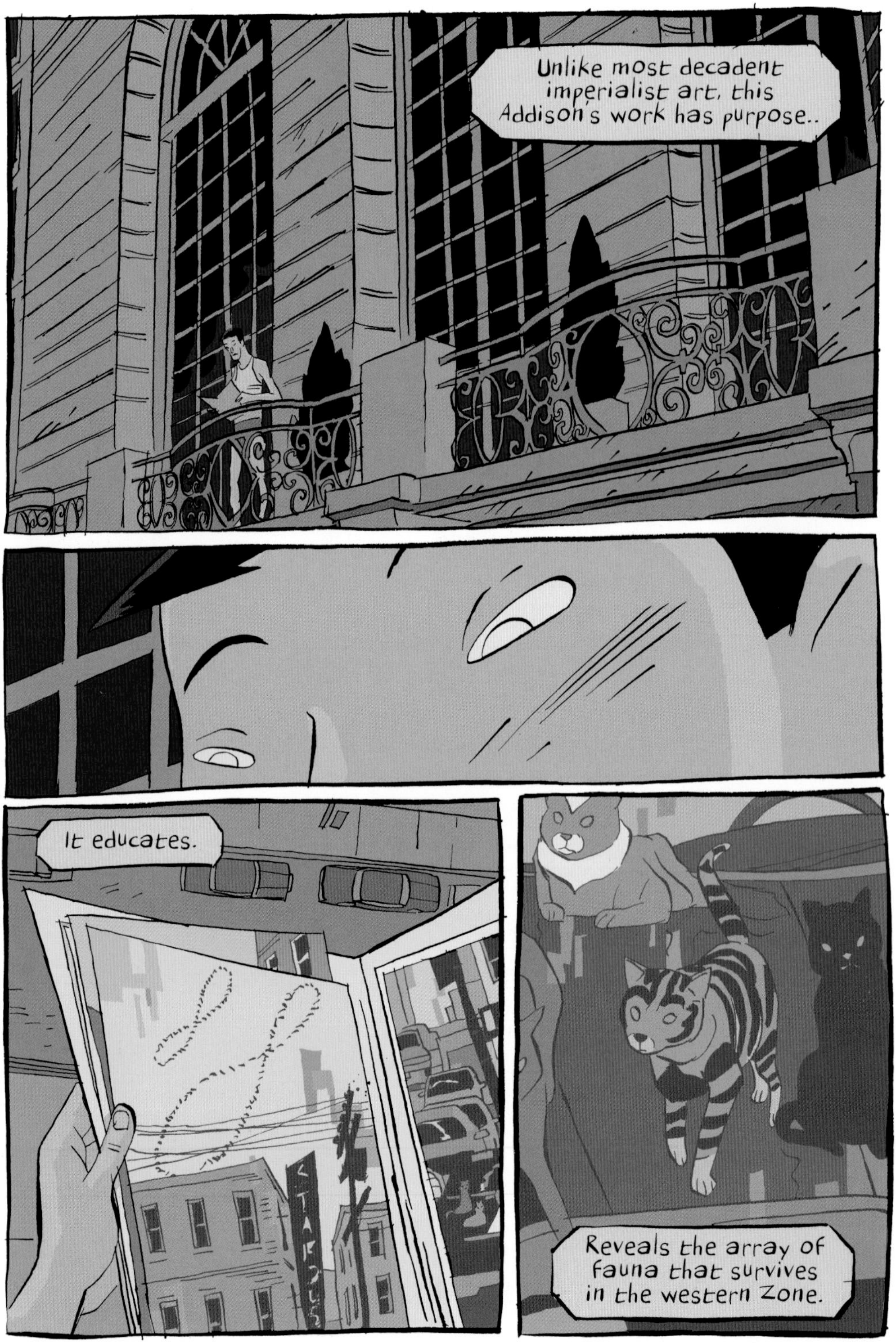
Unlike most decadent imperialist art, this Addison's work has purpose..
It educates.
Reveals the array of fauna that survives in the western Zone.

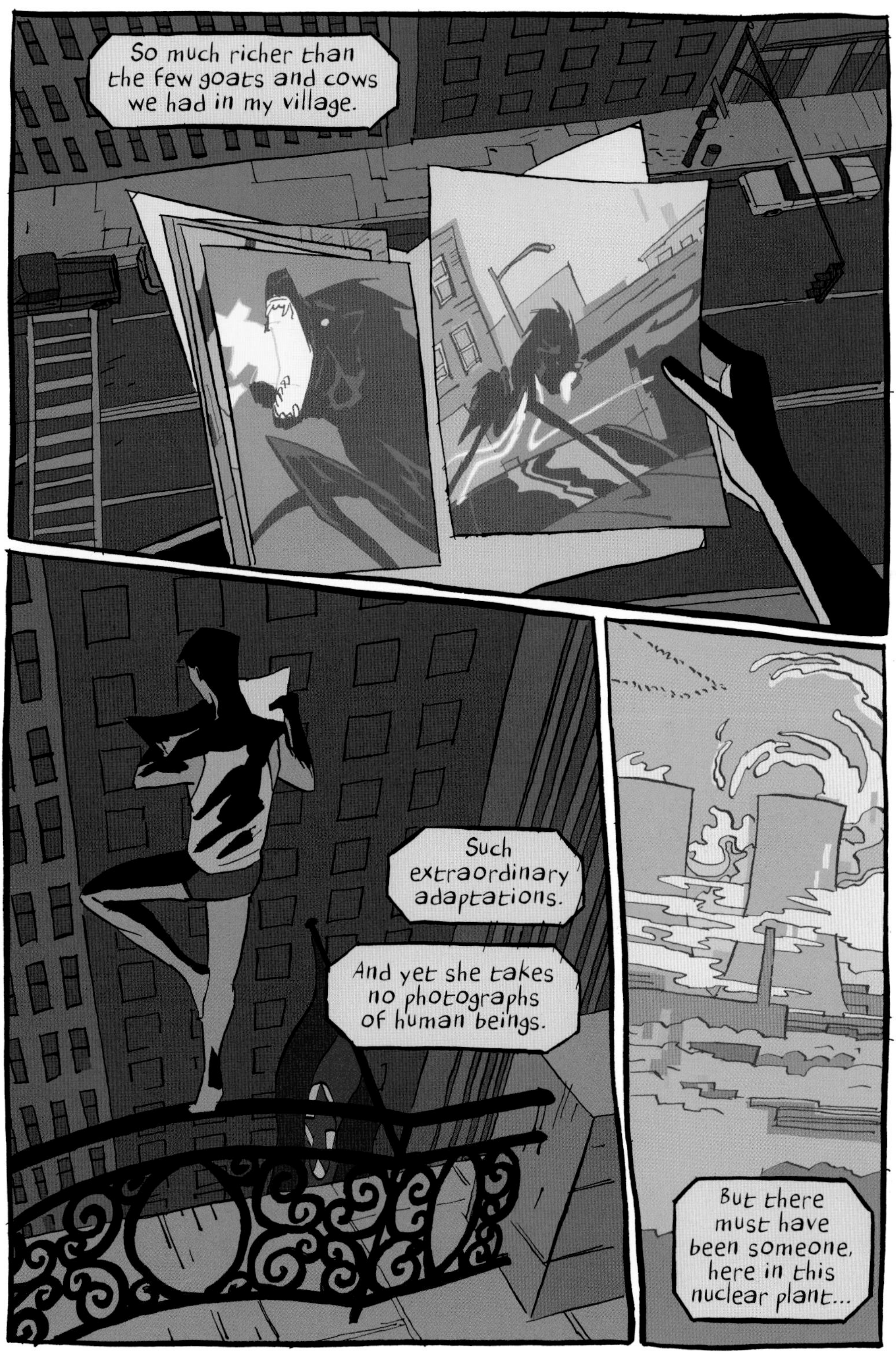
So much richer than the few goats and cows we had in my village.
Such extraordinary adaptations.
And yet she takes no photographs of human beings.
But there must have been someone, here in this nuclear plant...

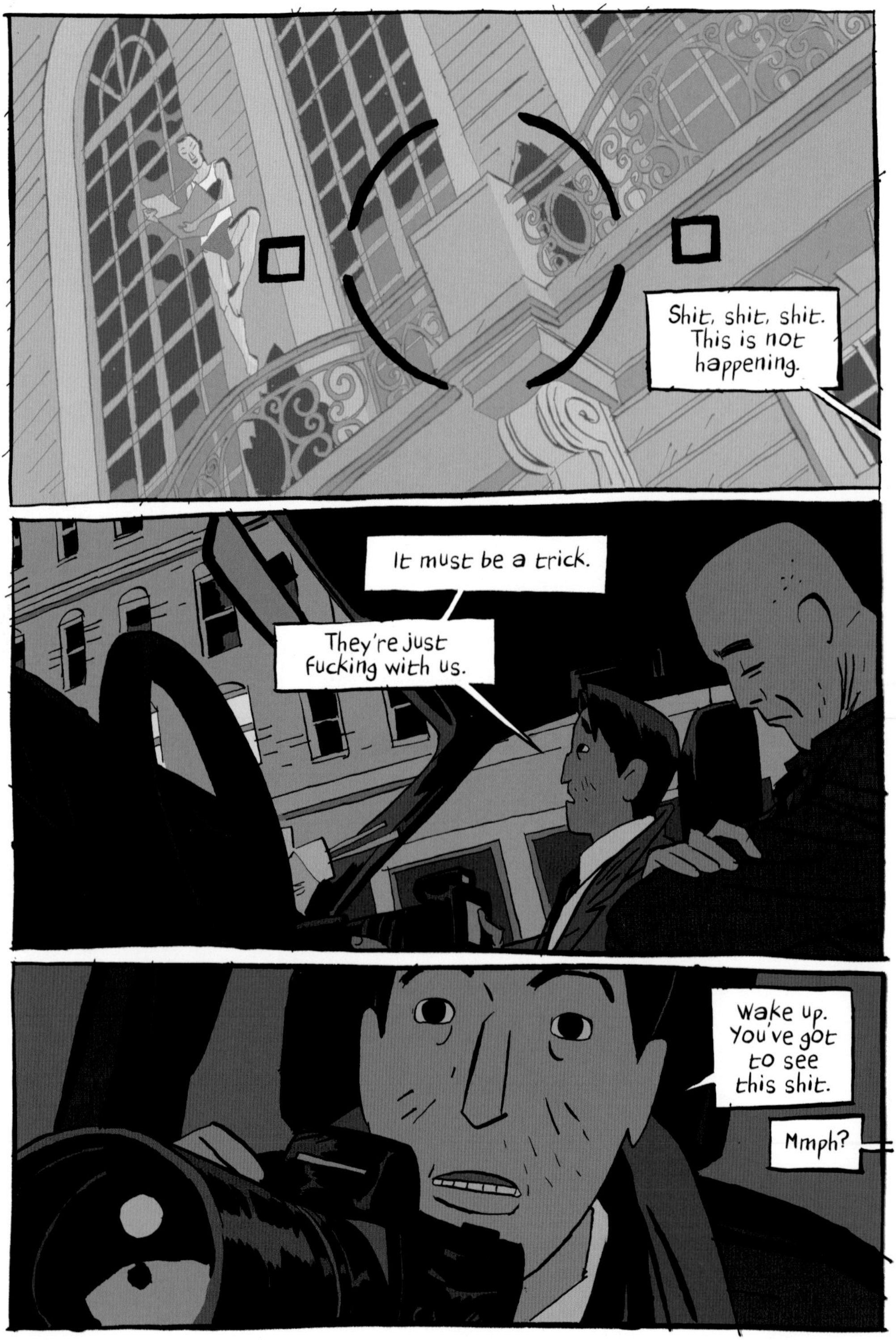
Shit, shit, shit. This is not happening.
It must be a trick.
They're just fucking with us.
Wake up. You've got to see this shit.
Mmph?

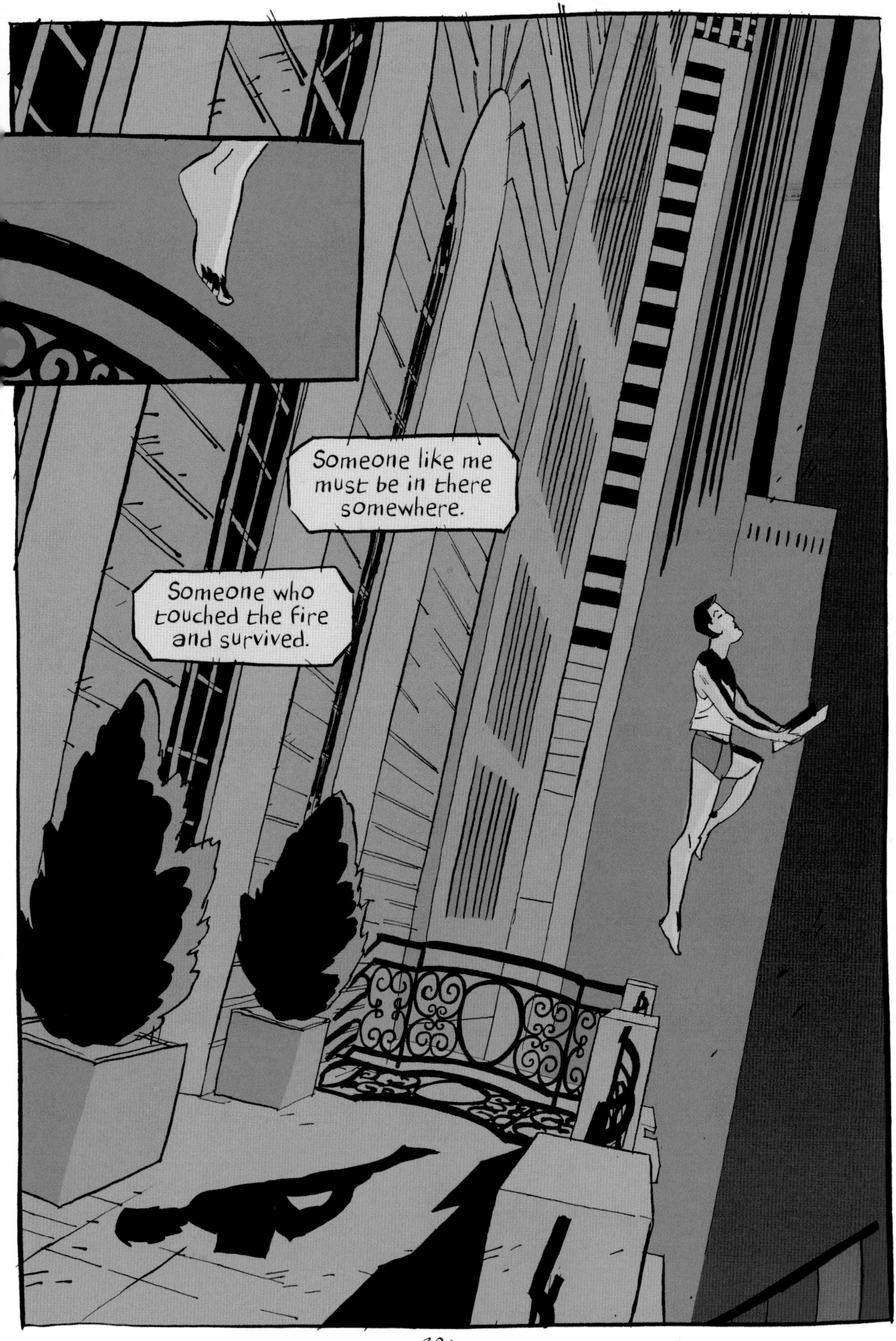
Someone like me must be in there somewhere.
Someone who touched the fire and survived.

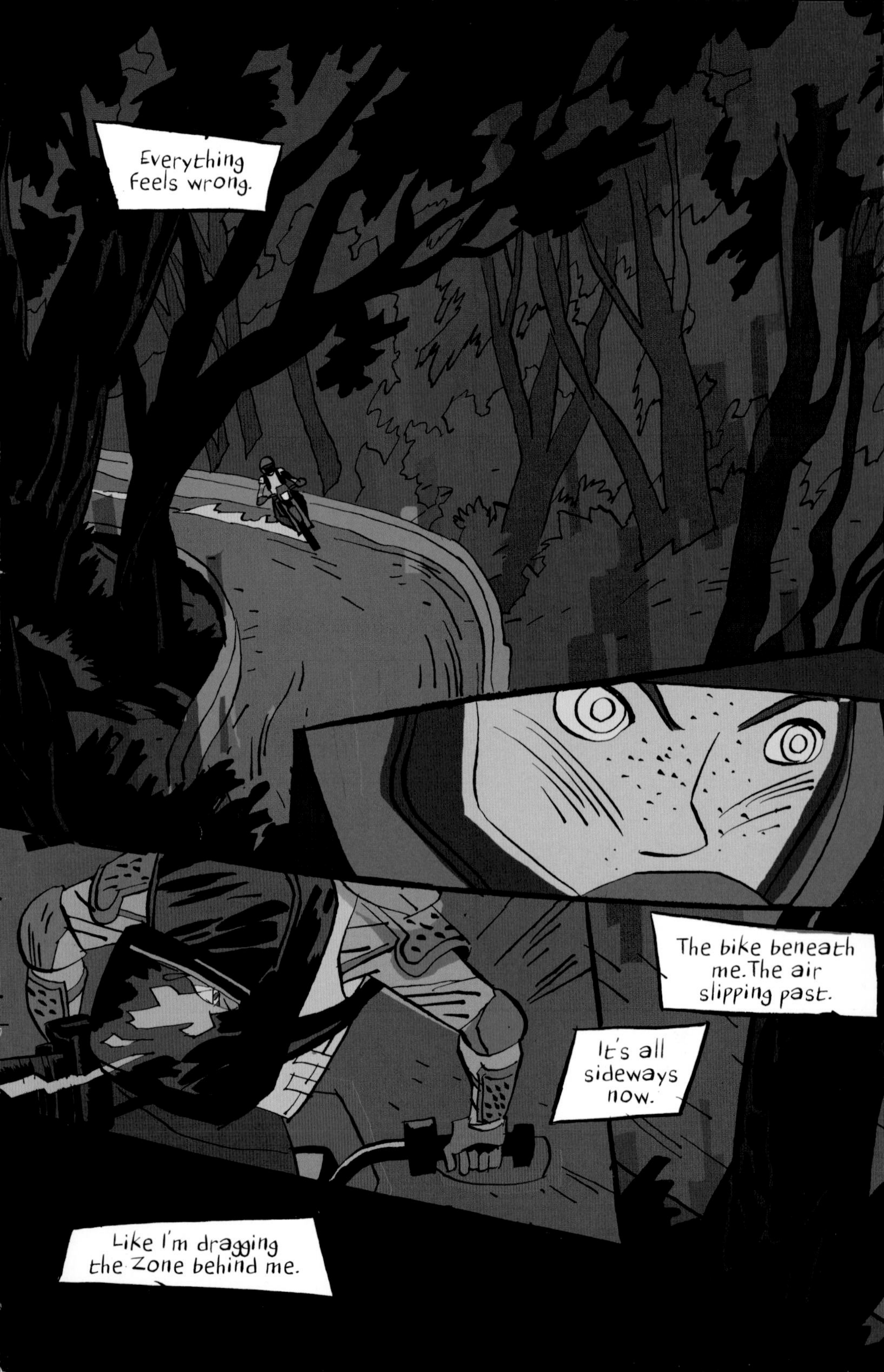
Everything feels wrong.
The bike beneath me. The air slipping past.
It's all sideways now.
Like I'm dragging the Zone behind me.

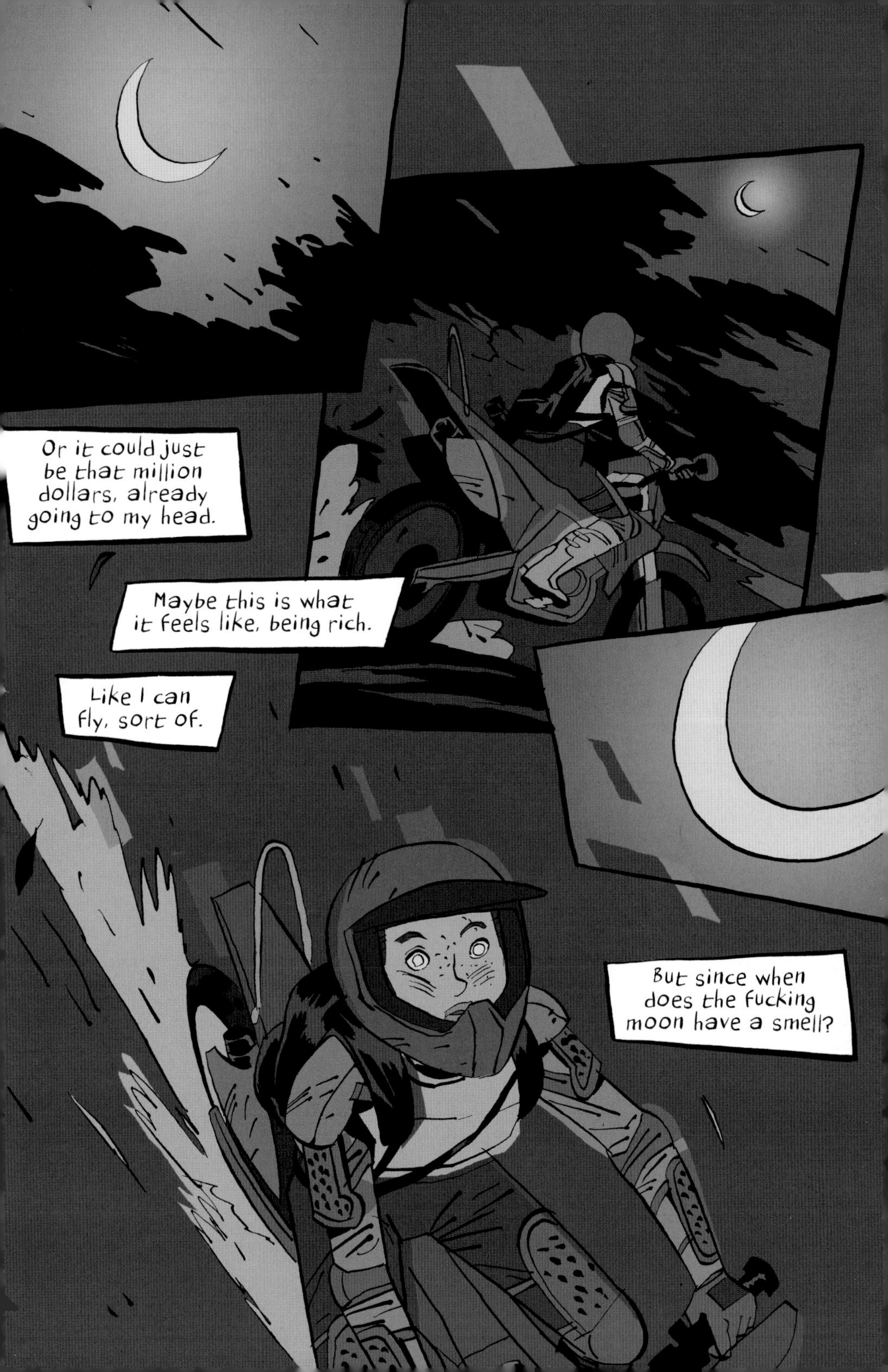
Or it could just be that million dollars, already going to my head.
Maybe this is what it feels like, being rich.
Like I can fly, sort of.
But since when does the fucking moon have a smell?

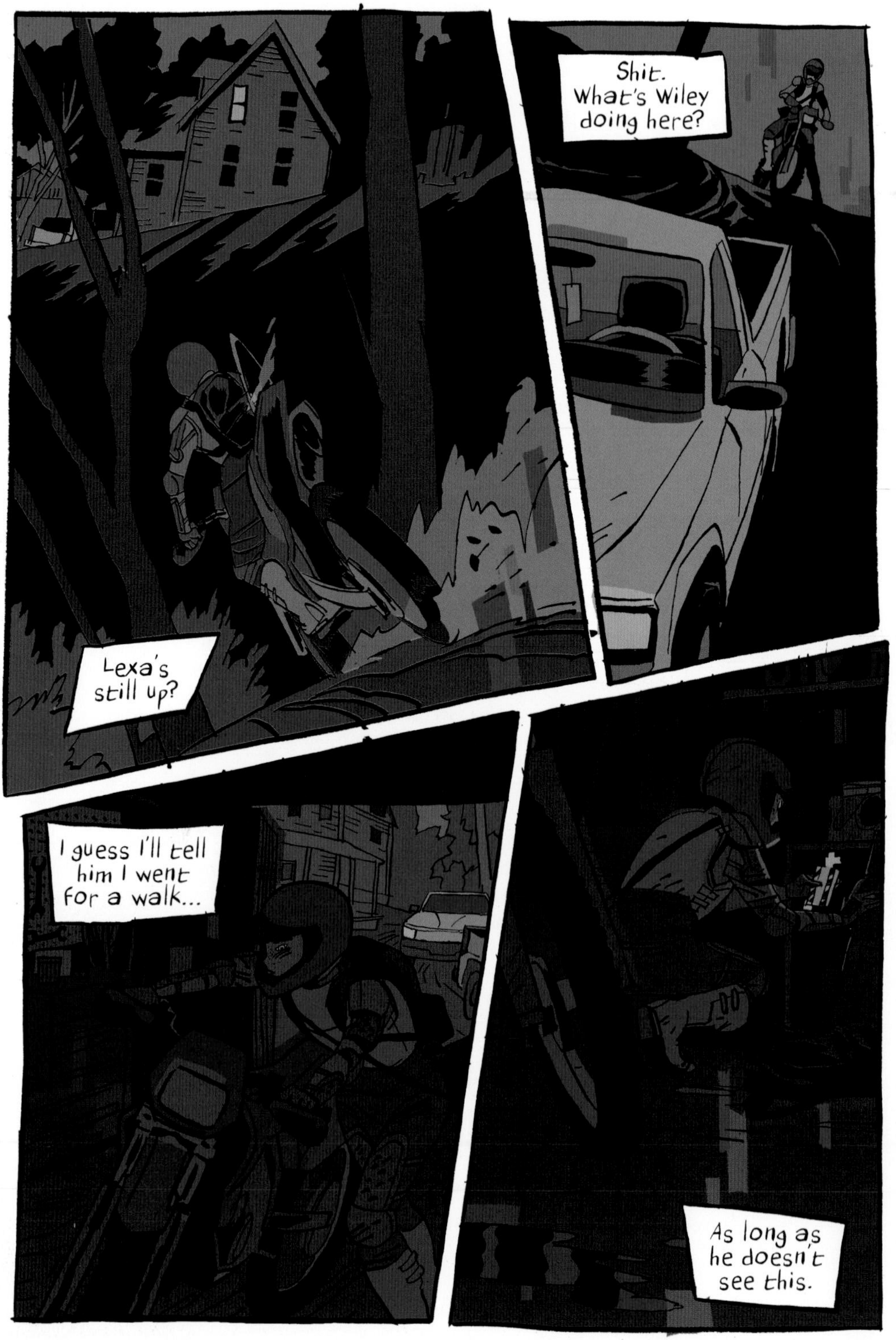
Lexa's still up?
Shit. What's Wiley doing here?
I guess I'll tell him I went for a walk...
As long as he doesn't see this.

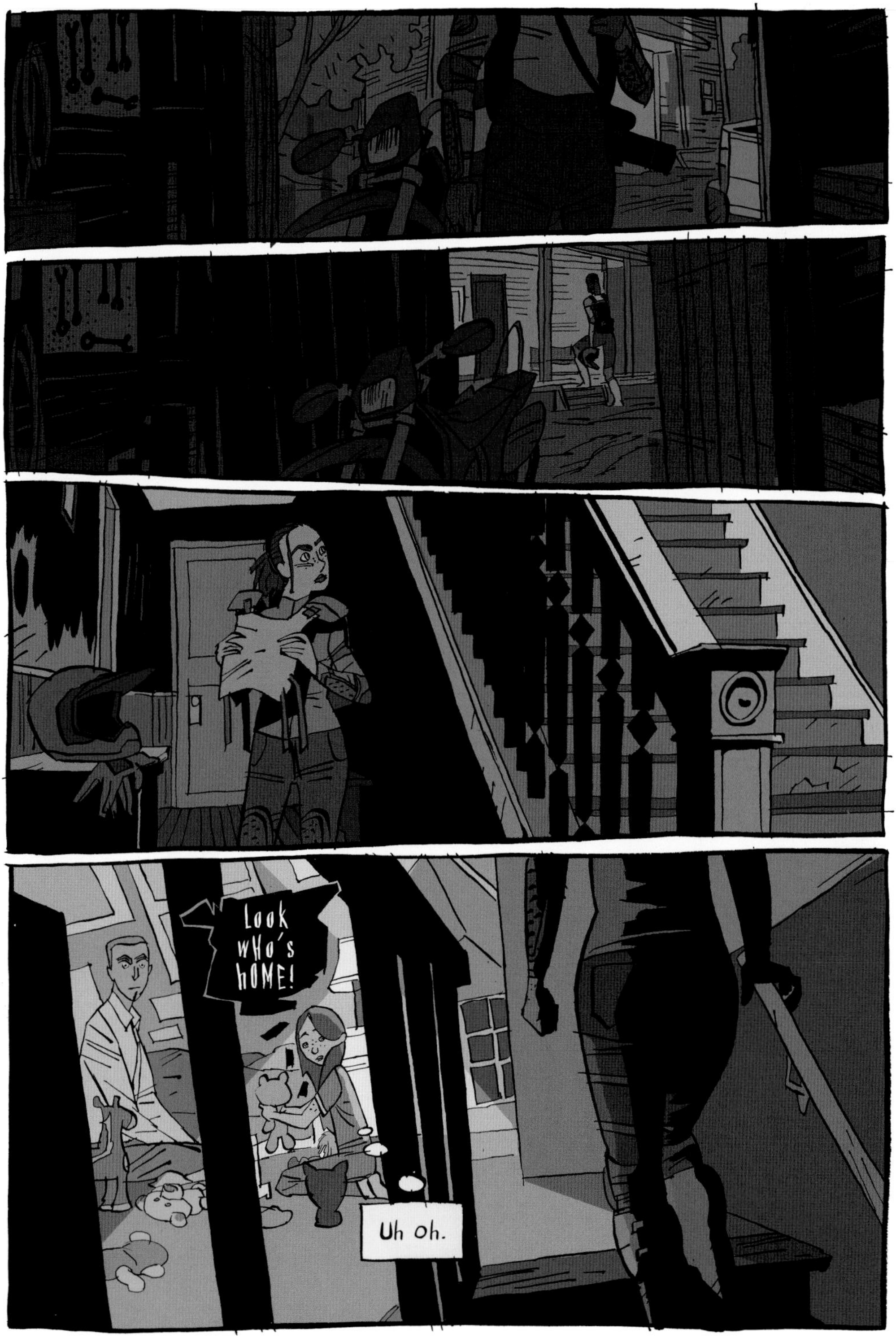
Look who's home!
Uh oh.

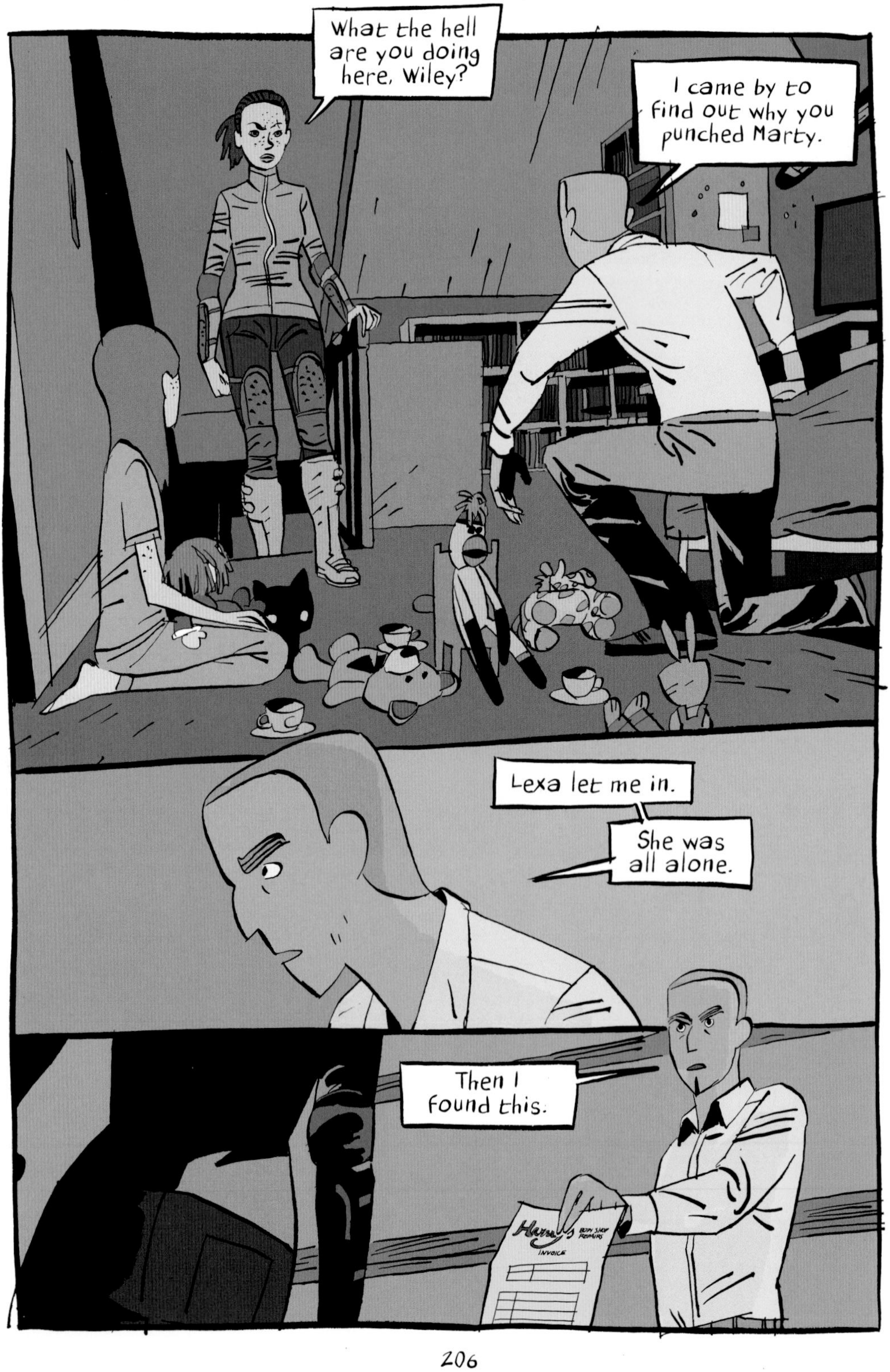
What the hell are you doing here, Wiley?
I came by to find out why you punched Marty.
Lexa let me in.
She was all alone.
Then I found this.
Harry's
BODY SHOP REPAIRS
INVOICE

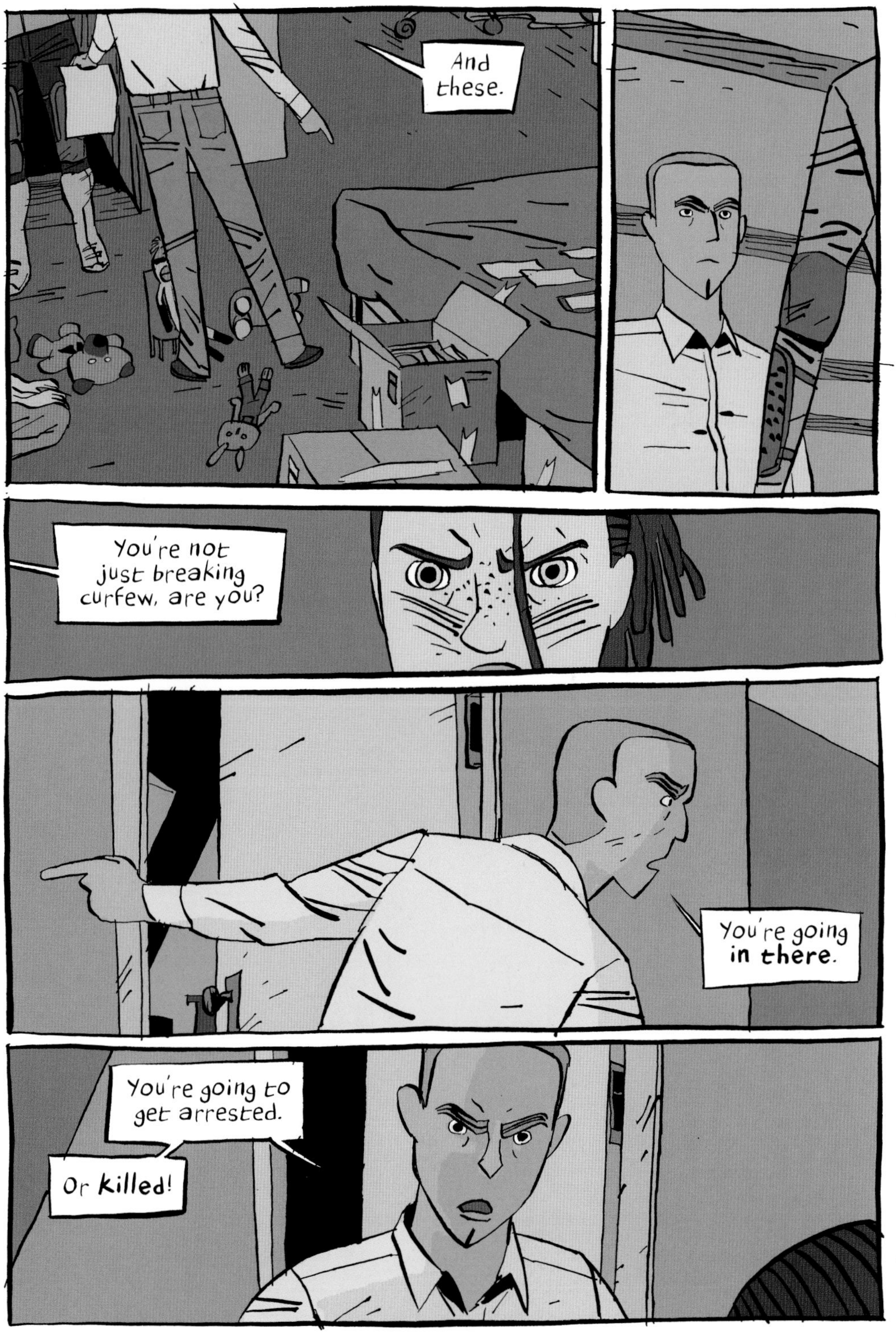
And these.
You're not just breaking curfew, are you?
You're going in there.
You're going to get arrested.
Or killed!

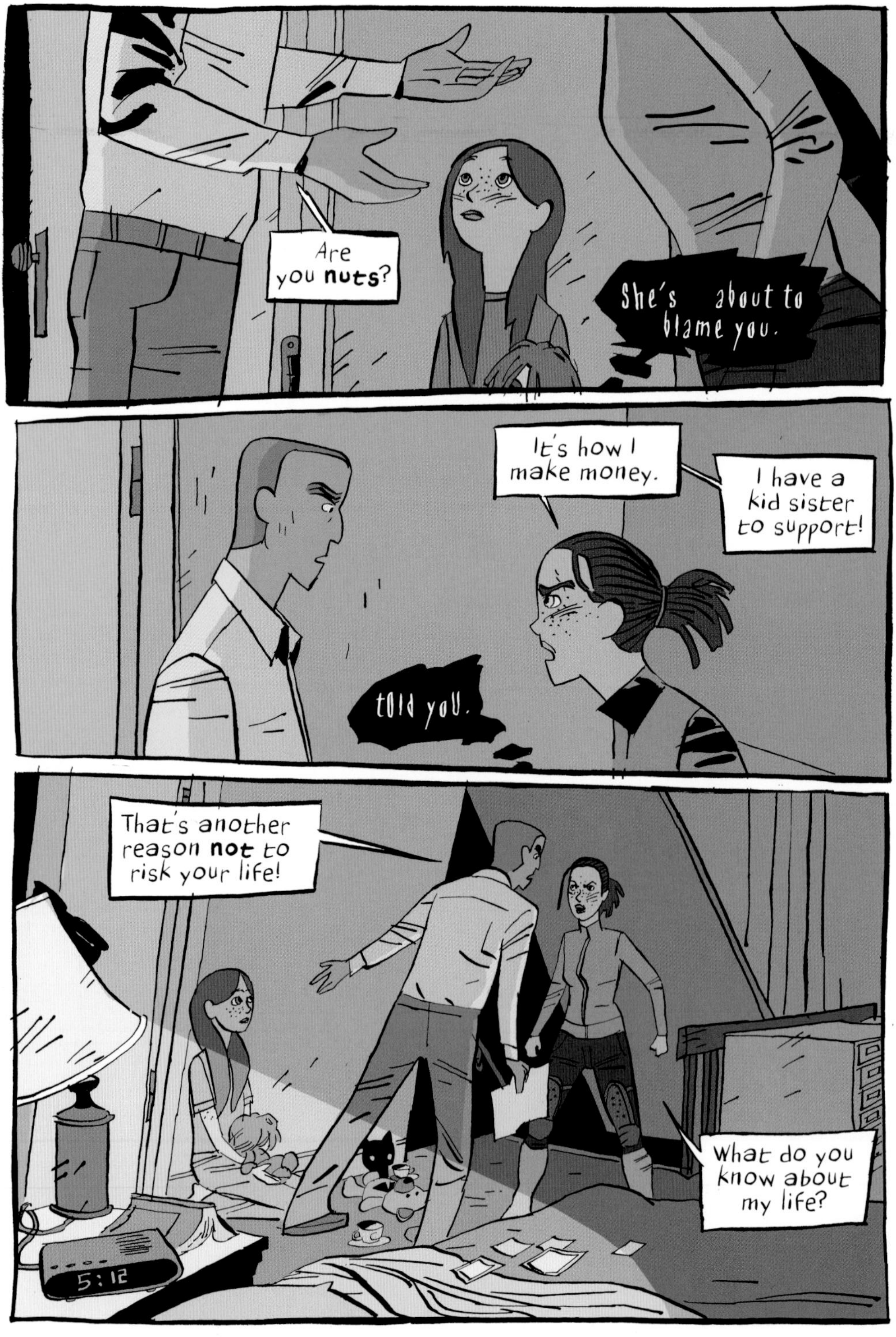

Are you **nuts**?
She's about to blame you.
It's how I make money.
I have a kid sister to support!
told you.
That's another reason **not** to risk your life!
5:12
What do you know about my life?

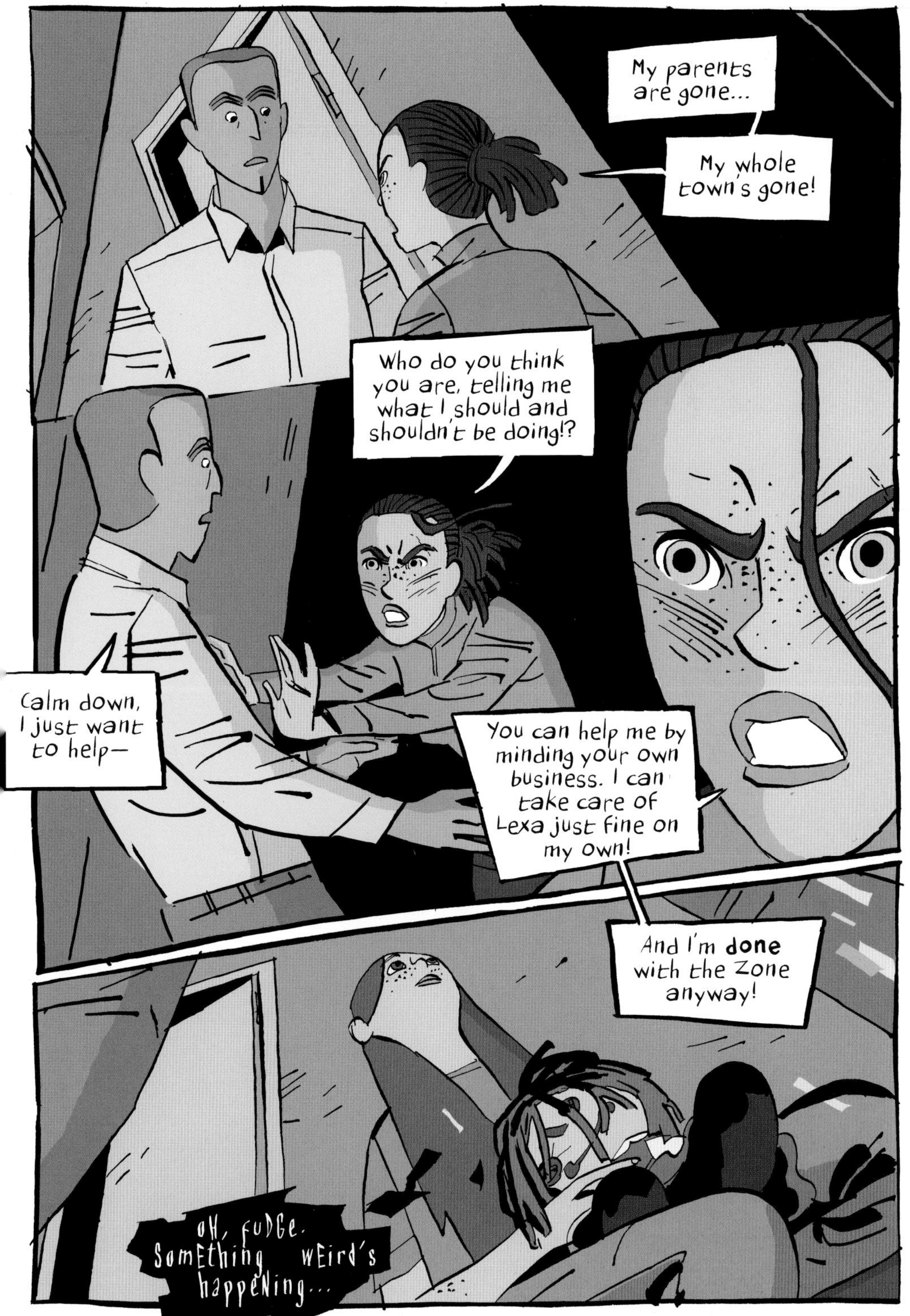
My parents are gone...
My whole town's gone!
Who do you think you are, telling me what I should and shouldn't be doing!?
Calm down, I just want to help—
You can help me by minding your own business. I can take care of Lexa just fine on my own!
And I'm **done** with the Zone anyway!
OH, FUDGE. SOMETHING WEIRD'S HAPPENING...

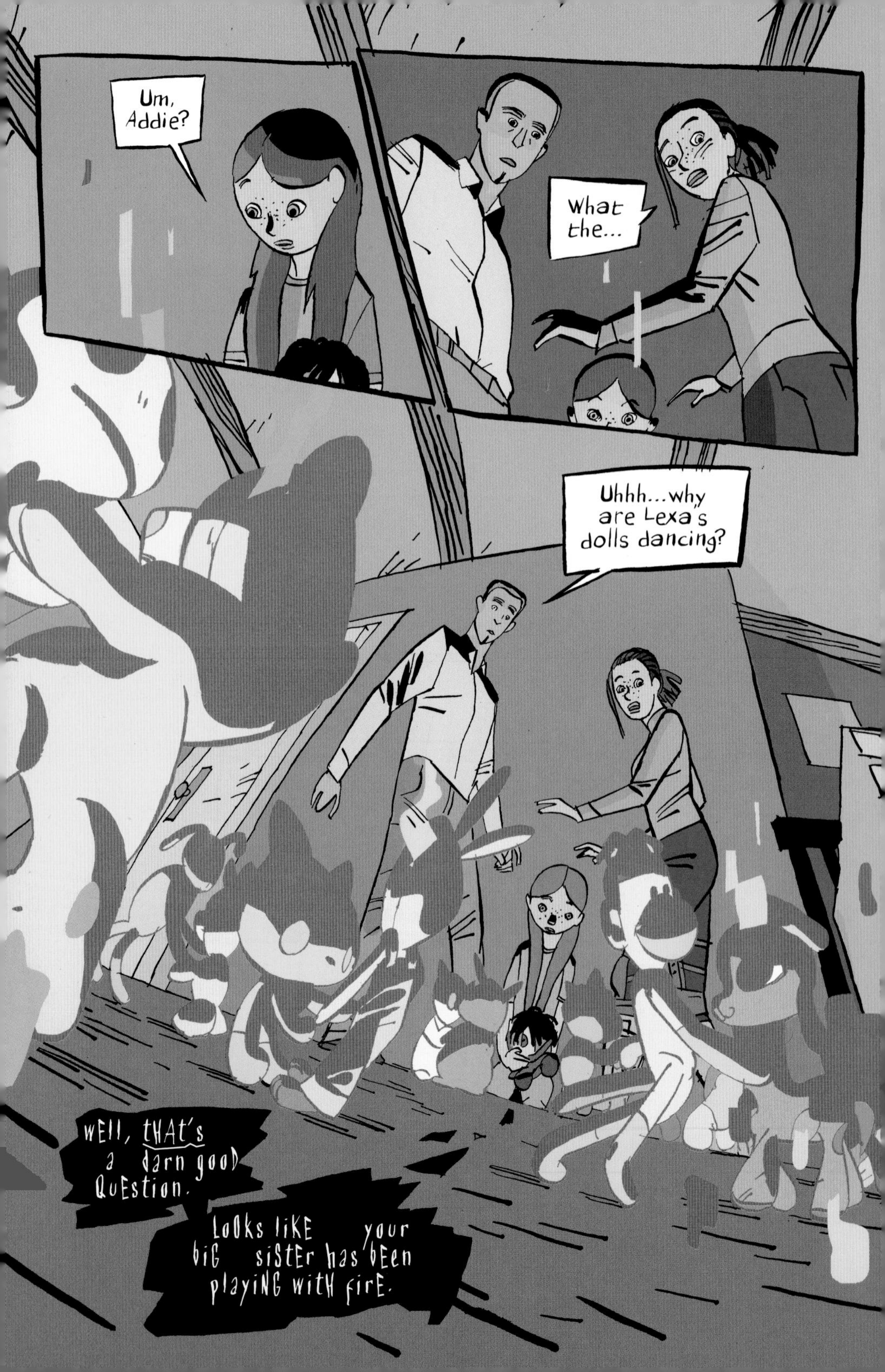
Um, Addie?
What the...
Uhhh...why are Lexa's dolls dancing?
WEll, THAT's a darn good QuEstion.
LOOks liKE your biG sisTEr has bEEn playiNG wiTH firE.

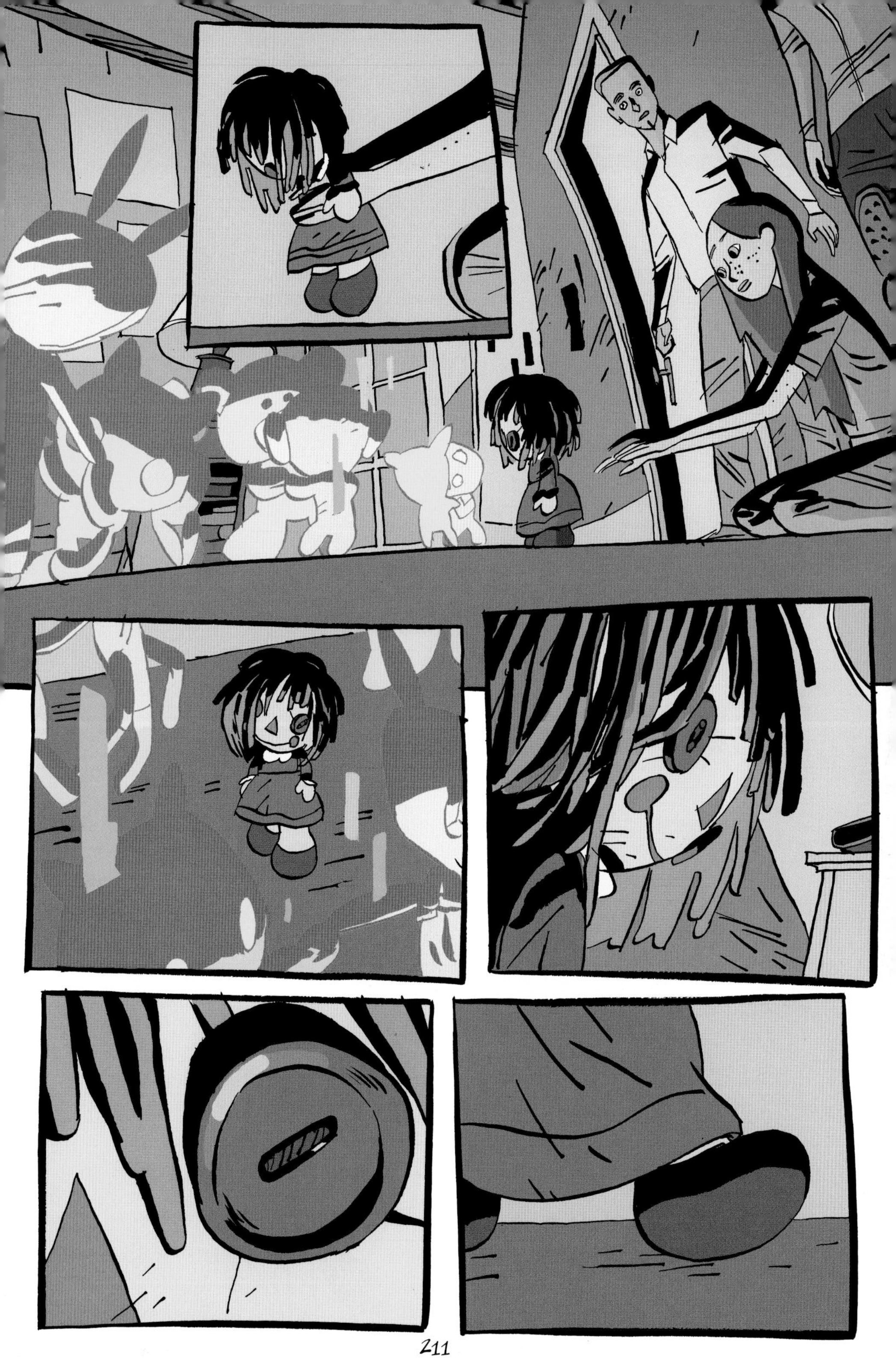

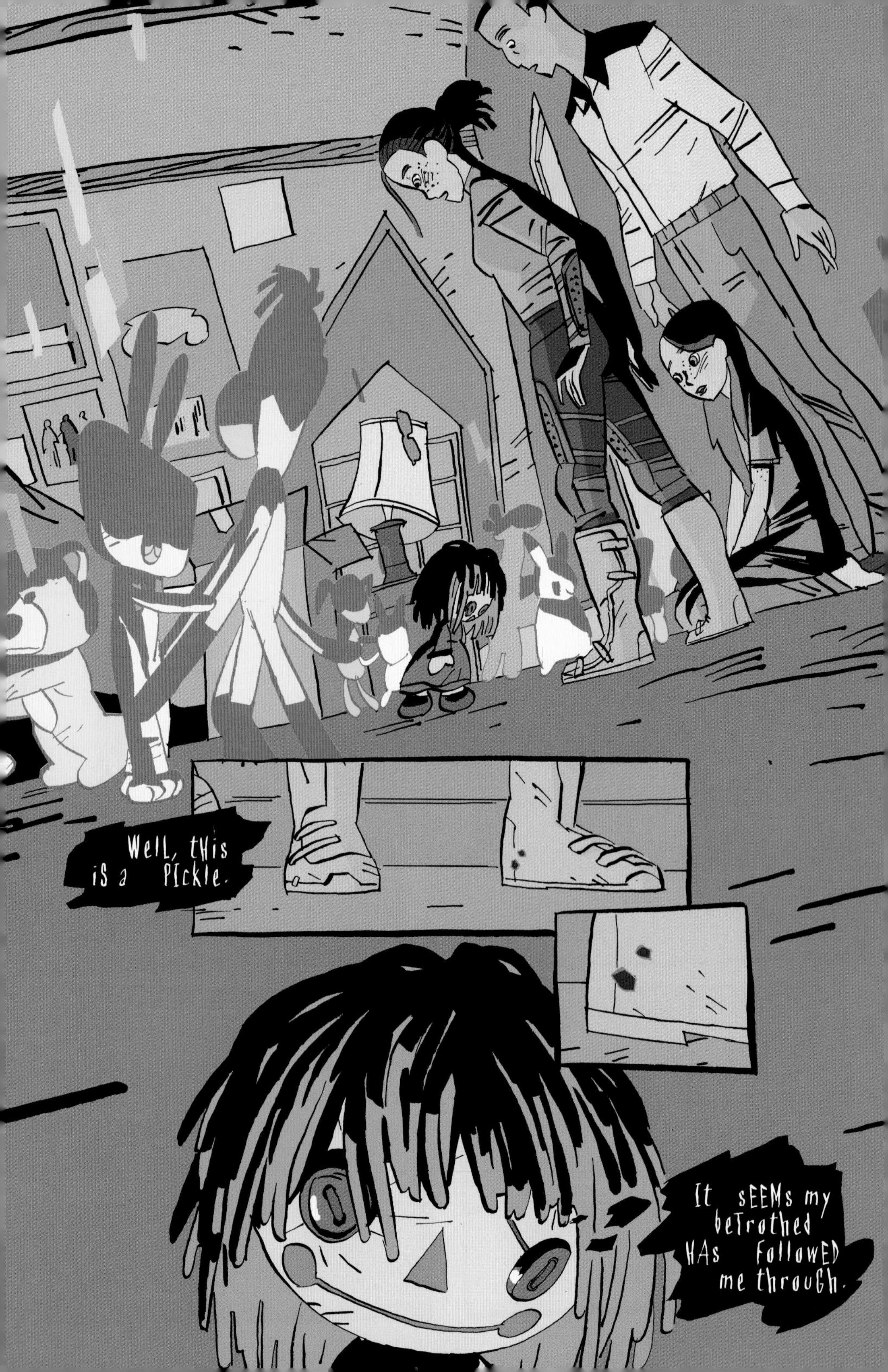
Well, this is a pickle.
It seems my betrothed has followed me through.

more to come

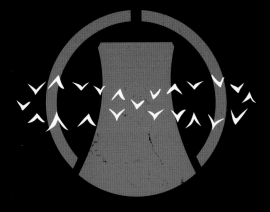

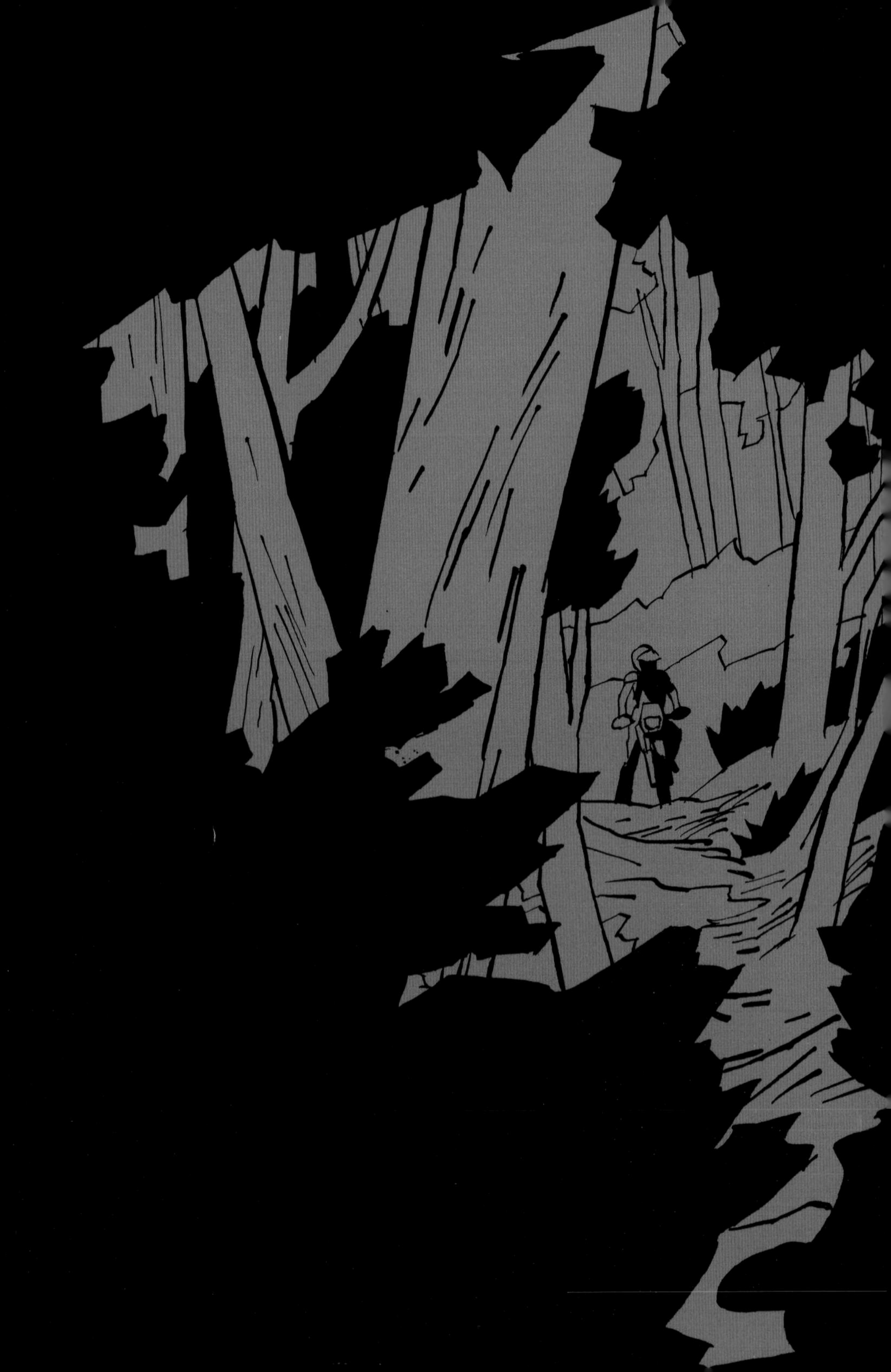

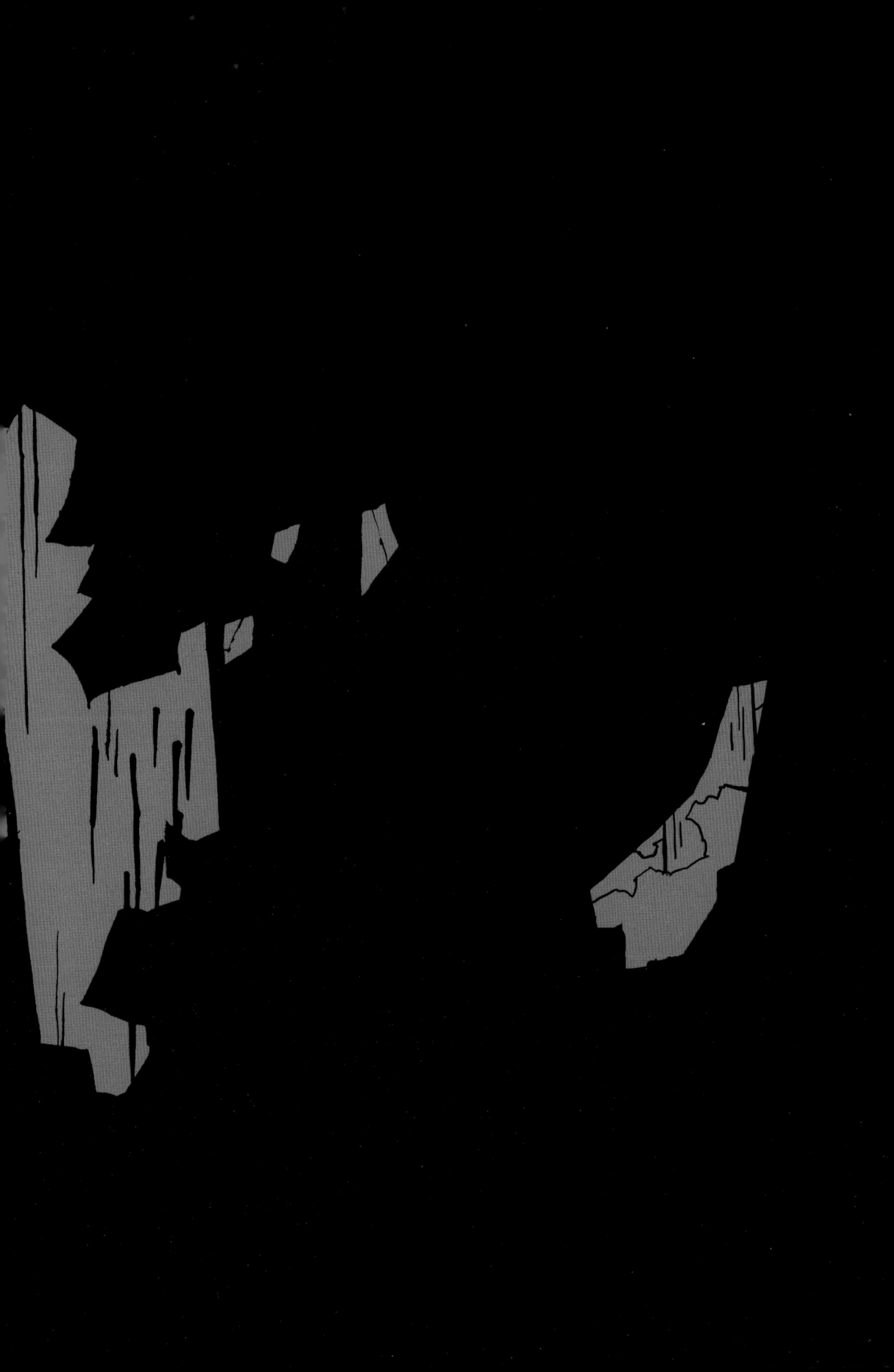

First Second
New York

Published by First Second
First Second is an imprint of Roaring Brook Press,
a division of Holtzbrinck Publishing Holdings Limited Partnership
175 Fifth Avenue, New York, New York 10010

Library of Congress Control Number: 2016945565

Hardcover ISBN: 978-1-59643-936-8

Our books may be purchased in bulk for promotional, educational,
or business use. Please contact your local bookseller or the Macmillan
Corporate and Premium Sales Department at (800) 221-7945 ext. 5442
or by e-mail at MacmillanSpecialMarkets@macmillan.com.

First edition 2017
Book design by Danielle Ceccolini and Rob Steen
Printed in China by RR Donnelley Asia Printing Solutions Ltd.,
Dongguan City, Guangdong Province

1 3 5 7 9 10 8 6 4 2

Penciled and inked on regular copy paper
with a Speedball pen nib number 103 and a Pentel
brush pen. Colored digitally in Photoshop.